The Mexican slut & the redheaded freak get naked. White flesh against tan. The woman smells so good. Flutters her hands all over Rusty's body. Kisses her face, neck, arms; squeezes her shoulders, feels & appreciates the strength of her biceps, and talks steadily, complimenting Rusty, telling her how she deserves to get what she needs. Gives her the full pleasure treatment.

"Most butches melt between my legs. They tell me I'm so beautiful, they don't know what to do with me."

Rusty knew what to do, and she did it. "You're good!" The slut commends her.

Also by RED JORDAN AROBATEAU:
Boys Night Out
Dirty Pictures
Lucy and Mickey

ROUGH TRADE

RED JORDAN AROBATEAU

Rough Trade
Copyright © 1996 by Red Jordan Arobateau
All Rights Reserved

These stories originally appeared in *Cum EZ Lesbian Stories with Feeling and Meaning, Volumes 1–4*

No part of this book may be reproduced, stored in a retrieval system, or transmitted in any form, by any means, including mechanical, electronic, photocopying, recording or otherwise, without prior written permission of the publishers.

First Rosebud Edition 1996

First Printing December 1996

ISBN 1-56333-470-4

Manufactured in the United States of America
Published by Masquerade Books, Inc.
801 Second Avenue
New York, N.Y. 10017

ROUGH TRADE

ROUGH TRADE/HARD CUM	7
PLEASURE IN THE GLITTER GUTTER	83
GANG RAPE	153
AFTER THE TRICK WAS TURNED	251
DO THE SLANG, SLANG, YES!	275
REFLECTIONS OF A LESBIAN TRICK	329

ROUGH TRADE
HARD CUM
Chapter One

'A lot of thoughts pass thru your head while you stand against the bar watching the girls.'

The Venus Nightclub had a circular bar. Lesbians gathered there from all surrounding towns & suburbs. Just 3 blocks down, they mopped up bits of people off the freeway to get there—car accidents of a major metropolis. So everybody was in a hurry. However, Rusty felt she was late. That she was trying to catch up, that she was slow.

Red taillights arc up the freeway, curve like a snake in convolutions, far as the eye can see. The club was down in the warehouse district.

Black walls; gold and red lights were the rule. This place was better than many, had a patio out in the open centering around a waterfall. But the bathroom was a toilet.

House employees open up the door of each stall, throw rolls of toilet paper on the floor, then run off on other duties, so when they piss, women have to dive down onto the pee-wet floor to retrieve a roll, peel some layers of tissue off, & wipe their pussies.

This nightclub had an elevated dance floor that stretches the length of the place. Was full of women tonight, including a lot of blondes, both original and newly blonde.

Fanfare. Dance music. Girls came in to Show & Pose. Stand, or sit, drink in hand, or cigarette. And far too many get very intoxicated. Alcohol eats away their livers & the pretty girls do it for the same reason that hounded Rusty: Insecurity. Low Self-Esteem. And Fear they might not meet a woman tonight & have to live out the rest of the workweek—straight jail time—in sadness. Depression born of loneliness.

Rusty; tough. Red hair. A boy-girl. Thumb in the belt of her trousers. Black leather jacket. Flexes her shoulders. Had deep yearnings to take a woman—tho she was structured by biology thru the eons as a female, to be taken. And this was constituted in muscles, tissues, and nerves—her biological destiny. But who, like countless other humans in growing ability, stepped out of this role—in her case, to put on the male persona.

Up on a platform about 5 feet off the floor, a dancer worked herself into a lather of sweat. Her pounding feet started where the customers' shoulders began. Blonde —newly; short cut. Very attractive curvaceous body.

Buxom. The crowd below had lesbians in leather jackets, short hair, crew-cut butches; ladies in earrings & halter tops, makeup & lipstick. And a lot of girls didn't get the idea they were supposed to tip her a few dollars. Put a dollar in the waistband of her jeans, pushing their fingers down against her sweating stomach flat & white that throbbed with exertion as she danced; or into her cleavage held by the cotton halter top. They went on their way past, hunting for Someone. Bantered between each other. As Blaze danced her heart out in excited energy, her pretty face reflected nothing but a smile.

Rusty leaned against the bar & she had these thoughts. Or, alternately, she came back to reality and voiced them to her buddy Frankie. "It's a dismal little narrow world. So many battered & abused lesbians. It's hard to get your sexual needs met with them.

"These girls are closed & tight and keep to themselves. Thought when I left that small town it would be better here—where women are more plentiful. Well, they're more glamorous, they dress sexier, they're faster—but everything else is the same."

Stood, black leather jacket, blue jeans, boots, shock of red hair. Heavy shoulders. A mannish butch. Thought: 'Go thru life trying to find satisfaction for my cunt.'

Especially eyed this dancer. Rusty's hard face tipped up, gazing now from right beside the platform, jostled by elbows from the crowd; eyeing her lithe form from its black lace shoes & white sox up her curvy firm muscled legs in denim shorts, bare stomach, short halter top showing her round breasts; up to her pretty face, deep red lipstick, & blonde hair. 'Too bad the sex act can't be as rough and tough as the emotions I feel firing inside me.' And started fantasizing a sex act that would. 'Fantasize what I'd do to that blonde if I could get her to go home with me. She'd open up her eyes & see me like none others in this club tonight see me. See my ripped-open naked heart in pain as I stand here with a drink in my hand. Only in killing somebody would I meet face-to-face with my real angry feelings.' So, of course, Rusty focused this terrific pressure that gripped her, this emotion, onto the blonde dancer—because she was always up there in public, like a Movie Star; going on from Saturday night to Saturday night in a sort of Living TV serial rerun of a series that had never been. Rusty had her greatest contact of all—besides her buddy Frankie—(with the Feminine Gender) with the dancer, passing in an exchange of green dollar bills, mostly singles, a few fives, for a wink of her mascaraed eyes; black contrast to white powdered skin; or the touch of her sweaty cold hands, or a wiggle of her hips, thrusting out to the redhead Rusty, seeming to invite her love, to promise more—but it wasn't so.

This boy-girl works as a machinist, but only part time now; earns good man money, higher pay, if you count being laid off 4 months out of last year & having to collect unemployment & survive on $120 a week. Her pay is still less than a man who has seniority & been on the job since before, when only guys held these kinds of jobs, before Equal Opportunity Employment opened them up to females. She stands on her feet all day, helmet with thick glass visor, heavy gloves, cutting pieces of metal with fire from a blowtorch. Dons black leather, a mean expression, and a tough walk after 3 P.M. when the shift ends, rides the bus home; truck ain't working, can't afford to fix it because of too many shifts missed due to layoffs. Lives in a poor section of town; constantly has to do battle with the unpleasant people in her neighborhood who do things like park their cars across her driveway—when the truck is running. Garbage in front of her apartment door. All on purpose & not by accident. Because she is a he-she; a dyke. And can't afford to move. The killing irony is that she has to be grateful just to have a roof, any kind of roof over her head—for which the redhead is thankful.

Sometimes when the work comes in heavy & she got more hours, Rusty would have the truck repaired, pay back bills, maybe pay up the rent two months in advance. And had acquired the Big Money habit of always carrying two or three fifty-dollar bills, and a hundred tucked in her billfold as well as the ordinary twenties, tens, and fives. —In case of emergencies. —Like meeting a girl who liked the green stuff, or a pal who wanted to go out of town—maybe to Reno, Nevada, across the state line.

'And I always say...I just sit here & watch...& see... and everything comes my way...and I could be so happy happy happy....'

Rusty entertained this basically negative attitude tonight, tho it was intertwined with streaks of hope like silver thru a black backdrop. Early that evening, while preparing to go out (that meant sprinkling men's cologne on her boxer shorts & T-shirt, then slipping into a fresh pair of trousers and a nice shirt, combing back her thick red hair, turning her face this way and that in profiles &

quarter-turns in the mirror, then pulling on her boots, walking around the mattress on the floor of her semi-barren apartment) had toyed with the idea of masturbation. Horniness so bottled up inside. 'In all deference to Feminists who say lesbians need power over our bodies, and so it's OK to jerk off; usually, the fact is I'm doing it to myself because I can't get a girl to do it. Some sweet femme dyke to love my stale old nasty sex parts. They don't love you enough, these girls. These girls don't want your juice. They don't want to pick your pubic hairs out of their teeth or smell your cunt-stink on their breath, or put their fingers to their nose and breathe your aroma after—before washing their hands in the sink.

'These girls these girls. They don't love you *agape*, as in the Bible. They don't love you as in a Harlequin romance novel. Or as nothing. In fact, most would step right over your body dying of a heart attack out on the barroom floor & ignore you & keep on walking in pursuit of their Impossible Dream.

'I'm too tired and disillusioned with women. Women who don't want sex. Who don't want to be touched. Women who've been abused & raped; & victims of incest as kids. That's one reason they're in the streets now, wandering lost, or selling it, or they put it on ice and stay a virgin, & don't want nobody to touch them. —So I'm locked out.'

Gradually, with Rusty, who hasn't been raped nor was a victim of incest, nature takes its course. And she feels her sex, moving inside her, get hot, get turned on.

And she watches the blonde dancer, & eyes the sea of women who wiggle on the dance floor.

'I've seen life from the underside.

'The Lesbian World is a very hard world.

'It's really a mean, tight world and it gives little.

'Lesbian Life is a circle within a circle—it can be a very lonely, isolated life.'

Most of her life, Rusty was used to going to bars, telling her problems to strangers & being supported by them—tho often they were drunk. So now she talked to Frankie, a woman her own age, in her 50s. "All the years I lived up in that room, nobody came to visit. No one called on the phone. Nobody knew if I lived or died." Frankie still drank, hadn't chilled out & stopped like Rusty, & had let her body go to fat. The aging process had hit her hard. Maybe it was just genetics. But her looks wouldn't get her a dime in this bar of pretty women, while Rusty still had a shot at the brass ring. The lines of age not as deeply etched.

"Herpes. That's how I got it. Doing sex cunt-to-cunt. Really, I think the bitch who gave it to me was determined to pass it down to every dyke she knew.

"Two other women in the bar came up with the disease right after they slept with her & then she left town.

"She was angry at the way some dyke had treated her, who had left town before her & so she infected every woman she could, butches and femmes. And then she left town herself & then so did I.

"She's still carrying it for all I know. Open bleeding sores. I hope it rots her cunt out, the heartless bitch.

"I'm lucky. Mine went into remission & ain't come back."

"They say it does that when you get to be our age. It's worse in the fertile years; that's why you didn't get it as bad."

Conversation about their dyke lives. Outside, in part of her brain, out of time & space, while talking, Rusty's watching the platform and the blonde dyke Blaze; pretty go-go dancer onstage dancing for wages plus tips. And the butch incorporates this blonde into her fantasies.

"We're both butches. And some lesbians treat us as if we have no feelings. Like they treat men. And some butches, in fact, don't have feelings. They use a lot of alcohol or drugs for that express purpose—to have no feelings. Like you, Frankie."

"I know, I know, man. I know I should quit. It's just that I don't have the willpower you got. Some got it, some don't."

"Yeah. Well, at least it keeps you in a happy mood. Me, I'm more angry & having these violent thoughts I never had when I was mellow on alcohol…unless I got mad. Then it was a rage & I couldn't control myself."

Their words tossed over the sea of noise, so each could barely hear the other. Basketball-court-sized field of capricious women, a crowd of 350. Nothing but females as far as the eye could see in any direction. Most with nice jackets and slacks, feminine or unisex; very few black-leather-jacket SM types; almost all white, hardly any over age 40. Glasses tinkling, music pounding, dancers swaying, & they charged $6 at the door.

'All the glamorous dykes walk by and they pay me no attention.'

The two butches stood near each other, not talking,

each lost in her private world. Frankie had given up the chase. But from time to time Rusty would speak to a passing girl, or spy one she liked at a distance and leave their station down beside the platform & plunge into the lesbian sea to go after her, just nearly 99 percent of the time to return dejected and empty-handed.

'Do I have to Stonewall my way into the hearts of these lesbians? Grandstand & jackhammer & sandblast my way into their attention?

The fantasy is the blonde dancer Blaze—she wants my cunt. Wants to suck me until I can't cum no more. She'll get in several kinds of freakish positions & suck my clit, or let me suck her, & drive it, pound it to her —my 3 fingers. I tie a belt around her neck & hold the end & pull it back & pull her pretty white butt into me & drive my dick into her ass.'

Evening shifted into late gear. Women walked to and fro.

'This blonde has put herself up as a sex object by the way she dresses. In fact, she's dyed her hair blonde. And she's purposely left a black tail in back to show it off.'

She'd do it—till sweat poured off her. Young body tossing in ecstasy just as now she pranced onstage. Clit cum, cunt cum. Rusty had cum from the Magic Carpet ride of the sex device at the base of her strap-on cock; & then she'd get on Blaze and ride her. Then cum for a 3rd bang, oral sex. But of course she leaned up there at the bar all by herself.

'People are a lot like mechanical dolls, except we're human. God puts a human heart in us instead of batteries, and it finally runs down.'

Rusty felt her heart run down by age 50. After all the desires of youth and all the places these desires had led her like a rampaging bull with a ring thru its nose; all the cities of the plains thru which she'd passed; and the arms. Perfumed embraces. Legs wrapped around her waist, fucking. Their erotic female scent; going for a long, deep ride. Girls' fingers probing her cunt as well, as masculine as she was. —Remembered some of them like it was yesterday. And time marched on, stark.

Then, in the meantime, Frankie's eased her big ass off the bar stool they've grabbed, and lumbers off to queue up at the women's pissoir.

'You see old age gain on you. Now, that's something else to be reckoned. Along with the regular Lesbian Hell. And the scarcity of sex in this sex-negative world.

'When I had the straight women for a long time, I gave up on lesbians. Now, after 25 years have passed, I have to justify myself all over again—Why I want a straight woman. In my teens it was, why I want a woman —period. Go thru all these difficulties because I'm relating to straight women. My ex turns gay. Then another straight woman. And the hookers before them who were also straight.

'Lack of sex among my own female dyke counterparts.

'Women. They know how to turn it on, they know how to turn it off.

'Love you with the full treatment—good, tender love. Then they don't have time for you.' Rusty thinks this, muses; bottom lips twists under her teeth, light-colored eyes bore into space. Strokes her pale white hand alternately over her red hair, then down pensively to stroke the side of the glass of a soft drink. It became so boring not having any women to talk to, so her mind reflected: 'Next woman I date, ain't gonna wait till weeks later to find out she really don't enjoy sex. I'm gonna ask: "Can you lay back and allow yourself to be penetrated by my lesbian fingers, to be ridden by my lesbian clit, to be fucked by my lesbian cock & sucked by my lesbian lips?"

'Then who should walk by (I always say, just stand here long enough and everybody comes back to you—at least one more time in a lifetime) but Nancy and JoAnne. These two pretty girls—one a bleached blonde —both individually took my telephone number, had me write it down for both of them on separate pieces of paper; and gave me their number. When I call, a man answers & they're never there. I see them— they're best friends —surrounding another dyke like they did me. A handsome butch, off-center, more soft than me. Bet they're giving her the same old line.' When they swirl their long bare legs down the aisle, arm in arm, Rusty plunges into the crowd to confront them.

"How come you gave me a phony phone number and some man keeps answering & you both took my number and you never called?"

The two petulant children reply: "But we were having a contest that night to see who could get the most numbers!"

"Yeah! Well, thanks a lot, girls! I should have figured as much! They threw you out of the bar because you were drunk!"

"They threw us out because they thought we were straight!"

"They always do that! They always think we're straight! They think we're straight hookers who come in to work the dykes!"

"I *wish!*"

"*Joanne's* a *schoolteacher*—isn't that a scream? And they think we're hookers!"

'So is it right to tease my lesbian cock, you bitch?' Rusty thinks, smiles hard; her red hair had been combed neat, back, but now it's mussed. Says: "So you both take my phone number & have me thinking yer gonna call?"

The girls smile, mutter an excuse, then fade into the crowd arm in arm.

'Go up with a bunch of other mad butches & dykes they've pulled that game on. And gang-rape them. Me and Frankie and a few more man-dykes. I'm sure they'll be glad to…. OK…. Yeah…I understand. There's no reason why they owe me their bodies. It's not their fault if my life has wound up to be a struggle to get a bar stool, not even a woman, not even the chance of a woman. And these last years I get it so infrequent when I'm not living with a woman. I respect them. It's not their responsibility—my problems. Then, likewise, also, it's not my fault if I'm pushed over the edge—by their coldness, and lack of response to me. Not my fault if one day I can't hold out any longer.

'So that's when I break down and lose my judgment or lose what civilization has gone about teaching me from the cradle—that's when I formulate the plot—since there is no exit—to entice a willing female home and kill her. Watch her struggle and die.

'Bust my nuts in her soft sweet dying mouth, my

pussylips in her lipsticked lips. Ride her, fuck her, cum all over her. Rope around her neck. Work her down to the last gasp of breath & my final orgasm. This is what thoughts I'm reduced to, standing up here at the bar.'

Rusty remembered somewhere, dim, in the recesses of her mind, words from the Bible. "Mother Mary says: 'I'll give you the victory.' The one wish in my life is, I'd ask Her for victory over these gay bars. For mastery of sex and love in my lifetime which has eluded me for so long.

'I'm not an unsafe Top. —When I do negotiate a sex scene in advance with a woman, I respect our rules. But what do we say to negotiate feelings? It's those feelings that permeate every sex act. It's the feelings that make me alone after she's gone, even when my body needs no more. Now, as of yet, I have not tried to trap some girl under false pretenses. But the pain gets so bad, I have these vengeful thoughts.

'For one, I was in a relationship. I ended it—and that was a mistake.

'When our marriage ended, I was broke down into the raw, brutal, lesbian world. Alone.

'I can still hear Judy run after me, and I'm not even gone yet. "I've done talking, and I've heard all you got to say. Better go fuck your new woman, Rusty! You're too hard on me anyhow! I'm tired & sick of your bossing me around!"

' "And you take this woman's word over mine?" '

So Rusty got down on her hands & knees and had begged for forgiveness. And Judy got down on her hands and knees with Rusty and Rusty said, "I'm sorry, baby—please take me back. Yes, there is another woman —but it's all over, it never really started." And she cried.

So Judy cried, too, and said, "Let's never do this again; don't let this happen again!"

Two weeks later, they're still arguing. Two fiery personalities that don't get along. "You're lucky I did come back to you so you can jack your hot clit off in my mouth forever so long as we both shall live."

A month later: Judy has on a tailored, lady suit, high heels, hair piled up on her head & ringlets down her neck & a suitcase on wheels.

"How can two people forget all they've been thru together?"

"I CAN GO AHEAD AND FORGET YOU!" And she slammed the door.

Can we forget—the death of faith thru time?

So resentment sets in on both sides. Now, Rusty is not the middle class, nor professional, but low-class & a street dyke. So she don't go to counseling or any self-help group to get over Judy, but just bears the pain stoically.

'A person deserves to become twisted after a while. Nobody expects you to be so moral. You been thru it. What society and living this life have done to you.

'Rage, that somehow society don't think I don't have to get it—raw sex. Or even love. No outlet for me, a lesbian butch. So here I sit on a bar stool, and something has got to snap.

'So I have memories first, & then fantasize. —Then heavy sex fantasies that degrade into plots.

'I remember the times I have crossed over and had their women. Stolen their wives. Paid their whores.

Fucked both these varieties of their kept sex workers.'

Rusty reached back into memory and thought about the whorehouse, and remembers the Mexican in particular who serviced her. Her, a boy-girl. And then thought about Judy, who had been a straight married lady before Rusty had seen her and noticed something special in her glance that lingered; and Judy had seen in Rusty the perfect dyke, what she'd always dreamed about—a he-she who was big and handsome; so Rusty brought her out and they were lovers 2 years. Stormy years of two clashing tempers. And thinks about the sex clubs where she ran off to hide from Judy and prove her butch masculinity in an anonymous way. And mulls even over this bar she's currently walking thru, with its waterfall & open air patio. A nightclub that's not even a lesbian-owned business, but just rented from rich fags for Saturday night.

'It's sickening all the things men have for themselves. Makes me enraged to think about it—I have to go back to my narrow world. Go. Our world could be so sweet if lesbians would just say "Yes" to each other instead of "No."'

ROUGH TRADE
HARD CUM
Chapter Two

Line to the toilet snaked forward; women wait, one by one & in couples. 'Know I can't get sex from any of them. Why are lesbians so dead & sexless?' Rusty stood beside a public john waiting for a whole row of women to piss.

Mouth tight, face flat, white, & without emotion; like a man's. But underneath were these feelings, boiling. 'Woman, I'm out here trying to live on the fringe of society. My soft pussy wants yours. My hard jackboots walked a million miles to be near you....'

When the gay community disperses, as it has to—by dawn's early light, we travel back home by pairs, or as individuals, into loneliness. Of restricted worlds. Of desires within straight solitudes.

The gay times are all too few—Rusty tried to learn to

create a home in her apartment. To preserve herself, to make an order in life. To fill loneliness.

'First of all, must tell about myself. I'm a Top. A butch Top. Dominant. Tame. Age—having passed from repression of the fifties to sexual freedom of the nineties. My name's Rusty—it's unimportant—that's only a label —not the meat of what I am. Age 50 is old for gay life —to be out in bars trying to cruise & pick up a woman for the night. And women my age I've been acquainted with, who've sat side by side with me for decades, have disappeared suddenly, one by one. One even has gone straight. —Most feel they're too old to be seen in here. I'm one of the few left. I look about ten years younger than I am. Some, like Frankie, hang out in this place on Saturday night for no better reason than not to be home alone shut up behind walls. But without hope of getting any companionship.

'So I had other women at the same time as my marriage to Judy. It was over-sex. Craving for extra eroticism. There is no medical reason for this. The clinicians report that a butch dyke who is very sexually active, mannish, & dresses in drag has no more chemical differences in her body than a femme. So this sex must be all in my head. And speaking of butch clothing, that, and my size which is big, and manner, are disturbing to some females. It reminds them of being straight & as a consequence limits my chances.'

Why was she evil? The fantasies—would they become acts? Was she possessed by a demon? Did bad things happen to her when she was a child? Did she just plot to become the hooded torturer for no reason?

Images. Billboards, advertisements on TV, on buses, trains, planes, picture straight people who kiss. Have sexual intimacy. We see no dykes doing the same.

Rusty had searched the entire daily newspaper for just one item about lesbians.

It was just the wearing away like water on stone.

'Women have come from all over to live in this part of the world. From Copenhagen, France, Iowa, Minnesota, Greece, Iran, Sri Lanka. All to be in San Francisco. And we still can't be ourselves in this stupid place without a fight in the street. Or defend our own territory. —Bars have closed down. There isn't but two bars owned by women in the whole city.'

Rusty dresses rough. 'Not a lot of women want to be with me just because of that. But I must do what I gotta do. Be myself.

'I've almost come to accept it as natural—before snapping back & catching myself. —The inferiority of myself as a female & a lesbian.

'What's wrong with us?

'Why don't we support each other?

'I've spoken my mind before and got beat up for it.'

Now Rusty was out on the street. Venus Club closed down for the night. A few lucky couples were released from the palm of its hand; newly joined to bridge the hiatus until next Saturday, when Girls' Play Night came again. Rusty began the long walk home. No buses ran that late & wanted to save money & not spend it on a cab for just herself alone, & was angry. And didn't want to bother Frankie, would rather save her pal for when she really needed a favor emergency ride if she picked up a girl. In a few paces, Rusty became separate from the festive throngs of women. Those together in groups or pairs, laughing, exchanging phone numbers. Her, alone.

'Could have bummed a ride from Frankie. But people get tired of bums fast.'

And she thought back to her teens, and twenties —about those times she'd spoken out and acted up. —In defense of her soul.

'So many times when it ended, me having to bow my head in tears.'

The black streets echo with Rusty's footfalls. No other activity. Warehouse buildings loom, sightless windows. Neon lights march down the row. Suddenly a scream rends the air. "CUNT!" Redhead butch turns, fierce, hand seeks the weapon, a small handgun inside her jacket. It's a crazy man hurrying along. He flails his arms in protest to the high court of another world. As he passes by, cries out: "CUNT!" At everything. Everything. Yells it to the tops of buildings. To the stars. At a newspaper caught up under his frantic feet. At the corpse of a white Styrofoam dinner tray, glistening on the curb. "CUNT!" Then he's gone & all is silent once more, but for Rusty's feet in steady paces.

'Tired of bowing my head and slinking by in a black leather jacket.' So she'd come out here to California. There was a whole lot more gay people concentrated all in one place. She wasn't a freak. Wasn't nearly as much harassment by straights. And by now after the years of straight people's scorn, & hate heaped on her from their narrow minds, she wanted to kill them, too.

'Wiping the blood off my face.

'When I came out to San Francisco, blood was still in my mouth from being slugged in the head, two ribs cracked as showed in X rays at the hospital, my nose swollen up twice its size, one eye puffed up, black. Lips ground against my teeth. Compound injury.

'Later Judy slaps me with her perfumed hand with rings and pretty fingernails, and it hurts. —It's not the beating that injures me, but far worse, the Grand Slam to my heart.'

So there's an old dyke with an old lady, maybe her femme, in a neat small older car with the hood up—it won't start. They have problems. This is in front of the only gay bar in town back in the Midwest, where Rusty was born, and the dyke who owns the place asks somebody to hold the parking spot next to the car vacant so she can go get her own car and hook up their batteries & jump start it. —She needs this space next to the elderly dyke's car. And Rusty's out in the street. —Here comes a car with two big men in it, fags. Rusty motions them to move on & find another place to park, but they won't. Men are so inflexible, they won't move. One rolls down the window and yells at her. He is not simply gay, but a female-hating man. The grey-haired dyke wrings her hands in dismay. She and her friend can do nothing. The fags pull right up to Rusty, stop inches from her, she can feel the heat of their car's motor thru her white shirtfront; they've been driving a long time. & the man in the passenger seat is a maniac, he's yelling, the car is trying to force its way in—regardless of the disabled car, whose hood is up in distress; and this dyke is blocking their way. The car is bulldozing its way in, and the driver presses his foot down on the accelerator; Rusty weakens and steps aside; the car pulls into the spot. She's so mad, she kicks the side of the car, glistening metal imprints with the mark of her boot.

Hell breaks loose. The passenger hollers, breaks out of his door screaming and charges Rusty. She races around the end of the car; he runs after her. His voice is much louder than hers as they yell, and there's terror in hers. She runs back behind the cars, casts a brief look of 'help me,' but there's no backup, just the old grey-haired dyke & her lady. The man is enraged and reaches her, grabbing at her in a split second. "YOU BITCH! YOU KICKED BILL'S CAR, AND YOU'RE GOING TO PAY FOR IT! YOU GODDAMN DYKES NEED TO GET THE HELL BEATEN OUT OF YOU! YOU FUCKING CUNTS! I'M GOING TO WHIP THE SHIT OUT OF YOU! YOU FUCKING DAMN DYKE!"

Rusty swings her arms out to block the man's lunge. For all her butchness and bravado feels herself pulverized by fear. In that split second, Rusty prays for help, catches the eye of one old dyke—they look at each other across 10 feet of space and see each other's weakness, both afraid, butch and femme alike. And the blows start. Rusty is punching back, her fists wild, but a big blow hits her. Stunned, she goes down. Then his feet are kicking her; the man is screaming & his companion has jerked open his door on the driver's side, run around to the front of the car to where the redheaded dyke is on the ground, body curled in a ball warding off kicks; he grabs his friend and struggles with him, yells; "JACK, FOR GOD'S SAKE, STOP THIS! STOP IT RIGHT NOW!"

Rusty struggles up to her feet, holding the front of the car for support, blood runs down her face & in the webs between her fingers. The man breaks out of his friend's grasp, and Rusty's ready, throws her fists out, punching, and gets off a good kick that makes him jerk back & scream in pain. And like a hen and a rooster battling in a chicken coop, the hen always backs down; she's smarter. The rooster fights until he's dead. Bleeding, Rusty draws back. The enraged man's companion gets a bear hug on him & pulls him back still kicking & screaming. Rusty is no longer afraid, but dazed. A tooth is knocked loose in her mouth; later it will have to be pulled out. She slumps against the side of the old dyke's car and they are pulling her away, back inside the bar. The fag pushes his friend into their car, guns it up, backs out in a fury, and drives off.

"Big, the two of them. A lot bigger size than me. Goddamn rich faggots. And they call creeps like that *Mister*. And give them all the respect; and they don't even look gay. Fucking fags!" Seated now at the bar, colored by amber lights, ministered to by the bantam he-she characters in trousers & shirts and short hair, and their ladies, until they decide by the amount of blood and pain that somebody had better drive Rusty to the hospital. As she leaves, the grey-haired dykes stand by the car—hood still up; and one goes with her in an entourage of dykes off to the emergency room, and one stays to survey the dismal scene of one stalled car with a dead battery, and crimson blood spattered over the street.

Age 50, Rusty had her revenge. For she had lived to

see the death of many big men. By their own hands. By their own vices & self-abuse. By a faster rate than women. And death by AIDS. Death brought an end to their stubborn hold. Like so many males, rich or poor, in their selfishness, stupidity, and inflexibility which just brings tears to women's eyes—women, who live to pick up the pieces.

Redhead Rusty took it personal. Held a grudge. Shifts on a bar stool, interlocks her fingers together in rage that she doesn't let show, that simmers. If Rusty could have seen the underlying brutality in all of society—not just against her, a dyke. To take it to the roots. The underlying force of rich against poor, of which she was one. Of strong against weak. And that many, many, were suffering, not just her kind alone, so she was in good company. But it did seem that women suffered the most. Those women at the bottom, with the crushing weight of others upon them.

Redhead dyke was cut from a genre of women who lifted weights. Who made themselves strong. Independent. Who fought for their rights & would settle for nothing less than their rights. Now, here in San Francisco when the bantamweight strode down the streets there was plenty of other queers to back her up.

Thru all days and nights whose composite made up the history of a woman's struggle under oppression of the current reign which is called Patriarchy.

Raging, hurt, & defiant.

'So I'm facing the straight world, which on one hand conspires against my way of life, despises me as inferior because I'm a lesbian. As a near-man, masculine—I get all the shit. The type of women I like—femmes—by their physical appearance are viewed as straight. So straight people accuse me of being the corrupter of women. When surely these femmes are as lesbian as I am—they crave pussy bad. Bad, in their lipstick and short leather skirts and eyebrow pencil. —They really do crave pussy.

'Just expect fights in the street. Rude yells from passing cars—just being who I am. And I'm always ready for it.

'Sad part is, when I'm in the arms of a woman & I know it's only for this one night, when I'm out there doing battle with the brutes of this world—men on the job harassing me, evil straight women and men in my apartment building laughing at me; then, silently, having to do a different kind of battle—one with slow punches, with soft curves surprising and sneaky out of left field. A pink battle with the ways & wiles of women. It's so hard. Hard. So when I get her naked, yielded to me, open up her thighs and her arms, she puts herself in my hands and trusts me to love her—it's a pink pussy trap. I fall into her aroma, her scent, the attention she gives me, her caresses, her motion. —But the hardness of her mind, I know this also. That mind will snap shut by dawn's early light, in sync with her evaluations of me. —I'm good for a piece of trade, for rough hard sex, but not for a permanent partner. So I can pack my dick and slip my muscled shoulders back into my black leather jacket and depart when it's light, down the back steps.'

Rusty saw her age. Had got to be less & less of a commodity on the sexflesh market of lesbian trade. Was a cut-rate item for sale on the meat rack of lesbian bar life. The courting dance, the glance across the room that cuts thru smoke to hold eye to eye for precious erotic seconds, the phrases 'Can I buy you a drink?' 'Do you want to dance with me?' 'What's your name?' 'Do you come here often?' This picking each other up.

Every human has a time to shine. Easiest is the age roughly between 25 to 35, when you're old enough to appreciate what you have & have an idea of what you need & yet still young enough to attract favors from the world on sheer good looks.

Her time was passing by—sand grains of time near gone. Within one more sad decade it would be impossible to pick up any woman on the strength of her looks alone. And Rusty didn't have any money, & was afraid to think she had an empty wasted life.

This year could easily be the last bar pickup of her life. —End of an era. Closing of a way of life, which had been a means of sexual gratification encapsulated within hours of socializing.

Like a ballet dancer, or a baseball player whose ability is limited by age; so her lined face marked the end of her rope. Her ability to attract & make love in the ways she had known come to an end, fast.

ROUGH TRADE
HARD CUM
Chapter Three

'I observe the women here tonight. Everybody's got her own life & of course what she wants to do with it. Some dykes smoke—shorten their lives like that. Others—always see a glass of liquor in their hands each time. Or tossing back a shot & wiping their mouths, eyes too bright.

'Down thru the ages, women have found ways to love each other. To have sex with each other.

'Because I have enough courage to get my sexual needs met. To be out here in a gay world does make me brave —I have to keep reminding myself—and not a coward who is fearful of physical battle. And not weak like I keep accusing myself, when pitted against men twice my size, and a world full of hate overwhelmingly large.

'It all makes me feel more like a seeker, a wanderer….

'Twelve midnight.

'This place is full of women.

'And it's been—count it, 7 now—I've approached.'

"Want to dance?"

"No. I've got these 5-inch heels on, I'm sorry."

"That's OK. My name's Rusty, what's yours?"

"I don't feel like talking."

"Oh…. Can I buy you a drink?"

"No. I'm waiting for somebody."

'Just want a woman to put her hand on my sex and her mouth on my mouth, and enfold each other for a while in this place and then drive off together in her car, to her place or mine, and make love to the fullest extent, for 3 hours…. Why? Because I want to cum. I want to feel wanted.

'The ultimate insult is that lesbians don't take care of each other.

'If we can't do something for each other, if it's something we need—even sex between two women, then what good are we?

'I want to have it. The right to pleasure & happiness.

'Seems like it should bother other lesbians too, that there are so many women who come into the Venus Club & leave not getting their needs met.'

Rusty hated men. And the next girl she approached smiled, was friendly to her, but then does something odd. With Rusty standing 2 feet from her, dangling in space, waiting, still making conversation, she turns and proceeds to start talking to a male friend. Rusty waits, patient, believing it's just for a moment, but their conversation never ends. Stretches from one song to three, then over a half-hour, in which the redheaded butch folds back into herself, leans against the wall. 'This man is here monopolizing the whole conversation. A gay girl talking to a fag and she could be talking to me.' Rusty tires of waiting. Takes the woman's arm in a firm grasp of strong freckled white fingers. Interrupts the conversation: "I'll talk to you some other time." Stares down at her a moment so that there's plenty of opportunity for the girl to beg Rusty not to go—she looks up at Rusty; lipstick with gloss, shines; tastefully made-up face; a man's suit jacket, sleeves rolled up femme style, revealing a length of gold bracelets on both arms, hair in ringlets down her shoulders, short skirt and dark stockings & high heels.

"I'm sorry, this is a friend of mine I haven't seen for so long." Says this sweetly, and so the butch is moving on down the line. Red hair bristling on her cunt in heat.

'Women in need of sex, not able to get it.

'Women in lace garter belts.

'Women stand up at the bar together, blabbing.

'These women have families, or friends, or are strangers. I'll talk to somebody 3 hours every night I come in, and they still consider me a stranger.

'People toy with other people's feelings. Women don't give.

'Wonder how long I can keep on. When I'll break and become mean and violent and hateful of women.

'Women are hot.'

Rusty thought: 'All these fucking bitches and all their fucking lies.' Her face, downed lightly with red fuzz, twists in an emotion which she swallows. She watched as glamorous, much more feminized lesbian types circulated thru the bar.

'There's a woman out here somewhere. She's gonna take me in her arms and love me the way I want to be loved. And get in any position I tell her to, and talk to me dirty & sweet; the things I want to hear.'

To watch Rusty was to see the sinking of the human heart into despair. A sea of them—lesbians, but no access for a lonely heart.

Finally stood beside the platform that raised its star up into space. Black leather jacket unzipped, underneath, a rough shirt showing muscular torso, small breasts. Silver belt buckle, trousers met black boots with a shine. Handsome. Needed no cap. Shock of red hair was a highlight. So Rusty had made the rounds again, and fluttered back into home port. Held up two dollar bills folded together; a tip for the blond dancer, for her attention and the flash of her eyes.... Smile of recognition. The 22-year-old Blaze is friendly & warm. Shimmies down on the stage, thrusts her hips in and out till she's squatting, then grabs the $2 between her knees and jerks it from Rusty's hand. Rusty yells and claps her hands in applause. Blaze takes the $2—it disappears into her shirt, down into her bra with the rest of her tips; and she dances away, turns to the east, then to the west to face the other customers, that smile still on her face, body wet with the sweat of her work.

'Then I get to fantasize what I'd do to her. We bump into each other in the toilet. Blaze pulls me to her...tight, and lets me pull down her sawed-off blue jeans over her tan thighs to her knees and lets me go inside her blonde cunt and fill her. She says, "Oh *Rusty!* It feels so good, your hand inside me."

'Loving her, petting her nipples. My tongue in her mouth & my hand goes in and out of her, faster, harder, so sweat beads on her alabaster body. She's barely old enough to be in this club, and she has the hard firm flesh of youth. I fuck her with my hand; she moans in orgasm.

'Then, still in the black-walled toilet, she gets down on her knees & says, "Rusty, I've really wanted you all along." And pleasures me in her mouth as I stand over her.

'The session's over, and suddenly we lie side by side, and stay that way the remainder of the night. Jazz is on the radio, very faint. White walls, clean apartment that she shares with her lover. Her mattress on the floor, like mine.' And Rusty pictures this because she's been there before—in that geographical location, once, a long time ago. One period of time when the truck worked, Rusty had driven Blaze home after work at 1:30 A.M. And had come up to use the bathroom, nothing more. So she knows the layout of the apartment & knows Blaze already, but not the way she wants to know her, wants to know a woman.

Lights flashing, strobe; music pounds. Blaze's feet, in black shoes with treads that grip the floor of the platform, kick; then she goes down in a split. Rusty claps in time to the beat of the music, hollers, a wicked grin on her face, enjoying herself & breaking loose in a rodeo way. Gets a five-dollar bill out of her wallet, waves it, Blaze dances over, red lips smile, eager; Rusty lets her take the five, shoving it down her fly front below her navel. Blaze scrunches up her nose & winks. Then Rusty beckons her to come close, wants to tell her something. Blaze leans over, patient (she's heard it all before). Rusty's mouth to her ear, has to yell over the driving music: "I'll give you $150 to sleep with me tonight."

Blaze laughs, shakes her head No, & dances away. Keeping up the lather of sweat on her young body. Rusty is ego-deflated, but still happy. Knows that $150 could be toward the $500 she needs to get the clutch fixed on the truck, but is a fool, and continues to carry it with her anyway, for an emergency—like if she meets a woman who will.

Blaze towers over the sea of lesbians, strangers to her, too, most. She's come to look at Rusty as a kind person she can count on—who is always there and never messy drunk, but who wants her, which is irritating, because she's told Rusty she has a lover. And the butch is way much older than she is, but she is intrigued by her red hair.

Blaze had told Rusty on several occasions while she was off on her break, "You ought to hear the bizarre comments I get from weird lesbians. They want to marry me and just saw me for the first time 5 minutes ago. They want to take me away on trips to Europe. It's weird the trips they lay on me."

'Now the blonde dancer—she don't know how many times I've used her in a fantasy to cum with.'

Rusty stood under the platform. The dancer was a Madonna look-alike. Dyed blonde hair, and the black tail was its natural color.

Saturdays, for many weeks perched under Blaze,

giving her tips, slowly they got to know each other. One night had the pleasure to drive the young woman home again, in her buddy Frankie's car, to where she lived, still with the lover, in a basement flat. Rusty slips a ten-dollar bill into Frankie's fat hand—to pay for gas and her trouble driving, but the big butch shoves it back; one masculine fist to the other, they fight over it. Finally Rusty gives in and puts the ten back in her wallet. "Give it to your little go-go dancer, that's what you want to do anyway, you dirty dog," Frankie comments drolly.

"Yeah. I like her. Blaze. She ain't but 22 years old. She's been a lesbian all her years & will die one," Rusty confides. A lot of lesbians are conservative and fucking uptight about sex. She's free. Her dancing is an art form, she says. Blaze is a free spirit. But she's bolted down by security right now, in a relationship with a butch who ain't no butch. Who is a wimp. I know her life's history. She's the only person I ever talk to in this place. I like a woman to show me some attention."

"Don't we all." Frankie's eyes bored dully out of a flaccid face, having tuned out the spectacle of all the untouchable girls whirling around them some time past 12 midnight, when she'd given up heart.

"I sit up here every Saturday night one week to the next and nobody notices me—to see if I've grown cobwebs on the bar stool or not," the redhead adds glumly.

Lights flash, probe, across the floor. Music loud, rhythm increases. Laughing, gyrating bodies on the dance floor. Blonde dancer on her platform wet with sweat did splits, shook hips, touched her toes, then leaped up in air, half-spun around & had made less than $15 in tips all night. It was near 1:30 A.M. when the shift was finished.

"She'll never leave her lover. They been together a year. The woman is such a wimp; she's supposed to be the more butch of the two, but Blaze has to make love to her."

"Huh!" Frankie grunts.

"Needs her to pay half the rent." Rusty growls this confidence. Frankie smashes a big hat down on her head. The stage is empty; Blaze has gone to get her paycheck for the evening in the back of the bar with the other employees.

The three drive off, Blaze & Frankie in front, the redhead butch, big body folded into the backseat of the compact car, pressed up against the front seat to be as near to Blaze as she can get.

A minor plot unfolds: Blaze must have what is owed on the rent tomorrow—Sunday—and the banks are closed. Has received her night's pay plus a bonus check for having waitressed two nights as a fill-in, and needs to convert this check to money. "I'll cash it." Rusty tells her. And hands over the secret $150 cash from her billfold. Blaze endorses the check to Rusty and passes it back over the backseat.

"You've saved my life Rusty, I really thank you. Really." Her young face sparkles.

"I'd rather give you your check back. Keep it and let me sleep with you." Rusty grunts, a shy smile creases her tough face, holds the girl's shoulder in her hand a moment.

"NO! I WON'T EVEN DIGNIFY THAT

COMMENT WITH AN ANSWER!" But Blaze is smiling, intrigued, & thinks it's funny.

"OK. I apologize. I'm sorry. I'm wrong. I'll be good."

"You *better* be good." Blaze informs her.

They drive to outer San Francisco. It's a nice neighborhood. Their flat in the basement is cold and damp. "It's so cold, mold grows overnight & there's no heat; so we have to use electric heaters. It dries the place out and I always catch the flu, and it runs the PGE bill sky-high."

Night is dark, stars, & they're there. Rusty's face is 6" from the back of Blaze's head, so she can see the black tail emerging out of the blonde close up. "You know what I want?" Rusty whispers. Frankie has turned off the motor, looks out the window to the deserted street. This may be a long good-bye; she knows from dykexperience.

"Tell me." Blaze laughs, a little tinkling noise. Sat very still in the front seat. Could feel Rusty's breath over the short space between them.

Rusty says, "I do a lot of thinking—but not enough talk. I want a woman to serve me sexually any hour of the day or night that I ask.

"I want a woman available on a 24-hour basis.

"I want a woman to hold me in her arms, encourage me sexually—tell me I'm the greatest, & I'm powerful & tell me how strong I am, which I already know I'm strong but I like to hear her say it. And I don't want her love just the vanilla way, but the use of dominance and consensual force. And…" Rusty raised her voice over the hum of the car engine pumping exhaust out its tailpipe layered onto the asphalt and simultaneously blasting heat into the space that contained them. Frankie had switched the ignition back on; she knew it would be a long good-bye. "...And I don't want a single lover, but a tribe of lovers."

Even Frankie was taken aback.

The blond dancer is amused. Rusty smiles; it cuts across her coarse face while she watches Blaze laugh. —She thinks her idea is ridiculous, too. Her heart's desire. Never in 50 years, 34 of them a dyke had she ever approached having this. But, well; humans can dream, and dykes can hope.

"If I had enough money to buy women, or I was very young and very popular...it would be OK. It would work." Rusty had tried to buy an evening with the blonde dancer for $150. Asked her on more than one occasion. The answer had always been a joking "NO." Now Blaze wasn't sure—maybe the butch really did mean it; but she wasn't that kind of girl. Rusty sat in the backseat pressed up as close as she could get to the 22-year-old, her long legs folded & cramped into the compact space. Blaze would go in to be with her lover soon. —Loneliness would settle into the butch's heart, but this minute she was alive, in the spotlight of attention. "I imagine that's a terrible thing to have to do," Blaze mused. "To pay another woman, when there's so many women who will do it free like it's supposed to be; but they're hard to find, I suppose."

"Yeah, especially my type."

"What is your type? Dare I ask?" Blaze's voice comes across the closed container of the car.

"You're my type. Pretty, blonde...young.... You got a nice body," Rusty says.

It's silent. Blaze looks back at her. "Loneliness is the worst thing," Blaze says finally. "You won't believe this with all the attention I get from women, but I get lonely. Because it's the wrong type of attention."

"No." Rusty mused. Pensive, stared into space. "There's something worse than loneliness, but I don't know what it is.... Then comes loneliness after that, and then next worse is probably having to buy a woman. —Unless it's *you*." Blaze reached back and mussed Rusty's red hair. That's one benefit. Her red hair worked like a charm. Women always wanted to touch it.

They talked briefly about her lover. Frankie noticed from her silent vantage point behind the wheel that the young woman was in a state of despair. But Rusty didn't notice. Then the girl went in.

The two butches watch the dancer disappear into the basement flat. Then Frankie guns the motor, shifts into gear.

Rusty climbs into the front seat, belts herself in. After they drove off, she says, "She lives with a wimp. The woman uses her. She won't even get up to go to work if Blaze don't yell at her."

So the magic glow of being a butch in the spotlight of a femme's attention is gone. And Rusty is in despair. And does not let it show like most dykes, the boy-girl type, or any type. As Frankie drives past all the lonely places, drugstores closed for the night, deserted street corners, neon streaking black-glass interiors—all normal things of day, to share with a normal woman in a normal lesbian relationship that none of them really has, none of the three, Frankie, Rusty, nor Blaze.

Frankie, an old-timer who has given up the search holds onto that train of thought.... Finally, as asphalt disappears under the car wheels & they eat up the streetlights of the road ahead, she confesses she ain't been with a woman in 5 years. Rusty chokes. Is shocked. Gulps, turns, and stares at Frankie, a hulking form tall as her but wider, bundled up in a coat & hat. Filling the grey upholstered bucket seat in a blob-shape bulk. "Well, OK, I had 3 pickups...but just for one night. And I had to do what you were telling that girl you wanted her to do, so, Rusty, to me that don't count."

This bit of information mellows the impact, some, of her own life. Music plays faintly on the radio, & Rusty thinks: '500 women must have passed thru the club tonight at various times. All these women, and she ain't had contact with another woman's cunt.... Yet, lesbian is what our lives is all about.'

Redhead mused. 'I don't know how she does it. I haven't had a woman in 1–1/2 weeks, and I want to kill.'

ROUGH TRADE HARD CUM
Chapter Four

She lived a gay lifestyle. Had lived in apartments with gay lovers & roommates & currently was in a studio rental, alone.

'This lesbian life seems so empty.

'So, after taking the dancer home, come home, wish my answering machine held a woman's voice accepting me, wanting me. Bleak. "You have no messages." And a light, steady, unblinking, that signals any recorded calls. 'Not even my ex-lover to phone & harass me.

'Just barren and fruitless wherever I turn.'

Rusty was just hungry.

Cum hard now, alone; harder than she might if there was some roommate to hear her silent ejaculation—breath forced to be quiet; mouth hot against the sheet, riding a pillow between her thighs. Thrust. Her lanky white legs downed with red hair tremble. Red bush, cunt wet discharge on the sheets. Frequently this was her practice, after every other attempt at sex had been exhausted.

'Somewhere in my mid-40s, decided I hate women, most of them. Yes, I hate females.

'Thirty-four years devoted to the lesbian cause— which is my own cause. My own sexuality. Everything that can be done to a person has been done to me by lesbians.'

"I know you've had a lot of bad experiences along that line," Rusty's ex had said.

"I'm not a substance abuser, don't use drugs, so I can't hide from my feelings. It brings out my mad feelings." Rusty had confided. "And feelings of that nature I keep well controlled, down in the pit of my psyche." Rusty had then told Judy about this wanting to kill women. And was sorry she had.

She'd storm inside and nightmare in sleep. And took the long walk home from the clubs at night instead of spending for a cab—pumping muscles of her legs; lifted her weights; did the self-denial of exercise. Her pumping arms like her mad thoughts. 'But isn't that what it's for? To push the body to its limit?'

"You're being a Lone Ranger about it," my ex tells me.

Craved some femme energy.

Had been thinking about it far too long.

So sometimes Rusty passed out of the arc of light that is lesbian life—bar sign blinking pink/green in the night, or a meeting hall of several hundred females, or a woman's bookstore; these common grounds—and went outside of the community, went off alone, the She Wolf to a motel with some unheard-of straight lady, or whore.

'I'd cover her with my whole body. Like to cum on top of her. Like to use her, & let her use me.

'Femme, willing open herself up. I scoot down, she spreads her thighs, her furry cunt open, smooth slick & wet inside, trusting me to pleasure her.' Rusty was passionate & highly sexual.

Femme, responsive & yielding to her aggressiveness. A femme lesbian who responds to her maleness. Who desires her for her ability to wear & need to wear trousers & a black leather jacket & short hair. And to lift weights, and open the door for ladies, and walk in protection between them and the howling wolves of male destruction that are everywhere. And what she likes, and how she carries her body and what she does with it—a butch!

So she had been a frequent visitor to this whorehouse. Sat around with the girls and have to go hide when one of the male clients came to the door so she wouldn't scare him away. Broad body in black leather jacket strode behind a screen across the entrance to the kitchen to wait there until a prostitute took him down to one of the rooms, & heard the door close, & their voices grow faint. Rusty had met the Mexican by answering a sex ad in the personal column of a gay newspaper. The woman brought her there to turn the date, which rapidly developed into a friendship, of sorts.

The Mexican gave Rusty cut-rate prices when the redhead was broke, and took her money when she was flush. The girls were intrigued by this big butch in their midst & so she whiled days away on layoff from work.

It was essentially a straight world. All the girls in the

house arrived with a real name, interviewed for the job, and if hired got an assumed name. They all had a sexual identity; when if asked what that might be they would reply; "Pansexual. I like all kinds of sex." Or, "Anything goes." Or: "Trysexual. I'll try anything once. If I like it, I'll try it again." Practically all of them had had sex with another woman at one time either for fun on their own volition, or had a female lover currently in addition to their boyfriend, or had done lesbian sex in the line of work. —A show for a customer.

"Now, you'd never hear a lesbian say *that*." Frankie had informed Rusty when she told her about the house. "I'm *pansexual*. *Ha*. Hell, no! A dyke is a dyke."

It was great being a butch in a whorehouse surrounded by females in all their array of lace & garter belts and corsets and leather bras & panties—sex work clothes, or the racy outfits they liked to wear in their everyday lives. Had to listen to jokes like—the gist of it paints a verbal portrait of a lesbian with her head between a woman's thighs, who likes nothing better than to suck pussy all day for hours and hours. —This says all lesbians do for sex is to suck pussy, which ignores the fact that some lezzies don't like oral sex, and it doesn't take into account the variety of other things dykes do, thus emasculating them. The fact that some dykes penetrate women with their fingers & cocks & can outfuck most men.

So Rusty went to the house frequently. Sat on the sofa with 6 or 7 girls seminude, in nightgowns, and was bodily close to them—where she was accepted, but was not their basic desire.

After the tricks go, the girls talk about them bad.

Negative stuff. Once every few months, a trick would come thru who was good-looking & had sex appeal & was nice. Then the girls' mouths would water; they'd have a hard time concentrating on business & not let themselves go in pleasure—but this was rare. The red-headed butch sat on the sofa with two pretty girls on each side, another at her feet, and two across the room on another sofa, and others lounging on the rug & a few coming and going naked from the shower to their lockers, stepping over half-clad bodies of females; & the phones ringing several times per minute from the great volume of advertising; & listening to the girls talk business on the phones & gossip to each other, & she would feel a pleasant glow & float farther & farther away into her own world.

And even took Frankie up to the house to celebrate her birthday with paid-for sex. But warns her: "The girls are bi—10 percent lesbian, 90 percent straight. Rosa has a girlfriend you might like; she likes a butch every now and then.... She claims she has to have a woman fuck her every couple of months. You two might like each other, I'm not making any promises."

But nothing had happened. Frankie just sat, sullen. Didn't want to spend the money. Wanted a real woman —that is, a lesbian. And Rosa and her girlfriend got mighty tired of this behavior fast. Because that's how whores can go broke and wind up in the streets among the homeless with their suitcases full of EZ-money finery & thigh-high leather boots.

The rooms are decorated 1950s motel style—an outdated era. Beds always made. Each room has a dresser, nondescript, stocked with latex safe-sex supplies, and a wastebasket ready for their disposal. Cum towels. Lube. Sextoys. Whips & paddles & handcuffs & chains.

The Mexican slut & the redheaded freak get naked. White flesh against tan. The woman smells so good. Flutters her hands all over Rusty's body. Kisses her face, neck, arms; squeezes her shoulders, feels & appreciates the strength of her biceps, and talks steadily, complimenting Rusty, telling her how she deserves to get what she needs. Gives her the full pleasure treatment.

"Most butches melt between my legs. They tell me I'm so beautiful, they don't know what to do with me."

Rusty knew what to do, and she did it. "You're good!" The slut commends her.

'I melted between her legs in cum, red hot. Then, for the second go, she received my cum in her mouth.'

"I love to suck a butch's pussy," Rosa said.

All the anger drained out of Rusty, too—all for the price of $50, that goes to the house, which they would have spent anyway for a motel; and $50 to the woman.

Rusty took her hard with the strap-on, which rubs against her clit fueling excitement toward an orgasmic plateau.

Rosa wore a garter belt; over her bare flesh & pubic hair, stockings & high heels. A lace bodice that pushed her naked ripe tits up and out. Dressed in lace, yet revealed her breasts, cunt, & ass. The butch reached over to her trousers that lay on the chair next to the bed, pulled the belt out of them, wrapped it around Rosa's waist & used it, holding it with her hand to pull the hooker's ass into her & fucked her hard, doggie-style from the rear.

'But none of the violence of which I had promised myself remains. So, yes, I did melt. She took this from me.

'I need a Mexican slut. She's a slut in bed, yeah, she takes my cum. Takes my anger with it.... It takes a Third World slut, or a white whore who's sexual and to whom I'm a cross between a trick & a playmate, who's liable to tell me anything freaky—and not a cold just-say-no-bitch. —Those are the ones I want to kill.'

The Mexican Rosa, too, has self-lies. She will retire soon and be a lady. Will own a house with a yard and a flower garden on the patio & work a square office job and have kids.

They slip & slide in each other's sweat, stomach to stomach; spreads her pussylips, press their clits together and Rusty pounds away; 180 pounds of cum loaded, ready to discharge. Cum together.

'My fingers in her.' Rusty took her hard and long. Then strapped on a 9" dildo. She took Rosa with long, deep thrusts, slow and masterful, then, at the finish, faster, faster pace of her hips. Rosa rose up to meet her thrust, moaning, giving herself; being taken by the thrust of Rusty's cock, and the cock rubbed the magic carpet at its base on Rusty's own womanhood making her clit hard, bringing her to orgasm at the same time. Then she takes the dildo off.

The motel bed creaks; the green/blue patterned spread & flat pillow under their weight. Rosa's tan body stretches under Rusty. Draws her knees up to her chest, holds herself open for her with her hands pressing her knees back to spread her pussylips wide. Rusty got in between, opened her own pussylips for a clear shot for her clit. "I want you to be able to feel me. Feel what I'm doing to you. I want you to feel it, baby."

To be accepted. Held in somebody's arms. Loved. By a cheerful, positive woman.

Rusty came. Came hard.

Tongue hung out of her mouth. Relaxed her grip on Rosa's tit. Sweat rolled off her back. Heart returned to its normal beat.

Then they lay nestled together in the motel-style room; with girls & clients going in and out of rooms next door timed by a clock to half-hour or hour intervals; ofttimes ten minutes if they could get away with it; lay there, Rusty back in her T-shirt & boxer shorts & they'd hold each other and talk.

"I had a butch lover when I was young, in Mexico. She was 28.

Carmen always had young girls—until their families found out—like mine did, and ran her out of town at gunpoint.

This is what the dykes in Mexico do—they go visit the Convent to have sex. Carmen slept with the Mother Superior of the Convent. And this other butch, a friend of Carmen, she was a real hard butch like you; she was seeing a Novice in the Convent. They were both going over there. Carmen's pal's girlfriend, the Novice, was younger of course. She wasn't a full-fledged nun, she was a practice nun. When Carmen saw this younger Novice, she started going out with her and the Mother Superior found out and got mad and got in a fistfight with the Novice. Carmen said the nuns were always getting into fistfights and rolling around on the floor of the Convent. The Mother Superior told Carmen she had to sleep with her only. And they're actually rolling around in fisticuffs over this butch because she wanted the younger girl. The Mother Superior made life hell for that girl after that. And the girl was very young."

'Being with a prostitute. Very loving—for her price. Hands caress all over my body. Talks to me. Loving me.

'So then, it's so long in between time to see her again, I even forget what it's like.

'Flutter tips of her painted fingernails. Smell of her perfume. I think of it time to time as the days pass, then weeks pass; where can I get $100? Since I been laid off a full shift, they just call me to work a few times a week. I can barely make rent.

'Haven't got the price no more....

'Living a bleak existence in my studio. One room with bath & kitchen. —Eating cans of food off the shelves that I had stocked up for emergencies. And thankful I'm not eating out of garbage cans, like the poor & homeless.'

And days pass till Saturday night comes again.

At the whorehouse, Rusty consulted the schedule pasted on the refrigerator door. She was hiding in the kitchen while a girl led a client to a room. Saw when the Mexican was on her shift; & would return there and sit on the sofa among sweet-smelling ladies frantically answering phones, waving manicured hands in the air to dry their nail polish, giving directions how to get to the place, running to and from their lockers to get their scanty costumes; going to the rooms with the men, getting their money; gone for a time, then reemerging to see them to the door.

Since they all had 2 names, it added to the confusion. "Who's Alice? There's been phone calls for you!"

The girls want to know: "Who around here calls herself Lola? There's mail for you at the Post Office Box!"

"Will you please make sure people know what name you're using?" The Madam who owns the place tells them over & over and they never learn.

Rosa. So pretty. Soft in her white gown. She's all business on the phones. "What kind of girl are you interested in? What do you want her to look like? The girl next door? Wholesome?—Or provocative, erotic, a nasty girl?"

A season passed, and Rusty had heard it a million times.

Go into a room, alone with a woman. Door shuts. Never locked. Nobody ever barges in—that's a rule. Knock first & that's only if there's a fire & the house is burning down.

Lie down on top of the perpetually-made-up bed. Half-naked female. Her body feels so good. Her aroma. Touch of her hands that run over my back.

Rosa had peeled off her white gown, dressed in a garter belt, stockings, and a bra that pushed her naked breasts so they stuck out, for Rusty to feel & squeeze & suck. Lies back and opens up her pussy with her fingers, and the butch goes down & licks it and goes inside her wet chamber with three fingers, four, & then her fist.

And her clit starts to work its magic. Soon Rusty is moaning & groaning on top of the woman, her body writhes. Rocks in her arms till it subsides. White freckled skin covered with sweat.

'Realize that these girls like butch dykes, but it's just one facet of their sexuality—20 percent at most. The rest, they like guys.'

So, long days pass on the sofa in which Rusty's surrounded by sexy girls, but her mind drifts to the Venus Club, and its Saturday-night lesbian crowd.

Sits at the bar amid the clatter of women condensing a gay life out of a 7-day week into a 3-hour meeting place. Talk. Cruise. Just sit and get quietly bombed on liquor, watching only. Drinking in the sight of other lesbians.

Rusty leaned against the platform, the dancer's feet inches from her head. She could still savor the taste of the Mexican in lacy lingerie, in whose wet cunt and mouth had got off five times in their last session. Her feet wearing silver high, high heels, long legs folded back; arms around Rusty's shoulders as they fucked cunt-to-cunt in erotic play.

She let the fantasy memory drift over the palate of her consciousness like a delicious meal—and licked her lips.

ROUGH TRADE HARD CUM
Chapter Five

'Saturday. Call from an ex-girlfriend. Hangs up on me. Last direct human contact I've had.'

"I don't believe you're acting like this! Not with all the women out there who want me! Who want a woman! —And I haven't even met them yet!—But I know they're out there! Who want a real lady like I am, and not an androgynous lesbian! You think about it, you bitch! Rusty, you'll come back to me on your hands and knees! I'm a lady! It's no problem for me to get a butch! I never had a problem with that! —My only problem was at first making up my mind to come out and be a lesbian & stop lying to myself & avoiding my attraction to women! Once I made up my mind, women flocked to me! *You're* the person who says it's so hard to meet a feminine woman, the type you need to satisfy you! — Like *me!*

"A butch like you are—you need a very sexual woman. You *need* someone like me!"

'A butch is someone who kind of loiters around, waits for women to see she's somebody.

'Pry painted fingernails under the lapel of my black leather jacket, pull me close & blow in my ear.

'I'm packing. Dick in my pants.

'Showing off on the dance floor. Stalking other women.

'No car, so, that all-too-familiar scenario, traveling across town by bus and by foot to be in the bars.

'With no money, gone back & forth to gay clubs daring the heart of darkness in dangerous streets.

'Times I need pussy more than I need my life.

'I'm both. Not a man. not a woman. Feel my femaleness & my butchness. A borderline gay. More a transsexual. Not sure if I really want to be a man. Sure I'd like to have a dick to fuck her with, but not sure I want to give up my cunt. —And in so doing, the whole race of lesbians who desire me for it, even if they don't fuck it like I do theirs. Definitely don't want to get a change of sex and blend into the world of men and be grouped in with them and have to be around men and do things men do. Talk men's talk. Have men sit next to me on the bus, thinking I'm another man. I'm not a man in my heart. Definitely don't want to have a hairy body and face.'

Regardless of what Feminists think about her as a butch:

Fact: she paid the dues of a woman loving other

women all her life with no exception—in quest of that love had ghettoized herself from the privilege of being a straight woman—a white one with red hair moving in a straight world. Even her underwear (men's) was a firebrand of defiance against patriarchy. That she wore it was a sin against all churches and organized religions of that day. Rusty paid her dues to love sensually, to lie down in bed with a woman—defiance that could not be challenged. Tho they called her crude and semibarbaric with women, her loyalty could not be denied. Rusty could not pass off as straight anywhere, in any way. While other dykes vacillate back & forth between straight & gay life; between their heart's love and the advantage & freedom hetero society affords, it was an outstanding fact that she truly was a lesbian. —The original archetype. No doubt what she wanted. A woman. No secret what she was, a biological female. A butch dyke.

She had been considered to be the lowest of the low by straights & her own people—Feminists—alike.

A lot of Feminists really don't understand what's going on down in the heart of a butch woman.

Rusty sat at the bar and watched—saw the procession in her mind's eye. 'Ingrid, Inez, Irma.' Names. Got thru to the J's, before she quit. '600 women I've bedded since age 18. Six hundred pussies wet, melting against mine in cum since I learned to fuck.

'Six hundred tufts of fine pubic hair in my mouth—I like blondes. And their lips and tongues, 600—pleasure me as I stand over them in my jackboots.

'Acts of sadism every day. All kinds of brutality, savage acts go on between human beings and animals against each other. I'm one of the people whose spirit has been broken down to bits.

'I used to cry for the animals, for the children, for the innocents. Now I don't feel nothing.

'The pain on the inside of a human being is so great....' Shoved her glass back across the bar, clenched her hands together as thoughts struggled thru that red-haired head....

'To wound her in her vagina as they have wounded me in my soul.

'Six hundred. How many have loved me? Five or 6. How many have I loved? Nearly all,' Rusty concluded.

'Faces I've seen before—I forget their names. Faces I've slept with before, it's all a blur. Looking up from under me.

'A million women trip past thru this place, in reverse gear.

'As I say—I just sit here and see everything come my way.

'You see everybody again.... Everybody. And there, around the bend, comes my ex—turning 'round the end of the bar.

Femme, curvy. Gaining weight in middle age. Stops. Puts her hands on her hips. "RUSTY! IS THIS YOU!?"

"NO !"

The redhead pushed the lady back on a bar stool. Viewers could tell by the way her body dived in toward Judy how bad she wanted to fuck. Fell into her open arms, buried her head of red hair into the fluff's chest—a bosom, full, round stretching its sweater. Wrapped her muscular arms around Judy, pulled her up off the bar stool into her in a mighty embrace. Then set her down and leaned over her, one thigh between Judy's legs spread on the bar stool. Judy wears toreador pants, the sweater, a necklace, bracelets, high heels, naked feet. But it was an instant only. To no avail. Nothing could mend their broken relationship.

"How's it going? Are you happy, *baby?*"

"No."

"Well, *try*. Remember how it was when we were together," her ex says, beautifully made-up eyes flash with the acid remark.

"Yeah. I'm out here chasing around like a baboon on a roller coaster," Rusty mumbles. Stretches out both arms in the black leather jacket and holds up her hands in surrender. Judy runs her fingers thru the red head of hair and sighs.

And so here she stood, caught by a slice of her own real life come to wound her with an angular cut, amid fantasies of destruction of women.

Butch & femme. Their scorn, their anger faded. For a moment, they had that peace inside each other they had had in the beginning.

Then Judy pushes Rusty off her, tired of smelling that familiar men's cologne in her nose. "So what are you doing for your hot pussy, baby? Still can't find a girlfriend? Well"—Judy's mascaraed eyes flash, tilts her jaw up, and turns her head from side to side—"I see a lot of women in here, Rusty!… Of course you have to have a femme, so that narrows it down. Well, there are different types of sex. Do it yourself, then! A lot of girls do, I understand. I wouldn't know; I don't have to."

'Sex has got to be right for my head. Masturbation is not one of my types I like. Neither is having an androgynous sexless woman,' Rusty thinks.

Later the ex returns to her girlfriend, who also has painted fishlike eyes. They survey the dance floor. Rusty stands at the bar, hitches up her trousers; black jacket satiny under gold bar lights. Tall, handsome, a soft drink in her hand. Sad—they can tell because the corners of her mouth turn down.

Judy brags, "She's walking around town jacking herself off. She's walking around town, her hot clit in her fingers, because I'm not going to do it no more. And she can't get a new woman to do it. She sees me and she hates me. She had it good for two years, and let it go. —To screw another wench. Her new woman don't like sex. So she dropped her, and now Rusty's alone. And that was 6 months ago."

Judy taps her pink painted nails on the bar, eyes flash, narrow, watching the redhead down thru the crowd, silhouetted by flashing lights. "She's so mannish. Too much male drive. She has to have it every night. She thinks she has to have it.... But they did a study. Lesbians don't have any more testosterone than regular women, so I think it's all in her head. She wants me to come back to her. She says she's dying. She's not dying, she's lying. And she's got nobody to cook for her anymore, & she's got an ulcer from her own bad cooking.

"She's an ex-alcoholic, neurotic, and she needs help." Her femme friend nods in agreement.

"She's a fucking good-looking butch." The companion eyes Rusty. "That red hair is amazing. Does she have it all over her body?"

"Yeah." Judy exhales sharply, stares at Rusty. "She's tall, strong, handsome, highly intelligent. Very, very smart. *Too* smart. You can't tell by looking at her, she seems casual. But she broods too much. Dwells on things. Believe me, I know some of the thoughts that pass thru that red head. I lived with her 2 years."

Stereotypes about redheads are—that they are fiery, emotional. It was true. Rusty was emotional, but kept it well hidden except from people who knew her.

People responded to Rusty because of her hair. As a true redhead, she was different.

Blondes and redheads aren't the same at all. Scottish and Irish, they are different nationalities from blondes. There are fewer redheads than other colors. —They're special.

Women expected Rusty to have a really hot temper, to be irrational and out of control. And expected her to live up to it. And a lot of redheads do.

"Red hair shoots out of my head; it grows out red," Rusty used to explain. When she was younger, dykes use to say, "Hey, baby, is it red all over?" People are fascinated by the fact that all her hair could be red. Red under her armpits and pubic hair. Just really conscious of red hair.

Carrottop. Red. Rusty. That's how she got the name. Her actual name was Maureen Mignon.

Like all redheads, she was secretly proud of her hair. Proud that she was different from anybody else.

And she looks down on people who think they have red hair, such as strawberry blondes, or auburn, but aren't really redheads.

Maybe it is her red hair, maybe it is the full moon, but controlled violence, thinking about ways to do it, shaped Rusty's thoughts. The way a madwoman bent on revenge oils up her shotgun.

ROUGH TRADE HARD CUM
Chapter Six

'There is no way a cute pretty blonde gal like that is going to go home with me—but I give her a $5 tip, then a second $5 in singles, to make it look like a lot more.'

Does all this on the strength of three $50 bills she carries to be prepared for emergencies, which is crazy because she has barely enough to meet the rent and don't know how she'll eat the rest of the week, but her sex life is more important.

Across the barroom, bottles clink. Music's pounding sexual beat pours out of the speakers.

Above the crowd on her platform, the dancer fights gravity. Leaps in air, thrusts her hips as if trying to shake them off her body, gyrates, shakes, spins.

'Can't unless the sex is right for my mind.'

Rusty was strong enough, brave enough, experienced enough for the blonde to surrender to her.... 'Never thought she would...this blonde....'

A slick, strong lesbian with confidence like Rusty, it excites the shit out of femmes. Femme lesbians like confidence on the street & in bed. Rusty had it.

So, a few more months had passed, & the Saturday-night ritual of the blonde dancer, using her platform as a leaning post, from which to plunge into the crowd, going after some lady. And having no sex in a sex-negative world.

And kept hanging out by the blonde dancer; was there. Was there when she steps down, breathless, to take her 10-minute break.

Rusty knows she has trouble getting home. Young, has no car.

Leans against the platform. Girl wears tight spandex shorts, a halter top over her full breasts which strain under tight, hard nipples. Red lipstick, gold earrings, & short hair.

Rusty beckons the girl, who leans over, stops her dance a minute; and the butch thinks: 'I just want to fuck your cunt, baby, so bad, so bad. Exchange body fluids.' Smiles at the sweating dancer. 'Suck up my discharge in her mouth & see her swallow it.' And Rusty's saying sweetly "Let me take you home—in a cab tonight."

"OK!" Blaze shouts over the music. "But I gotta go straight to bed. I have to get up early tomorrow. I got a new part-time job waitressing. So you can't come in."

"It's OK," Rusty says.

Thinks about the $20 she's spending for the cab, for maybe nothing.

It's cold. Blaze sticks her hands in the sleeves of her coat & hunches down like a turtle. "Driver, turn the heat up for us," Rusty says. Blaze turns to the butch and tells her life story. Her old lady has stopped making love to her months ago & is threatening to move out & Blaze can't afford the rent by herself. The wimpy butch has stood her up & left her stranded at the club tonight, & she's so thankful for Rusty's help.

"Fine butch! If it was me, I'd be waiting for you right at the club to make sure you got home safe."

The cold melts from the blast of the heater. Blaze's painted lips press together; her eyes get big. As the cab rattles over San Francisco city streets, she tries to explain the situation that is gnawing at her like a dog chewing a bone. Of course it's the age-old lesbian story: ever-present drag—never having quite enough money. Bills. Struggling to have the rent paid on time. If the wimp moves, she'll have to find a roommate quick, or move also; put her stuff in storage, find a rented room & start all over again.

And the cab flies fast, negotiates the twists and turns. Blaze nods her blonde head, lips tense. "The worst isn't the money, but our relationship. She won't make love to me…I don't know why. She just died on me one day."

As Blaze talks, Rusty nods, "Yeah." And her mind drifts to her own needs. About how she has to lie with a glamorous sexy loving sexual fast very loving erotic woman for the sex to be right for her mind.

The blonde intones plaintively: "Seems like it's

continuing morning noon and night. More and more and more. She's out all night, and she's on the phone all day with somebody else. But they're all friends; it's not like it was a lover or anything."

It's dark except for a few streetlamps. Blaze gets out of the cab, black shoes & white sox, shorts, & a coat wrapped around the rest.

In the yellow interior of the cab, Rusty pays the driver. Envisions the long way home—20 blocks to the Geary bus line, which is the only one that runs all night. If Blaze won't let her…. Even thinks vaguely about asking to crash out on the sofa until morning's light. Rusty's footfalls cross the sidewalk and the cement steps down to the basement flat, join Blaze. Shadow figures, they stand by the door of her apartment. Rusty thinks, 'Hell, what is she gonna say next?'

And Blaze continues on the theme she'd spent many evenings telling Rusty: why her "soft butch" is better for her; superior, as it were, to a "hard butch," which is what Rusty is; tho in not these direct words. Rusty nods her head dully. Man's shirtfront shows, for she has unzipped her jacket in dull hopes she might get a good-night hug and wants to feel it full on her body, not thru inches of leather. Strong fingers clench together shoved down deep in her pockets. Clit anesthetized, and her emotions numb both with the cold & the words. Then Blaze is finished. Her blonde hair is neat. Rusty's is rough having combed her freckled fingers thru it again & again anxiously. "Good night," Rusty whispers, takes the girl by her shoulders and draws her close, kisses her under the starlight; full lips touch Blaze's lipsticked mouth.

Hot. Their lips part open, and Rusty's tongue probes the girl's wet mouth; and Blaze responds, parting her lips and touching the butch's tongue with her own.

Rusty don't know what's happening, only follows as Blaze moves apart from her, gets out the key, opens the door & motions for her to follow.

The two go in. The place is cold, damp, & silent. Blaze switches on the lights and looks thru the 4 rooms. "HA! She's not here! I can't believe I'm actually happy!" Wraps her arms around Rusty again for a moment. Then breaks away & stares up at her. "I'm going to let you spend the night with me because I need to get back at that bitch.... And because my body needs to.... Well, Rusty...you don't know anybody we know...and I don't want this getting out that we slept together!" Frowns, and a worried look crosses her smooth young face in the dim light of the living room.

Rusty grabs Blaze in a terrific bear hug and pulls her lovingly across the room into the bedroom. There it is, mattress on the floor, just like at her own place. Like so many dyke places, with young lesbians on the run from bad relationships, from bad neighborhoods, from one city to a better city.

Rusty is happy, happy. They collapse down on the mattress together.

Small amount of light from the living room silhouettes them to each other. Blaze ran the tips of her fingers down Rusty's face. "You still think a butch should have two femmes?"

"I'd love it."

"Some weak butches aren't enough for one woman. How about a femme with 2 butches?"

"There are plenty of butches who have that now. They just don't know it. —I'm the other butch a lot. That's how I know."

They lay together under covers on the mattress. Red hair & blonde, of their heads. Pubic hair red & black bushes brushing each other. "God, Rusty, you're red all over your body! Aren't you! I can hardly see!"

Soon Blaze was on her back, thighs parted so she could get done. Get lesbian sex.

Wet & slimy, her juice made it wet everywhere. Cuntlips, sheets, mattress, thighs, Rusty's face & fingers.

Duly, during lovemaking, Rusty recalls: here's a woman she'd fantasized killing, just a few hours ago.

Her sweet dripping wet cunt. Smells of her own pussy now on Blaze's fingers & in her breath, as her mouth presses close to Rusty's ear, exhaling short excited gasps. 'I can't get this with a dirty magazine.' As she goes in with 4 fingers, thinks: 'Here's the real thing, right here with me.'

"Love me!" Blaze gasps.

"Try to relax." Rusty coaches, her face strains with tension, red down on her upper lip in an almost-invisible mustache.

"It really excites me. Makes me feel like I'm a sacrifice. Giving myself up to her," Blaze had said once before.

Rusty coaches: "I need some more lube."

"I want your fist in me!" Blaze gasps.

Rusty holds her hand in front of Blaze, who lies back, head on the pillow. Makes a fist. "Is it too big for you, baby?"

Blaze looks at it. "Your hands are bigger than hers."

So Rusty puts it in gently, by working her fingers thick with lube in with a screwing motion. Blonde's knees are drawn up to her chest, feet off the mattress, thighs spread wide; then Rusty turns her hand once more, and her fist slides in.

Time ticks by like a gallant ship on the night seas of time. Two females on a mattress on a floor. Lean bodies. White walls hold their groans, their sighs.

Books in homemade shelves on the wall mark it as a lesbian world by the titles that stare down at them. The rainbow flag. Posters for the Women's Music Festival.

'I could turn into rough trade on her and fuck her raw.' Rusty's face scowls hard. 'Can do anything I like. She's in my control.'

Blaze thinks: 'Sometime's it's very uncomfortable when her fist goes in…I let a butch do this to me…let all my guards down. And become very vulnerable. She has me literally in the palm of her hand. I feel like I'm putting my life in her hands.'

Rusty's fantasy of whipping her, loving her, fucking her, killing her… Blaze draws her knees up to her chest, surrendering to the fucking.

Plunge of Rusty's fist in and out partway, then back in.

So then, from the back burner of her mind, Rusty thinks: 'I could just kill her, just like this. I thought about it back in the club.' Now that idea seems so far removed from what she's doing.

Rusty gazes down at Blaze, as she crouches over her; fist pounding in her cunt, arm tense with the action and the strain making sweat bead over her naked skin. "You can kill a woman like this, you know," Rusty says; simultaneously fucks her hard and slow.

Blaze just opens her eyes, looks up. Her fit white body trembles & she moans, "Don't talk like that! Just fuck me, honey!"

Rusty thinks: 'I could kill her, but I won't because she's giving me all this erotic sex, so I won't hurt her—any more than she consents to be hurt. No surprises, baby.' "Baby, baby, baby," Rusty coos. Leans over her, pounding carefully, and strong with her fist.

"Ohh! Ohh!" The blonde cries in time.

Time ticked by, neon outside and no sound here but their lovemaking.

And felt Blaze clamp down on her hand. Arm between those legs, in the wet chamber leading to the womb of life.

'Most femmes are smaller and weaker than me. A few slugs in their painted face with my fists, and they'd be down. Quivering in obedience. But here I got my fist right up her cunt and she loves it; tossing and turning, humping. Enjoys. And I'm enjoying.... And she's gonna have my genitals in her mouth again and suck me long and hard soon. Long and good, to a hard cum before night's done...'

"So lonely, I just can't feel no feelings no more. Never should have broke off with my last girlfriend." Rusty's voice breaks the silence. Fist is out of her, wet with mucus. And she straps it on: 8" of female cock rising from out of the red fur of her pubic mound.

"You handle that thing really well," Blaze informs her later.

With her, loving her. "Just tell me when you want me to leave," Rusty heard herself say.

Dawn was creeping in thru the window.

"You'll have to leave," the blonde whispers. "But not yet. Don't go yet; I want you near me."

'Make the ecstasy last between my thighs as long as I can.

'I come hard and long, and it's real good. Real sweet.

'This trade is rough on the heart.

'This blonde, I know it's just for tonight. I got lucky. Because she's hurting and sad about her girlfriend. Blonde dancer. And I won't kill her, ever. Because she favored me.'

Descent into this honey pit—this woman trap of naked thighs in garter belts. Breasts, cunt, cuntjuice, touch. Then the emotional cutoff. —'She won't want to see me again.' How many times had Rusty heard those words: "You're too much like a man; you're too hard. I never let my lover fuck me like you did. I'm usually the aggressive one."

"But you liked it!"

"Yeah, I loved it, and hated it. You've heard of pleasure and pain? I can't fuck like that every night."

"You don't have to do it every night," Rusty cajoles her.

Blaze stops talking and just stares into space, held in the butch's arms. Like she's a million miles away…or thinking about somebody else. Rusty gazes down at what she holds in her arms. Thinks about Blaze. She's a sexual being. A woman who knows what she wants from another lesbian.

Enters her vagina once more before it's time to go. Fingertips rub her clit, then go in her, & pull out, & rub her clit until she bucks up for more. Hips slap the mattress, her hole strains for Rusty's fingers; who slides 3 fingers in, then thrusts hard & fast, nonstop until she feels an orgasm rock Blaze's body.

Lay there exhausted. Sun came up brilliant, even to a basement apartment.

Rejection.

"But it's nothing about you. Nothing about you, Rusty." Blonde speaks wearily. "It's all about my lover," Blonde went on. "I don't like a woman who reminds me too much of a man. I was never with a man, but I've worked around them for 3 years. A butch, a hard butch, one like you who looks like a man, acts like a man, fucks like a man... You've crossed that line. You look like a man. You're a stone butch."

"So what's your lover? She's a butch!"

"She's a *soft* butch. She might wear high heels and a dress one day if she needs to—for her job, and she likes to. And look butch as hell the next day. It's in her nature. She's a soft butch. Then a stone butch sometimes. Sometimes she pushes it right up to the line like you, & looks & acts like a man. Other times she looks like a total woman, and you'd never guess she's gay."

Blaze stares at the ceiling. Dawn is born. Doesn't want to let Rusty go. Eyelids flutter. She falls asleep holding the butch in her arms.

So Rusty thinks: 'Maybe I should kill myself. Maybe that's the answer. I can't kill Blaze, she's let me use her body. I came twice. No...I can't kill myself, and I have to kill some woman who won't touch me at all. So I'm rejected. And she's still holding my body, and I won't let her go for nothing.'

Day rose in full. Blaze's lover still had not come home. The two women got up, washed, dressed.

They move around the 10-by-15 foot room. Rusty picks up her clothes. Got her pack with the rubber dick & harness.

Rusty notices that Blaze asks her an awful lot of questions & feels guilty. 'Maybe she could tell by my face I was thinking about killing somebody. Maybe she thinks I'm dangerous.' And Blaze looks at the butch oddly, as if sizing her up. But Rusty didn't attach any importance to this.

Day. Rusty's left, goes to work, starts a new shift; & Blaze is late to her waitress job. So go the lives of the working poor.

Rusty grumbles to herself: 'If I was a man, I'd have a regular shift, and not have to fill in on Sundays. Not enough emotional input from the girls—that's the other half of my troubles.'

She was a traveler in a lesbian desert. Women poised at the bar in Show, offered no release.

'I'm a fellow sister. Traveler in a lesbian-landscaped crater of the moon with no answers, no exit, but my sexual release; and their love. A barren landscape of moon craters & dead volcanoes; but once in a while, just every once in a blue moon, a crater opens and a verdant rich land hidden underneath—that nobody could have guessed was there—emerges.

'I'm angry all the time. Angry.'

Unlike the past, hurt when a one-night stand proved

to be just that and not the beginning of a lifetime commitment, a mature Rusty was glad. Glad she had loved Blaze & cum in a warm release in a woman's receptive body; & not the awful loneliness & emptiness which had been her recent fate.

Rusty stood tall. Blazing red hair.

A macho boy-girl. Macho because that's all she had. Owned a few other things—clothes, radio, TV, a truck, a gun, some lesbian books. Had rented a series of rooms or apartments all her life, and women interchangeable with the rooms.

Nothing else.

So she was macho. —Struts around, especially when she feels a femme eye her. Up to a point, her whole social life has been in the bars shooting pool.

'Not too often you can get intimate with another woman. —Get naked. If you missed it from your mother, too bad.'

Rusty. Was one of the crossover people. A he-she. Was a human being and was entitled to joy.

'Feel I'm a coward.'

It wasn't to be expected for her to beat up men twice her size. And to God she walked tall indeed. And to a few femmes. —Nobody else, not even to herself. Rusty walked with power on a very exceedingly hard journey.

Rusty never would have thought she could have been soothed and received by the lesbian community which had given her its collective cold shoulder; into whose Femme arms she was received finally. Never would have thought that having a cunt between her legs, and seldom used the whole thing—besides her hot clit,—that would qualify her to belong; that (not as a man) as much of a boy-girl as Rusty was, she still belonged with them, her sisters; and that she would one day know peace in a woman's arms....

ROUGH TRADE HARD CUM
Chapter Seven

Blaze is up on the platform, dances blithely. Sees the redheaded butch approach. Leans down over the edge: "I'm taking my break." Hops down, goes off to the bar & Rusty follows. Blaze orders a long tall glass of water with ice cubes. She wears black slacks, her cutaway shirt shows bare arms. White face valentine shape, pert mouth lipsticked red, & short blonde hair. —So cute, so lesbian.

"I've thought about what you said, Rusty."

Petulant, looks up at me; rosebud mouth, bright eyes. Just spills it out, point-blank. "Can you take care of me? I'm tired of being poor. I'm sick of having nothing. I'm tired of living in a basement flat. And having a cold I can't get rid of. You're always joking about paying me

$150—well, that's not what I want. But Rusty, maybe we could get together. We'll be lovers and friends. But not married. Free. You'll do your part, I'll do mine. You won't stand me up, will you?" Innocent, yet mature, a 22-year-old woman who's tired of it all. Rusty looks down deep into her brown eyes and sees Blaze in the real flesh & not her own perverted fantasy. 'Young & pretty, yet she's sick of it, too. Just like me. Tired of this lesbian life, living in basements and insecurity.'

"I thought maybe we can live together. I'm not going to be your woman; I'm nobody's woman. No more. But I'll sleep with you, in the same bed. I don't like to sleep alone. I promise I'll make love with you a lot. You're good in bed. We'll be more than roommates, but we won't be married."

"I want to, Blaze. I'd love to…. You like me in bed?"

Blaze's face furrowed. Her rosebud mouth tipped up. "My lover was such a wimp compared to you. You're strong. Yes, Rusty, you're very good in bed. You gave me what I wanted."

"You gave *me* what I wanted, too." Rusty grabs her on butch impulse, holds the fluff in her arms in a tight hug.

So the bar nights ending long & bar lights shine bright on its patrons long left over, thinking about their misspent lives. So it ends. The bar tunes pound out the last song. Blaze hops back up on her platform to finish the dance. Next view, the Venus Club has thinned out considerably. Strewn paper napkins on the floor, piles of glasses & bottles on the bar.

Rusty leans against the platform, overwhelming flood

of joy hits her. Lips fuzzy with red down. Happy. Even her. Who was stoic. Angry. She is amazed.

It's just barroom madness concocted in the whirl of personalities, rejections, and acceptances; interchanged between members of a lesbian tribe. For Rusty wasn't an alcoholic, drank little these days, and could see clearly, and new hope peered thru the too many bad memories.

'So the long night ends—I'm drained. Still haven't done it—killed some girl. It's just flesh and ringlets. Ringlets of hair down her back. White shoulders and arms, face inviolable, having just turned her back on me and talks to someone else, younger, with more savoir-faire.... But I couldn't care less, I'm so happy, happy, happy tonight because I've been made an offer I can't refuse. Refuge. A harbor in a woman's thighs. Companionship & she's young & pretty & smart and works, and she likes me.... I forget about the killing ground, the rape, the blood, the intentional murder I'd planned... I'm so happy happy happy.... As I've said, a lot of thoughts pass thru your head while you stand by the bar watching the girls.'

PLEASURE IN THE GLITTER GUTTER
Chapter One

It's all about the Puss-y.
—Anonymous quote

Glitter Gutter. Miracle Mile. Folsom Street, San Francisco, South of Market—SOMA district, 1984.

This new arrival to the club was of little interest to the glamorous lesbians who worked the door.

Five-feet-three-inches, 135 lbs. Age 45. Medium build; tan complexion; a brown-haired butch.

Educated in the middle class, but fallen from grace because of a broken home & mental illness. Life in a spiral of centrifugal force, a long process of dissolution —and struggle to remain a top.

Her vocabulary consisted of popular words—less esoteric than an educated person that no one can understand but a scholar or an artist.

The high-class edge had worn off, and revealed she had nuts and grit, and soul.

Wore dark jeans, designer stitch; handsome brown boots, brown leather jacket, and a man's satiny shirt that glittered.

Under, men's boxer shorts; stripes red & blue on white; and a black T-shirt.

'Prove my prowess as a lesbian butch.

'Not the world's best, but not the worst either. I know I will find a woman in this glamorous place.'

Warm, willing, and very lesbian.

Carried a backpack; in it, besides the can of Mace for protection, a notepad & change of underwear, was a dildo & harness. 'Have to penetrate. I want my woman to feel something. Four fingers will fill up her wet pussy. And this.' And a tube of K-Y & a few condoms, 'in case I get weak & let her do it to me.'

So this stranger, hat brim pulled over her eyes, signed in the hotel register, name & home address which was across the Bay Bridge in Oakland. Paid $35, got a receipt and key. Door person indicated the entrance that connected thru to the hotel from the club. Went thru & up a stairway carpeted & silent.

'Is it wrong to want the love of another woman in my clit and my cunt?' Life had answered this question 30 years ago. 'If not, then why is it so god-awful difficult to get to?'

Her clit throbbed.

'I wish they'd stock these hotels with women.'

Opened the door with the key, went in, & set the backpack on the bureau.

'I wish they provided as one of their services—women.'

Room was 12' x 10'. Double bed, closet. Very still.

'Maybe those sweet young things reject me because I'm too butch?. Or too old... Maybe because they can tell I'm not quite white.... Blacks reject me because I look white. What a problem!... Also, I'm too picky. I want a glamorous glitter lady.'

Pushes the hat brim up on her head. Had had her share of women by now. Took her boxer shorts & T-shirt & clean shirt out of the backpack.

'Fill her up with my rod. Uh. Bring her up here, maybe one of those hot strippers that's gonna perform here tonight.'

Over the years her luck with ladies got better. Just come out of a 2-year interval with 4 women in a row. —Two black sisters older than herself who, when they had broken up, had been very nurturing; & they'd still remained friends. A Jewish lesbian sex relationship. —They had agreed on these terms, asking nothing more than a hot dependable lay. And the last, a sweet blonde blue-eyed fox who had left her for another woman with no warning & who then went straight. This cold separation had nearly killed her.

Her heart was on the mend.

During this period, she also struggled to survive economically. Now, having some financial success, it was her first time out on the prowl in 2 years. Butches' Night Out!

This newcomer had earned a livelihood as a janitor, bartender, warehouse worker, nurse's aide, on & on. Many people have an avocation as well. —Hers was being a writer. This something she saw, beyond the daily grind—a goal. In the meantime, she was a telephone salesperson, a sort of con artist.

An Undesirable.

Part of the Underclass.

Our territory as gays are the clubs, the neighborhoods, the restaurants; and books. The rainbow flag flying proudly from windows & cars; purple, blue, green, yellow, orange & red.

What a struggle!

Two strippers from the lesbian sex show that was due to begin in an hour had been in the entrance at her arrival. Now the butch didn't know this—one woman, a tan beauty, almond-eyed, had looked her up and down head to toe & inquired about her.

At 45, she was used to being devalued as a woman and as a dyke & didn't fully realize the power that lay within.

"Wow! Who is that butch there?" Zarina asked.

"That's Red... Red something...a strange last name." Roxie replied as she flitted about, some last-minute fliers in her hand to be posted. "She used to go to the shows all the time a while back."

Nobody knew the butch intimately, but most had seen her around forever & knew her on a first-name basis .

A she-man. Masculine.

"That's the type I like." Zarina giggled, following the statuesque blonde back-stage. Soon all the strippers were in the bathroom changing clothes.

Hands on the Mickey Mouse watch said 8 P.M.

Evening events had begun earlier. —In a suite of

rooms across town, a ramshackle Victorian building, once a residence, now used as an office for a fly-by-night phony telephone scam supposedly for the benefit of crippled children.

Days on the job were 12 hours straight. Lying into a telephone receiver to the customers in their homes at the other end, or in their places of business. Her index finger ran down a list taken from the Reverse Directory of the phone company. Sell. Sell it verbally. —The concept that the show tickets—$12.50 apiece—are going to help a disadvantaged kid. Clear voice into the telephone receiver.

The businesses might purchase a block of tickets worth $500. Her commission at 20 percent was then $100. An individual usually popped for $25—$5 in the butch's wallet.

Why was it, as a member of a racial minority (barely visible), a dyke (extremely visible), and former street person with mental troubles, that she found most of the jobs she ever had were illegal? 'World, explain this to me!'

Four-room suite. A garbage can on the second floor. So much $ passed thru this craphole; $50,000 in 2 months before it would close down and she would go on to the next one.

Day began at 9 A.M., when the first business owners came in. Twelve noon lunch, grab a big bean burrito dripping with cheese. Then resume toil; ear glued to the telephone, boots planted on the floor that is littered with cigarette butts, talking shit & scribbling out names, addresses, & amount of the cash donation. Until 5:30.

Then, take a half-hour break walking around the semi-gay neighborhood, and back on the night phones until 9 P.M.

Took the BART train under the bay from Oakland on Saturday to work people's homes for 4 hours, for an extra $50.

And was so busy working, didn't have time to see her loneliness.

Police had raided the last office the butch worked in San Leandro, so she was back in The City, on a street quite near the Gay Mecca of Castro. Lying a new lie, according to a script written out by the owners; spinning new fabrications—waving a tan hand in the air as she expounded on the theme of the crippled children: 'Yes, we pick each child up at their house & deliver them to the facility & take them back home. We do this every year." Using her safe-sounding voice—clear, sincere, and proper white English.

'They call me the Silver-Tongue-Devil.'

She remembered them well—those long-ago days beyond the statute of limitations.

We don't see people crawling all over each other trying to survive; don't see them prostituting & eating out of garbage cans here in the United States so much —there's too much opulence.

But this is the only job many poor souls could get —some visible gays, the mentally troubled, etc. Always the last in line, and never hired.

So Red had finally discovered another place besides bed where she had power. —Phone Power. White Middle-Class AmeriKKKa responds to her because she sounds like she IS White Middle-Class.

It's the voice.

In fact, at one job, they had nicknamed her The Voice. —Until plainclothes police broke down the office door with a warrant, wanting to know who inside was impersonating the Mayor of Alameda to sell ads.

'I apologize for what I've stolen!'

No one else is in the office now, only this hard worker who seeks a living from lists of age-old givers, called Tap Cards.

Boots planted on the floor, itchy in a rough work shirt, corduroy slacks, & funky gym shoes. *Hand on the Mickey Mouse watch says: "It's time to go, or you'll miss the show!"*

The butch got up, stretched mightily, grabs her backpack and goes into the toilet at the end of the two rooms 30 feet away from her desk.

It's a public craphole. Holes in the floorboards, sink with a bucket under to catch dripping water. Toilet seat always up and never flushed, brown & yellow piss; pubic hairs all over it that fall off the bodies of the pissers. —Nobody cleans this toilet. The manager & his secretary in the other rooms have their own private toilet. It's very clean. She squats over the shitty one and pisses. Then, gingerly, begins the maneuver to change clothes while touching as little of the walls or floor of the filthy room as possible. Off go the corduroys and stinky work shirt and funky boxer shorts and T-shirt; slips on the new striped shorts over her slender tan legs, over muscled arms a black T-shirt. Fresh deodorant. Satin shirt, fancy dark jeans. Modern boots. Brown leather jacket.

Clit throbbed in anticipation.

Strode out of the craphole. —Was the only one who ever flushed it. Went to take a glance in the mirror.

Mirror over the mantelpiece of the tumbledown Victorian catches a butch combing hair back over her ears like a man. Splashes on masculine cologne—Brut. On her neck, under each armpit, & slaps it on both sides of her face. A brute some femme might want to take into her arms and romance.

So, first night out in 2 years. Opulent—has earned $350 this week, no tax. Nice clean clothes, fresh from head to toe—for a willing femme to examine.

Friday. Receives her pay in an envelope, in $50s & 20s. Deposits some in the bank and carries a roll of $150 in her wallet. 'Now where are the girls?'

Strode out into the night, down to 7th & Mission.

Area in the first block gets rough. Better-lit area is behind. She can't afford a car. Buying a house is a miracle & little is left over.

Darkness. Tourists from Market Street hotels grow distant; she walks thru the factory sector.

San Francisco wind, cool, blows papers in the gutter.

A car full of white males drives along. Suddenly they scream: "FUCKING LESBIAN DYKE! FUCKING QUEER!" Her hand hits her pocket, knife flips open, ready; the Mace is in her back pocket. Anger stretches her face, and fear. 'I am going to fight you with every bit of power I got!' Karate kicks, judo, her mind whirls with frantic plans of defense. Her guts tighten into steel. The knife is out, in her hand. 'I'm going to fight you bastards! And hurt you somehow—no matter what you do to me, I'm gonna put a hurt on you!' But the car sails by. A dyke across the street is running in fear. Then she realizes: 'They didn't even see me, I look so much like a man.' They've driven off. It's the other lesbian they were harassing. Her guts ooze into jelly. Fumbles to put the knife away while passersby stare at her as if she is the danger. Mercifully, the hand of the Great Protector has brought peace. —For this time, anyway.

Being a dyke is being always conscious of the brutalization of herself as a lesbian, as a female. And of her gay brothers, too.

Two more blocks, arrives safe. 'Whew.' So, had peeled off 2 $20 bills from the roll, & got her room at the Bay Bridge Hotel upstairs.

'Think I'll meet a woman here tonight. Out of all these beautiful women, it's got to be EZ. Take her upstairs and make love. Sweet passionate love.'

As she turns from the desk to go thru the passageway, there's a spectacle unfolding at the entrance.

"YUH DON'T WANT ME IN YO' FUNKY-ASS CLUB 'CAUSE YO' PREJUDICED!"

'It's Sugar Bear!'

There was a friend. Satiny brown skin beaded with sweat; body like a pear, big butt, wide hips, huge tits in a man's shirt & trousers and jacket & boots and a cowboy hat. Furious, swings her fists in the air. The white door checkers won't let her in because she's drunk. They've summoned help from the bartenders at the front bar, and 5 women are hauling the huge Sugar Bear out into the street. "YO' PREJUDICED! YO' DON'T WANT NO NIGGERS IN YO' FUNKY ASS CLUB!"

Red squeezes out the door, past a line of pretty young things waiting to get in, slings her backpack over her shoulder, and runs out to minister to her friend.

Sugar Bear is in the gutter—glitter of neon light, nursing a bruised lip. Her shirt is torn open, revealing a huge breast. "Red! Oh, gosh! They tried to kill me! Oh! Oh! I'm gonna die! Oh, Red! You can go in there, they think you're white! Go in there and get us some white girls! Get you one and get one for me, too! They'll let you in!" Her dark face contorts in a howl.

Red pries a skinny hand under Sugar Bear's wet armpit and helps lift her up out of the gutter, and the two stumble off thru the gutter away from the amused eyes of the line of gals waiting to get into the club.

Sugar Bear's face turns, beaded with sweat, stares down from under her cowboy hat at her smaller friend. "I must have a white girl right away! Beautiful white skin. Must have it!"

"Don't start, Sugar Bear!"

"I must—" Saliva drips down her chin.

"Down, girl!"

Sugar Bear tries to push away out of Red's arms to get back to the club, whose party lights fade in the distance as their boots stride along. Passersby gawk at them. They struggle down the pavement fronted by warehouses & buildings silent by night.

Shows Red her knife on the sly. "I got something for them," she says.

"Put it away! It'll get you in more trouble than it's worth!"

"It's for protection!" she growls.

So they walk arm in arm, and Sugar Bear calms down. Angry, but calm. She's always angry.

Moonlight. Stars. Warehouse & artist lofts of the SoMa. Set down on a doorstoop. Puts an arm around Red in a huge bear hug. "No." Red takes the big butch's arm and drops it back at her pear-shaped side, then puts her own arm around Sugar Bear, who promptly cuddles her huge self up under Red's arm. The butch felt Sugar's pulse beating thru her own body. The night was young.... The wind blew glitter in the gutter....

"Oh, Red...I don't really need a white girl," Sugar Bear confides. "It's just they all looked so *good* back there.... If it had been a black club, I would have said I wanted a sister. I just want women so bad!" Sugar blusters. Tears roll down her face. "I'm a lover of females.... Oh, Red... Back home, when I use to go to the whorehouse...it was so *embarrassing*...wanting a woman so *bad*. When you get up there, you have to bow your head & explain to the women that you're a female. And when you open your shirt and you got tits, and you drop your pants and you're a woman, too, and you got to explain, 'I have the money!' It's so cold-blooded! I open up my jacket, see, I'm a woman, yeah! And I want to love a woman just like you!' And you have to explain how you want her good hot pussy just like any man would, in case they didn't figure that out—you wearing man's clothes and all——you go up in the whorehouse and it's so humiliating, but they take you. They take you," Sugar Bear confided from under Red's arm. They sit on the stoop in a pale yellow pool of moon.

Sugar is blubbering. Cries. A drunk wobbles past,

white, skid-row type. Alkie. "THEY SHOULD SEND ALL YOU PEOPLE BACK ON THE BOAT!" he yells.

Sugar Bear fumbles for her knife; the drunk weaves past. Red pulls her back down on the stoop. Back into the recess of the crevices of South of Market, where skid row touches the artist colony and New Age rocker bars and gay men's sadomasochistic clubs. A few wandering derelicts go by….

They held each other a moment in this space. The butch felt the big butch's heart beat in need, and her mind drifted thru that true red beat into a different time zone.

It had been a party up in the black ghetto which once existed on Fillmore Street. Party had ended. Leftover people. Bottles strewn about, empty. Ashtrays overflowed with cigarette butts. Most of the guests had gone home in cars, or by riding with friends. Sissies & dykes lay around on sofas, on the floor. Everybody was passed out. So they had had to tiptoe lightly because it was dark and they might step on somebody. Made their way to the bedroom. Sugar Bear leads this new butch Red by the hand. "We can stay in here; the lady whose flat this is is a friend of mine." By the hostess's good graces, people with no way to get home can crash out till dawn.

Now, this is how the Third World makes love in a house full of people and not enough beds.

It's 3 A.M. Red don't have a car, so is trapped in this house in the ghetto. Everybody's snoring in alcoholic sleep but this big dyke who don't live here, who they all know. Big, brown, 220 lbs. 5'9". They step over black dykes in baseball caps, tight slacks, loose tank tops showing titties & strong rippling muscles slung over the arms of the sofa, hard faces relaxed now, sweaty Afro curls. Single earrings and nose rings.

Dyke who owns the house is poor, but safe. It's very secure. Car parked in the driveway behind an iron fence.

'A few more hours until dawn, before I have to go out in the streets and take on the world by myself.'

The smaller butch notices a bulge in the big butch's trousers, pointed down the left side. Can't help but see it. Sugar Bear sees her looking. "I'm a real woman, honey; don't worry, this is made out of rubber. I been running around all night like this, but it looks like all the women are taken." Pulls her shirt out of the cowboy belt; brown flesh with tan yellow creases & a black leather harness. "See?"

So, to make a long story short, she catches this butch in a moment of weakness.

They go into the bedroom, small, nicely furnished, double bed; & collapse down on top of the covers.

"Baby...do you want to get plowed?" asks the brown woman. "You're all alone and so am I." Her brown lips close, whisper. "Let me fill you with my love.

"I know you're butch," she insists. "I know you want a pretty femme, but we're both women, ain't we? Please just let me hold you in my arms...I know you're probably just as god-awful-lonely as I am."

"Baby." She touches her lips to the butch's pale neck. "Let somebody else do all the work for a change.

The smaller butch is tired; it's the wee hours before dawn. Tired of struggle. Tired of no money. Tired of IT ALL.

"After having all those white women, won't it be good to have some lesbian soul?" Her breath whispers, licking behind Red's ear.

"I know you want to." And her arms come up, encircling.

"We have all night. Let's play."

The healthy husky dyke immediately gets on her knees, kissing the cloth of Red's clothes; kissing her body; her fingers caressing. "I know you're a butch. And your pretty white skin, it's just like a white girl's. I know we're the same—soul, but you look white. Please!" Her sweaty body crammed into her nice clothes; beefy legs and arms. Knelt before Red who gazes at her, bored, tired, unable to come to a decision. "Don't take this wrong, my darling." Sugar Bear takes her hand and kisses it. "But I have $40 in my pocket. It's all I have—you can have it!" And holds her gaze a moment with liquid brown eyes.

"Forty dollars! I have $120 in mine!"

"I'M SORRY! I'M SORRY!" And falls to kiss her boots. "Oh, my darling. Is there anything I can do? Is there anything I can say?"

Great big hug from Sugar Bear. A brown honey bear.

"Your features, your hair, just like a white person. Oh, baby! Oh sweet, sweet butch!" And kisses up her arm under the shirt, on flesh; as far as the sleeve will let her go.

Sugar Bear opens her shirt. "See these breasts? Please, touch them if you want. Even the touch of your shirt against me will be ecstasy; you don't have to do anything."

Bends her head full of tight Afro curls that smells like hair relaxer. Brown skin sweats.

She opens up her fly. Trousers stretch across her huge hips, fingers reach into her pants leg and pull out the tool. Red is unzipping her own pants; pulls them and her blue boxer shorts down by one finger under the elastic band. Then her friend's brown fingers probe her stinky tan cunt over and over. It's wet. Sugar's other hand takes her tool and pushes the tip of it against Red's hole. Pain & resistance. Then, working it around and around, the tip goes in. The little butch sighs. Sugar Bear works the finger of her other hand over and over Red's clit & waves of pleasure roll. Jerks the tip of the tool in and out, just a few inches. Hot flashes of desire.

Sugar breaks open a packet of lubricant and runs it over the tip of the dick and down its shaft to the base. Strokes her own bare nipples with the remainder of the substance so they glisten, poking out of her man's shirt. Then Red unbuttons her shirt too, pulls off her T-shirt; while Sugar Bear strokes her; admiring. But doesn't ask where the scars came from. Gently they massage each other's tits, then, firm, Sugar holds her cock and runs the tip up and down Red's clit. "I'll be gentle, I'll take it slow."

"I don't trust shit!" Red says. Her body is tense, but excited. Still remains on her guard, ready to push the butch away if she gets rough.

"I know," Sugar answers. So, they lay there side by side, legs spread. Red don't trust her enough to lie on her back yet & be pinned under Sugar's full weight; and the door is not locked. So they start caressing & probing with the cock, whose base bangs up against Sugar's clit where it's harnessed, exciting her, too. And this is too good to be true....

A knock on the door.

Enter a stately black woman, bent over, holding her guts. One of the roommates of the flat.

Sugar quickly hides the dick that's strapped around her big thighs. Throws her shirt over her crotch.

The woman looks nauseated, falls into the bed. "I have to lay down because I have cramps, I'm sorry, ladies, you'll have to go somewhere else. There's sofas in the living room. Ohhhhhh!"

Only thing, there's a bunch of people passed out there after the party. And the ebony lady's holding her guts and flips over on her back & then over again on her stomach.

So they go out and look around. Nowhere to do it —no mattress. No empty sofa. And the floor is dirty. "I'm not laying my back down on that damn floor no way."

"I would for you, my darling, if you want to ride my cock."

"I'm not putting my *knees* on that floor, and not around all these people!"

Now the ghetto night howls outside; no way they want to walk thru blocks of deserted territory to find someplace, so they have to make do here.

So that leaves only the privacy of the bathroom.

So they stand in its doorway, under a shaft of starlight thru the window.

"If somebody makes a sound like they're coming in, we can duck inside and lock the door."

Her cock is 8", but only 3" is in Red; standing up. So she's banging it in and out those 3", and it hurts. The butch tells her not to push so hard; if it don't go in more than 3", it's 'cause they're standing up & because it's been a long time. A long time cumming that way.

"I ain't doing nuthin' for you, Sugar Bear."

"Yes, you are. I can cum."

So, they're standing up there in the doorway, legs spread, bare-chested, tits rubbing.

'This is like one of the first times fucking in my life, on the highway in a gas station. I was 18. Life has come full circle. Me & my lover. We didn't have rods then, just used our fingers.'

Moonlight. Star bright.

"Sugar Bear!"

They stop, turn, and listen.

"Don't worry, my darling! Nobody's here! Just somebody having a bad dream."

"OH. Huh. Shit!" Red thinks: 'Of all the white people's houses I've cleaned, dykes, doctors—with tons of bedrooms and beds & sofas; bigger than this whole flat; and here we have to stand up in the doorway next to the toilet to get pleasured, in a neighborhood I'm afraid to go out in.' And they listen to the occasional traffic roar by outside.

"Thank You. Oh, Thank You!" Sugar Bear shoves her cock in and out and bends her head to nestle in the crook of Red's neck, and their breasts, tan & brown, mingle.

Red hears that slapping wet fuck noise go all thru the silent house, thinks: 'God, they can hear me get fucked.' But they are hard-drinking & hardworking dykes & sissies, and everybody's passed out.

The session goes on about an hour of sheer pleasure. Stopping & going.

"I don't have vaginal orgasms unless you play with my clit."

In and out her big dick thrusts. Fast. Rams its head in her hole, back and forth. Cunt muscles have relaxed. Banged with a stiff cock up against the wall. Tan dyke; sweat breaks out on her upper lip.

Sugar Bear's cunt smells strong, her pubic hairs curl over the harness ring; her brown breasts bounce bubbly; aroused as the cock bumps her clit, too. She has all the womanly working parts.

'Must we meet like this?' Red thinks.

Heavy-muscled body of the bigger dyke; Red hangs on to her for a moment. Having sex, her legs get weak. Her body trembles.

Sugar guides the dick out with her hand and runs the tip up and down Red's clit over and over; pushing it fast, fast; it's banging her clit, and she cums against the base of the dick. Red feels her heart beat. Then Sugar hugs her with big arms and grunts. Sweat beads on her back. The dick still sticks out of her pubic mound. And she guides it back to Red's cunt. A brown, sturdy body, perfumed, wearing one earring; beaded in sweat performing her labor of love.

'Here's this dyke fucking me & her with this dick. I'm suppose to be the man, but I'm enjoying it.' They hold in a sweaty clasp.

"So much soul. It's so good to get off with one of my own people. After all those old white blondes." But they both know this butch-on-butch thing will just last a minute.

Just a moment of compassion between people servicing each other's needs.

Cunt smells & sweat & men's aftershave fill the bathroom.

Hard dick wielded in fast, short thrusts. Turns her head from side to side in ecstasy. Hot streams of lust go running rampant. Sugar Bear holds the cock now so the base runs up the butches clit and the tip goes in her hole & it's getting too hot to hold back. Going in and out and up and down. Pounding her vagina; muted fire suffusing her body. "UH OH! SWEET BABY, UH OHHOOH." The big butch clutches her partner tight with one arm, feels her near the moment of orgasm.

Just lean up against the wall, yielding, arms at her side, not hugging at first; but now it gets too good & hard and fast, and she has to hang on. The dick goes 3 inches into her hole and the base runs up her clit, and it's between her legs like she's riding it, fast, back and forth.

"OHHHHHHH!"

Sugar clutches her. "Oh my butch, I've waited to fill you with my love! I'm filling you with my love! Filling you with my love! Fill you with my love!" Butch in harness pumps, going to town. Yes, butches get fucked. Leaning up against the wall, hard cock; BANG BANG! So good! Cum hard. Feet jumping off the floor. Hips pump forward; try not to fall out of the doorway, now she's bringing her over the threshold, pounds over her swollen clit, in and out of her. Red pumps her hips up and down, and round and round; rides it; big pussylips swollen and wet. Sugar runs her hard cock, rides along Red's clit, and she's so close, it's rubbing her into a fiery heat; feels her tits against Red's tits; the little butch cums, feet dance up and down on the floor she cums so hard. Sugar holds her in her strong arms & Red's knees sag; feet jump up and down on the floor in orgasm riding her dick, and they clutch each other, their thighs & cock & legs wet with liquid discharge & lube pouring out.

Moonlight. Star bright. They slide in the sweat of each other's arms.

Moments pass. They pick up their pants, button their shirts, and go into the living room, fall asleep on the sofa beside some dyke; held in each other's embrace. Sugar Bear's heartbeat strong & true.

Image fades.

Night. Outside on a doorstoop on the Miracle Mile of the Glitter Gutter.

Sugar Bear asleep under her left wing.

Shakes her awake. "I've got to go, honey." Runs the tips of her fingers over that kinky hair.

"I'll be OK," Sugar Bear mutters.

The butch takes her shoulders firmly, points her in the direction of the lights of busy Market Street, where the all-night bus runs and the BART trains go underground. They walk, Red guiding her. When they reach Market Street, she says good-bye. "Put that knife away unless you absolutely need it," she cautions.

Red heads back to the club.

At this time—1984—gays referred to Folsom Street as the Miracle Mile. —All gay, SM, leather clubs. Bay Bridge Inn for Lezzies. Miracle Mile originally was a term for the straight theater row of restaurants, nightclubs & pizzazz of towns back East, such as Chicago,

New York. —They all have a Miracle Mile. So this is the gay version.

Glitter, lights, artistic persons; leathermen & SM dykes with handcuffs on their belts. —Civilization where once were only drab deserted warehouses.

And goes back up to her room to get ready for an evening of fun, flirtation, & lust.

Went up the winding stairs, carpeted; rooms quiet. Makes a turn, goes to the low numbers.

Bed takes up most of the space, a bureau runs the length of it; sink, a closet. Toilet down the hall.

And a view of rooftops stretches to infinity outside. Up to the giant monoliths of the Financial District, upon whose outskirts she makes her living and from whose businesses she cons her sales. Throws her pack down, lies down on the bed in boots, hands folded behind her short-haired head. Visions—to come back up the stairs with a beautiful woman; her smell of musk. Round ass & tits under a slinky gown. Guiding her masterfully into the room; romances her with pets & kisses & lovewords, then removes her clothes & has good hot orgasmic sex.

On top of her; stud her in an embrace. Finish with oral sex.

Casts a brief look at the bed, which holds high hopes for tonight. With covers pulled back, pillows in place, it can become a playground for sex.

Lies there; readies herself to descend the staircase at 9.

Lesbian Strip Show begins at 10.

Already booming music from downstairs dance-floor reverberates thru the place. Echoes up thru the floors.

PLEASURE IN THE GLITTER GUTTER
Chapter Two

*I was really surprised to hear you
and others talk about the strip shows.*
—Zarina Yasmin

What is the interdynamic of the lesbian class struggle?

What is the interdynamic of race & color in public establishments & meeting places for dykes?

What is the importance of Age vs. Sweet Young Thangs?

Where is the love that could have been?

'Where are the whores? This is a tease!' thought Red, growling, as she watched the show. Everybody in the place is a regular working dyke with a single partner. Others are in groups.

Hand on the Mickey Mouse watch says 11 P.M.

Room dark. Spotlights illuminate the players.

Muff diver's glimpse of heaven —spread legs, cunt.

Chair act. Dim lights. Women hooting, clapping, & wolf whistling.

Red has a ringside seat at a small table shared by a group of women; it's crowded with glasses. The Strip Show is in full swing.

'The Lesbian Strip Show is a tease, as I knew it, calculated to arouse erotic feelings in women, and to portray art & statements, mostly in motion, nudity, and suggestively. And to make a dyke hot and wet her crotch in lust.

'Roxie & us, would be in the bathroom, & she used to say; "Oh, those girls in the audience will really be turned on tonight. Their pants are really going to be wet."

'Now, me and the other women there thought the butches getting turned on was kind of funny. It's fun if someone gets turned on, but you don't think about them getting upset about it.

'I really doubt if anybody in that show ever thought about that—we certainly never talked about it.'

Zarina Yasmin was a stripper who worked the shows two years:

"My memory of the strip show was being in the bathroom, because you spend most of your time in the bathroom. I got tired of being in the bathroom. We never had a nice dressing room playing at the lesbian clubs. Once or twice we had a nice dressing room with a table and mirrors, and we made money. We talked a lot in there. Talked about the audience. 'Oh, this audience is real lively.' 'Oh, this one's real boring.' Or a dead audience. It was all very cramped. All those women in that tiny little bathroom, and we had to throw our butches out; they had to wait outside. And we were always trying to keep people out of the bathroom.

"I had taken classical ballet all my life and was truly an artist more than a stripper. I was the most organized one there. Roxie would always have forgotten part of her costume. 'Zarina, can I borrow some bobby pins?' Usually I had it, and always would be loaning everything out. A lot of them forgot some part of their costume. Roxie forgot her music a few times and had to drive back to Oakland to get it.

"I had more a variety of acts. And more costumes, and I was more creative. Most of the time I felt jealous, or competitive, or self-conscious. Some times I felt sexy. I felt kind of dissatisfied.

"I was surprised that after the first few years the crowds began to dwindle. Roxie had to pay money out of her own pocket to pay us. We didn't make enough at the door. We had big crowds at first, then they dwindled away."

Butch sat at her table. Shadow darkened her features.

Unlike facilities set up in the hetero world, there are no working businesswomen to follow thru with this erotic arousal these naked ladies create as they bump and grind and spread their cunts and dance on the glittering platform.

When the butch had worked as a cashier in a burlesque house, and sex-film houses of the sixties, she had seen men stumble out of the turnstile from the lobby, go out under the marquee, and down North Avenue into the night to find prostitutes that abounded in that district. Likewise, at the 16th and Mission Street burlesque show, the services of women were there. But there is no follow-up for dykes!

The strip show was over.

A stripper, brown skin, big hips, curvaceous, peered out of the bathroom. Saw the butch she'd noticed earlier —now seated glumly, alone at a table littered with glasses. A tough dyke. The kind the pretty woman liked. Enough glamour—the tailored blue jeans, the leather jacket, the boots & rings on her fingers.

But, as she'd danced naked before her, this butch had taken no notice. Her tongue hanging out, eyes bright, raising up in her seat in heat instead over glamorous blondes. Ex-straight strippers who had crossed over from the hetero world.

Later Red went to the back bar, ordered a mineral water & watched the lively party from the sidelines.

Suddenly the heavyset woman comes over. "Can I talk to you?" she asks shyly. Very pretty. Bats her almond-shaped eyes.

"Yeah, sure. Have a seat." Red was so picky. This woman was not up to her expectations, for the lovely brown girl now wore a plaid shirt, boyish blue jeans, and lace-up construction boots. Full figure disguised as a boy —or a dyke with correct politics. Even her makeup was wiped off. And the idiotic butch didn't even realize it was one of the strippers.

Their conversation led nowhere. The stripper picked up her pack, rejected, and walked out the door. Moonlight filtered over her. Silently put the pack in her van; red taillights gone into the night.

Lounged at the back bar, hands shoved in blue jeans; $100 boots. Had approached a few women whose answer was a polite No. *Mickey Mouse watch hand ticks toward 2.*

'I know I am not adequate. I am a piss-poor butch. A

usually frigid dyke who refuses to be touched in certain places on my body & look too masculine to pass myself off in the greater world to hold a decent job. This is my problem.'

Glasses tinkle around her. More and more bar stools are empty.

Musical calliope grinds on. Back exit is open, notes spill out into the alley—Clementina Alley. 'Oh my darling, Oh my darling, Oh my darling Clementine, You are lost and gone forever, dreadful sorry Clementine.' A door guard with a flashlight sits by the exit.

'How many hours have we waited here, looking for devices to spend the time?'

'Music grinds me to mincemeat, then spits me out of itself into the alley.'

"INGRID!"

"RED!"

"Gosh! Ain't seen you in 20 years!"

Tall European woman in a diaphanous gown that clings. Tiny straps hold it up. Rings on each finger. Fur coat. Golden high heels with tiny straps. Beautiful Ingrid.

Dykes foam at the mouth, wet their crotches, turn to look. 'And here I am, held to her bosom. Yes, I have screwed her; have been between her milky thighs in the distant past.'

Ingrid, with a swish, sits down next to Red, briefly. Assembles the gown under her round hot ass. Immediately a bunch of dykes in plaid shirts with sweat stains & blue jeans and boots, long straight hair whipping, go mad over the sight of her. Ingrid caresses Red's head.

Pulls the butch to her bosom again. Butches fall over each other trying to buy drinks for Ingrid.

The European woman is an expert of love. Sees the dykes begging for her favor, smiles, & whispers to Red, "Boy, are they asking for it. —To be trained to the crack of my whip."

Soon Ingrid has risen—goes off on the arm of the escort who brought her. Briefly her hand brushes Red's, who wisely knows that this is like trying to hold onto liquid. —Ingrid will always pour away toward some stronger gravity.

Hands on her Mickey Mouse watch say Last Call!

Two A.M. Night is over. Glasses empty. Cluttered tables. Bar lights go up, tables and chairs empty. Women dissolve en masse. The last fringe of them sweeps out in coats, stomping boots; with the toss of a head of wild hair, over a bare floor littered with cigarette butts and bar napkins.

Strippers have gone home long ago.

Slowly, ascends the staircase to her room.

'Times I wanted to commit suicide. A slow-motion race to get thru the unloving day, in back of my mind thinking about cutting the cords to life.

'It seems strange, but to have a high sex drive & be very shy is frustrating.'

Goes to the toilet at the end of the hall to piss.

Cunt-smell hangs in the air. —It's a cruel hoax—the girl has gone.

'She's had her legs up in the air holding them open by the ankles for some other butch, ran into the john to piss, then flown back to their room to resume the love-play.'

Pussy good. Oh, so good.

Emptiness.

Glances out of the window; a dim figure back inside the room;—out into the highways, byways, triways, & gaily forward thru these cities of the night.

So this had been the short adventure in The Life, at the Bay Bridge Inn.

See her under yellow light, in a pair of boxer shorts—white with turquoise stripes, and a black T-shirt. —Nice new fabric. Not threadbare, but thick. Not like her sheets at home, worn-out threads so it's like sleeping on knots—all the fabric worn out.

Just come out of a long economic dismal darkness.

—And had money to spend.

And no woman to spend it on.

'Not even a whore can be purchased at the Bay Bridge Inn! (That I know about.)'

In lonely frustration.

In spiritual transmigration.

In horny rage!

She tossed & turned on the bed, ran tan fingers thru her hair. 'Would my life be better if I had a dick? Used to torment me as a child, the idea that if I was a boy, my life wouldn't be so unhappy. Or humiliated. Always was a tomboy & tough. Now I have more luck with the ladies, more access. Yet I'm still going thru life as a 4th-rate person. A she-he. Too shy. And not making the grade. Maybe I should have a sex change and go over to the other side.' Yellow light gleamed down. Feverish testimony issued from her. 'I been so busy trying to survive the last 5 years, trying to pay for the house &

take care of my animals, I forgot about me. Maybe I need a dick to ever enjoy this world. I'd get more respect in public, a lot more. Might get a lot more women. I could go in the whorehouse boldly & not feel ashamed. What more is there in life? Would I be happy being a male? I don't hate my femaleness...I do kind of like myself...but it's not making it. My luck with the ladies...well, my last so-called marriage was hell. She goes & leaves me for a dyke, yeah, but then I find out she's got married to a man. If I was a man, I could have women like Ingrid full time.'

Her thoughts were a burning rage. Hellfire red. 'If a woman would just value me as a butch! Put her arms around me as a butch, and respect me as a butch, and be female for me and sexy & yield herself to me as a woman —to a butch. That makes a difference. For her to encourage me. To appreciate me for the way I make love to her. I don't even know if I do make love good. The last girl—the white one—just up and leaves me. I don't know why. Just leaves me for an older woman & then turns straight!'

The hotel quieted down for the night & she was alone.

'Don't know if I've got the right equipment between my legs... I've passed as a man; I know the respect I get then. People are more cheerful, friendly. But...basically...society isn't what I'm concerned about. It's loving a woman, and for a woman to stand by me. If being a man enhances this—that's the test. A buddy of mine had a sex-change operation, & now he's got a great job and a straight woman. But actually, it's not what society thinks about me. How I'm treated in straight establishments. I don't care if I *am* a 3rd-class citizen. If I go to restaurants and they seat us way out of the way by the toilets so nobody can see us…that's not it.'

Hands folded between her legs, lay on her side, studying cracks in the wall. 'It would be so nice to be able to make it with this cunt between my legs and not have to go get a dick. —Go thru that expensive sex change surgery up on the operating table…. Just keep wearing my boots & butch it up & me and my lady enjoy our lovemaking to the finest degree.

'How I want a woman to wear her lipstick off on my cock.

'To appreciate me for what I am—not a female, not a nice person, but a *butch*. Not pretend I'm a man—I'm a *butch*.'

Feet in sox twitch. Tan face scowls.

'A woman who's going to make me feel like I'm a man, or a butch; not like I'm another dame like *her*, but a *butch*,' she thought bitterly.

'There are so many dissatisfied people who walk the face of this earth.

'I feel so bad about myself; maybe being a man is better.

'I know this stuff is supposed to come from within, I've been to enough counseling groups. "Happiness comes from within." That's what people say.'

But it was life's gifts that count as well. Lost in a fantasy. "So good." A woman under her, runs hands over her; "Oh you have such a strong back!" Moving for her, telling her all the right words she craved to hear; how she's so masterful at lovemaking. So potent. "What a butch!" A woman to build up my ego. "My hard strong lover."

'Instead I feel tore down by these ladies.'

Had been struggling for economic security the last 2 years. —Lies across phone wires. 'Feel low & inadequate most of my life.' When suddenly there is no more struggling to survive—which takes a tremendous amount of energy—she stops. Looks and listens to her life & sees she's not happy. She thinks: 'Get a gun and put myself out of my misery.'

How peaceful is death! No more turmoil.

Yellow light snapped off. Starlight, moon-bright illumination thru a dusty windowpane.

So this had been her adventure at the Bay Bridge Inn.

A big glitter BANG! Deflated like a balloon.

'Lesbians need some ways to find other lesbians & above all to have our sexual needs met—besides masturbating.

'So I am reduced to this.'

To warm up, she pictured Ingrid in the satin gown, peeled it off. Big tits, round hips, milky thighs. —A lay from the past Date Book of Memory.

So in the photo album of her mind, Ingrid spreads the lips of her labia—"Come and suck." Red examines her from front to back in snapshots that show pussy.

The pillow has two purposes:

Put under the ass of a willing female to tilt her cunt up so when the butch lies down between her thighs, cunt & cock meet, & she can ride to an orgasm.

If no female, butch mounts pillow and rides it. Rubs clit on pillow to an explosive orgasm. So sad!

Butch went to town. Put pillow under her, straddled it, hands on the mattress; hips pump up and down driving her clit up and down on the pillow. Mouth closed in a line; intake & exhale of air thru nostrils. Up and down. Build fast, fast; under her, the empty bed. Before her the headboard. And out of the window, a view of rooftops stretches to infinity. Fast, faster. "Uh, uh, baby. Uh! Uh! Baby!" Cum. Discharge spot wet on the pillow.

Bang Bang. Cum two times as usual. "Ohhh, Baby!" Bang Bang! As she does with a woman.

Rolls over to face her inquisitor—conscious. And wants to die. The loneliness is terror.

Four A.M. Hands on the Mickey Mouse watch. Rolls over solemnly. Yawns, runs her fingers thru her hair.

Legs swing over the side of the bed, goes to the toilet. Yellow piss.

Falls back asleep.

Five A.M. Sounds in the hall, laughter, the bathroom door slams shut, then again sleep.

Six A.M. Light of day is burning. Out in the littered sidewalk—papers scattered from night.

Wind blows papers, and the Oakland trees.

PLEASURE IN THE GLITTER GUTTER
Chapter Three

Mickey Mouse watch says: "It's time to remember where you came from."

Mental illness had been a major force in her life. When Red was born on the South Side of Chicago, in the black sector, in 1943, chances were she would be killed, die of suicide, drugs, alcoholism, or be an untreated victim of mental disorder, in a higher percentile because she was a member of a racial minority, female, from a broken home, and had one parent suffering from schizophrenia.

Age 9, 10; a tomboy stayed away from home as much as she could. Mother holed up in a room locked in spiderwebs of gloom emanating from that mind, slowly poisoning the house. The sickness was catching.

Child strove to have a warm, loving relationship; by tugging on mother's dress, staring up with big brown eyes, trying to communicate; instead was beaten & denied. And driven into mental disorder herself.

In adolescence showed raw signs of being sick. For the first 20 years of her life, her worst fear was that she'd lose her own mind.

Age 13:

Self-conscious. Terrified at school. See if she could make it thru the day without going to the toilet & throwing up.

Always sick. Flu. Missed 1/3 school year. Afraid she wouldn't survive.

Discovered she was a lesbian. Afraid she wouldn't survive again.

Age 15:

Out in the streets in mismatched clothes, shoplifting food. No one helped. Few friends. Cut off from them, suddenly realizing she was gay. Did graduate from a special adult high school downtown in the Loop, for dropouts.

Loneliness. Out of school. Wandered the streets. No women in the streets. Men meet men in the streets, but few lesbians. Racial hatred rears its ugly head. Moves to the Near North Side. Haunts the semi-gay sector. More at home there with her tan face among whites then among blacks.

Spent life in daydreams. Wrote poetry on scraps of paper. Walks the beaches. Holds onto sanity. Waits for a miracle to change her life. Sneaks into gay bars, underage. Holds off from committing suicide—not sure how to do it, anyhow. The beaches, the streets, the museums, library, the elevated train. Eats from one sack of potatoes all week, & food stolen from students' lunches at the university she haunts; and digs in garbage cans.

As a teen, discovers the joy, the pain, and the power of lesbian intercourse.

One of the first times is in a public toilet of a gas station off the turnpike.

Leans up against the wall. They stand on tile littered with toilet paper & urine, by the sink. Both drunk. Pet each other's tits, pull their pants down around their knees and go to it. Fingers seek into her soft warm nest; jam into her. Runs fingers 'round and 'round inside. Sighs. Moans. Paw each other's tits thru their clothes. Sticks her fingers into Bess's cunt & works the juice out of her, then kneels on the piss-stained, toilet-paper-littered tile floor, mouth between Bess's thighs, her seeking tongue in Bess's hot cunt, bringing her to orgasm.

Five feet three inches, 120 lbs. Kept living. Hoping for tomorrow.

Narrow room 10 by 15 feet. Thirteen dollars per week. Sink. Bed. Closet with a few clothes from the thrift shop —which are men's trousers, shirts, used boots, gym shoes. A table. A sack of potatoes. Seldom meat. Begs for spare change. Lives off handouts. It will be 2 years of hell before she is eligible to receive a $125-per-month welfare check. Is too isolated and needs to be around people. To touch people & there is no way....

A lonely existence.

Every morning she awakes with a cleansed spirit; seconds later, a thick grey depression meets her on the threshold of sleep & must wade thru this all day.

For 25¢ can ride the El train around forever. From Wilson Avenue north, back down to Cottage Grove south.

Too nervous to sit down and eat, but sneaks in restaurants and finishes food off the plates people have left behind.

Bad nerves. Trembling body. Madness of her mother.

Afraid to be around women, yet wanting a woman terrifically.

Five years she rode the El trains, haunted public libraries, & walks the beaches. A mass of sensations, no thoughts.

Hangs out in bus terminals, art museums. Lonely. Goes to gay bars & stands outside when she can't get in. In the street, follows women she doesn't know.

Age 16:

"Follow me up to my hotel.... Do you live on the beach? Do you even have a home?... Ain't nobody showed you how to wash yourself? Don't you ever wash your clothes? Don't you know any better? Come on, baby. Come to me."

Immediately the woman lies down, holds her knees back with her hands to spread her thighs open even wider, her cunt open. "Come on, ride me, little butch. Don't be so shy.

"Are you tired? Come on! I want to suck you!"

So the teen scrunches her nasty cunt up to the woman's face. She gets right in and licks it, loves it, takes all of it; lapping & sucking. "I'M A PARTY GIRL! ALL THIS HERE FOR $10!" And spreads her cunt with her red fingernails, lies back for the butch to come do her, too.

So she endured & grew. Knew women like this twice a year…. Knew women met in gay bars also once or twice a year…. Loneliness seemed forever stretching out far as the eye can see—down the sandy beach curve, over the billowing waves.

To kill time, writes stupid stuff. —Pencil & paper are cheap.

In a slow evolution begins to realize she is definitely attracted to feminine ladies.——To her they are the real thing.

Time passed. Age 21. Fat & muscle flowed over her thin body and settled into a body type—strong less than stocky. The mind & body that housed her grew more certain of itself. The awful period of growing up between age 13 and 21 was over.

Twenty-two. Finally starts making money. Gets her hair dyed red. Styles big. Dons a pair of shorts, men's, still a male shirt; gym shoes; still masculine but not as much and walks down North Avenue, Wells Street, Division Street; that area. Head turned to look back over her shoulder, if you know what I mean.

Once a week for money. Rest of the time, all the rest of the time—the other 23 hours per day searching for a woman—combs the red styled hair back behind her ears, goes severely butch. Trousers & shirt. Collar turned up at the back of the neck. Arms muscular from push-ups and karate practice. Tough jacket, & the same gym shoes. Searching for sex from a woman, which is what she really wants. Goes in the gay bars, & when they get raided and closed, is cut off from her community again. Loses her 2-room apartment when the city tears the building down for redevelopment. Is sleeping in hallways; catnaps on the El; goes home with straight women acquaintances—a waitress at the restaurant at the intersection of Wells & North streets; or a straight alcoholic couple from a bar she frequents. Staggers this so she never sleeps at the same place twice in a row. Or with 3 airline stewardesses she's met—soul. And nobody quite knows what her scene is—her real woman scene.

Then goes downhill. —Meets some chippie broads who are dopers. Is introduced to drugs. Soon, becomes recentered. —'Drugs are too good. They are love to me. Love drugs.' She is making a life of drugs. A short life.

She gets too accustomed—to drugs. It effaces her butch personality as water wears away rock.

Sits at the dopers' house & uses drugs all day. Screws men as little as possible for a living; submerges her wants & desires. Always hungry. Few clothes. Still writes, & awakes to discover she can't decipher her writing the morning after. It gets smaller and scribbly, letters scrawl; reverting to the pre-alphabet eons of developing humanoids.

Dying. —Because instead of getting toe-to-toe and fist-to-fist in the great struggle to be with a woman; to be a lesbian, to maintain a lesbian world against the massive intrusion of the heterosexuals; she sinks deeper into drugs. Mayor and his Vice Cops still raiding gay bars. So hangs out with this—the only female companionship she can find—sinking deeper…into the pit. In this pit nurses all her old wounds of childhood. Mother who rejected and battered her. All the racial things the world hurls in her face—not white, not black. Face held tough, nursing herself on the tits of the drug genie. Drugs to help to enjoy unwanted sex. "Having sex with women is hard to get. Drugs is a very attractive sidetrack. Mainline heroin. Drugs make me passive. Takes away my maleness. And gradually begin to hate myself. Seems my main problem is it's hard to get a lady friend. Chasing these chippies who don't want cunt, they want *drugs*.'

Going back farther into the hurt of time passed. Nursing it in drugs & enjoying this & the decrepit drug-shooting galleries & falling-down rooms where we nod. Frustrated & angry when her spirit awakes.

City of Chicago. No gay bars this week. Maybe next week the Vice Cops will accept the payoffs again, and the Mafia will open a new playground for gay kids.

These metamorphoses all come down to The Puss-y.

It's all about the pussy & how women treat each other, and the availability of the stuff, and its quality, etc. Starting about 1958—this Journey to Woman; Morning in the Village; Beebo Brinker, etc. Come full circle.

Decide: 'I got to get out of this town. Get out of Dodge.'

Out of here and find a city like New York, where there's dykes. Gays in the street.' So as to make it easy for a shy and semi-crazy butch like herself who eats with her hands & talks to herself out loud—and answers, to find a lady to lie down with.

Vice Cops' continuous pressure on the gay bars. 1967. Too much repression.

'If I stay in this city I'm going to become a prostitute for life, and shooting up with a needle will become my paramount act.'

So God prevailed. While doing The Love Drug with chippie women, who tied The Love Tie around her arm, making her veins bulge green, if you know what I mean; contracts a serious blood disease, must be hospitalized & while in confinement, loses the yen.

'I know in my heart of hearts it's a woman I want to bed. And to write these books which are my life. I won't find it giving in to the degeneracy of drugs; the environment of drugs, the ladies of drugs; nor by loving those drug women and semi-chippies of heroin, and mainline whores of drugs—and their multiplicity of Speed, Crank, Uppers, & Downers.

'So I got to get out of Dodge City!'

PLEASURE IN THE GLITTER GUTTER
Chapter Four

"SLUT! FREAK! PUSSY! QUEER! FUCKING BITCH QUEER!"

BAM! Side of her face goes. Manages to kick one of them in the leg, inflicting pain on him, & then she's down. More kicks. Blood. Feet run. A car zooms off. Having fought back, a show of strength as blows came crashing down she defended her face & her spirit.

Hobbles around in pain. These are the post-heroin days after hospitalization & she is deathly afraid that drugs will destroy her liver, and also of the genie in the bottle that tried to murder her in her teens. So she takes nothing but aspirin to kill the pain.

So she goes around town with a cold towel pressed to her eye. Her ribs feel like a throbbing mass of jelly. She

...ps. Leg wrenched out. And a huge black area runs down her side, turns purple. And she writes with tremendous ferocity. Strings words together. —The only power she has to combat the world.

Big bruise on her face which sticks out 3 times larger on one side. Eye is swollen shut.

Friend the waitress stops work, sets down her tray of dirty dishes & takes out the time to care. "Who did that to you?"

"I don't want to talk about it."

"That's why I left my husband! Because of *that!*" she confides. "I hate to see that happen to a woman!—*Any* woman!"

"It's the nicest thing anybody's said to me."

So, lame & with purple bruises, the butch sits in the restaurant sipping free coffee & doughnuts, by the window in a pool of sunlight—last dying light of autumn, blood-red sun.

'I don't hate them. I'm just sick of their world. They're interlopers in my territory. *This* is my territory.

'So I've got to get out of here.'

So she lay on her back one last time, allowed herself to be fucked by a male dick, about 30 minutes. Then it's over. Gets him out of the room, puts his money with the rest, and there's a hurt in her side; chances are it's a vaginal infection—all for 30 minutes of somebody else's pleasure. Then begins the cleaning-up process, all that crap dripping out of her, her own discharge, semen, & K-Y jelly; then, hair slicked back behind her ears, trousers, men's shoes, shirt, collar up in back, goes out in earnest search of a lesbian woman to have sex with, to love. Goes in search of her own dick & her own power.

Buys a bus ticket out to the West Coast.

She has been lucky in life. Only diseases she contracted were VD once, & hepatitis of the liver thru a dirty needle which almost killed her, but saved her because she'd squared up in fear; and a variety of vaginal infections & abrasions. Was beaten by men only a few times. 'Am still walking around. I see stars, blood on my face and hands & a terrible pain and wonder when I came back to consciousness, determined to live. Could life be worse than this? Is it worth it? Being hated. The Hate. HATE. Because of being a lesbian, member of a minority, looking white among blacks, and a stranger among whites. Yet kept at that karate training, kept on doing those push-ups. Kept on pushing that pen across a page. To fight back against The Hate. It kills.'

Thru all this to bring her love to a woman somehow.

Only one suitcase, a guitar, and the clothes on her back.

'Another city, and try to start my life all over again —this city didn't work.'

She had seen all the lonely people, where do they all come from?—Dead-end lives, who exist in cities where nothing happens. Big blocks of buildings downtown sun-streaked; windswept main drag; a few restaurants & bars where special kinds of people loiter.

A people who want for something—a book, a friend, a vision from God—to inspire their lives thru the decadence. To help increase their territory.

The stigmata on their hands was not The Christ, it was from working menial jobs. From fighting back. And yet it was the same suffering. —A tiny bit of the huge universal suffering. *And, the hands on the Mickey Mouse watch said: "It's time. It's time—COME!"*

Come! Come into the city of San Francisco!

Come, come into a lesbian community.

Come, come into the knowledge of yourself!

PLEASURE IN THE GLITTER GUTTER
Chapter Five

Do you know what that girl said to me? "Baby, you got me so weak, I'm trembling—I can't stand up." They're looking for someone to love. —And boy, are they asking for it! They need to be trained. *Like cats respond to the whip!*

—Ingrid's Law

So that's when she got out to San Francisco. She met Ingrid. Had been in town 6 months, got situated on welfare. Starved & struggled, worked a few odd jobs; Christmas work in department stores, delivery job, etc. Ticket taker at a movie house. Is still clean—no drugs, no alcohol. Buys a manual typewriter for $10 at a pawnshop in the Tenderloin, where she lives in one room. Red has grown out by the roots, leaves only the name. Hair reverts to its natural color—brown & looks very butch. *Always.*

"Here's $15 to help you out with that phone bill."

"Thank you, darling." She winks & a smile cracks her face.

Now Ingrid's male lover don't bring her any money; he has a wife who takes his paycheck. And her live-in female love is broke—she gets welfare, too.

Ingrid lets her robe fall back, revealing sloping white shoulders; then removes it to show large breasts, round belly, & sleek thighs. "Hope you don't mind, it's just us women."

"I hope you don't think of me as just a woman! I'm a butch, and you're turning me on! I'm sensually attracted to you! You're a beautiful woman, & dykes like you, & you know it!"

"Are you in a hurry, darling?"

"No. I can wait as long as you want me to."

"Because James is coming over. I have to spend some time with him. Do you want to wait? You can be with me after that."

James never spends the night because of having a wife. And the live-in-lover lady has her own room.

Her youngest baby is in a cradle right in the bedroom which was once a living room. The dining room a few feet away houses kids by night, and turns into a recreation/eating area by day. Upstairs are 2 more bedrooms & a second bath, for more kids and the lover. Their house is too small.

It's 12 midnight. Having no car, Red traverses the streets by bus to get there. And so she waits her turn on the stairs in between the live-in lover upstairs & the current lover down in the living room.

Four A.M. She comes to the bedroom; removes her clothes & in cold hard strength gives herself to Ingrid until she knew her.

"Darling, you're good."

Because of the two lovers, Red don't take her serious. Just as a party girl.

"When can I see you again?"

"Tomorrow morning, breakfast."

"Can I bring anything for breakfast?"

Ingrid fixes her with a 'please, darling, don't be ridiculous' look—she has 5 kids. That European accent sounds just like a movie star.

So Red comes over with a shopping bag full of 3 packages of bacon, 2 cartons of eggs, 2 gallons of milk, and several packages of waffle mix. Will be broke now for the remainder of the month.

Ingrid's delighted to see the carton of food. "Oh, darling!" Kisses her & gives a gentle caress.

Breakfast takes an hour to fix. Stacks of pancakes in butter, piles of eggs & sausage & toast. Five kids & 3 adults seated at the big carved wood dining-room table.

Eats with a tablespoon. Eggs, bacon, waffles—everything in a spoon. 'Amazing!' Red realizes, mouth full of food. 'This is one of the first real breakfasts I've had in the last 15 years.'

Red proves to be right at home in the Snow Queen's Palace. Blonde, European accent. But Ingrid likes Third World persons. The black male lover comes over for a few months, then is out of her life. Her live-in lover is a Filipina butch. Her tricks are old Chinese men in Chinatown. And she's let Red cum with her 3 times so far.

The kids reflect this multi-ethnicity. She loves her kids.

Poverty is not going well with them, and they are rebelling against her.

Red is the color of a couple of the mixed-race kids, so the butch fits in quite jolly.

Evening, Red is invited back. They sit on the bed.

Kids climb all over her body. Touch her face, play with her hair. Small hands, little bodies. They giggle.

Ingrid says, "You know, I get all the touching & closeness I need because of the kids. I'm never alone. All I really can use is romantic interests—and *sex*, darling."

The butch gets sensually aroused from the kids touching her. Not erotic, just touchy-feely. Ingrid alternately reads romance magazines and does her nails. Wears a nightgown under her robe. Orders the kids to change the record on the stereo music machine. Gives orders like a Queen. Kids play over the bed, wrestle & touch & play in Red's hair. Butch enjoys this and keeps looking at Ingrid's nightgown. Large breasts full of milk poke out. Her lean white thighs, blonde pubic hair in wisps; wet pink cunt with sweet juices which she's sucked before.

The butch thinks: 'Giving her the $15 for her phone bill means nothing. It's not a bribe for sex, it's just to help her because I have a heart.'

Ingrid opens her robe and lets her youngest child, age 2, suck from her breast, while feeding the baby at the other. The older children are jealous. Red crawls up to Ingrid, pushes a shock of blonde hair aside from her ear and whispers, "I'm waiting my turn to suck." Ingrid casts her a dreamy look amid sarcasm. And chastises, "Don't be in a hurry! Let it flow, darling!"

This is how poor white people make love in a house with not enough privacy.

Baby is in its cradle next to the bed. Younger kids in the makeshift bedroom 5 feet away thru the sliding wooden door. Older ones & the lover upstairs.

Pleasant sensation lingers on Red's body from all the

kids. Now they're tucked in & Ingrid has kissed them all good night.

Long filmy lingerie parts, & Ingrid invites the butch to suck her breasts. Suck the milk out of them.

The kid & baby had pulled on her nipples, and they'd got large & hard.

It's milking time.

Butch's pants are soaking wet, so horny.

Crawls across the bed, comes to Ingrid's beautiful breasts, opens the nightgown. "Come & suck," Ingrid moans, eyes closed. "Milk my tits—they're sore."

Red must help relieve the pressure in her breasts by sucking. White liquid milk comes out, not like milk in the refrigerator. Ingrid's tits are painful unless she's milked regularly, and must have a butch do the job.

Ingrid taught Red how to suck, & press down on her tits by hand, 'round rhythmically until liquid spurts out. Sweet milk, warm from her body, into the butch's mouth. Stiff nipples. The whitish substance is a different texture & taste from dairy milk.

"See?" She squeezes her tit with a pale hand and squirts it out in an arch that hits the bed.

Fills a glass up with it. More the color of coconut milk than dairy.

"There's so much milk, the baby can't drink it all." Her Filipina lover don't enjoy drinking milk—she's very thin & doesn't like eating. Just smokes cigarettes & marijuana. Her other lover don't like it—thinks it's nasty.

Squirts mother's milk juice.

Red cups Ingrid's full tits in her hands, puts one thigh between hers, rubs her clit up and down on Ingrid's thigh while milking her; still wearing her clothes. And her trousers are soaking wet. The bed's rocking.

Ingrid is aroused, but it takes her 2 hours to cum—if she can at all. No one, female nor male, including herself can achieve this too often.

Red lies there in her clothes, humping; Ingrid's nipple in her mouth.

As she sucks, the butch grinds her pussy against her nude leg, and this delicious feeling begins to grow. Feels heat from Ingrid's cunt so hot and willing against her own leg. How she wants to take it. Now, as she sucks milk, thighs locked into the woman's thighs, clits rubbing, oh, how she desires to spread Ingrid's legs back, mount, and get her cock onto Ingrid's cunt.

'Don't want to cum in cloth. Want to press my cock up to her pussylips & cum rubbing in her hard, but...I can't rush her. I can't rush her...'

"Enough." Ingrid pushes her away to suck her other breast—milk is running out of it. And the fire between the butch's legs is so great; totally wet pants, almost cumming. Heavy squirt of milk in her face, warm thick creamy milk in streams. Both Ingrid's big swollen tits squeezed in the butch's hands.

Craves her cunt; to pull open the filmy gown and to suck there. To ride her hard. Moving her clit fast, faster, in Ingrid's cunt. To bust a nut.

So she's found a butch to service her tits.

The stiff, swollen breasts are ripe for the taking. Butch takes her lover's aching tits.

"I could sell this milk. I always produce too much. Some women don't have any."

"Sell it to me, baby. Uh-huhhh."

Ingrid swats Red with her ringed hand. "Don't be crude!" Then runs her fingers thru her hair as the butch fondles her.

So sexy. But privately both know it ain't easy for Ingrid to get her rocks off. Red strokes her big beautiful tits. Milk drips. Sucks. 'She is a sex object to be fucked, but seldom gets her own pleasure. I want to ride her so bad. Her under me. Feel her hot pussy against mine.'

Now it's time. Masterfully, Red pushes Ingrid down on the sheets, one big ripe tit in her hand, gown half-off & the woman surrenders without a word. Yanks the gown off her round shoulders past blonde hair; pushes Ingrid's knees back, spreading her thighs, mounts her, between her legs, so her clit can bang Ingrid's juicy cunt. Goes around and around on her wet, juicy cunt.

Hard contact of her cock in the wet, hot cunt. Streams of desire rush as she forces her clit around, hips move around and around, all the way up and down, rubbing, enjoying it. Whole body pushes down on Ingrid, who receives her in her arms. The woman holds her tight. What the butch needs—to lie down with a beautiful woman and screw and be held tight all night.

Now they were rocking, doing it—cock in her cunt, rolling around in her sweet pussylips.

Rubbery soft, hot, pubic hair; clit banging away. Bed going up & down to meet the thrust of their bodies.

Red about to cum, her reward for lustful milking services.

Presses her clit up in Ingrid's cunt, hard, rub; feels the warmth, the hot currents, the passion. Up & down thrust hard, riding clit & cunt embrace, presses tight; Ingrid pulling the butch into her; tight fusion of their bodies. Cum works out of her.

Her cunt, clit, whole body going crazy. Moves around fast, cum twice in succession.

Red had brought her dick over in a bag.

On all fours, knees & hands on the bed, slides it in between Ingrid's beautiful thighs, and it glides into her. Slow thrusts. Keeps up this rhythm.

But the European woman can cum only with clit contact; and only if you work her over good.

Porn magazines by the bed, & trash novels. They don't work, just give her a low level of libido.

Finally the butch begins the long process of sucking her off while filling her cunt with cock.

Has tried everything. —Mounts her from behind. The woman raises up on all fours dog-style; cock slides in & out of her cunt. Red's hand reaches around Ingrid's hip to rub her clit.

Then slides down between her legs, parts blonde pubic hair & lips, and seeks her clit. Her tongue licks, sucks gentle, then hard. Simultaneously, hands reach up to her tits, grabs one, pulls it, milk spurts out. They are fastened together. Red holding Ingrid's tits; Ingrid's thighs holding Red's head firmly down in her crotch.

And the bed is wet with milk, spit, and cunt juice. The sweet smell fills the bedroom.

Raises up, bends half over her, three fingers up in her vagina; it's warm, wet inside. Her thumb rubs in a circular motion over Ingrid's clit, presses the pulse. Head bent down to suck tits. Finally arousal begins intensely;

its level rises, then fades away. Ingrid loses it. Red feels her body straining to be released.

The butch removes her fingers; takes Ingrid's gown, wraps it around her midsection so it pushes those ripe tits up erect. Kinky and erotic; lace & milky tits. Now fingers glide into her wet chamber around and around, while her thumb rubs Ingrid's clit steadily; pubic hair soaking wet, bedsheets wet; fingers going around, lips suck the ripe, hard nipples on her breasts pushed up over the gown.

Slowly, inside her cunt felt her contract. Building, moaning. Ingrid pulls Red's hair, scratches her back; thumb rubs on her clit, hard, fingers are now tight in the swelling cunt, keep moving fast; streams of desire throb. Ingrid is cumming. Arches her back. Whole cunt wet and hot with liquid; & she shudders in an orgasm. Clamping around Red's fingers.

Butch keeps fucking her harder & harder with her fingers, thumb rolling on her clit. "Stop!" Ingrid tells her.

Clenching inside, but the butch keeps on firmly & don't stop screwing into her; cunt muscles squeeze on her fingers, fucking her harder, and her vagina accepts it, & Ingrid has a second orgasm; more intense thumb pressure hard on her clit, three fingers inside gripped tight. Body shudders.

"Oh, my God... Oh, Darling!... Darling...."

Bed is wet with milk, cum, cuntjuice, spit. Sheets must be changed.

Mickey Mouse watch said: 'Cum together. You are my children. Cum together, over me.'

PLEASURE IN THE GLITTER GUTTER
Chapter Six

I had just settled down for a long winter's nap.

—Red

December 1984. Holidays.

Life grinds on. It's work work work. Finally out of debt with this illegal job, after poverty over years of minimum wage as a nurse's aid ($3.50 per hour); so poor, not a stick of furniture in the house besides a bed & TV; & stealing food off the old people's trays so as not to starve.

At the job in San Leandro been taking home $600 per week for 12 hours daily labor, in unreported income; in a red wallet inside her white beach trousers. Finally money. A few hours of leisure time on Sunday, and she realizes she is alone.

A stark bare house, some animals, & no humans but her.

'I want a woman's love! I want to party! Want to cum!'

Thus had gone out to the Bay Bridge Inn, saw the strip show, leaned at the bar, cruised; & didn't cum. Not even a party girl to pay. And slung her tool in the backpack & trod forlornly down the steps of the hotel into the light of day.

'When I was poor & lived in the red light district, there was always girls around to pay for their sex services. Few times I got it free; my oral services exchanged for theirs. Now, here in this regular working-class neighborhood, there is nothing.'

Red was a nasty person. Rude & selfish. Very selfish. Uncouth. And shy & quite often stupid.

Sometimes she was too immobilized to sit in a chair at people's houses; must sprawl out on the floor. And also, eating with her hands. —This proved to be another stumbling block—labeled antisocial.

Ate with a big tablespoon in public, & with her hands in private.

Now this was a great contrast to what she projected over the phone lines—sounded very middle-class, businesslike, and authentic. As if calling from the sanitized offices of a charity—instead of a decrepit room whose floor is littered with cigarette butts, amid a group of winos & dopers.

So, sleep & work at the craphole, & sleep, & work. —Nose in the files of customer cards. Received her pay. Too tired to be horny except on her one day off when she masturbates & gets depressed.

Often sad, moves thru the days, this burden on her.

—Then frustration, anger, & sexual frenzy engulf her.

'I gotta go down to the Tenderloin and find a prostitute. A young one. Not a mean one...I need some...compassion.... I need someone to hold me.... Maybe a prostitute won't do....'

PLEASURE IN THE GLITTER GUTTER
Chapter Seven

Is this trash? Use it for your garbage can!
—Red

Suddenly it ends.

That long trick turned day after day in empty pages of a Date Book Calendar on the Celestial Mandala.
—It's done.

Happiness!

So! A happy ending! Finally, a young woman likes Red. Twenty years minus 6 months younger. Likes her. Likes her cunt. Likes her rod.

It's the lesbian stripper. They'd met at the show 6 months back.... Oh, those lonesome 6 months in between.

No more shame lying in bed listening to other broads pump; beds creak fast, BANG! BANG! Groans of pleasure in orgasm.

No more shame!

So, we don't meet on the Miracle Mile of the Glitter Gutter, but in a little hole-in-the-wall bar in Oakland. Pretty brown dancer.

Talk, dance, buy her a carbonated drink. This time, Red appraises her—she's wearing lady clothes; that's why Red's immediately gone to sit next to her, recognizing at long last that Zarina is femme. They meet again the next night.

Miracle: Zarina's there, just as she promised she'd be.

Zarina speaks: "When I first saw you at the strip show, I thought you were very butch. I thought you looked good. You had big shoulders—or your jacket had big shoulders. That looked really good. I wondered how much was the jacket. You have jackets that come out to here—(demonstrates)—they make you look bigger, & had those boots on.

"I was 19 when I first saw you, I was somewhat... well...I was scared to talk to you. You looked very imposing, a little scary. You looked white, possibly some Latin or Indian.

"When I hear you say that you couldn't get a woman, that it was a *tease*, a strip *tease*; well, I was very surprised. Thought it was very presumptuous of you to think you'd be going there to get a woman in the show. Was even kind of surprised that you were getting turned on!

"I don't think of it that much when I'm dancing— because it doesn't turn me on that much while dancing. So I don't think I'm turning women on. I'm thinking of it in a different context.

"If I was 18 again, I'd do a lot of this different! I'd have started dancing & making money. I would have been a femme from the start—not wearing those stupid clothes; those dumb plaid shirts & jeans and construction boots!

"I would have been bolder! And gone up to your room where you stayed that night and knocked on your door, & told you I'd be with you if you wanted me!

"I was so stupid to dress in those blue jeans and plaid shirts. I looked like a boy, and you disregarded me."

"Baby, if I'd known God was sending you into my life, I would have saved my money and not spent it all on hookers so we'd have more security.... *Why* did you wear the plaid shirts, jeans, and gym shoes? *Why?* You could have worn a dress and lady shoes, a skirt and sweater! I would have been all over you like white on rice!"

"I thought I was *supposed* to! Mostly everybody else was! I figured, for anybody to know I was gay, I was supposed to do that! A lot of dykes do!"

Zarina is a good companion, and intelligent. Very beautiful, and is of mixed race like Red. Not sure of her racial heritage. It's lasted 5 years so far. The butch gets her sweet love every night.

Happy ending to this bittersweet tale. Zarina Yasmin steps into her life on time—*right out of the Mickey Mouse watch of fate*. Tan, almond eyes, bodily charms, fleshy not skinny. A stripper in Roxie's shows.

Least nasty of all the strippers. Zarina is an artsy performer. Belly dances in a G-string made of chains & coins, and takes this all off in a strip as well.

Zarina confides: "Tips!" Anger flashes in her beautiful dark eyes. "They all made more tips than me and I was mad about it! I'm prettier than them!"

"That's because you don't work the crowd. You're not slutty enough. —People appreciate you as an Art Form. —Belly dancing is matriarchal. It's tribal art."

Zarina is not a bisexual, so there's no competition with men. Not a prostitute. No disease.

She is a nice middle-class girl. And her mother was white.

So then, after the strip show, the butch had someone to take home and bang. Oh, so good! Tender tan thighs spread, her arms wrapped around the butch with love.

They are poor. Excitedly she counts her money from tips—lengthwise-folded green single dollar-bills. Red has the house & Zarina moves in, bringing additional animals.

Red stops lying on the phone and gets an honest telemarketing job with a reputable business where the only person cheated is her. —Wages aren't half of what the frauds pay.

Not only their personal relationship, but our whole world is in change.

Drive down the street & see dykes everywhere:

"Is that one?"

"You see them everywhere!"

Dyke daydreaming.

Not only my relationship, but my whole world is coming to power.

Before—the late 1950s and 1960s saw a few of us slink down the streets visible, smoking cigars, wearing men's suits, in drag; & meeting in trepidation at gay bars raided by Vice Police.

Now bold dykes are everywhere.

On TV, always in the news in a great sea. Lesbians & gay men waving the red, orange, yellow, green, blue, & purple banner; fists in air!

"I'm busy! Every time I go into the bedroom, you follow me in and keep coming in and having sex with me!" exclaims Zarina.

This is how some Third World people live—servicing the homes of AmeriKKKa. Janitorial supplies all over our house—we've started our own business. Bedroom littered with clothes, no time to wash and the washing machine broke 6 months ago, no money to fix it, so we have to wash our clothes by hand in the kitchen sink & use the dryer which still functions. Too tired to clean our own house. Used condoms for the dildo we share & sometimes play with a 3rd woman, lie by the side of the bed. Plus dirty magazines. *Cunt*, *Pussy Eaters*, *Lady Mud Wrestlers*. Big tits with milk in them—Memory Mammaries. Come And Get It.

Little animals everywhere. Pet birds. Dogs. Cats. Ducks. Chickens. Pigeons. Rabbits. A Parrot. Cockatoos & cockatiels.

Five stiff dicks in the nightstand, plus harness. Tubes of K-Y jelly & bottles of lube. For our cunts. To love each other.

First thing was her mouth straining upward with a kiss for me.

Strap on my rod, big dab of clear K-Y on its head and down the sides. Use my hand and guide the rod to enter her. Fuck my woman long and deep with it. She wants my rod; in and out of her hard, fast. Then pull it out, slow; hold the tip with my hand up to her clit and rub it up and down to excite her, then penetrate again, long & deep. The black leather harness holds the base of the cock against my clit & fire grows in me. This cock is new —never used in any other cunts before. Fifteen minutes of steady thrusting, then she asks me to come out and do her clit with my tongue.

Lick and suck awhile, and now use my fingers on her. Three, in and out & continue to suck. Hard, fast, she's crying & tosses and turns, her hips thrust off the bed wet with juices; orgasming, her cunt tightens around my fingers pushing them out. Her body arches up; she cums and cums.

Tonight I choose oral sex as my pleasure. Stand over her. Zarina kneels before me; my cock in her mouth. My woman sucks me off hard; my hands in her hair pull her head into me. An intense cum.

Gone is the shame of lying here wanting a woman and not in my power to get one.

Mistakes I've made are covered by time.

Learned items about lovemaking with Zarina that one never finds out in one-night stands.

Slow love, experimentation. —In penetration. —Had started out letting my women penetrate me in my late teens; and now again, nearing mid-century.

I write this within the treasured substance of a relationship of 5 years. My first in life, by age 48.

Sat there in her boxer shorts & T-shirt, after finishing copulation. Her woman spread under the blanket, satiated. By light of a yellow bulb; (it's 4 A.M., when ghetto noises are at their least) she wrote her confessions. 'I must be mentally deficient to have gone this long without a happy home. —Am tremendously embarrassed to admit that Zarina is the first of my relationships to go beyond 4 months, in my entire life.'

Dragged herself thru this world 40 plus years, until it became a ballet, and she finally began to dance! A musical dance of life! 'Never thought life could treat me so good!' —Finally, romantic love. A house become a home. Enough money.

Under a yellow bulb, the butch finishes in masterful strokes her orgasm. —The Cum EZ series. *Dirty Pictures; Lay Lady Lay; After the Trick was Turned; Pleasure in the Glitter Gutter; Lesbian Cum Stories with Feeling & Meaning*. Red Jordan Press ground on its wheel within a wheel on the Great Mandala.

I, Red Jordan Arobateau, take pen in hand to write about the face of things that have been—shape of gay worlds as the butch knew it; rough period of time of sexual activity 1959 to 1991 the present; and to testify to the great loneliness of the bulldagger.

To mention if dykes shared cunt like guys share dick there would be a lot less loneliness & isolation.

And that females should make love harder, not rougher, but more aggressively take each other in each other's arms.

Is this trash? Then use it for your garbage can!

Dedication: To all dykes who lie with a vibrator, or fingers between their own moist thighs; with a Dirty Magazine full of naked women, wishing it was the real thing.

No matter if you are a dyke doctor lying up all alone in a mansion with 5 bedrooms & 3 separate baths and a maid to clean it and money & too embarrassed to find a date with a whore; or some poor woman surviving on welfare, doing what you must do, up in a hotel in the red light district.

Hope you never have to flip the 2-sided coin, turn a trick, or be tricked.

And, the long, long loneliness—pray you don't have to go thru in your life what I was forced to in mine—but maybe that's better still than not having done anything!

One wish, yes:

'I wish more women had taken me in their arms.'

So, dear readers, forgive the self-indulgence of this semi-autobiographical essay.

Can this be a story of triumph of the human soul?

We are all part of each other in a circle dance. —Some experiences are mine, & the others, they lay in my arms & told me their stories.

It is transposed with magic!

This is a story full of blood, guts, and cum—especially mine, on every page!

Truth & love are their most outstanding feature.

The Spirit of God came to me in a dream within a dream. She came to me in a Heart of Gold, within my heart of flesh. Spoke: 'What you are doing is great, but you must give your all.'

We are all dykes! Let the boundaries of our territory grow! Let us suck & fuck cunt to our hearts' content and not postpone this, nor put our desires, our lives, on ice for anything, or any reason ever again!

Funny thing happened at the Xerox place. Had a sack full of the last pages of this story resting on the floor

—guess because I look like the garbage person, a lady comes up to me with some crumpled-up garbage in her hand and drops them in my sack & asks, "Is this the trash?"

I ask you, Dear Readers…

GANG RAPE
Chapter One

It was a hard time; those early 1990s. AIDS, that plague of the century murdering tens of thousands. Herpes, a disease that could set the stage for cancer of the cervix. Women dying of breast cancer and uterine cancer. Gay men dying of AIDS, plus an ever-increasing statistic of females.

And sex runs rampant in the streets. Women's pornography; clubs with hot lesbian desire, as nowhere before. Lesbian sex illustrated, advertised.

So it was the best and worst of times all at once.

Sam's light brown hair stuck to her scalp. Face shone with perspiration in the hospice room. Hot, the odor of death, an unmistakable odor once you knew it—of the body's functions failing; the medicine, the waste, the heat.

Informal: slacks, flat shoes, a shirt. No white hospital uniform here, only her name tag: DR. SANDRA ANDERSON, M.D. emblazoned in plastic with a serpent twisted over a staff: symbol of the medical profession.

Moments ticked by in the dying hour toward the end. Dr. Sam thought about it: 'People who live safe lives are the worst ones to face death. But this one is already reconciled. She never had control over her life, she exerts little now, and she's going easier—if a human being can go easily.'

Conditions of the body change drastically from day to night. She'd cough, sweat, spit up. Then be at peace. 'Some think there isn't going to be any emotion. They just want to get it over with. They look up at me and beseech me, "Is there going to be an end to this?"'

The patient's sleep was fitful. In pain, her body spasms. Is jolted awake by a spasm.

Her face had altered dramatically from the ravages of illness over its progression. Had Sam not learned from 3 years' experience, on returning 2 weeks later she might have thought this was a stranger placed in this patient's bed. Somebody else.

Spasm awoke her. She reached for Sam's hand. Her eyes were cloudy now, no longer clear. Her legs had been gone a long time. Just her hands still had enough strength. Reached for Sam.

And then the patient died.

Dr. Sandra Anderson drove home thru the streets of the city.

She put the dying room behind her in memory, relegated to a hundred other such scenes. It was time to live.

It's summer. A massive amount of heat. Like it's your duty to fornicate. To have a woman. —To take that girl on her back again. —Or on all fours. Fuck her from behind, your dick inside her cunt, other arm wrapped around her waist, fingers in her pubic hair, rubbing her hot clit.

Pictured that girl, the blonde; how she'd taken her, crouched over her; girl's legs wide, hairy cunt open as she lowered her cunt down on top of it, screwing around till she got the right contact, & began to fuck her. Hands on either side of the girl, on the mattress; loving cunt. Fuck. Just fuck until she got an orgasm & not even think about the patients, the girl's feelings, or about being nice. Just fuck.

Hot Summer Desire.

Drove thru the city on the main thoroughfare that reckoned 8 more miles in distance to the hills where she lived.

Heat. To abandon herself to it.

Sam felt like a dog. Intense heat had come up on her. —Hormonal.

Her short hair clung wet to her face. Cunt was wet in frustration.

'Pussy. I want to get some pussy. Dirty old pussy. Any kind of pussy.'

Past intersections and passersby & taverns and all kinds of places, in which she knew no woman would be waiting,—for her kind of sex. None. The hills ahead, her empty home, with just 5 dogs to wag their tails in greeting.

See it in a vision,—in bed with her head between the

girl's legs, delicious cunt-smells, and her own cunt; making orgasms together. The girl's sweet tits. Sam was fired with desire to pull a woman to her, to suck her off, to jack off her own clit in the woman's soft, wet cunt.

To taste, and touch, and fuck.

On the thoroughfare passed a gang of hookers who hooted at cars in the street; short skirts, long bare legs in high heels. It was obvious that they were selling their female bodies for sex. Sam had never thought to approach one before—not in this kind of setting.

Now even that desperate idea crossed her mind.

Of all people, the doctor knew how dangerous it was to have unprotected sex with a high-risk partner. These girls shot drugs intravenously, had partners who did. Had multiple sex partners frequently. Today; so wild, needing a woman, Sam was actually torn by the idea of stopping & trying to meet one of them. But she didn't.

Outside her small estate, the dogs set up barking when they heard the familiar car motor climbing the last grade of the hill.

Trees. Horizon of the bay & grey city be163
neath. Even-ing began to settle.

Wind blew hot.

The physician worked 16-hour shifts. Often in the past she'd taken her pleasure on nights off like these. —A ready woman at her disposal gleaned from her own black book of tried, tested, chosen names.

An active sex life was vital in her line of work. With all the emotions and responsibilities bombarding her, Sam had to work at it. Most were women she'd met in respectable clubs and parties where professional women gather. Women of her own class. But the list had gotten dusty these last 6 months. After stumbling and bumping her head in an emotional way with the current girl-interest, Sam had ruthlessly gone back to that black book of phone numbers—just to find out none of them were available.

Had tried out a call girl once, a long time ago; it was much too risky. It could jeopardize her job if caught in the illegal act of solicitation to buy sex. It had to be an adult woman who wanted her for her own sake.

'I can't wait any longer.' Her whole body trembled. Could see her own life pass before her eyes. Felt her guts shake like they wanted to throw up from wanting. And her mind unglued.

Paced in circles around her house.

The phone didn't ring & she'd called every woman she knew.

It was a bad time for Sam.... Summer heat... Too many deaths.... Dying all around. A sex drive pounding inside her that wouldn't go away, and out of her string of ex-lovers, no woman to handle it.

Tried to cool down by putting on soothing music. Ethereal outer-space music. It helped, but didn't work. Music she used for patients who were dying. 'Now I'm living and it doesn't work for me.' Music to soothe the savage breast.

And answers lay all wrapped up in time.

GANG RAPE
Chapter Two

Blood was everywhere, blood of a sustained natural cause, not violence.

Blood was in her mouth.

Blood on the sheets, on the hot towel that had been heated by water, compressed & squeezed out & used to wipe her lips & cunt.

Parted her lover's pubic hair, smelled the sweat & cologne and cunt & blood; her own hair in ringlets touched by that liquid, as she worked between her lover's thighs, did cunnilingus, then put fingers inside & blood streaked the doctor's face.

So close, side by side, ran her hands over the length of the woman's body. Fiddled with her tits and, as she pushed three fingers into her wet hole, heard her moan.

Peggy's cunt was heavy and swollen from being sucked and fucked. And Sam knew when she climbed back between her thighs, their cunts would make good contact. Lubricated in blood. And she would cum.

The sweet blonde was worked up to a sweat over her whole body; with her hands held each knee pressed back to spread her legs even wider for Sam.

Worked in the gash of hot cunt, in the blood of menstruation; her cunt against Peggy's, screwing, until her white neck arched, head thrown back, legs trembling between Peggy's from the impact of her cum.

So this was memory. The delicious first and only time. Six months of game. And a doctor in heat going crazy.

That evening her professional woman's club gave a party. A great party. A wonderful party. Five hundred lesbians. Five hundred bottles of champagne. The best event. Every woman got balloons. Vanilla ice cream floats, a swimming pool. Hot tub.

Light brown hair, nearly blonde, very curly; expensive tweed suit; as masculine as possible and still be recognizably female. Dr. Sandra Anderson was there —with a party name tag that read: HELLO! I'M SAM! on it. And no stethoscope around her neck.

This dance hosted by the National Lesbian Women's Professional Association was a prodigious affair. The Star Room of the Highton Plaza Hotel, $60 a ticket admission plus another $20 for valet parking in the bowels of the mammoth structure some 30 floors below. This doubled—if the doctor had had a date, $140 would have meant absolutely nothing. She could do it daily, if such events for lesbians occurred daily. She was rich by birth and by trade, and was a big spender by heart—when she could get her mind off her career enough to see someone in need of help.

Pants suit; eyes sky-blue. Curly hair, light, barely touching her ears; butch/female appearance. The doctor definitely looked gay.

Toasting with long-stemmed glasses; the banquet hall roused in the echo of women's voices in a salute. 'So many great sisters. It's true, we lesbians are no longer alone. There's so many of us.' And Sam knew that by next Christmas she'd find another woman out of all of these; her equal in power & wealth & education, and hand in hand they'd go vacationing on one of the remote beaches of the world, at some luxury resort.

Two attractively dressed lesbians down the length of the doctor's table were discussing something. Tanned; one non-gay in appearance, wore a backless black gown, diamond necklace & dripped diamond earrings to match. The other, masculine, wore white; a lady's suit, white tie, and also ruby earrings; tiny studs like blood drops. They looked at Sam, who sat just out of earshot: "Well, she had really frowned on that sort of thing; keeping a woman for all those months; but she told me, 'I'm doing it because I want to get out of my condo in the city and back into my house in the hills. And I don't think the relationship will work with me being absent so much because of my practice, so I don't want to bring her into the house because it'll be harder to get her out once she's in.' So she lets her use the condo in San Francisco for months.... She's so softhearted."

"It's her work that does it."

"*Sandra Anderson.*" The tone dripped acid.

"Hah!"

"The famous lesbian lover who lays them and leaves them."

"Hard to believe it's the same woman."

"Remember that little *dive* we girls use to go to years back, that *place?* And some gal had carved, not written, but *carved* on the door: INTERN DR. SAM ANDERSON IS A MOTHERFUCKER! IF YOU WANT A GOOD TIME, SEE DR. SAM! SHE'S A COLD-BLOODED SLUT! SHE'LL WINE YOU AND DINE YOU AND FUCK YOU AND LEAVE YOU WHEN YOU NEED HER THE MOST!—AND SHE GIVES GOOD BLOWJOBS! And her phone number after that."

"It even rhymed, I thought."

"Yes! Yes, it did. And on the stall door in the toilet of the hottest lezzie dive in town. Can you imagine! Having your professional title slandered for every dyke who pisses in the place to see—on the door to the toilet stall?"

"Now she looks so desperate."

"Won't speak. Won't give me the time of day. Next week she'll be on the phone begging us to come over and barbecue on her deck & dip in the hot tub."

"Her people are from money. Old established money. Money always acts funny. Always."

"Well, *I'm* from money, and *I* don't change like the wind."

"She's like a lot of upper-class people. I bet her parents are conservative and uptight. I bet they sent her off to Catholic boarding school so they could jaunt off to

Europe; she goes straight thru grammar, middle school, college, & never got enough love and affection & had no power over the situation, and is trying to make up for it with every date she can get. The love, the affection, then the power trip. —When she kisses 'em good-bye."

"Lucky bitch!"

"Oh, she gets 'em, honey. Watch her in action sometime."

"So she's hurt now. Some gal finally put it to her like she's been doing it to everybody else. —It's her turn now; she's got to go thru the shit, pardon my French."

"I feel no sympathy."

"She's never had any problems with anything in her life. Nothing bad ever happened to her. Got her degree. Tells her parents she's gay. They think it's wonderful. Tells her straight friends she's gay; they think it's wonderful. Comes out in the hospital that hires her on staff; they think it's wonderful. —Now she gets a slut who loves her and leaves her, and she can't take it. Wants to give up her practice and move away to the tropics, where life isn't so fast paced."

"That one named Peggy.'"

"*Yes*. Who's not even a professional or a business owner, but a stupid little secretary stuck in a canning factory which will probably have to pick up its base and move out of San Francisco with the rest of the blue-collar businesses, and she's been there all her life. It's pathetic."

Dance floor reeled with shattering light from a multi-faceted ball hung in the heavens casting a prism of colors upon 500 dancing women.

Sam picked her way thru the crowd, drink in hand. Sometimes a hand would reach out to tap her arm, and a friendly voice call, "Hello, Doctor!" And Sam had all but forgotten her mission. —Often her ringed fingers rose up to comb thru her curly hair, for she was deep in thought. Remembrance of how good the woman had sucked her off caused a sly grin, followed by the pang of loss. And admonished herself, for she was at the party to get her mind onto a happier plane.

So that's why she was on the 30th floor of this grand hotel, amid her professional colleagues; partying with her own rich class—trying to forget Peggy.

Found an alcove where she could sip the intoxicating beverage & lose her mind amid the swirling couples & dancing lights.

Figure hunched on a cushioned divan under a frieze of carved stone. One trousered leg crossed over the other. Hand, pale, very short manicured nails cupped her chin. 'God or the Devil sent her into my life. Whoever it was, they knew what they were doing. Peggy is a very hot and desirable female. A very sensual and erotic woman.'

The way Sam had met Peggy was at an affair just like this. —Spied a cute blonde not far away, approached, and struck up a conversation.

The minute Sam saw Peggy close up, she knew they were from different classes. The eye-catching low-cut halter top matching the tight figure-fitting women's slacks was a shade too bright in color, and lots of brass bracelets clanking up and down her arms. And the way she carried herself. —Assertive, plucky, energetic. Not mild, reserved, but with power—like a lady to the manor born.

Not surprising, few lesbians Sam actually met in the gay life were. Many rich heiresses were only rumors in the old family circles; the country club, the Republican Club—the gays among them had to be unearthed. Like turning over a stone to discover them, living hidden gay lives.

As the cute blonde chatted away, Sam had gazed at her, wondering vaguely how she got there.

And Peggy answered her question, openly, honestly. "I go to these dances; they sure are nice. I'm going to go to all of them—I have a calendar. Sixty dollars is a lot for a ticket, but it's worth it. You meet a higher quality of women here. —I go to better myself."

'Ha. So that's it. She wants to meet a rich dyke. Maybe she's a gold digger.'

"I'm not a professional, I don't own a business or anything. I'm just a humble little secretary and part-time computer operator. Just plain little Peggy."

And there was nothing simple about Peggy. Not the wiggle in her walk, not the way she talked.

The blonde was 5'5", two inches shorter than Sam, clear blue eyes that could be big and full of wonder, or half-closed in mirth. Tits, full, filled out her halter top and a bra strap showed thru on one side. Hips and a nice round ass all piled up on slender legs on high-heeled pumps. Peggy talked a little too loudly, ate quite a bit, and drank too much. She wrapped her hand under Sam's arm and wouldn't let go, rattling on in conversation in a very amusing manner. It was the slight touches of her fingers on Sam's curly head, the pats on her arm, and a dreamy gaze from those blue eyes into Sam's deeper blue ones.

And Peggy said yes readily. The doctor was surprised it was so easy; smiled, blinked, and squeezed the woman's hand. And they went home together.

Winding up the hill toward the house, fog settled on the inner city far below. The huge concrete buildings of downtown had become child's alphabet blocks by time they got there. Highways were ribbons, far distant, with tiny cars like toys moving at insect's pace. The bay, then the ocean far beyond surrounding in blue. A half hour ago, they had passed the last dividing line of poverty —houses that are technically houses, but more like shanties. Shacks; compared to hers, which fit snugly into the mansion class. Houses with only one bathroom and 2 bedrooms—that tacky kind of stuff.

The broad road had grown narrow.

Hardly any people could be seen. Privacy. Tranquillity. Nature. At peace. Blue jays flitted thru the trees here, & deer grazed. Just a 45-minute drive above hell.

Dogs barked. One first, then the others took up the chant. Crickets chirped in the underbrush; sound of tires of Sam's expensive foreign car crunched over the gravel driveway.

Sam's mansion was on 3 levels. Three full baths and one 1/2 bath. One point five kitchens. A full wet bar. A wraparound deck supported by redwood beams, which went 3/4 way around the house commanding a view of 3 major bridges and the inner city below, and of the 2.5 acre grounds. A hot tub was set in a smaller redwood deck off the living room, entered thru sliding glass doors. A garage large enough for 4 cars. A fishpond in the wooded acres. A service elevator connected all 3 stories plus the full basement. A 2-million-dollar house, it was one of a kind, set back in seclusion and tranquillity. A heated swimming pool was an aquamarine gem on the lavish property; and neighboring estates touched hers on three sides to form a private forest.

As Sam escorted the blonde up the front walk, hand firm in the small of the woman's back, feeling her hot flesh under the sweaty satin garment, fire rose in her thighs. She felt in command. Saw awe on Peggy's face and knew she was impressed. And this made Sam hot and lusty & wanted to lead the woman into her master bedroom & give her a long hot screw.

The two women went thru the entrance hall, and stepped down into the sunken living room. Immediately the blonde looked up, blue eyes wide, at the cathedral ceiling zooming 40 feet tall above them, its huge glass windows illuminated by starlight; vast as a planetarium. A huge log-filled fireplace whose brick chimney shot up into the darkened recess of the ceiling; logs flickered embers—prepared by the maid, just waiting to be brought back to a blaze.

Miniature palm trees in expensive oriental ceramic pots dotted the grand sweep of the living room. Plush wall-to-wall carpet in every room and upon every stair except the basement stairs, which were tiled. One wall of fabulously expensive music equipment; tapes, CDs, and a massive eight-foot wide TV screen. Sam saw to seating her guest in one of the luxurious wraparound white leather sofas;—like the mansion itself, once a person fell into it, she never wanted to leave.

Fixed beverages at the wet bar. With shrewd cunning she had memorized Peggy's drink, to keep her libido liquored up and willing for love. Turned on some soft, erotic music with an insistent pounding beat, to match the rhythm their hips would make soon, locked in each other's passionate embrace.

A handful of crumpled *Wall Street Journal*s & some logs, and the fire was roaring.

Sam thought: 'Perfect setting for a night of love.'

As the doctor moved around preparing the drinks and the fire, the woman appraised her.

'She's very nice. An almost childlike simplicity about her. Very attractively dressed… This house alone has knocked me off my feet. She works with dying people. What a job to have. She's strong, in a quiet kind of way…. A tranquil quality. —A childlike tranquillity. Maybe it's from working with sick people so much. And this house…it's perfect. She has a very nicely kept house. She says she has a maid that comes in every day. Imagine that! Every day!'

Firelight flickered on the two. Sam handed Peggy a drink and sat down near her.

"Part of my job is to try to talk to them about dying. And to prepare them to accept this. But they don't want to accept it. And they think they're not going to die."

Nurses see a lot more of patients than doctors. Sam was an exception. Spent many hours of volunteer work among the dying as well as in her practice, which ranged over a variety of care.

Sam worked hard and played hard. And as often as

she could—got her body next to a female, and got themselves all wet in each other's juice and spit and cum.

Fire streaks red light. Black heavens towered in the night thru cathedral windows dotted by silver stars.

Now, curly brownish hair and blonde together, intermixed, heads move in slow passion of a kiss.

Music's heavy beat was sexual. Love was intense with the doctor. She had seen death, so she lusted to make life happen.

First thing Peggy noticed was that Sam wasn't as kinky as she might usually be attracted to, but the fervor with which the woman held her, caressed her, kissed and stroked her; the holding she did was super-real. 'Maybe it's the line of work she's in—being with people who have come to the end of the line. She must have a lot of need built up in her, too. She's emotional.'

They kissed a long time, romancing, tongues in mouths; but when Sam finally made her move, hand at Peggy's back trying to unhook her halter top and get to her tits, the blonde stopped her hand. "I'm on my period tonight, so I can't go too far."

"That doesn't bother me at all. I'll get a hot towel."

"No. I don't want to. No, Sam!" Peggy pushed her away. "I don't want to keep kissing; you'll get all hot and bothered."

"So *let* me get hot and bothered."

So as the fire raged, and the fire inside them both, they sat and necked and loved, just like the old-days lovers did in the parlor, or on a swing on the front porch. And Sam knew: 'I've got to have this woman.' Felt those tits as she crushed Peggy to her, warm and light and forcing her body down against her, the heat between the woman's thighs. "I want to love you so bad. Blood doesn't bother me. We've talked: I know you're clean."

"I'm bleeding heavy."

"Ever thought that might excite me?"

And Sam's thinking: 'She wants me in her body; I can tell. Why won't she let herself go? I hate it when they tell me no and leave me frustrated.'

And Peggy thought: 'She wants me now; she's practically begging for it. But when I tell her what I want her to do, that'll be the end of it! I hate it when all they want is ordinary plain sex, it usually leaves me frustrated... It's like having a woman who won't go down on you or something.'

So the blonde finally gave in & lay down for the butch doctor. And let Sam love her.

Climbed stairs to the master bedroom. Undressed. Sam had brought in towel heated by hot water and wrung out, set it at the side of the bed.

And got down.

Turned the night-light on her. To see her body, pale pink-white. Soon, in lovemaking, red blood streaked her thighs.

First it was oral sex; blood all over the sheets and thighs and face sticky from clots. And Sam wiped it off, and Peggy clinging to her moaning, holding her, rocking back and forth because she'd cum hard. And Sam went in the bathroom and got a fresh hot towel; and the sheets got full of blood, pussy discharge, cum, and sweat as Sam rode Peggy's pussy, moving her cunt fast around and around, hips pistoning, grunting in her own climax.

Peggy saw the vibrating sextoy under the bed, its cord trailing to an electric socket in the wall. "Aren't you going to use that on me?" And noted that Sam looked back at her hesitantly, as if she'd never used it on a woman before.

"Do you want it?"

"No. You don't have to."

The doctor was passionate.

Soon her fingers thrust in and around inside Peggy's hole.

Room smelled of cunt.

Going in and out of her cunt, sucking her tits. Licking her clit with her tongue tip. It was really good sex, and Peggy felt herself let go. 'Why not?' she thought to herself, and got into it. Thighs spread to receive her lover's hand, humping and groaning, and let it go, hips going 'round, back arched in ecstasy.

Sam's hand was bathed in blood & cuntjuice. Was tired & happy. Her own body's inside being rocked in tides like the sea from multiple orgasms. Was tired & happy. It was a lot of fun.

"It's so good being with you. Thank you so much for coming here with me & coming upstairs."

Sam lay on her, kissing, breathing in Peggy's ear. "So good." Smelled her perfume. And Peggy's hand with painted fingernails caressed the line of curly hair at the back of Sam's neck.

Flickering firelight.

Sam would not soon forget the power of their cunts pressed together, the cumming.

First time, blood was on the sheets. Stains remained. Tho they'd gone thru the washing machine in the basement twice in hot sudsy water.

Yet, what lingered most was memory of the fire that came up thru their thrusting cunts into orgasm; cum up from the very center of her being.

GANG RAPE
Chapter Three

Their second date, like all Dr. Sandra Anderson's dates, was at a fine restaurant.

Good table, fine linen. Filet mignon and lobster.

Champagne, vintage 1953.

Flaming baked Alaska for dessert.

Credit card tossed down on the monogrammed tablecloth to pay for a $240 meal, including the tip.

Sam wore a man-tailored jacket. Open collar, satin shirt, tanned skin, expensive gold pendant on a chain necklace—male style. Betraying the first roughness of a dyke past her mid-thirties.

Laughed, tipped her curly head back, at ease, a lion in the throne of her chair; secretly surveyed across the table her conquest for that evening's pleasure.

The blonde looked a bit showy; naked shoulders, cheap jewelry, but soft & sweet. And that moved Sam, bad. They both chatted. Sam thought: 'I'm telling this girl my same old line of bullshit...it works. She loves it. She's going home with me tonight and getting laid. Maybe this will last a while before I get bored. Or she'll decide she wants someone who'll get serious about her.... My career is my wife. I can't have a permanent woman, I can't give them the personal attention they need, I'm too busy. But tonight it's still sweet. She thinks I'm falling in love with her...And she'll move her sweet pussy for me tonight when I get on her, and I'm gonna cum so good because it's been so long. Five days since I've been with a woman—Peggy.'

Peggy laughed. Her wispy blond hair shimmered by candlelight. The white-gloved waiter had returned the credit card on a plate with a receipt to be signed. As the doctor bent over the table, pen in hand, Peggy mused: 'Well, she sure has the money to spend on me. That's definitely good. I never see money. It passes right thru me from my paycheck directly to the landlord & the bills. I never eat in nice restaurants. There's nothing left after my outrageous rent and money to keep the car running.'

The doctor sipped the last of her champagne, watched Peggy in the flickering candle's flame. Soft violin music filled the air, and distant metal clink of the silverware. Sam felt no pain, was slightly intoxicated. 'Guess I'll ask her now to go to bed with me.... No... Maybe I'll ask her out in the car so I can demonstrate with a kiss.'

The two women walked out slowly. In the privacy of night they joined hands, and bumped into each other in a romantic closeness.

Sam had learned more about her. Peggy had an apartment she shared with another lesbian in a very nice neighborhood. It was too small for them both, but safety was a priority to her. That place had no problems. This was very important.

And paid dearly for it. One thousand three-hundred a month.

Had an ancient car she kept fixing up whenever it broke down. Kept her appearance stunning. All her money went to this, and nothing was left. "I like a location I can walk around in night and day and not be hassled."

"Yes," Doctor Sam agreed. "Personal freedom is vital."

So Peggy had to have a roommate. "We both want a neighborhood we can feel comfortable in, yet still remain in the inner city near work. It just means spending so much money. I like walking down the street to the store and not having to feel afraid for my life." Peggy laughed, a tone that was merry, yet cutting at the same time.

The parking lot was quiet, neon-lit. The doctor opened the passenger door for her date, locked and closed it, then went around to her side and got in. She slid past the steering wheel, over next to Peggy. Silver light shone thru the windshield.

Sensual mouth close to hers. Scent of mint. Felt warm breath. Kissed Peggy full on the mouth.

Pulled away. Specks of saliva on her full lips; Peggy's

blue eyes opened slowly. Under the neon parking-lot lights and moon rays; for a second Sam glimpsed a tiny scar, its white hairline across her upper lip. Had noticed it the first night at the dance, forgotten, now saw it again.

Dr. Sam put her mouth back over those sweet lips, ran her short-nailed fingertips over Peggy's warm breasts, stroking her; and began to breathe heavily. The woman's hand came up to hers as if to stop her, but didn't; just stayed, resting lightly on Sam's hand as she petted her tits. Motion of their tongues going 'round and 'round each other's. Peggy's strong response. And nipples grew firm under her touch.

The white hand with pink nails finally tightened around her own, pulling her fingers away from her breast.

"Ohhhhhh!" the doctor moaned amorously. But Peggy was firm, held the hand down.

"Come on home with me. We can have a few drinks and use the pool."

"Not tonight, Sam."

'She's turning me down!' The doctor's ego took a nasty turn. She tried once more to lift her hand back to Peggy's tits, but the woman was firm. 'She had an excuse the first time I asked her, too.'

"We can just take a swim...no sex." She lamented. Felt deflation. Her spirit sank.

"I love your house, but I have a job assignment tomorrow working overtime, twelve hours, I can't. Anyway... Sam"—Peggy toyed with the doctor's strong fingers—"let's not rush. Let me get to know you.... Let me grow on you first.... So...if I do anything you don't like, it'll be too late to leave me, because you like me too much. We made love on our first date.... I hope I didn't make a mistake. Sam.... I don't want you to expect sex every time with me." Then wrapped her arms around—tight—for an instant. Then let go.

Peggy faced straight ahead.

Couples, straights, in tuxedos and evening gowns were crossing the lot.

Sam heaved a big sigh and moved away, back to the driver's seat.

The doctor was restrained and civilized. Had a good bedside manner. But after hugging & petting Peggy's pretty tits, and probing her sweet mouth, and feeling her warm tongue moving in unison with her own, up in the front seat of her car, she felt like coming out of her slacks right there, just ripping off all her clothes, getting naked. Red-hot sensation from head to toe. And fuck the woman in any manner she wanted to do it.

Drove Peggy home, thru the commercial area crossing town. Past two police squad cars; officers had a man under arrest, hands in steel cuffs with a chain thru them, wrapped around a lamppost. Calling in the report over their police-band radio. "GOOD! Lock him up!" Peggy applauded, looking thru the window.

Just the sight of rough men like this made her afraid. Sam looked sideways as she drove, and saw the woman's body shaking. "I try to be as far away from this element as I can." Sam was to witness later that Peggy would literally get up and leave an area and go somewhere else whenever she saw this type of character.

The doctor was very embarrassed. When she got home, the crotch of her slacks was soaking wet. From the pets & kisses & hugs. And from seeing the blonde over the restaurant table all night, curvaceous and sexy, & having prematurely envisioned what she'd do with her. Headlights bounced along the winding road; caught the flash of a deer bounding thru the underbrush. Then it was gone, upturned tail leaping off on strong haunches, just the dusty brown earth of the road focused between two lights remained. Plus mystical music on tape; the scene was aloneness on the way ascending the final stretch to her home. She hadn't planned on being alone tonight. 'Star bright...Star bright...First star I see tonight...Wish I may, wish I might...Have this dream... Come true tonight....'

Let the dogs in the house to woof and roam at will.

Sam thought of all her conquests. Girls had followed her around everywhere like puppy dogs.

She and her dogs trudged upstairs, past the study. There was a grant for $5,000 on the desk for a research project she was involved in. —A check she'd not even taken the time to cash.

Passed on to the bedroom, showered in the master bath.

Before, in her days of intermittent sexcapades, she would have lain in bed and taken care of herself.

Vibrator between her thighs, or fingers, or one of many purple or pink flesh-colored cocks.

Now her whole focus was Peggy.... She'd missed calling up other women during the brief interval they'd been together, as was her habit: dating several women at once, so she could always depend on the sexual services of one of them.

Lately had been so busy between the hospice, her humanitarian love, and the hospital, her career; & along with dating Peggy & calling and chatting together on the phone, her schedule was so busy, she hadn't gone cruising.

So tonight, in the yellow lights of her spectacular mansion, peering out thru vast glass windows into the dark, she was a lonely figure.

This left her to the solitary pleasure she could devise with a lesbian sex magazine and some toys.

'All my other women have gone on with their lives.'

So, for the first time in several years, she was alone.... And this was a weight, groaning on her mind, as heavy as the groaning of her pleasure on Peggy that first time, in that sweet release.

Night-light on.

Lay in bed. Reached automatically for her vibrating dildo.

'No. No. I'll wait. It'll make me hotter when she *does* sleep with me.'

So the weeks passed into months. And she did weaken, and masturbate; and felt bad that it wasn't Peggy. —That was her inner feeling.

Outer reality was a whirlwind of dates, shows, movies, dinners, flowers, a lot of conversation; dancing close in lesbian bars and parties,—all with Peggy;—& no sex.

'She's using me. Using me to be wined and dined. But doesn't want to go to bed with me anymore.

'Why not?'

So, this remembrance; as she huddles in an alcove beside hotel windows in a star-filled night; an event costing nearly $100, and the money meant nothing, wished it had been $200 and that at her side would have been Peggy, in her tacky satiny gown, or the other pantsuit lady-style outfit.

SHARING YOUR LOVE!
ARE YOU SHARING YOUR LOVE?
ALL YOU HAVE TO DO IS DO IT!

The band rocked. The party was emblazoned with big red hearts and festoons of silver chains.

Tanned, curly hair, by herself at the edge of the dance floor, upon the cutting edge of her sexuality, Sam watched the festivities at the National Lesbian Women's Professional Association party.

Remembering their first & only love night.

It had been some night!

Scarlet color panties,—barely a strap across her pussy, blonde tufts of hair sticking over it.

Hot, moist, her cunt responding to Sam's touch.

The woman had even done a show for the doctor. 'The first time it was so fabulous! Peggy's worked as a go-go dancer. The sight of her sweet white body tossing that blonde hair.' Peggy took off her clothes slowly, flung them away so they sailed thru the air and landed where they might. Curves, tits, ass, naked in front of Sam. "WORK OUT BABY! WORK OUT!" Sam had hollered, excited, to her own Private Dancer. Sam, the cunt expert. And Peggy was erotic, fully undressed but for her pair of high-heeled pumps; naked legs spread, bouncing her tits, dips down to the floor, thrusts her hips up in a fucking motion. Gets on her back on top of the rug, writhing, and humping—just for a second's tease.

And Sam would never be the same again. 'So this is what the guys have been getting all along,' she thinks. Sits in her slacks and shirt at the edge of the bed. Peggy prances about, turning to show her sweet round moons of ass; dips, thrusts her sweet cunt, wiggles. Then comes over & sits on Sam's lap.

And her delicate hand works, sliding down the front of Sam's stomach and across her thighs; pale, ringed, doing an expert job. Way in the back of her mind a question's taking shape: 'She learned to do all this go-go dancing?' But is too busy to think.

And the butch pushed her down on the bed, stripped her own clothes off in a hot hurry; mounted; felt herself cum right away.

Hips, tits, so inviting. Plants a kiss on her mouth, hands on her shoulders pull Peggy into her. That perfect body, not a blemish.

That she was on her period made no difference. Sam cherished the bloodstains still on her sheets as a trophy of war.

Had cum twice. Cunt to cunt, like the center of their souls was mixing.

GANG RAPE
Chapter Four

So they had many dates after this torrid first night; but it finally established itself—without words—that there wasn't going to be any more sex. The doctor was too busy to ask why. —And too afraid to know. Took up her vibrator once more; but remembered the great way Peggy gave oral sex, so kept the memory alive.

Then, in July, it happened.

Peggy called Sam. Not unusual. But her request was a first. "I'm very lonely. So blue. Come over…and we can make love."

Sam rushed over in her fancy sports car. Right away she saw Peggy did seem blue. "I've been trying to call you for three days! Why didn't you return my call?"

"I was going to! I was waiting until I had time to

really sit down and talk. I didn't know it was important!"

Blonde gave a resigned look. She looked sexy, but so sad. Wore a filmy Japanese kimono, pants to match, and high heels. Sam tried to take her in a fierce embrace.

"Not here—we can go in my bedroom." For the few times Sam had actually been in Peggy's apartment she'd only been invited into the living room to pick her up and take her somewhere, or drop her off.

As Peggy led the way, Sam ran her hands down over her sides and curves. Felt heat thru the filmy material. "My roommate's away at her new friend's house. *Damn it!* I think she's going to move out, and that leaves me stuck with the rent!"

She whirled around in the doorway. "My fuckin' roommate, she won't tell me the truth, so I don't have time to advertise and get a new one! It's $1,300 for rent alone! And I only earn $1,500—before taxes!"

And the doctor was such a fool—or so absorbed in her career—she didn't do anything with this information.

Sam walked into the bedroom for the first time and was surprised.

It was a sex playground.

Pinups of women on the walls. Hard-looking women in leather. A red night-light shone down, and the curtains were drawn tight, so it might as well have been night.

A pile of lesbian magazines nearby—some open to nude lezzie centerfolds; and unmistakable sex devices—not even hidden.

Peggy lit a candle in a dish, and a piece of incense.

She came to the bed, wasting no time to deliver on that promise she'd made over the phone.

"I know you've been waiting for me. I can tell. I'm sorry."

"Wow! I don't know what to say! This is nice…for a change. I've been…missing your…affection." Sam's hands fidgeted in her lap; she twisted nervously on the edge of the bed. In no time Peggy had stripped out of the kimono top; her large breasts bounced, topped with pink light.

Heat suffused the doctor's whole body. A special sensation in her tits and up inside her cunt. She wanted to cum really bad. Wanted to give her partner the greatest sensation she could.

As she looked around the pink room, Doctor Sam was astounded. Everything a dyke might want. This little woman was ready. Sam scratched her curly head. "This girl's way ahead of me." Took a visual evaluation of objects around the bed. There was fluid gel, and K-Y lubricant, handcuffs hanging on a nail on the wall. Tit clips. A row of dildos out in the open; plasticine purple, pink, & beige wiggly sex organs. A body harness of leather & silver studs. Some photos of light bondage on the wall. Then she was shocked to see packets of condoms.

The blonde anticipated her thoughts moodily. "It's for that"—pointing at the row of toys—"cock. My stupid roommate borrows it all the time. It's the best one of them all. Flexible. Nice size. I don't want to pick up any of her goddamn diseases. Shit!" She threw her kimono down on the floor. With a flounce climbed into the bed, pale feet, red-painted toenails, kicking off her pumps.

Sam unbuttoned her shirt slowly. Peggy nestled up beside her, then lay down, still wearing her silky Japanese pants; naked tits and belly under the pink lights. Peggy continued to chatter: "Oh, this is driving me crazy! I took yesterday off to worry about it. —With pay, they owe me sick leave. I tried to call you! Why didn't you answer?" Sam muttered some excuse in reply. "I'm going to make you happy today, Sam," Peggy added nervously.

'Huh, she's so willing & obedient.' Sam thought, eyeing the pretty woman warily. 'Lying down in the bed half-naked already. And she's been so cold before.... And so hot at first...It doesn't make sense.'

Sam bent over her. "So today you want me."

"Do anything you want," Peggy said, in a soft resigned tone. —But she seemed preoccupied. Sam caressed Peggy, leaning down. Kissed her mouth, touched her blonde hair, streaming, bathed in the scent of perfume & pink.

"Don't you have somewhere else to go?"

Peggy turned and looked at her sharply. "No."

"Thank God!"

'All these months of saying no, it's confusing,' Sam thinks.

Sam knelt down and Peggy lifted up her rump to help her pull the pants off.

Her long pale legs naked, swiftly she turned, leaned over the side of the bed. Peggy picked up her high-heeled pumps and put them back on.

Sam's stomach churned. 'This is kinky.' Licked her lips. 'She's doing this for me!'

Fiercely came to her; lust in her crotch suddenly ready to explode.

The high-heeled shoes turned up the burner of sex higher.

"Do whatever you want to first."

Hot steaming sex session started. Peggy lay, pale pink, soft on the bed, thighs spread, high-heeled shoes on her dainty feet; otherwise completely naked.

Reaches down with red-painted fingertips, pushes back her own wispy blonde pubic hair, opens pink folds of her pussylips. Sam climbs between her spread thighs, wiggles her clit around feeling wet, smooth meat. Then her hips start humping. Peggy holds her. Sam's riding up and down and around. "Can you feel it, baby? Is it in the right place for you, too?" pants Doctor Sam. After getting worked up to a red-hot fire of desire Sam slides down Peggy's legs and puts her head down at her pussy. It's red blush color; big with passion, and so wet, pussy-hairs—blonde wisps around. Sam's sweet lust. —Lips dive into her cunt; sucks and licks; her hands stroke Peggy's thighs meanwhile; and tits. "Tell me when to stop and come back up. We can cum together."

When the blonde called her up, Sam's whole body was hot and wanting & shivers ran down her spine. Mounts her once more, sucks in an intake of air. Peggy heaves a sigh. Her gentle hands pull Sam's ass into her, their cunts meet, & the butch starts screwing.

"So you like it, baby?"

"UH UH UH..." Sam is humping; lust runs in mad passion toward a climax.

"Could you do it with me every night? How would

you like to get it every night?" questions the little voice from under Sam.

Curly head stops bobbing over Peggy; a pensive face looks down. "Of course," Sam pants. "Why? You want to give it to me every night?" Sweat rolls off her; the question hangs in space.

"I don't know." Peggy was worried and confused.

Sam starts back working between her legs again; takes a quick glance up at the woman's feet, held up in air to accommodate the position, one now bare, red-painted toes; the other in its high-heeled pump; thighs open; "OHHHHHH...." A long groan escapes her and lust charges up thru her rutting clit to a near explosion. 'One more minute and I'm done.' Thinks. Hot. Humps. Loves the idea that she is a lesbian using another lesbian's cunt; pussylips open, working in it.

"Let yourself go, baby! Come on, talk dirty to me! *Talk rough!* I like it!" Peggy whispers hoarsely, clutching Sam's ass with her red-polished fingernails. Humps her little cunt around against Sam's cunt.

"OH, CUNT! CUNT! OHHHHHHHHOOOO *CUNT!*" And cum burst out from between her legs.

As her clit rubs into the woman's cunt, as the courses of hot lust run thru her, Sam felt her power come back strong. Felt: 'This is what it's all about...this is what I want in my life, and always have wanted. Anything else is secondary, and just fills in space until I can come back to my joy and pleasure once more.'

The sweaty sheets clung lightly to them. Bodies touch, now side to side. Sam has rolled off because she's too heavy to rest on top of Peggy. Looks at the woman she's fucked before and knows she will fuck her again. Her cumming was fast.

"You didn't come."

"I will."

Little room, pink-lit, very quiet both inside the apartment building and outside. The blonde put on some sexy music & was playing in a new position. Had the doctor up on all fours, her ass stuck out, and parted her buttcheeks with two small hands. Peggy's tongue ran around the rim of Sam's ass with a feathery touch. The hot cheeks closed on Peggy's nose and face pressed into her crack. Smell of her butthole & womanly scent.

"Want me to suck your ass, baby?"

"OK."

"Want me to? Do you like it? Come on!" And Peggy was exuberant, sucking the butch's asshole, probing her tongue into it as her hands kneaded the flesh of her rump.

It gave the doctor a sensual feeling. She enjoyed it. Emotionally it empowered her. 'She must think I'm very special, or she wouldn't be doing this.'

Peggy got the K-Y gel off the nightstand, lubricated her finger, and gently went into Sam's butthole. Her other hand reached underneath, to Sam's furry crotch and stroked her clit. "Ride my hand, honey!" she exclaimed boldly. And moved her finger in and out of her asshole, as Sam humped her hand; hips pounding so hard the flesh on her asscheeks shook, and the bed gyrated.

Pushed her finger in and pulled it out. Then Peggy jammed her face in between Sam's buttcheeks once more and sucked her asshole with renewed fervor, runs her tongue into it.

"No one's ever done that before," Sam said.

"Orgasm's more intense...a number of people have done it to me."

Doctor Sam had helped 500 people die over the last 3 years; yet she felt she'd lived a sheltered life.

Pink lights streamed down. The blonde pushed wisps of hair out of her blue eyes, blinked, stared at Sam. "Come on, baby." Spanked her ass. "I know what you like. You can cum 3 times. I got a good memory, huh! Come on, Daddy, get up! Stand up so I can take it in the mouth!"

Sam was amazed at the transformation of this lovely creature, from mild-mannered secretary and amiable dating companion, to sex worker, overnight.

"You can go another time, Sam! *You can!* Don't just stare at me!" And she was down on her knees by the headboard of the bed, naked, breasts with hard pink nipples, full hips, butt resting on the heels of her bare feet. "Don't keep me waiting!"

Sam got off the bed and stood over her. Peggy indicated where she should stand, and Sam saw that the blonde even had a place for her to hold onto the headboard of the bed, to keep from losing her balance while Peggy sucked her off.

"Come on! I like to satisfy my man. Can I call you that? It's OK?" Peggy winked. Had a pixie look about her, as she got up momentarily, rising like Venus from an alabaster oyster shell. "I'll put some hot music on, honey. —It'll make you cum good.

Music of a woman singer; deep, emotional tones that rose up the scales in passion, then descended into a blazing, panting need. Drum's rapid-fire staccato kept up the insistent rhythm of life—and sex.

You could make your body move to it and cum with it.

Sam admired the well-prepared love room.

Jungle music played. A head was at her cunt, tongue licking, searching into her pussyfolds, mouth sucking her pear-shaped clit, pulling out lust currents to ebb and flow and come back stronger; each new wave harder then the last.

It had to cum!

BANG BANG BABY! OH, SO GOOD!

The doctor looks down at this woman on her knees, whose face is between her thighs. Peggy looks up now. Blue eyes meet her own. Lips, cheeks, wet; with Sam's cunt discharge, cum, & her own spit. Swallows it because she wants Sam, and wants her so much she doesn't think it's dirty. Doesn't go spit up in the towel like other women have. Sam gazes down at her, into her eyes that look back. 'She's a lesbian who wants a woman bad. She's proven that.'

"You suck it good." Sam spoke aloud.

Peggy smiles. Rubs her hands up Sam's thighs as she kneels before her. 'Not like some women, who just lick with the tip of their tongue, no, she gets into it deep.'

"So, could you, baby?" Peggy sits back on her heels, on the floor, waiting. "Could you do this every night of the year for 365 days a year for the rest of your life?"

Sam didn't answer.

When Sam began to make love to Peggy in her gentle vanilla way, careful, considerate, she didn't see that the body under her was wrestling—in simulated struggle. Was seething, with intense emotions that cried to be let out.

Hand squeezed a tit, one finger in her wet vagina. Two, then three fingers. "Tell me what a good pussy I have." Peggy breathed hoarsely, into her ear.

Sam was embarrassed to say the word, but was learning. Stroked down into Peggy. "You pussy is good, honey. It's sweet." Sucked on her tit, pushed fingers in and out of her; feeling her cunt clamp inside. Her mouth came up from the hard nipples of a tit. "Your pussy's so hot and good. I can't live without fucking your pussy! I need your pussy! I WANT IT! I WANT IT!" Running her fingers in and out, pinching her nipples with the other hand.

Peggy felt heat rise up thru the thermoteter of her body. Then she told Sam to stop.

"You've seen my collection of toys." Sam gazed at the cocks with harnesses, the tit clips and other sex paraphernalia. "I didn't want to ask, but you never used your vibrator on me! I was happy to see it." Blue eyes wide, lips petulant. "I hate to ask for things. It's so much better when somebody just does it...I have a favorite cock." She selected a purple toy made of a rubbery substance, picked it up. "The bitch just takes it and fucks with it, and puts it back on the shelf without telling me until it's too late, and then I get an infection. Don't worry, it's cured. I been to the doctor."

And Sam listens, as she's been trained to listen—to a unceasing parade of patients & their problems; notes: 'She's used this thing and I wasn't doing it. So either she can masturbate with it, or she's got somebody else screwing her.'

"Do you use yours a lot, on your sweet honeys?"

"I don't have any sweet honeys. Just you, and I'm not sure about you."

Peggy's blue eyes filled with mirth. "Don't be so mean!"

Sam sighed.

"Do you put that vibrator inside you?" Peggy asked wickedly, with girlish curiosity.

"Very seldom," Doctor Sam confessed.

"Don't your ladies ask for it?"

"One did; that's why I got it." Pink lights bathed them, turning the room into a pink sea. Curtained windows, walls, held them in a womb. Sam thought: 'Of course I am masculine, yes, I can be defined as butch. But I'm light-years behind these young girls in experience. These young women are getting fast. They fist-fuck. They use all kinds of equipment. I've been out of touch. My head in books 8 years thru medical school; and my practice is just 3 years old. I've lost 10 years of my life...while they've been running around bars and sex clubs and play parties like fast hot pussycats doing nasty things with other women. I'm so jealous, it makes me sick to think of it. I just get on a woman and screw her with my clit, a good long hot screw, and service her orally and fuck her long and hard with fingers. They mastered the art. They use handcuffs and tit clips and buttplugs—all this paraphernalia. And that collection of dildos which strap on around the waist.... We always used cucumbers.... I thought that was enough. How I regret wasting 10 years of my sex life to those damn textbooks! I want to get on her and cum and cum and fuck my brains out, fuck her with this cock, and let her fuck me, too, if she wants it. I want her oral service from now to eternity & I want to throw her down and ride her from here to the moon.'

Sam took the harness, mumbling under her breath. Fumbled with it; black and silver studs contrast against her tan thighs.

"It's my favorite! I think she must have used it in the ass! The dizzy dyke!" Peggy's hands tugged and pulled, helping Sam into the harness. "I can't afford to get another infection; it cost me $125 just to see the gynecologist." The cock stuck out purple, 9 inches long from the doctor's pubic nest. —She kneels, knees dug into the mattress in front of the blonde femme, who expertly rolls a translucent condom over the cockhead and down its shaft. As the doctor waited, she felt desire bursting inside her sex. "I never know when she comes in here and borrows my stuff, and now she's moving out without telling me!"

The blonde lay on her back, spread her thighs, raised knees—heels up by her ass. Sam climbed in between, held her purple cock in one hand, and slowly manipulated its firm round cockhead thru Peggy's soggy pubic hair up to touch the wet, hot meat of her clit. Stroked it up & down over and over her clit a while, then, fist around the thick dick, dropped it lower, searching Peggy's hole, and entered her slowly.

"Talk to me, Sam!"

The doctor didn't know what to say. "Oh, baby, I do desire you! You're so sweet...Uhmm...." she managed, but was horny. Hot as hell. Began to hump, fast, pumping the cock with swift lightning-fast strokes into the woman; and Peggy moans. Hands tight on Sam's back. "This is for you, honey. Let me make you feel good. Sweet baby!" The doctor pants, then another flurry of thrusts.

"Darling!"

"That's enough talk, honey," the blonde said breathlessly, wiggling under her; temperature of her body rose to a hot passion as she received the torrent of hot strokes into her pussy.

Sam drove it into her fast for a long while. Until Peggy tells her it's enough.

Exhausted, Sam comes out, and they both unbuckle the harness; the cock bounces down on the bed, stiff.

Sam looks at her.

"Now just use your hand."

"I can still go with the cock."

"You look tired!"

Sam picks it up and goes back between her legs. There are techniques you can do with a dildo in your hand that you can't do when it's strapped on. Sam twirled the thick rubber cock around, made it go in & out with big circular twirls. Lay down on the bed midway down Peggy's body and used a finger on her clit while driving the cock in with her other hand.

The condom's thin latex sheath was halfway worked down the cockshaft when Peggy decided she was finished. Sam kissed and held Peggy, and went back to just fingers again, lowering her face to the femme's cunt to suck it simultaneously.

As the doctor serviced her, Peggy puzzled, eyebrows

arched quizzically, staring at the ceiling, as if trying to come to a decision on her back.

Fingers with blunt tips, no nails; three sturdy fingers of the right hand went in and out of her hot, wet hole, fast, in quick lightning-swift strokes. Tongue made hard contact on her clit. And Peggy was in orgasm, lifting her hips, clenching around Sam's fingers. "AAHHHHHHH-HHHHHHAA OOHHHHHHHHH! OOHHHHH!"

Cunt tight; so Sam could barely move her fingers, but kept on, and made her tongue hard on the woman's clit, slipping over it back and forth in spit and juice.

"OHHHHHHHHHHHHHHHHHHHAAAA! HHHHHAAAAAA!" Peggy came a second time; head thrown back grinding into the mattress, back arched up, feet slapping down. Solid heat; her whole body hot, sweating drops of salty water. Sam made her cum so good.

Sheets with stains of their lovemaking. Candle burnt down to a pool of wax in a dish. Echoes of sobs of passion marking their golden moments spent. The sighs, the climaxes, their arms, their thighs, the sweat, the aroma, the love.

So sweet.

"A lot of women aren't so loose. Believe me, many won't use my dicks at all." Peggy ran her finger down Sam's lapel. They had got dressed to go across town to the mansion to feed the dogs and go swimming in the heated blue pool.

"Sam, you have a more mellow attitude about life."

"Life is how you find it."

"Some women look at my handcuffs and get frightened."

Sam cast a look at the metal cuffs. "They don't bother me."

"You don't have to be frightened with me, Sam. I won't ever ask you to do anything you can't do."

"I want to please you, Peggy. Whatever it takes." Placed a square hand on her cheek. "Life is short, I know that. Just tell me what you need."

"I think I want to be with you, Sam."

"What do you think I've been dreaming about all these nights? I want to be with you, too!"

The couple wakes up the next morning. Naked, Sam hooks her bare foot over Peggy's ankle. Listens to her breathe beside her. Wants to do it once more with feeling & meaning. On top, clit in her slippery pussy, lusting in it. Motion of their bodies. —But there isn't time.

The woman's body is warm and sweaty from sleep.

'Wonder what it is she wants me to do for her. Maybe she wants money.

'She excites me. Then turns cold. At this point, even being hustled for my money is OK. This woman is so erotic, the feeling she gives me is worth the price.'

Later, when Peggy awoke, Sam was at the dresser, grey pants suit on, white hospital coat over, name tag in place: DR. SANDRA ANDERSON M.D. Came to kiss her, bent over the bed, and then in the sudden light of day noticed that scar again. "I've been meaning to ask you...that scar on your lip, what's it from?" With the curiosity of a doctor whose been trained to notice physical details.

"Well"—the blonde began sitting up in the sheets,

pushed hair out of her eyes—"you might not want to hear this, but I was raped." She paused and turned her head. "There's another scar here." And there was, down the side of her forehead under the hairline.

"I'm sorry." Sam looked very concerned, her eyes, steady, usually tranquil, now flashing a spark of anger which melted into feeling as she said, "Tell me about it when you're ready to. It's good to share things like that, with other people who can be sensitive. Don't keep it bottled up!"

Doctor turned, went to the closet, got her medical bag, attaché case, and a stack of manila folders. 'Scum who attack women ought to be murdered,' the doctor thought. 'They shouldn't be walking the streets ever again…She's been farther down on her luck; I thought so.'

GANG RAPE
Chapter Five

Sam really felt ugly and angry. Like she wanted to punch somebody in the jaw.

Her patient had just died.

She'd seen one too many.

Lived in the Mansion on the Hill, owned two expensive foreign cars and a year-round heated swimming pool, had a medical degree from Johns Hopkins, one of the finest medical schools, and had power in the world. 'Yet I can't stop them from dying. I can't hold back the tide of death.'

Went to the wet bar across the vast living room; pulled open the sliding wicker doors. A full liquor cabinet, seldom used but for entertaining. Reached into its solid oak interior and pulled down a bottle of sherry.

'I need fun. Fun for *myself*.'

Peggy was acting funny again—it was an added wear and tear on her nerves. 'I need her now. I really do. Let's put her to the test. —And all those pretty promises she's been making the last few weeks. Let's see what she'll really do for me when I need her.

The doctor reached for the phone, punched out Peggy's number by memory. The line was busy.

It was happening all over again. Three weeks had passed; Peggy was distant to her one minute, then cuddly and sweet. Then declining a few invitations to expensive restaurants & a lavish party thrown by one of the doctor's associates, as if she didn't care.

So Sam had begun buying her presents.

Now every time the two went out, there would be a small luxury item for her afterward. A necklace with a diamond. A jade bracelet. A leather coat.

For the pleasure of sitting side by side on the sofa, petting & kissing a while.

And then having to drive her home.

And, in solitary, took care of herself. Slim body lay under the sheets—fresh, changed by the maid;—and masturbate to a show of nude airbrushed photos of glamorous females, & cum.

Shadows zoomed 40 feet up into the cathedral ceiling. Doctor Sam dialed the phone once more. Stretched out her legs in comfortable slacks, wiggled her toes in blue argyle sox. Pensive face framed by curly hair. The number was busy again.

So, head buzzing with effects of the sherry, she made a rash decision—to go over to Peggy's in person. Sam was seldom this bold.

Cap set on her head at a jaunty angle, tweed jacket, and grey slacks matching threads of the jacket; a lavender shirt open at the collar, and gold chains dripping down her tanned chest. Firm tits, sleek hips; a perfect portrait of a professional lesbian.

Drove thru the main thoroughfare, & saw streetwalkers there. 'Wish I was a man for just an hour. I'd go talk to one of them, have sex, get it over with.' Hot dampness between her tweed-covered thighs. Squirmed in frustration as she drove.

Life wasn't that simple.

"YOUR LOVE! YOUR LOVE!"

Shouted over radio airwaves. The beat grinds on.

Pushed her shoe down on the accelerator, hard.

Unannounced, Sam came up to Peggy's door.

When Peggy opened the door, her face looked pissed, tho she didn't say so.

"Come in, Sam."

The doctor fumbled for words. "I'm really sorry... this is very inappropriate of me. I must have lost my head—I had a glass of sherry." Sam looked confused; then she stopped in her tracks.

There was a man in the living room. Short, dark, square body. Thick black hair. Shirtsleeves rolled up, feet on the coffee table. Obviously very much at home.

Sam stared a moment as the man glared at her with a fixed look of hate. She dropped her gaze. Not knowing how she got across the room, Sam found herself sitting down in an armchair very uncomfortably. 'So *that's* who the condoms are for! This guy, he's a rough customer.' All her fears boiled to the surface; hoping he was a friend of the roommate, knowing by the words transpiring between the two, that he wasn't.

The man looked at Sam, directly in the eyes; a look that went clear down into her soul. —Danger. She sensed it. Ten feet separated them across the living room. Fear clenched her stomach thru the haze of the sherry. Suddenly Sam felt like a trapped animal.

Then Peggy had taken his hand and guided him into the bedroom, & the door shut.

'Ominous,' Sam thought worriedly. She didn't like him. Hated the fact that he was there.

Heard muted voices thru the door. "You bitch!" came thru recognizably. The door opens, hard; slams back against the wall, and the man heads to the front door, jerks it open & walks out, slamming it so hard the walls shake.

They were alone.

Peggy came and sat down next to Sam; her weight light as a gentle dove indenting the sofa.

Sam just shook her head, then looked into Peggy's blue eyes. "Who is that guy?" Angry, disappointed, and afraid to know, but having to find out the truth.

"He's not a guy." Peggy smiled with odd resignation. "Mack's a female. —Don't let him hear me call him that."

"Mack's a female?—A transsexual?"

"Mack has the same equipment we have."

The doctor heaved a sigh. Now, just surprised because he was such a tough-acting person; angry because she was jealous.

"So, you're seeing this Mack?"

Hesitant, Peggy replied, "Sometimes."

"I asked you if you were seeing anybody, and you told me you weren't!"

Peggy made a grim face. Blue eyes strained, large. She looked old.

"This really isn't fair, Peggy! Somebody else has been taking care of you—your needs." Hurt filled Sam, and it showed. "And nobody's been taking care of mine!"

Peggy dropped her eyes. "I'm sorry, Sam. You don't understand how it is between us. If Mack made...that much difference to me, I *would* have mentioned it. She—Mack—is not somebody I love. Is not somebody I want to live with...the rest of my life, or any part of my life."

"But you sleep with her! *Him!* And I'm spending time with you, thinking you care for me and go home having to take care of my own needs...while you're laying up with somebody else!"

"I'm sorry. Yes, Mack is taking care of my needs...but he means nothing. In fact the way he treats me, I actually can't stand him...to be honest."

The dam had gone up. Tears almost ran out of her eyes, welled, checked. Lanky legs folded at the knee; lavender shirt sweaty with adrenaline rush; Sam shook her curly head from side to side; would allow no tears to flow. Thought of the nights after their dates, after the flowers & dinners & the expensive $300 and $400 presents, having to crawl home defeated and press a vibrator against her sex; so horny. Hold the end in her fist and pound it inside of herself; feeling mad and powerless for having to use that instead of a woman's love to fill her. "GODDAMN YOU, PEGGY!"

And the blonde came to her, wrapped her arms around Sam. "Listen to me! It's you all the way! I mean it! I...I love you. I respect you. And you're a good person—Mack isn't." Peggy pulls Sam's face around to gaze into her eyes: "It's just...some things we have to get clear! —You and I!"

The living room whirled in a buzz of confusion. Absentmindedly, Sam noticed the phone lay on the coffee table, purposely disconnected.

Sam felt horrible. "I thought we were mature adults. I thought we had an understanding. You've been cheating me."

Blue eyes sparkled. Next to her, Peggy was animated as she explained. "I lost my roommate! Remember? I tried to break the news to you gently, Sam, but you're so thickheaded! I told you she was going to move out! I can't pay $1,300 a month all alone! You've given me some very lovely, and very cherished presents, and they mean so much. The jewelry and the coat.... It's expensive stuff. But I can't live on it! Mack is paying part of my rent!" Peggy wrung her hands.

"So she's living here! She's moved in, to take your roommate's place."

"No! She's *not* living here."

Sam just stared, frozen, hard.

"So she's giving you money."

"Yes."

"In other words, she's paying you."

Peggy looked back, eyes flashed. Said nothing.

They stared at each other a moment, then averted their eyes.

The silence was heavy.

Finally the blonde spoke, in a coarse tone, heavy, which Sam hadn't heard from her before. "Look Sam, I'll spell it out for you. Mack gives me $600 a month. If you can make it $700, I'll put her out of my life. —Or let me move in with you."

"Oh, God." Sam heaved a sigh.

Peggy gently put her arms tight around Sam, pulled her closer; then hugged her hard. "Don't hate me."

Time ticked by.

Heartbeats. Sam's lavender shirt rose and fell. The world was a hard place. It was a hard decision to make.

"So I'm your preference?" she said at last.

"Definitely. Sam! I'm trying to survive! She gives me $75 or $100 a week, regularly. Just hands it to me—no fancy presents, no dinner dates, just *cash*. I can't pay for this goddamn place & a car & still eat, too! Now my roommate moved out, Mack's making it $150 a week! If you can do that, then I won't have to be with her!" Blue eyes flashed. "I really don't want to!"

"She calls you a bitch? You let her do that? I heard you in there!"

"That's the type of person Mack is."

"What does she do for a living?"

"She has a landscaping business. I met her in a bar. She likes people to call her a him. He lifts sacks. One hundred-pound sacks all day, full of earth and sand, and drags potted trees around, loading up the truck, and takes male hormones. It makes him strong.

"He's nothing. —Owns a house, but it's in a run-down section, & he's poor...because he spends all his money on women—too many women!" Peggy ran her hands up and down Sam's arms and thighs and pulled her close, into her bosom. "Sam, I'd love to come live with you! Mack wants to move in with me, rent out his house, and he'll have more money. But he's such a sleazeball. I hate him getting that close to me!"

Sam pushed Peggy's hands away from her body and held them a moment. Faced the woman. Wanting her, wanting to fall into her and rest & be at peace, yet having to hold herself back. "I would hardly be home because of my job. I've never asked a woman to put up with that before."

"I work during the day, Sam, and I could find plenty to do, till we finally had time together.... Honey, I would be there waiting, every time you needed me. I could cook, iron your white coats, lay your clothes out for you in the morning, *everything!*"

BEEP! BEEP! BEEP!

Doctor Sam stood up, ran her hand thru her curly hair. "I've got to get back to the hospice."

"One of your people?"

"Probably."

Sam walked to the door. Turned; and said, "Think about moving in with me, then."

The blonde came across the room after her to hug good-bye. —Sam shook her head. Didn't want to be touched. Turmoil in her brain. Reached for her wallet; inside it was thick with green currency. Peeled five hundred-dollar bills off the thick wad. "Here." Pushed it at her. "Don't say anything. Please. I've got to think. I need space." Headed out. Peggy held the money, blue eyes wide, worried, and sad; for the money was a great relief—and a great weight in her hands.

After Sam left, after Peggy put the money away, she heard a key in the lock and knew it was Mack.

Went to the living room; there he stood, wearing a sullen expression.

Mack wore men's suits; was 5'8" tall; had a naturally stocky build, made muscular from lifting heavy objects.

First night Peggy had picked Mack up at a gay bar, taken him home, they'd kissed and touched just a few minutes. "I can't stand this soft stuff," Mack had growled. Mack had dropped his trousers & boxer shorts and got his cunt off twice in her mouth, and liked hard contact. Then put his finger rough, inside of Peggy, then another. And then reaches into the recess of his jacket pocket and pulls out a dildo & harness. "I'll go easy on you, I know you ain't done it before. And Peggy had looked up at him a moment; saw the cold hard expression in Mack's face as he mounted her; put the cock in her pussy; and thought: 'I'm glad it isn't a man doing this to me, but with her, it's the same thing.'

Mack proved to be great in the sheets. Gave oral sex, and did it good. Could suck & fuck for hours. Took Peggy on top in the missionary position; rubbed his furry cunt in Peggy's till they climaxed together.

Got her on all fours and fucked her like a dog; entering her from behind, under her full round ass-moons, sticking fingers into her pink pussy surrounded by wet fur; the other arm wrapped around her waist, to rub her clit from the front; or jamming a plastic dick in and out till Peggy was hollering and rearing her butt up in passion.

Mack scowled at her. "Come here, baby!" Grabs Peggy and pulls the blonde up against him. "You do like them lined up waiting their turn to fuck you, don't you, babe!"

"Don't be disgusting!"

"BAM! BAM! Thank you ma'am!" Mack thrust his trousered hips up and down in air in a lewd gesture. "Well, I'm next, babe!"

"You're so sleazy and simpleminded!"

Mack grabs her roughly. "I'm gonna take my turn screwing you now that doctor bitch is gone!"

Peggy wrestled her arms free, threw Mack's hands off, and stood, mad, gazing at him.

Mack's pockmarked face twists in glee. "I could break that bitch's back in my two hands. Let me get ahold of her! I'll break her in half! I can tear her apart like this!" And makes a breaking motion between his big hands that are creased with dirt.

"Calm down!" Peggy grabs Mack under the arm of his suit coat, guides him into her bedroom, and they sit down, bouncing on her bed.

"Mack! She can do a lot more for me!—Stuff you don't choose to do! You know the arrangement we have! You use me for sex, basically! You don't want a relationship, or a marriage. You have all your whores and girlfriends! You don't need me!"

"Don't know no whores."

"Well, they might as well be! They sleep with everybody and everything! And Mack! You been using my cock on your other broads, you bastard! It must have been you! Or my sorry roommate! One of you! I bought it! It's *mine!*" Mack glowers at her. Peggy rants on, pissed. "You don't need me! Your wandering eye finds anything that wears a skirt, & you chase it. I could never have you to myself, and I want somebody for myself! For me alone!"

Tough, in trousers, man's hat; stance; yet even Mack could melt. He gets down on his knees on the floor, puts his black-haired head in Peggy's lap. "Let me make it all up to you. I know I chase women, but it's this need I have.... None of them mean anything! Let me give you my love. Let me love you. His powerful testosterone-strengthened arms reach up, his hands hold Peggy's hands. He rises up and whispers into her ear. "Let me love you." Lips press to her mouth, then move away, to plant a line of kisses down her neck. "Let me love you hard. Tonight. The way you like it." Then plunges his tongue down between Peggy's lips.

Peggy pushes him away. "Don't try that! You always try to make me weak, to get what you want! Then I'm stuck having to deal with you & those stupid broads you fuck calling my house, looking for you!"

"I'd be in trouble if you left me now!" Mack stands before her, balling up both fists in passion. Trousers, suit coat, face mean; then, again, he gets down on one knee. "I wouldn't know where to look for love. You're the only one I'm serious about. All my other women have somebody else they live with."

Peggy watched the dark, almost handsome, man-woman go thru his act. She sat on the bed. Her blonde hair is messed up, makeup worn off into pale shades.

The room silent. Buzzing of a fly trapped outside against the windowpane.

Then the dark-haired head is in her lap once more. A weary question comes out of Peggy's mouth: "What are you doing for the Fourth of July? Anything planned?"

"Nothing. I'll go up to the Gay Community Center."

Peggy feels the loneliness from Mack, emanating thru his rough man's suit coat, thru his laundry-starched shirt. Almost felt sorry for him, but she knows what a rough customer Mack is.

Thinks of all the lonely dykes out in the glittering street of gay dreams. These men-women like Mack, who have no place.

Mack in suit, vest, tie, & hat, with a pistol in his truck, who would hang around on the outskirts of the festivities, gruff; and try to find a willing girl to pull into his bed; giving up if he couldn't—and going off and getting raging drunk.

And Peggy had grown to enjoy Mack's kinkiness. Wearing his dick in harness sticking out from the slit in his boxer shorts, chasing her thru the apartment, to pin her down, anywhere—on the bed, the floor, the sofa; on the dining room table, in the bathroom on the toilet, against a wall—and fucking her fast.

It was just his/her low personality Peggy can't stand. His treacherous ways.

And Mack is speaking: "Am I moving in with you? Think about it, Peg. I can rent out my house; we'll have money." Opens his grimy hands.

"No.... I might be giving up this apartment."

GANG RAPE
Chapter Six

The doctor stood on the deck a moment, wind slips its fingers thru her curly hair. Thru a pair of binoculars surveys 3 bridges & major arteries of the freeway down, down, in the inner city.

Went back thru the sliding glass door, crossed the vast living room on stocking feet; goes to the liquor cabinet in the wet bar and pours a glass of cream sherry from the vineyards of Spain.

Sinks back in her luxurious sofa in front of a dead fireplace. Black logs charred & twisted. Fire was for romance. For nights and this was day. Sun runs thru the cathedral windows.

Her legs fell open, one hand drops between her thighs. Touches herself thru the fine fabric of her trousers.

Dull sensation.

Fire climbs up the interlacing of her nerves; fire idles in her sex, churning, building; desire spreads thru the cavity of her pelvis, and out, inflamed her breasts & throat. Burning with sensuality. Horny.

It's been a week and a half with no sex. Career busy. Time flies.

Sam envisions Peggy's sweet mouth swallowing the juices of her cunt in oral sex. Loving the blonde's sticky sweet pussy with her tongue & fingers. She can't stand it, so she removes her hand that's clenched to her damp crotch, reaches for the phone, and dials the number.

"I need to talk to you. In person." Peggy's voice responds, coming thru the other end of the phone line; shy and distant.

"Is Mack there?"

"No."

Peggy greeted Sam at the door. She was dressed in a sky-blue business suit, secretary style, which she wore to work. Very formal.

She had decided not to move in with the doctor after all, & would keep the relationship with her hardened man/lesbian.

"There's a lot of things you don't know about me. —Mack gives me things you don't."

Sam felt her heart fall.

Peggy saw the expression on the doctor's face, and felt bad, in empathy. "Oh...I'm not sure!" She wrung her hands a moment. "I can't make up my mind!"

"What does she give you that I don't?"

"Well, he's been good to help with the rent; all the

time before I met you. But it's not just money…it's the sex. And otherwise it's a bore.".

Peggy's mind whirled. Her sudden loss of a roommate had escalated everything. She was in a state of confusion.

"Is she trying to hold it against you—that she's helped you out? I can give her her goddamn money back—*all* of it—and tell her to leave you alone!"

"He's gotten it back already. Every time he goes to bed with me." Sam winced and turned away. Peggy was mad, talking without thinking. "But I'm not letting him live with me, either. Just for too many reasons! He has too many problems for me to seriously consider him as a mate. He'd be in my life, in my house, hanging me up & I'd never find anybody to have a relationship with."

Suddenly, out of the corner of her eye, Sam sees the door opening silently. Peggy doesn't hear it.

The door bangs open and Mack barrels inside, in a rage.

Sam sat, jaw opened; felt an instant panic, and had no time to get up and run.

Mack ran over fast. Peggy rises in horror. "NO, MACK!" The man-woman goes right up to Sam, his arm shoots out, fist striking down BAM! into the doctor's face, deflected by her arm. Sam rises up, blocking her face. BAM! BAM! Two slugs knock her back down. *"STOP, MACK! PLEASE!"* Peggy tugs on Mack's sleeve, throws her body against him. Sam lies on the sofa bleeding, holding her stomach with one hand, clutching her face with the other and writhing in pain. Blood spurts from her nose, and her aching guts are trying to heave.

Mack & Peggy struggle, Peggy throws her whole weight into it, just trying to keep him away from Sam. "KEEP THE FUCK AWAY FROM MY HOUSE AND MY OLD LADY!"

"THIS HAS REALLY DONE IT!" Peggy's blue eyes flash; her suit is torn at the seams from struggling. "MACK! YOU AND I ARE THROUGH, MISTER! *I HATE YOU!*"

Mack lowers his eyes, his passion spent. Knuckles bloody & beginning to swell. A rough customer, all the fight gone out of him in the series of punches that leave Sam twisting on the sofa, feeling like she's gonna die.

Peggy pushes Mack out the door, locks it with the sliding bolt & chain. "I'LL CALL THE POLICE IF YOU FUCKIN' COME BACK! I'M CHANGING THE LOCKS, YOU CREEP! YOU BASTARD!"

"YOU KNOW YOU NEED ME, BABY!" Mack hollers, sounding faint from the other side. "YOU KNOW YOU LIKE ME MORE! I'M BETTER IN BED! YOU SAID SO! IT'S JUST THIS WIMPY BITCH HAS GOT MORE MONEY THAN ME!" His begrudging voice pleaded thru the crack in the door. "GIVE ME ANOTHER CHANCE! DON'T LET THAT BITCH AND HER FUCKING DOCTOR BULLSHIT STAND IN OUR WAY!"

"SAM'S MORE MAN THAN YOU AND MORE WOMAN THAN YOU! —YOU JUST PROVED THAT BY BREAKING IN MY HOUSE LIKE A FUCKING ASSHOLE! HER MONEY DON'T MEAN ANYTHING! I WOULD HAVE STAYED WITH YOU FOR THE SEX, BUT NOW I'M

GOING WITH HER BECAUSE SHE LOVES ME! NOW GET AWAY FROM MY DOOR, OR I'M CALLING THE POLICE!"

And she kicks the door with a dainty foot. BLAM!

Peggy wrings her hands. Rushes over to Sam.

"She's gonna come back!" Sam moans.

"No, he won't. He's afraid of the police."

Sam was shaking as Peggy knelt beside her. "I'm leaving this apartment; I've made up my mind." Blonde wisps of hair sticking out all over her face; she looked very very old.

Peggy led the doctor back into the bathroom, and mopped the blood off her face with a hot towel. Kissed her. Then Sam lost control, heaved her guts up, yellow & red in the toilet. It hurt.

Took her to the bedroom, knelt down and pulled off her boots.

It was so good to be ministered to. 'It's almost worth getting beaten up,' Sam thought. Peggy had put a cold towel on the side of Sam's face and was caressing her, pressed down on her with soft full breasts.

It was 5 P.M. The money talked & the bullshit had walked.

Shadows ran over the apartment; end of a long summer evening.

"What did she mean, she's better in bed?" Sam asked, nursing her jaw. Peggy lay beside her, massaging & loving her.

Sam turned to gaze at the blonde woman. "Whatever it is she does better than me, I'll do it!—Teach me!"

Time ticked on the small clock on the bureau.

Night was silent, dark.

"You do it good...." Faint voice began. Saw the smile begin on Sam's face. "I see why women like you.... It's just...." Peggy pictured it. Sex with the doctor was satisfying in a vanilla way. Lying side by side, Sam, purple dildo in her hand stroking down into her. Her tender hands caressing. Mouth sucking a nipple, bringing her to orgasm. But sometimes Peggy craved more action.

"Sometimes it's too light. Like I'm waiting for you to start...and it's over. It's too soft. You never do it hard enough.... When you make love to me, it's OK...."

"Then that's why you had decided to stay with *him?*"

"Yes! Because he talks to me the way I want to be talked to. And he handles me the way I want to be handled!"

"You chose me, tho. So what are we going to do about it?"

"Well, I'm just going to have to train you!"

"Train me?"

"Yes! To do what I like and how I like it!"

Reaches over to the nightstand & opens the drawer; pulls out two objects, straps of black leather with buckles on the ends and white fuzzy undersides—which Sam vaguely recognized as restraints.

Then she got the dildo & harness; black leather with silver studs.

"She uses these on me. You did it with my dildo before."

Sam looked at the objects.

"Not all the time, just sometimes when I need it. —A lot of butches think it's fun. —It's just like your vibrator, really; it'll be easy."

"Mack is better in bed than me. I see why."

"Out of the bed you're better to me than anybody has ever been. And I love you.... Taking me out to dinner & buying me all those expensive gifts & putting up with me not sleeping with you!" Peggy was breathless, getting undressed; now helps Sam out of her clothes, too, both emerging pink & nude.

"You're more than I bargained for, Peg. That character Mack looks like he's had a terrible life. He's not too secure. He's definitely a thug. Yet you chose him over me. Well, at least it proves you're not after my money."

Peggy sat on the covers on her haunches, naked and white. "Mack started paying me from the beginning. He's smart. That's how he keeps so many women on the string. —Otherwise they wouldn't waste their time on him. Sam, I can't live in a bad neighborhood anymore. I'd rather turn on the gas, or take an overdose of pills & kill myself. I've been around too many rough people. Also, I like how she makes me feel.... She—I mean, he's —not a person you love. He's really a lowlife. A dog. Some of his women pay him. They fall for his bullshit; he gets them weak for him so he can use it to his advantage. One woman worked two jobs to support Mack, until she found out there were several other women ahead of her." Peggy ran her hands down Sam's skin. "We play games. He tells me things."

And Peggy explained it.

Mack not only provided stud service in bed, but reenacted the rape scene with full intensity and enjoyed doing so.

"It makes him feel more masculine."

Sam was lying back in the bed; lifted her lean hips; Peggy slid the straps of the harness around her ass, buckled them; the cock stuck out 9".

"Sam! I was just so confused. I didn't call because I was trying to choose between you two. I didn't know you as well as Mack, I didn't know if I could depend on you. Then my roommate moved out and pushed me to a decision."

Night. Peg switched on the pink light, they lay naked, side by side, the purple cock stiff, sticking straight out of Sam's pubic nest. "Now you know I'm not such a lady you can't act dirty with me." Peggy winked.

"Yes. We broke the ice."

The blonde showed Sam the way she liked to be restrained. A metal ring on each strap was fastened to a corresponding eye ring bolted into the bed frame with metal clips. The straps would be sealed around Peggy's wrists; one spread out to the left, the other to the right.

"I'm gonna struggle, but don't stop. Force it in."

Peggy got on top of Sam, buried her head in the crook of her neck; blonde hair mixing with brown. Naked. Straddled her; warm cunt sat on the cock, wiggled her ass.

"Baby, pretend you're a man raping me."

"Does it have to be a man doing it? Can't I just be me raping you?"

"No."

"I'll do it." Sam looked at the woman inches away from her, kissed her on the forehead.

"And I'll tell you what to say, OK?"

"Yes. Tell me. I've got a good memory."

Gang Rape | 219

"Sam, can you pretend you're two men raping me? In succession?"

The doctor sighed. And Peggy, pressed to her chest, rose and fell with their breathing. Sam's mouth opened, then closed in a tight line. "Yes, until you have enough."

"How about 5 men, taking turns?"

Sam's mouth quivered in a grim line. Looked at the blonde. Thought: 'Why? Did this really happen to you? Why must you play this scene? But she only said out loud, "OK. Tell me what to say."

And Peggy rolled off, was lubricating the cock with gel, working its purple shaft with her hands so it banged against the doctor's clit, creating hot thuds of dull arousal. Then Peggy lies down, pulling Sam on top of her, stretching one arm to the right for her wrist to be restrained to the bed frame, then the left. "You can do it? You're butch enough?"

Back in her mind's eye, saw the scene, 11 years ago; would never forget.

"Tie my wrists down tighter! Sometimes you can just pin me down. We can use ankle restraints. Any way will work. Just so I can't escape. That's all—it's simple. Say what I tell you. Don't stop."

Securely tied down, Peggy attempted to rise. Tension rippled across the spread of her arms & chest as she reached the end of motion that the metal rings would allow. Then fell back. Put her knees up, spread wide, heels back by her butt. Sam was over her, held the dick in her fist and ran its tip up and down Peggy's clit, then put it in her.

Then Peggy's wrestling, and Sam pushes her back;

shoves her hips and with all her body weight behind it, drives the cock all the way in.

"Keep humping. Pull it almost all the way out and drive it in. Don't stop. Don't give out on me, baby!" Peggy gasps. "Fuckin' lesbian bitch, Slut. Just say that, remember! —I've got a tight pussy, remember! —Can you say it?"

Shadows like flames seemed to lick high, turning the room red. Ceiling closing in. Time loomed. Peggy felt lost in the invisibility of dark, stifling as if in a closet's confines. —Like hell brimming over.

Sam was putting the cock in her. Red-hot bolt jamming like a piston into her juicy pussy, hard. Held her shoulders down, slamming her struggling thighs back down into the sheets with each of her lustful thrusts, overpowering her; this woman tossing and turning underneath. Rubbed by the friction, Sam's clit was hot, and coursing rapidly towards a climax as if on wings.

Then guilt overcame her.

"Wait a minute!" Sam pants, stopping her motion, and lay over her propped up on her hands, dripping sweat. Peggy relaxed, head dropped back on the sheets.

"Are you OK?"

Sam looked down at her, the harnessed cock still stiff inside her cunt. Peggy sighed, turned her face away. "I started doing this with Mack about a year ago, when we met. She brought it all out of me. She wanted to pretend she was raping me—and that's when I saw what a terrific turn-on it was.

"It all came back. I'd tried to forget it. Had blocked it out of my mind for 11 years, what happened. I met her, we went home, she did it. Then I told her what had happened to me. She wanted to know everything. Every word the attackers said, everything they did. And she's been in my life ever since. Her and her women.

"It happened at a party. I should have known better. I couldn't get away. They slugged me in the jaw when I tried to struggle. There were too many of them.

Sam raised herself up on her hands, leaned back on her haunches and gazed down at Peggy. The dick had come out, stiff, lying against her thigh.

Peggy turned and looked back up at Sam. Her blonde hair floated over the sheets. Faint hint of makeup. "Well, to begin with, they knew I was a dyke; that made it worse. Part of why they did it."

In her mind's eye, saw the mean hard faces, two of them young guys. Didn't want to talk about how she felt about it. Entering her body, fear of dying...that had been all behind her, like blue water under a bridge.

Talking to Sam, she saw them again, the first one, stocking pulled down over his face to distort his features as a disguise thru which glinted his narrowed eyes bright as razors; biceps bulging thru a denim jacket, boots, rough, taking down his pants.

"They just kept coming at me, and cumming in me.

"Just do the same damn thing! I tell Mack to stop, and she won't, not for nothing. Even if I'm in real pain. She just goes on and on like a machine. That's how I want you to be."

Sam muttered vaguely about taking her rifle and hunting them down and killing them.

"Don't talk! Listen! Pay attention! Don't argue with me!"

Her blonde hair wild, eyes held fire. "This is for *me!*" Jabbed a finger of her restrained hand at herself. "I'm the one who's important! Do it for me!"

Scrunched her knees up again, cunt bore down to meet the cock. "Now put it in me! Remember! Fuckin' bitch dyke! I'm shit! Remember! I'm not your sweetheart!"

Four cornered bed was a playground of pain.

"Well! Some butches can't do it! They think they're taking something from me; that's not true! They're giving me power!"

Sam was angry, angry at the men, angry at Mack. "Did you feel power when it happened?"

"Please! I knew you'd argue!" Peggy lay under her in a position of helplessness; cunt scrunched down, hot, wet, wanting. "Do it! Don't ask questions!"

"No, you did not like it when it happened, absolutely not!"

"Of course not! But this is with you, it's not them!"

Sam, naked, hunches over her. "I don't have that much muscle to rape anybody."

"It'll work," the cute blonde said, breaking their anger with a laugh. "I'll help you."

Glistening body beaded with sweat. Bed creaked under their weight. Sam put the cockhead to her hole, then dropped the cockshaft and put her hand up to Peggy's cheek and touched it. "You can be gentle too, Sam. I love that. I love being with you. I love necking with you. I'm sorry I'm such a mess." And so Sam put her hand back down to her crotch and guided the bulbous tip to her hole; Peggy started to struggle, testing the bounds, and Sam drove it into her soft pussy. Blood was on Sam's mouth from the fight with Mack, beginning to ooze out from the corner of her lips as the heavy pounding jarred the wound, opening it up again. Her body was sore. Her heart was sick, and her mind whirled in grey confusion. Peggy struggled under her, and she drove the cock in hard with a thrust of her hips, slid it up in her. "OHHHHH!" And Peggy was hollering like she said she would. And Sam remembered what she had been told to say.

"Expensive lady, givin' sex to all those bitches."
"OHHHHHAAAAHHH!"
"This bitch ain't had any kids; her pussy's tight!"
Slamming it into her.
"Tight pussy."

Superimposed shots of her rough lover riding her with no mercy, and memory of her own heartbeat like a drum inside her chest, knowing she was going to die, fearing they were going to kill her.

"Come on, honey, say it!"
"Lesbian bitch, how does it feel to have a real man in you?"

Sam's curly hair tousled, as she jammed her hips in and out, driving the sex organ into her lover's cunt.

"This is some tight pussy, & I'm fuckin' it good."

She pounds into her, and Peggy's clit is swelling. She's breathing hard, tossing her blonde head from side to side, twisting her body, arms straining up against the ties that bound her, pulling until blue veins bulge under her skin; fighting; as Sam lunges into her, keeping up her rhythm, bang bang, in & out. Sweat rolls off them.

Sam's hands push Peggy down on the mattress, driving dick into her cunt; exhausting herself.

Peggy saw the red walls enclosing her; the intense scene. The party. The mean faces. The boots. Trousers down, hairy legs. None of them took off all their clothes.

And tossed and turned under Sam. The purple dick fell out. Sam reaches down with one hand, forces it back up inside Peggy's wet cunt; it goes in easy. Their thighs are wet with cuntjuice, lube, & sweat. Sam's cunt is dripping, too, with excitement & the banging pressure of the cockbase at her clit. "LESBIAN BITCH! YOU PUSSY-SUCKING LEZZIE FAGGOT CUNT! I'M *FUCKING* YOU, CUNT!"

With each cock thrust, driving deep into her, Sam yelled something, and Peggy cried out.

"This pussy's tight, it's so good, I'm gonna go again.

"Dyke, how do you like this, dyke! I'm a real man! You got some real cock up inside you!"

"DON'T PLEASE! STOP! STOP! HELP ME, SOMEBODY! HELP ME!"

They're going at her again, in the red room; a filthy mattress, the men, the stinking odor of smegma, semen, male sweat, and her own wet cunt. Faces revolving above her as she lay on the dirty grey mattress, legs spread, her face broken in front & Sam—a lesbian,—pounding on her, driving her dick into her.

"STOP! PLEASE! PLEASE DON'T! STOP!"

Yielding to the moment, Sam kept on pounding; "SLUT! DYKE! BITCH! BITCH! SHUT UP OR I'LL KILL YOU!"

Peggy struggled as Sam unclipped the wrist locks and, wrestling violently, turned her over. "TURN OVER, BITCH!" Peggy got on all fours. Sam entered her cunt from the rear, guiding the cock in, then clutched her waist tight with one arm and worked her other hand on Peggy's clit. "DYKE BITCH, I'LL FUCK YOU LIKE A DOG!"

"Let me fuck the bitch in her ass!" came another voice; still the same voice. And the sweating, trembling woman felt a jab of pain in her rectum searing red-hot as she was sodomized. Bang, bang, bang.

Half an hour had passed in continuous fucking. Sam was exhausted. She threw Peggy back on her back, the opened restraints clinking a metallic noise; rolled a condom quickly up the dick, then lunged into her again. The dick went down into her fast and slippery, and Peggy yelled out. It was the final fast jabs of pleasure & pain mixing into an undefinable smooth liquid sensual fiery heat. Her clit was swollen and made better contact. Sam lay in between her legs, fucking as fast as she could; fingers twisting Peggy's nipples, and the woman's hips raised up off the bed, involuntarily; her orgasm held there, stark, too-real, cumming, hips rolling from side to side: "OOHHHHHHHHHHH!" Sucking in her breath, hips slamming down on the mattress. "OH, MY GOD!"

And then she was thru.

After, they lay panting, worn. Fell asleep immediately, exhausted from the session.

Just before dawn, Peggy awoke. The doctor slept lightly, & opens her eyes groggily. The blonde hugs her, hair tumbling down to soft shoulders. Had a cup of tea on the nightstand. Sat on the side of the bed & begins to kiss her. "Sam, I'm sorry I went to sleep on you. I'll do everything for you now.... Whatever you want—want me to suck you off? Do it cunt to cunt? Just tell me."

GANG RAPE
Chapter Seven

The next morning, Peggy was in a bad mood.

Sam stretched out on the sheets. Peggy had a cold pack against the blue-black bruise on her face, doctoring her and bitching about something.

"Hope you don't mind me asking, but are you always in a bad mood after a good sex session?"

Peggy pursed her lips, dug fingers into Sam's thigh, to soothe cramped muscles from the fight with Mack.

"How do you feel, Peggy?"

"Slightly depressed... No. Angry."

"Well, I *thought* you'd be happy, gay, and full of joy," Sam said sarcastically. Curly hair brushed around her tan face; reached up and stroked Peggy with slender fingers.

"This scene is your way of control over what happened

in the past. It's become eroticized. A hot image that gets you off good. But it degrades you at the same time and leaves a bitter aftertaste.

"So it's wrong. Big deal." Peggy replies. "How's your face?" she adds, too brightly, changing the subject.

"You want to be taken…. I do, too. Even tho I'm masculine. It's part of us…to want to be taken. At some time or at some point. All human beings, not just females. I'm not too butch to admit it.

"It's just…if you feel so bad about it after, maybe… there's a way you can be taken…hard, like you enjoy it, and fantasize something that won't make you feel so bad about yourself…. I don't know the answer."

"Maybe you're the answer." Peggy smiled, hugged her. Got her tea and took a sip.

"I hope to be a part of the answer."

Put the tea down, and lay her head on Sam's chest, pressed against her soft breasts thru her mannish shirt. Sam just held her.

Was there an answer?

Later, the doctor's slipping on her trousers. "Sometimes it's hard to see people dying around you, some so young. It's important that I keep my personal life in order. I don't know why, Peggy, but I feel something for you. I've been freer in the past, not wanted to get involved. In fact, I was known as a heartbreaker. —Yes, me." She gave a slight laugh. "I give enough emotionally at my job. That's why I tried to have so many women, and not fall in love with any of them.

"I just see people pass away…I've faced it hundreds of times. It's all about enlightenment…. And it's painful…."

Gang Rape | 229

Peggy's mind was a million miles off. 'I'll be with her, it's a safe place—with all those dogs, the burglar alarm. This is luxury. A heated swimming pool.... No worry about rent, and the sole responsibility of the bills will be off my shoulders. If I keep her satisfied, I'll never have to worry again, and I really like her.'

She lay back in the doctor's arms. Sam was pensive, eyes stared into space, scratched her curly head.

'It'll be a relief not having to pursue those babes just for a night of their love. —Spend a week or two to catch up with them... All that hunting & chasing has worn me out.'

Peggy demurred, "If I move in with you, I'd keep my job and pay you rent."

Morning crept over the sky. The beeper was shut off.

"I don't always cum with Mack. I came because I feel closer to you." And imagined herself ensconced in the doctor's second car—the convertible, open top, her blonde hair blowing back; one of the doctor's big mastiff hounds accompanying her in the rear seat; counting her money and being wined and dined and no longer a care in the world; keeping her job just to pay for an extravagant new wardrobe.

Peggy began to spill out her memories. "I was young, I was ready for the world. I was too wild.... Had too many problems...I did a lot of things, and a lot of bad stuff happened...not just that one time, it was the worst. I did stuff I could have gone to jail for.... Getting raped was just one of the bad things that caught up with me during that period of time.

"A lot of country boys out there have the wrong attitude about women.

"I was glad I was still alive. Maybe the only reason they didn't kill me too is that the penalty for manslaughter is greater than for false imprisonment and rape."

"Is that why you became a lesbian?"

"No, I already was. Yes, I had been bisexual in my lifestyle…but even back then at 19, I think I was really gay.… By the time it happened, I'd been completely gay for several years. It's just my lifestyles overlapped; those places I went, the people I was with.

"Everybody knew I was a dyke, and that was part of it. Some of them couldn't accept it. They hated me & singled me out even more.

"The way I was living made it easy for them. I'd go off and party with anybody. I used drugs, and was drinking then.

"I didn't take police action because I was so wild & the drugs I was using were illegal, & I didn't think anybody would believe me.

"It was the lifestyle I was living. I didn't care about myself, so I didn't take any action about my life, and that carried over into not following thru by calling the police against them. It just wasn't part of my world to go to the police. I was their enemy, remember, from being wild and into drugs; and doing antisocial things. The police were supposed to be the enemy, not people I thought were my friends.

"I knew it would be an ordeal going to court. I just couldn't focus & get myself together enough to press charges after the attack. My mind was a wreck for 6 months after.

"I thought about pressing charges, believe me. Not a

day didn't go by that I didn't think about getting revenge.

"So, you see I use to hang around with all kinds of people, even tho I was gay.... We were all friends, all drinking buddies, all party people.... We were gonna have a good time. I was so stupid." Peggy hit the mattress with her fist. Tears came to her eyes. "No, Sam, it's not just that I got raped, it's...all those years as a kid I spent running around...so open, freehearted, meeting women and men...being friendly.... It didn't get me anywhere but pain. In a lot of ways."

In a while, Sam pulled Peggy on top of her, and they lay in an embrace, blonde hair on her chest.

"My mistake was that I went to the party alone. No dykes would ever go anywhere with me.... I was always alone, out by myself. I was at the wrong place at the wrong time that night."

"You have that right! To be out alone! To go places without the threat of...being attacked."

"Tell the morons on the street that!"

"I said, 'guys, well, stop kidding....' And I was woozy from liquor I'd had.... And then I saw they were serious. One hit me in the mouth and knocked me down when I tried to fight. I scuffled, I tried to run, and they grabbed me and threw me into a table; that's where I cut my head; all along this side, under my hair, was open. I had to have 30 stitches. And my lip, too. I just gave up. There were too many of them. I knew I wouldn't make it out of there; I'd get beaten to death."

In a while, Peggy reached up shyly to touch Sam's tit. Stroked it, soft, felt the nipple harden under her touch. "Do you ever want me to take you, Sam?"

"Sometimes, but not like you like it! You can go inside me with my vibrator. I'm a woman. I like to be on my back sometimes. Yes, I like to be hammered in my pussy. I don't deny myself that."

They lay in each others arm's. "I work in a hospice; I've told you. I work with dying human beings. People about to pass out of this life... They spend their whole lives fighting back against what the world dishes out to them. They spend a lifetime being strong. Then they come to die and they can't fight it. So I have to show them how to fight in a different way.

"Their bodies are failing them. Nothing they've achieved can save them."

It was the morning after. In the woman's pink bedroom. All her lesbians in black leather outfits in posters on the wall smiled down. The doctor felt vague stirrings of responsibility. Was glad the maid could at least feed and give water to the dogs. She had dressed to leave, changed her mind, undressed, stayed. Hours had passed. She was buck naked, and still didn't want to go back.

The women looked deep down into each other's eyes and knew they wanted to cum together.

To use each other; together. Motion of their bodies and what they did, to work out their wanting. To love in a sweaty embrace, intimately aware of their partner's needs; timing it right, one waiting, loving the other, building her up, timing it right so they could both burst loose together in a wild, brief, joyous moment of ecstasy.

"So they used your body—and you got nothing for it but hurt, fear, anger, shame. —All the garbage.

"Now it's up to you to dump that garbage. To let go of it.

"I'm not a rape counselor; it's not my work. I don't know what to say to you.

"I just know that when people are dying…this is one of the kinds of things they become able to let go of. There are many losses, griefs, intrusions, that happen over a lifetime. You'd be surprised how many things seem small in the light of death. As I said, death can be enlightening."

"I really thought I was going to *die*, Sam. I really did. I've never come that close to it before. —It helps me cum."

"You can cum better.… It took you an hour. —That's not so fantastic. Some women can cum 3 times in an hour. I've had women cum vaginally—with fingers or a dildo, 3 or 4 times in a row. So, our first time, we had a soft vanilla cum. It was nothing great, I *know*."

"You're not that soft, especially when you ride me. Don't underestimate yourself."

"I should keep my mouth shut and keep raping you… because I don't want to lose you. But this is important! I've got to tell you this, Peggy, even if I never get to make love to you again!.… I mean, there are no easy solutions. It's not…like buying a brand new bed and throwing out the old mattress to rid yourself of the memories of all the old lovers.… I'm not that naïve… and I don't want you to be any different than who you are.… But also, Peggy, I don't really relish that scene like that Mack! Saying those degrading things that undermine both our self-esteems! But I will do it as long as you need it. If it helps us stay together, I'll say it & do it for a million years! It's not beneath my politics!"

Sam toyed with the idea of asking Peggy to get her shirt & slacks again, but wasn't sure if she wanted to get dressed and go yet.

Hum of the refrigerator from the kitchen. Still air floated on the carpet. Only Peggy's voice, melodic, hesitant, filled space.

"When I was younger I lived a life as a party kind of person. I wasn't a prostitute or anything, I was a go-go dancer. And I'd go out of my house with one bunch of people, and wake up the next morning in somebody's house I didn't even know with an entirely different bunch of people.

"I used to get loaded on drugs & alcohol.

"It frightened me sometimes, what I was doing to myself.

"I went to a nightclub where there was a lot of gay men and a few gay women and a lot of straights. These lowlifes told me there was a party. I thought there was going to be gay people there, and I didn't know what I was getting into.

"After a few days, a lot of people in the club knew, because they bragged about it. And the word got around.

"I should have pressed charges at the District Attorney's office, but anyway...I told you."

"So now they got away with it! They're probably doing it again! To some other woman! You have the right to press charges! This is America!"

"Afterwards, they disappeared. From time to time I might see one; he'd duck his head and go the other way.... Maybe they thought I was too drunk to remember, but I *do* remember each last one of those motherfuckers, and will till the day I die.

"It changed my life. —Not to be as careless, to watch who I meet, get to know them first.

"You see the marks on my face? Well, if I'd been in that life much longer, my whole body would be like that…. I'd be nothing to look at—I'd be howling & jittering. Lifetime alcoholics & druggies, that's how they get. There's no hope for them then. —They've made their decision a long time back. You'd walk right by me, Sam. —I know you like pretty women. That's why I turn it on for you. Wear my slinky satin stuff, and the high heels; and floods of perfume. I know what arouses butches.

"After that incident, I went downhill very bad. Didn't care about myself at all. Overate, used drugs & drank, —alone, safe in my own rented room and, stupid me, back in that same tavern. I'm lucky nothing worse happened during that time, I might have wound up dead.

"Then I started coming out of it. I had a job, was living a normal life on the surface during the day; that helped me get a grip on it, too.

"In a year I stopped messing up. Straightened out my life, kept working, & started looking seriously at myself, and trying to figure out a way to be a lesbian, with other lesbians, in our own places and ways of life.

"Didn't think about it again, until Mack. The way she… He took me. And then I broke down and told him about the attack—I'd almost forgot it…. And he wanted to know everything…. It drove him crazy, it seemed; he said he was jealous of the way they'd gotten to me, and said he wanted to do it, too." Peggy's voice trailed off. Felt warmth rising up from Sam's breasts and her thighs, close; under the sheets.

"You say Mack is that damn good in bed! Well, you should be having multiple orgasms! Not just cum once an hour—if that!" She heard the doctor fairly shout.

"I know what it's like, Sam—your job. It's depressing. —I had a lover once, a nurse. She used to say, if they lost a patient who was young—less than 40, 'It's a shame they died so young.' If they were really old, over 70 or so, she'd say, 'It's time that they died!' She didn't think death was depressing. She didn't like people to be hooked up to machines going on & on, half-unconscious, zoned out on narcotics. 'It's better to see them die than to have them suffer so much when there's no hope.'

"Some doctors are in it for the money. An 80-year-old woman is brought in, she's comatose, and they operate on her. Why don't they let her die? They're going to pick her apart over & over, and she's going to die anyway. Doctors do so many unnecessary operations.

"The nurse would come home and tell me how her day went; 'We had ten hemorrhages, 2 traumas, 5 car accidents.'"

Finally, in their reminiscent ramblings, Doctor Sam told Peggy, "You've done such a good job pulling yourself up so far—why not go all the way? When I first met you you said you wanted to better yourself, now here's a way. You can begin to deal with this garbage. Get into some kind of counseling. I'm sure I can find a therapist for you—a woman, a good one. I've had counseling for myself for other issues. It works."

Sam told her how in the sessions a lot of things were uncovered that she hadn't seen. And told her how she could take real power over the assault. And as far as her damaged self-esteem, and problems even before that incident; that no amount of external love can give what's needed inside. That everyone has to come face-to-face with truth within herself. Sam urged Peggy to go to counseling—money need not be a problem.

Secretly she hoped her lover would. So that they might not reenact the scene quite like that again and again and again, and their lovemaking become an insult to the doctor.

So that they might find an erotic power stronger—as they let go some of the mechanisms of the past—and yield themselves to each other in a night filled with love, and less hate; swiftly, and with power.

"So do you want to keep the people at your hospice alive, or help them die?"

"Neither, it's just to heal each minute. It has to be a deep healing. Spiritually. Because you know—and they know—that their body is dying."

The doctor put her hands on Peggy, ran them down her sides to her waist. "Glad I fucked you the way you wanted. Because it's what works for you right now. Glad I was able to do something for you."

"Most butches can't. They're too cowardly. They can't take it. —Unless they're superbutch, like Mack. Then they love it."

"I like the way I can make love to you, too."

"Everybody does."

"You give good oral sex. That's what kept me coming back, calling you on the phone. Now I've gotten accustomed to being with you. I like being with you. I enjoy going places with you."

Day moved across the horizon. To Zenith.

"In the process of dying, is the time for transformation. When they die, they are born, in a sense. To surrender... People are trained to think that to surrender is to give up, to lose control—that's what you did when you were assaulted. You had to survive and maybe made it better for yourself.

"When I deal with the dying, I have to teach them about surrender.... The Western way is to expect physical healing. To fight right up to the last minute. Doctors try to find a cure for everything physical. Some people fight death up to the end.

"The minute they hear they're going to die, they become hard. Vow they're going to go out kicking and screaming, —and before you know it, they've died like everybody else.... They go out aggressively & miserable.

"I try to get them to deal with forgiveness.

"To come to a sense of peace within.

"Some, in their enlightenment, see other people dying all over this earth along beside them. —Suffering in pain along with them in the final seconds of living breath they draw on this earth.

"In the billions of people on this planet, there must be 20,000 dying right along side any one of my dying patients; down the street, in the next block, in the next city, across the hemisphere.

"The best thing we can do is to have mercy, to make them physically comfortable. You see the pain in their bodies, and how that pain changes from day to day....

"A sense of something greater than yourself, is very helpful in the dying process. Those who have a belief go better than those who are alone.

"An atheist might go better than a believer with a church & a Bible—it's the state of belief in their heart.

"Dying is easy, the actual crossing over out of this mortal earth.

"It's working up to it that's rough. Fear, anger, sadness, grief...having to know they're going to die.... Kindness and mercy is what they need the most, in the end. Kindness.

"They perspire. Their faces might not be recognizable from what they were at the beginning. They look like strangers, unlike the individual you first met. You lean close and breathe with them. My hospice is residence & care 24 hours & they die all kinds of ways.... You have to keep your heart open for them.

"And it makes you think about your own life. To make your life work as best you can.

"When death stands there looking at you, very few other things make any difference.

"They're dying. Nothing can help them. All the things they possess, the material gains they made in this world thru so much struggle can't help them.

"Even their loved ones can't help.

"Their body has failed; it disintegrates fast.

"Some can no longer move. They lay trapped in their body, waiting for it to die.

"The only thing that stands between them and something greater, is their stubbornness—or their enlightenment. Whatever this greater state is, whether it's by an outward spiritual force which touches them, or power that comes from within.

"It involves a personal insight. Some level that each person must struggle to get to on their own.

"Then finally, you begin to see, death is imminent at all times.... And this brings either a heaviness of heart, which I bore for so long, or enlightenment in the mind."

"Enlightenment. That means you get lighter," Peggy mused.

"There comes an opening in time and space. They die. Then I pull their eyelids down for them.

"A lot of people do their first living when they know they're dying, or going to die.

"It awakens their minds and souls.

"So, I'm saying...it all has to do with the concept of surrender. Forgiveness of this world, and all held resentments in it.

"I know you had to surrender to those creeps. There were more of them than you, and they were more violent.

"And that you're angry about that.

"Cancer deaths. AIDS. They go by me.... I see them, young, so many—they struggle not to die.

"You were sexually abused; there's a lot of grief in that as well.

"As the pain increases, they're very grateful for people to be at their side. To hold their hands. To give them care. They are carrying huge burdens—the feelings of helplessness, feelings of loss. They've had sexual abuse. They've been poor. Some of them have never been appreciated. A lot of grief about a lot of things. They might regret how they've lived this life. They have anger— or more self-awareness.

"To be self-aware—awake.

"Don't try to stop our feelings. Examine them.

"So many deny and resist. They deny their illness. They resist death. That seems to work—but it doesn't keep them alive any longer than any others.

"Some find out who they actually are inside...and maybe it's somebody they didn't want to see.... And that's when forgiveness comes in. It's self-forgiveness. Not just to forgive those who trespass against you, but self-forgiveness. And enlightenment.

"I've been at the hospice 3 years, it's not very long, but I've studied it.

"I try to help them, so that as their bodies die, their souls are healed.

"Some accept their own children they rejected once, for an old unforgiven sin. They forgive the people they hated for a lifetime.

"They hold on, and they want to let go; and their pain is increasing day after day, night after night; sweating, fits, spasms, coughing.

"It's a heartbreak—and a new vision.

"The religious fundamentalists with their judgments and hates, who are so inflexible, are the worst at dying. Tho they have a belief. Because they won't change. Won't see. Won't surrender. Won't be enlightened.

"Won't have birth inside themselves; to be reborn.

"They cling to their tired beliefs, their prejudice, their scriptures, their doctrines.

"They need a birth. —To let go.

"I tell them, 'You fought back all these years, now surrender to it, and let it go—and be enlightened.'"

Dr. Sam had finally got dressed, combed her hair. And thus would be late getting to the hospital, and still hadn't been back to her home. Turned wearily to her woman.

"Peggy, maybe you can get into some kind of therapy about the rape, and come to terms with it.

"It helps. Therapy is one of the advancements of modern civilization. I'd be glad to pay for it."

Stuck out her hand in a good-bye handshake, but Peggy grabbed the hand, raised it to her lips, and kissed it.

GANG RAPE
Chapter Eight

Peggy & Sam sat together in a pew of Grace Cathedral with the rest of the Anderson family.

"THE BLOOD OF CHRIST IS GIVEN TO *ALL* OF YOU!" The priest's voice boomed over a microphone. Sam thought about Peggy's menstrual blood, its sticky salty slime in her mouth; that first night way back in summer when she was so hot and horny and in need. Blood's unmistakable taste, which lingers strong, so you must wash it out of the bedsheets well, in steaming water. How she had offered up her cunthole, her thighs, her tits, her body, for Sam to lay, & fuck to an orgasm. How she couldn't get Peggy out of her mind after.... Reached her arm in its white doctor's coat along the back of the pew, & pulled her woman close.

The priest was denouncing Satan from the pulpit. Sam's curly head touched the blonde's, whispered to her, "I hate the Devil, he's tried to destroy so many people."

"All those patients you work with, dying?"

"No. The spirits of people who are going to live. Live a long time, but just give up. I see them drag their bodies around like empty shells across a lifetime."

"WHAT IS THE COMPASSION OF CHRIST?" the priest intoned. "WE'VE SEEN HELL, NOW PARTAKE OF THE JOY!"

Peggy felt snug in her doctor's arms. Looked down into her lap, and once again was choked by emotion. —As she saw the diamonds glittering on her marriage finger—a $15,000 ring.

Now the combination of being in a cathedral for the first time since she was an intern at General Hospital, and having a new, deep love, made Sam watery-eyed. As for Peggy, her curvaceous companion, she had not been in church since she was a child; the spirit of the Christmas holidays filled her; as being lovingly accepted into the warm family bond of the Andersons, along with their other children & grandchildren, moved her. Held in the arms of her lesbian lover, Peggy glittered like a queen.

All these factors accounted for the tears that dropped down into her lap. 'Drat. I'll have to do my mascara.' Blue eyes stared, big, up at the multicolor stained-glass windows. The pipe organ bellowed from bass to treble, with gusts of hymns.

Mrs. Anderson loved Peggy. "She has blonde hair and blue eyes like your grandmother from Norway, Grandmother Sonja." Took Peggy's face in her wrinkled bejeweled hands and kissed her on the forehead. And Mr. Anderson shook Peggy's hand, a smile beaming out of his elderly face. "We're just ordinary folks, Mrs. Anderson told Peggy. And the blonde femme met Sam's sisters and brothers. They were a big family held by loving bonds. They were civilized and humane.

After the medical rounds were done, Dr. Sam Anderson walked the wards and would extend the touch of her hand in the dying room.

Fingers of weakened hands might reach out to her. —Sometimes there was not enough time left to reach out.

She was there while they transcended from matter and passed into spirit.

When she gave oral love to Peggy, Sam reached her short-nailed fingers under her butt as she pressed her mouth on Peggy's cunt and sucked the salty river from which issues the pageant of human life.

And she, too, was held in a life-giving embrace. Peggy, on her back upon sweaty sheets, grips Sam's ass tight, to pull that butch cunt into her own, as Sam worked, humping & moaning, passing over the orgasmic threshold into moments of sheer pleasure & abandon.

That week there had been seven dead. Who threw down their skeleton selves to run free.

Dying on the surface; slipped away in a moment, across this barrier which is terminal, to rest in timelessness.

"What do you say to them when they can't let go?"

"To follow the Light. If I can talk to them at all, I tell them, 'Let the Light lead you.'"

"What is the Light?"
"Something beyond us."
"Like the universe, or like God?"
"Yes."
"Huh."

"I tell them, 'From now on, you have to follow the Light. It will guide you.' When you see it, there's a melting away, a letting go, a forgiveness. Nothing else matters when you see the Light.

"Now, all they worked and slaved for a lifetime can't help them anymore. All the morals they held, the people they loved, the people they hated.... It's just time to let go."

"Fate, or the Light, or whatever... Sometimes I think certain people come into your life just at the right time.... You came into my life at the right time.

"I've needed a woman of my own. You taught me that."

Peggy undressed in the master bedroom of their mansion. Rolling pantyhose down her shapely legs. Flips back her blonde hair.

So the erotic desires of long summer heat, & the lamentation of dying; all the dying.... Thru Gay Life in San Francisco, God makes promises & delivers acts. What more is needed? Time. Time for those promises to unfold.

And there comes of this a new understanding. To see in a new way. And to Believe.

Joy does spring from the heart. Comes in the morning; after night's harrowing voyage; when God puts it there. An affair arranged for us at the end of a necessary journey. The conclusion of a vital process.

One promise, manifest; naked; to lie down in bed beside this woman, where before she lay tossing & turning alone.

This was their days & nights.

Came to her at 3 A.M. Peggy was sleeping.

Billowy blonde hair under moonlight. Nubile body sprawled under a sheet.

Came to her.

She had just left the room of a dying person. Just closed down the eyelids of the dead.

Light motion of the bed as the doctor lay down was enough to wake Peggy.

And she had said, "Wake me when you get home, I'll be there to take care of you."

And did now, gentle, tender, strong.

Loved Sam; hands squeezing Sam's small tits. Before the doctor knew what was happening, the femme's full body was on her, caressing, sucking each tit, pushed her thigh between Sam's thighs, groped her wet sexhole with her fingers. Her clit working hump, hump, on Sam's leg.

On top of her; Peggy's hands caressing. Sam felt her breath on her skin.

They did it different ways at different times.

Penetrated with the cock. Fast & hard.

Went down on her; while using fingers in her cunt and tongue tip licking over her pink clit simultaneously and got her off. Felt her vagina clamp down on her fingers, tight, so she didn't want to move them anymore, but kept thrusting, just to feel her lover's cunt open up, ripple in muscle spasms, wetting her whole hand with juice, and climax a second, then a third time.

Peggy had started cumming EZ because she felt so close to Sam, and really wanted to surrender to her.

And Sam became more experienced in sex, with Peggy for a partner in play.

Sandra Anderson marveled as the hot blonde climaxed on her fist. Clenched, knuckles, thumb tucked under her finger—inside the blonde's pussy. And cumming with her orally was the best of any woman she'd had…Every evening being there for her.

The future promise of love—it had seemed way off in the distance back then, in the long hot summer of 1991. Now it was right here beside her, looking at her & laughing in fun.

They watched love grow; it was intense.

Peggy knelt on the sheets. Paused a minute, looked at her love. "Do you want to cum in my mouth?"

No more hesitations; "Yes."

Felt the tugging reins of sexual desire course from her clit & sweep up her guts & spine and spread out in a fan of desire throughout her body, held tense with expectation; as her lover sucked & licked with her lips and tongue.

Outside, wind stirred across the deck with fragrance from a jasmine vine. The hills stretched into the distance.

Then they lay in the sheets which were warm from body heat.

Aroma of woman drifted to her senses. So good. Naked. Wanted her sweetness inside. Sucked the pink nipples of each tit. Stroked Peggy's long bare legs.

Got between her spread thighs, which Peggy held open to receive her, using her fingers to press her knees back farther. Sam jams her clit against Peggy's wet cunt and screws up & down & around in their juice.

'She takes me so good.'

On her back, holding herself open for her lesbian husband, so close, like a circuit completed; cunt-to-cunt, intimately building an orgasm together—one of the mightiest forces in this world.

Cunts fused into each other's, Sam loving Peggy hungrily, & her femme responding; so that they're cumming together.

They're cumming right on time.

Moonlight. Naked female bodies. Having sex together. Bedsprings creak under them. Use each other's wet, hot pussies to fulfillment.

Rhythm of their bodies begin the Dance of Life.

Which living on this mortal earth is all about.

Birth. Death. Sex.

The Fire of Death.

The Dance of Life.

AFTER THE TRICK WAS TURNED

After he'd paid his money, it was me she wanted. After the john came out of the room, I came back in the wee small hours and doors opened for me. A woman in a negligee showing me tan flesh, full breasts, hair tousled & tired, but expectant, awaking to my gaze. After the trick was turned, I came back, she opened the door and received me, naked, and I loved her all night long into the morning, for free.

Frankie was in her early 20s. Blue jeans & plaid shirt, brown leather jacket; about 5'5", sturdy frame. White skin, fair hair under a hat. Wallet big with papers & union card, on a chain that looped, fastened to her belt.

Year was 1968…before the advance of AIDS decimated gay ranks. When hippies came from all parts of the USA in caravans. Just when rents were starting to go up sky-high. Amerika sitting on the brink of depression still decades off, but already the factory jobs had moved out.

Frankie had been to the ocean. Blue waves crash in from across, from Europe. Vast. Drop off the continental shelf, where lie all the hulks of sunk ships of a woebegone age. Seaweed under her boots. The Pacific coastline.

Driving around town in her truck.

Those days between old loves and new loves when she was single.

Frankie had a room on the outskirts of the Tenderloin, just $13 per week, no bath—toilet down the hall shared by the whole floor. A piss-in-the-sink room, if you understand. Midnight getting out of bed she didn't want to go down a hallway back to that craphole past transients & winos, and rough people. So hiked her white butt up on the sink & with effort a yellow stream of piss went down the drain.

Her building was poor, white, old, a few blacks; alcoholics on Social Security & some transvestite hookers.

Five-thirty A.M., been at the union hall and waited all morning. Three men's names, 2 women's names, men's, then more & more and they weren't calling no more dames. At 10 A.M. it was all over.

'So I'm floating free, waiting for my next unemployment check to come thru.

A small amount of cash in my pocket, a tiny bankroll of $140 put in a local bank, checks still not printed, and out of a job.'

So Frankie's just going around the city, beach. Haight-Ashbury where the hippies are. She stood on

Haight Street; blue jeans, keys in a ring on her belt, shortish hair to her ears; rings on fingers, hands that women had told her were strong, with nails that she keeps very short so as to be prepared.... Light-colored eyes.

Had been to a peep show even; by the bus terminal, watching naked women gyrate & writhe on a screen; wanting sex.

Frankie had been all over town.

Then drove her truck by the gay bar she would hit tonight. There would nurse a couple of beers & maybe she'd meet some bitchin' woman, windblown blonde hair lighter than her own, in ringlets; smoky blue eyes, tight blue jeans, and open-toed shoes. A heartthrob.

On the way back down across town to her room had to cross Fillmore Street & thought: 'I'll stop and see how the Negroes live here.' Parked the truck on a whim & got out to walk. Street was crawling with people all the way down from Geary Boulevard past Eddy Street, Ellis, Turk. She was almost the only white. Past bars, record shops, shoeshine parlors, storefront churches.... 'Just going around this old city of yours, San Francisco... killing time by the dock of the bay until 9 P.M. then go sit up in the gay bar.'

On a corner, a black woman, 30s, ebony, and very bright red lipstick and dressed in very fine clothes. Satin stretched across her bosom & hips. Not the finery the blacks wear to their churches, no.

This black hooker is looking at her sharp, and Frankie don't have the price. Lady on her job standing by the shoeshine parlor. Soon Frankie is just moving on down the line, boots restless on a stranger's pavement.

"SAY, STRANGER!"

"Huh? Say, Man!" It was Slim, a man from the union hall who lives in the same apartment building in the TL. He's got a bigger apartment with a bath & kitchen and pays $68 per month—because he has to have something nice for his woman who comes over on the weekend.

"No work today."

"Yeah, Sport. I pulled MJB Coffee; they want me back for 2 more shifts."

"Lucky. You got a union book?"

"Red card."

The two talked; man was friendly, the outgoing type, showing his teeth as wind whipped their words. While he talked, Frankie glanced back; the hooker was gone from the shoeshine parlor.

"Say, sport." Slim says. "Do me a favor. I got a stop to make…this lady I know got a TV set for sale. I don't want to go over there by myself."

"All right, man."

Frankie had nothing better to do. She followed his truck in hers.

So Frankie's truck tails Slim in a caravan. They go deeper into the black sector; rows of apartments, modern, built in the 50s among old Victorians fallen down in disrepair; swarming with kids and adults & loud angry noises & old people falling asleep on the porches. Then around Lyon she sees him park, so with a turn of her strong hands on the wheel, she swings her truck to the curb amid crunch of glass slivers under the tire.

Go up apartment steps. Children were making noise

from everywhere, and cooking smells wafted out windows.

Walked up three flights; they got to the corridor, modern enough, went down. They got to a door, it opens; there's a colored lady, older, a spin off the black race in complexion, light. Nice-looking, but older. Crow's-feet around her eyes, & mouth weak, like maybe her teeth are bad. Wears a sweater & lady slacks.

Frankie looks in her face, says hello, takes off her hat, & steps in.

Frankie & Slim sit on a sofa against the wall, him on one end, her on the other. It's supposed to be a living room, but it's the only room. So the bed is in it also.

Bed is double, nice headboards & matching nightstands & dresser. Simple furniture that belongs to the woman that she moved in here with and don't come with the apartment. A bath on the side, tiny & crummy, and a larger kitchen that looks out over the street. In it, a dinette set, & there are boxes on the table with glasses and cookware half-packed.

Slim and the woman are talking & he's slapping his leg and laughing, showing his teeth because he laughs so big, about something funny they remember from the past.

And the woman seems so much more quiet; but talking.

So the story unfolds slowly. She works in a hospital and makes low wages, barely enough to live in an apartment on the bad side of town in any Amerikan city and to keep clothes, pots & pans and her own furniture, and splurge & get a new TV set every 5 years or so, and keep a raggedy car together—like any of the other nonspecialized minorities who service Amerika; and Frankie thinking how she, too, is drifting on the marginal fringe. From factory to factory in a dwindling blue-collar labor pool & that the woman is less than her because she's colored, but also her having an advantage because she is straight and wears lady pants and can work in an office.

"I want to die," the woman was saying. "It's my birthday next week. I thought he was going to ask me to marry him. He told me he had something to tell me. —That he has another woman.

"For my birthday. I'm 47. I don't mind telling that. I'm grateful to live this long. But I don't want to live anymore. I can't go thru this again.

"My people kept telling me he was no good. They knew it all the time.

"My friends at the office knew he had another woman, and nobody told me.

"I'm going back home to my people in Chicago, I'm selling all my things and giving the rest away. Gave notice on the job. Twelve years I been there. Twelve years. I can't be there no more seeing him every day. He ain't leaving, so I've got to be the one to go."

She sat on the side of the bed pulling the sweater around her, in her slacks and run-down shoes; glancing at a pathetic pile of clothes in the closet.

Noise of people moving thru the corridor outside, loud, then ceased.

The woman was tired. Spoke in a drained manner. "I'm giving up. Can't take it no more. I got to go home and be with my people. I know it's giving up, I've tried to make something work for me out here in California, but it's just not happening.

"Two years I go with a man, and it turns out he's got another woman all this time—his main woman—and I thought he was going to ask me to marry him."

And the woman looked like she'd been to the ends of the earth. Young Frankie was thinking: 'It's not enough black men to go around for the black women. She's lost 2 years of her life, got hung up, & she's almost old; she probably thinks she's not pretty anymore; and she hasn't made it out here in California.'

The woman looked like all the fire had gone out of her because of this emotional betrayal, and she was almost dead.

And Frankie felt sad for the woman.

Sat there, leaning back on the sofa kind of playing with her hat with ringed fingers, legs wide apart man-style; face solemn.

Woman looked over first to Slim, then Frankie. "Go get me some beer, will you? And some cigarettes." She looks at Frankie.

"I'm broke," Frankie says. So the woman gets up and gets her purse out of the closet, fishes in it for some coins. She's poor, too. "Here," she says. And Slim says he'll go down to the corner store.

TV was on, and the two sat. Frankie asks the colored woman, "Pardon me, I forgot your name." Her name is Esther, and she is going on and on about being betrayed & says suddenly, "You know I'm not prejudiced. I like your people. At the office where I work there's all nationalities. We're all friends. Just one big family. That's why I hate to leave, but I can't be there no more." And her voice chokes. And with a thin hand pulls her sweater tighter.

Frankie nods her head, sympathetic but underneath is wondering, 'Does she realize I'm a dyke? I'm a lot younger than her...maybe 'cause I'm white she can't tell.... Maybe it don't make no difference to her that she's spilling out her guts to a lesbian.'

Slim was back with the beer. Woman pats her full lips with a tanned hand & her eyes mist like she wants to cry; she goes around and pours beer in 3 glasses. Everybody's having a taste.

Now Slim and Esther are talking about old times. He's laughing, slaps his hand down on the sofa, goodnatured, remembering good times.

Esther sits about 5 feet away from Frankie in the small room; Frankie is looking at her in a nonsexual fashion. 'She's old. She ain't gay.' And she's the only woman around.

Esther is very passive in a beaten kind of way. Raises a glass of beer up to her full lips; and that look glazed across her eyes like she's had something stronger than beer or dope that has singed her with its fire.

And Slim says he's not taking the TV for his woman because it's not color; he didn't know this.

And Frankie leans on the sofa drinking beer, biding time, glad she's not alone. Thoughts drift up & out of this space back up to the bar in Haight-Ashbury, off on a fantasy of a bitchin' woman, blonde, slender with the fairest skin of white alabaster, earrings, painted toes in open-toed shoes, hanging on her arm. One of the Queens of this world. So a grin is on her face.

Heterosexuals are prancing around on the TV, & the three sit there sipping beer.

After the Trick Was Turned | 259

A knock at the door. Esther gets up from the bed, opens it, and a black man dressed in a suit with vest & coat runs in, frantic eyes, tie off; nods at Slim, stares at Frankie a second, & goes and sits on the side of the bed by Esther. He's very agitated. Soon he's shouting, slams one fist into his hand, and she's trying to calm him down. It's about some kind of problem he's having with a woman.

And Esther's trying to quiet him down, to make him relax, and tries to tell him how she's selling her TV and dinette set, and bedroom suite and taking the first flight back to Chicago. But the man in the suit sits on the bed with his broad back turned to the other two, ignoring them, pounding his fist in his hand and yelling because he feels powerless about something in his life.

Stupid, the man yelling, demands all the attention like a baby. Anger. Esther puts her hands on his fists trying to keep him from slugging the headboard; Frankie has felt the woman fade away.

And the man is taking off his coat & throws it down.

"We better leave." Slim winks at Frankie from down at his end of the sofa. "Leave these two alone."

Esther's pleading with him to calm down, and the man gets up and is unbuckling his trousers, still yelling. Frankie gets up: 'I'm out of here.'

Slim gets out the door first, then Frankie's shoulders frame the doorway, cowboy hat on her head, longish hair; and the woman has got up off the bed & the man is taking his trousers off. When Frankie got out in the hall the woman is right behind her, pulling her sweater tight, and puts her hand right in the small of Frankie's back. It rests there just a moment in a feathery touch. "Why don't you come back later?" she says in a low voice. The young butch turns around, looks down at her & she's looking right up at Frankie with a pleading look.

Frankie is surprised at this.

The two go down the steps. Head to their trucks. Frankie says, "Is she going to be OK?"

Slim says, "They've been dealing together for years." Gives her a knowing look.

Cold on her hair. Frozen sky. Neon dripping icicles. And time had passed.

"Let them do what they have to do."

And the story comes out that it's some man she used to see as a boyfriend, and he already has another woman, and Esther's dropped him a long time ago, but he gives her money as a bribe to keep seeing him; to run to her when women are driving him crazy & he's powerless. And she needs his money to keep from being in total poverty as the wages she earns are just the minimum, and the rent keeps going up, & continuing to climb.

And Frankie finds this out from Slim.

So she can't make it on her own, not with what they pay her, and she had thought this other chump at the job was going to marry her, but she knew better...deep down in her heart she knew better.... And the wind is catching his words. Two figures separate, and the night has set over SF. Winter. Early daylight saving time. The gay bar twinkles not far off. Passersby walk along.

Slim drives off. Night has fallen completely. Building tops obscured in blackness. It's cold. From inside her truck, Frankie can see up to the 3rd floor apartment where they just were. And the lights on...

She sits in the truck, thinks: 'Why did she put her hand on me? Said to come back...why? Now...it might not be what I'd like to think...maybe it's just friendliness because I'm white or something...or her way of apologizing for that crazy guy.... She touched me with her hand when she said it.... And looked me dead in my eyes like she's trying to tell me something.... Maybe it's because she's so lonely...she wants me to talk to? Or...does she want me as a lesbian?'

Cold air rushed by, and the night crackled with voices laughing & cigarette embers died out in mean streets. Embers. So Frankie didn't budge. Frankie turns the ignition on so the heater will warm up the interior of the truck, and just sits back watching the stars in the night; enjoying the buzz from the beer. Mellow.

So she waits.

'I'm not prejudiced...it's just there are problems going over to the dark side to drink sweet nectar from a dark passion fruit.' White face in the cab of the truck looking about at the crummy neighborhood, ready to drive off if there's any trouble.

She looked in the rearview mirror in the direction of a loud voice, but it just passed by.

Thought in disgust: 'These glass-littered streets... they can't even throw their trash away, it's like these people are beaten down.

'I'm not too proud to lie down with a colored woman....' She thought ironically: 'If she's not too proud to lie down with a dyke.'

Frankie wanted to screw. She wanted a woman, hard.

And she really wanted to drink again, from the cup of that dark passion fruit.

'It's because their lives are harder...and they give up because of that.... I don't cross over here very often; I have before.... It's just that their world is meaner, and their lives are rougher.' And Frankie looks at her watch and thinks: 'How long am I going to wait, and for what? I'm missing a night at the gay club; it's alive right now, all those glamorous women...' the bitchin' blondes of her illusions; 'but this woman says to come back to see her...and hardly anybody in the bar talks to me yet.

'Some of my friends would despise me...say I lost all self-respect...to be out here in the cold, waiting for a woman old enough to be my mother, 30 years older, and not of the white race...and *straight*.' Frankie was embarrassed. 'She's so old, and a colored woman....' Then she's thinking how it would be if she, Frankie, goes to where the woman works in her boots and leather jacket & blue jeans & hat, and the woman touches her there, & looks into her eyes in front of the whole office saying, 'Come back to see me.' All the straight people would faint dead away. And, most of all, as the night enclosed her in the cab of the truck, night air blew in drafts and the waves crashed to the ocean's shore...most of all, Frankie wanted that hot gash. What every lesbian wants, what every woman has between her legs; no matter what age, or color.

And this was funny because they'd both been despised and had both been to the ends of the earth.

Night ticked on solemnly. 'Been about a half-hour,'

she thought. 'And she's taking the first flight out of town. If I don't wait tonight, and instead come back tomorrow she might be gone. She's in a big hurry.'

Dull sensation had been glowing in the 22-year-old as she'd roamed around the city for the last few days. This wanting a woman. The bed. Wanting one bad, as well as a companion to stretch out the days.

'If she lets me fuck her, that man will have used her before me. Her cunt's full of semen. Jesus Christ! I hope she uses a rubber...and I'm out here waiting for this?' Gritted her teeth. And Frankie sat there. Her lust for pussy was stronger...and she would go thru anything to get to it.

Wanted to get cunt. To get in it. To get her cunt against it. To climax with it. And the moon rose & roamed across the sky; waiting a little while longer, as the wind blew the minutes past.

Her hand, white, ringed fingers rested on the seat beside her; other arm draped over the side door.

Solemn shadows of the trees behind which no ghosts hid; she had as of yet no memories here for she was new to this town on the western seaboard.

Reaches under her belt; rising up in the seat, Frankie slides her hand under her belt down into her trousers, jabs two fingers down into her hot sex, moving over her clit in one rapid motion. And, in a bolt of fire, sex responded; hit her senses in a rush. Just once she touched herself down there, then, hastily, pulls her hand back out & straightens her belt. Jaw tense. Turns and gazes out the window seeing nothing. A film over the windows. Fog from the ocean moving in.

'Will she want me? How long is she going to let him spend up there?' And Frankie switched the ignition on, gunned up the motor again, and bathed in warmth. Upstairs, dim light in the apartment still shone.

Wind whistled and the trees bent.

Forty-five minutes had passed. Suddenly Frankie looks up. Lights in the apartment were out.

To take a risk. To try…. Frankie heaved a big breath out of the pit of her guts. Moving around, gets ready to go; then she has an idea. Before she leaves the truck, she removes her hat so her light hair shines in the moonlight; set the hat down on the seat & got out.

It must have been about 12 midnight. The butch went back up the steps of the building, up 3 flights of stairs, down the corridor, finding her way back to Esther's apartment.

Knocked on the door.

"Hey! It's me—Frankie! I think I forget my hat. Sorry to bother you!"

The woman opened the door, tired look on her face, feminine…liquid eyes, brown. Wearing a bathrobe. "I'm glad you came back, baby," she says in a husky voice, and takes the younger woman by the hand and drew her inside.

Frankie looked around in a quick glance. Saw they were alone.

Door was shut…the bed unmade. And the woman is standing right next to her…passive, and Frankie's wondering, 'Does she really want me? What should I do?' And her eyes drop to the woman's breasts, the housecoat loose over them; full, not saggy, not what they'd once been, but nice. And she wanted to take them in her strong hands, to reach out and pull the woman's hips into hers. But she had to stand her distance... 'Will she?' And Frankie then realizes the woman hasn't turned the light on, it's still dark, and she looks so damn good, gentle, standing there in her bathrobe, waiting passively, for Frankie to make some kind of move, or word, or gesture....

'She might slap me, or scream, and all these colored people in the building will be watching me run down the steps like a fool.'

And the scent of the woman, good, from her body; and the robe almost parted...and Frankie reached out and touched her face.

Frankie looked down at her, and ran her hand down Esther's face, and the woman reached out and put her hand on Frankie's neck, the back of it under her hair & a thrill swept up her nervous system, and her lips reached to Esther's...And tho she'd left the lights off, city dwellers, like birds roosted on the side of the mountain, see by lights of all the other lights from other houses & by neon outside, shining in, illuminating this room.

And Frankie was pushing her toward the bed, while experiencing her warm flesh; crushing the woman to her, running her lips along the woman's face, tugging open the robe, bruising her hands over the woman's full breasts, & Esther was hugging her even more fiercely in return, worn hands with red-painted nails clutching her & they came face-to-face, lips kissing, tasting; Frankie bent down to suck from her lips again & again & the bathrobe falling away in a heap on the floor. Frankie held the woman tight, kissing her tanned body, running both her hands over her full breasts... A woman...such a long time...eyes opened to look at what she had; then she pressed Esther back down on the bed, and they were loving; her stroking the length of Frankie's body as far as she could reach; & the butch still had her clothes on, hands wrapped around her & kissing her deeper, deeper, tongue into her mouth.

The 22-year-old was a good lover & slow. She petted the woman's breasts, squeezing the dark nipples, orally loving one, then the other. Tongue probing the recess of her lover's mouth over & over.

The clock says 1 A.M., and they've been necking all this time; now the woman's lying back on the pillows silent, not making a sound. Frankie sat on the side of the bed, pulled off her jacket and shirt, and tugs off her boots, pants; strips down to her underwear, and pulls the rings off her index & pinkie finger, and her watch, and sets them on the nightstand, and took off her underwear finally, and turns, naked, and looks down at the woman she's just held in her arms...anticipation rising, on fire. 'She couldn't want money from me; she knows I'm broke...she knows that....' Thinking in the back of her mind: 'And she's straight.'

And then Frankie says, "I got to go to the bathroom." Went in the bathroom first, before sex, because of holding her piss all that time out in the truck.... Switched on yellow lights. It's a small crummy bathroom which the woman has tried to make nice. 'Well, at least she's got a toilet in this place; it's more than I got.' The toilet is rammed up next to the sink, that's next to the tub. A shower-curtain rod—feminine things hang from it. Stockings, bras; and there's a douche bag. Pisses. After, Frankie is sneaky, she examines the douche bag—it's wet. Like it's just been used.

Naked white body, small breasts, young, filmy blonde-brown hair in her crotch and armpits, Frankie walks back across the room lit by twilight from neon, tho it's still the pit of the night.

Esther hasn't said anything. Lies back waiting for her, yellow legs parted. The butch holds her in her arms, hand goes between the woman's legs, to touch her sex, hot, parting the pubic hairs, at the same time kissing her mouth in a long, deep kiss. 'I better take her as a man; that's what she likes; she's straight.' Now Frankie's tool was back in her room down in the Tenderloin. 'Whoops! damn, I should have driven back down there while I was waiting & got it so to be prepared.'

Cupping her breasts in the other hand, Frankie's sucking the nipples. The woman's got her eyes closed. Frankie's sexing her with her fingers. One finger, resistance, then pushes in. "You want me inside of you, baby?" Then two fingers. Meanwhile, she's sucking each nipple alternately; then she pulls out, and three fingers push back into Esther's pussy; and the woman's moaning, veins stand out in her neck, turning her head from side to side, and, thrusting her fingers deeper inside, Frankie feels the grainy IUD device up in her cunt that women use for birth control; and pushing her strong fingers in and out of her wet hole, sucking Esther's lips, touching her everywhere, loving her. 'I don't have my tool with me, damn it, which she probably craves right about now.' And the woman is moaning, her full breasts rising & falling, her back arching. 'If she wants it, fingers will have to do.' Probing that hot slippery cavity. Bed moving with them up & down & up & down; & Frankie enjoying it immensely.

"You like me inside you, baby?" And Frankie pushes in again with four fingers. 'With straight women, you have to prove you can do it.'

And Esther reaches down, touches her hand and says, "Be gentle, baby." Then Frankie knew she didn't want her like a man at all; she pulls her hand out. "Baby, love me." Esther says in a little voice; & opens her eyes to look at the butch who realizes: 'She wants me to take her in a more womanly way.'

"I cleaned up for you baby, real good." Esther says, embarrassed, looks away. And Frankie, gazing down at her, knows what she means.

So she did, she did.

Went down on her. Esther reaches down for Frankie's hand, takes it, squeezing it...and the taste of her cunt strong like an older woman & good, and it was like nobody else had been there before, a clean odor smelling like woman from juices deep inside that Frankie had worked out of her. Frankie's down there, hands moving back the pubic hairs, kinky, tight curls with her white fingers & thinking: 'This colored woman is old enough to be my mother, & she still looks damn good.'

Esther moaned. Frankie stayed, lips on her cunt sucking her clit, licking her tongue up & down on it, then finally using her fingers right inside the wet canal while sucking her clit too & after a long while it seemed Esther was just finally warming up to it as she reached down and grabbed Frankie's hair, pulling it & her back arched, but nothing happened. And Frankie's thinking: 'Why is it taking her so long to bust a nut?' She works Esther over steadily. And her mind is starting to wander & the sex act has become mechanical because of taking so long; drinking, licking, & sucking & pushing her fingers in and out of Esther's pussyhole. 'It's embarrassing...if my friends could see me now with this colored woman who's old enough to be my mother & if she was to see me on the street in the light of day with her straight friends, she'd be too embarrassed to speak to me.' And finally she stops. Reaches up both hands liquid wet, face wet from cunt & strokes the woman's thighs, raising her head up. 'She ain't gonna get a nut. It's been an hour & I'm exhausted.' And the clock said 3 A.M.

Frankie raised herself up on her elbows, climbed up next to her, and asked, "You already came earlier?" But the woman said nothing; she just shook her head back and forth. Sad, ironic smile on her lips.

So Frankie had tried to satisfy this woman, and she had to have it now herself. And she pushes her legs apart; the woman is going to let her screw her. Frankie rises up on top, spreads back the woman's thighs to take her. As Frankie moves on top of her, she can tell she's never been with a butch before—she has to show her how to put the pillow under her butt so to get her cunt right up where she wants it; has to tell her to hike her legs up a little more to accommodate her, so she can press her wet sex & clit up against the woman's cunt.

And she's breathing hard, and starts to fuck.

Frankie knows she's going to cum quickly, from wanting a woman all the month she's been here, and from all the playing and touching that's just gone on. She always satisfies a woman, a lot of times this way too, cunt-to-cunt climaxing at the same time & she has to have it now herself, regardless.

Pumping faster, harder. And from beneath her Esther whispers, "Take your time, baby. Make it last." And Frankie moans & keeps on fast, wants to so bad she can't help it. Has her head tucked down on the side of the woman's face lying on her, but when she got ready to climax, it was so hot & good, she raises up on her arms, hands on each side, pumping; Esther's arms wrapped around her ass, caressing her making it good to her, really sweet. Sweat rolls off Frankie's back; keeps fucking hard.

"I'm gonna give you my love, baby. It's cumming, baby, Uh uh. I'm gonna give it to you, uh uh uh." Deep voice filled with passion groaning from her guts & tho Frankie was trying to be quiet because of next-door neighbors behind paper-thin walls, from her guts it escaped: "UHHHHAHHHHAAAAAAAAAAAAAA-AAAAHH!" As she felt the cum just pouring out of her. Out of her sex, out of her soul, out of every fiber of her physical anatomy. And collapsed back onto the woman, still pressing her sex hard up against the woman's cunt, and the woman holding her so tight, then rolled off to the side, their arms still around each other and wet discharge on their legs mingled.

Apartment building was quiet, near morning. Soon in

a few hours would run with the yelling of children; people, too many crowded together in their multicolor cells.

Daylight breaks in the window.

"I know you're unhappy," Frankie told her. Her pounding heart had evened out its beat a long while back; & so relaxed from getting to fuck.

Lay there side by side, and talked. "I know you're sad." Frankie told Esther. And the woman caught her breath. Suddenly her fingers took Frankie's, clenched around those white ones, and Frankie turns to look at her face, and a tear, a single liquid tear on her worn cheeks; she's crying silently. Frankie sits up. "It was stupid of me to say that. I just wanted to tell you I know how you feel." And the woman held onto the butch's hand tight, and don't say nothing. But puts her hand around Frankie's head, and pulls her down on top of her & puts her mouth on Frankie's, seeks into it with her tongue. Esther lies there, the sheets over her knees, holds her a long, long time, Frankie just basking in the sensation. Starts thinking about this woman whom she'd just ridden, who let her cum, who pleased her. 'Everybody's getting on her & getting a nut & getting off & she's not getting nowhere, not even to cum herself.'

So she slides down her body one last time, for one last try, moving aside the sheets, spreading Esther's kinky pubic hair with her fingers, strong; her tongue seeking her vagina, puts her head down there & goes down on her again, loving her again. 'My mouth is tired, & my tongue is numb, but I won't stop.' Cupping her bottom with her hand, and caressing her thighs, one hand reaching up to squeeze the nipples on her breasts, twisting them hard, fingering her pussyhole, then licking it, then fucking it. 'Doing everything I can think of.' Putting all the soul she knew how into it.

Sun is rising fast.

Then Frankie has an idea. "I'll get her to talk.' She strokes the outside of Esther's cunt, then plunges her fingers in hard. "Baby, I'm in you; I'm inside you. Do you feel my fingers in you? Do you feel it?"

"I feel it, baby...ohhh!" Esther breathes.

Frankie's fingers come out, & strokes her clit, working her hand, alternately sucking & biting the nipples of each breast, rubbing the clit up and down, holding her tight with her other arm, & the bed's bouncing.

Rubs her cunt. "Give it to me, baby. Tell me you want it."

"Uhhh, I want it."

And puts her fingers in hard. 'You're so pretty, baby, you're so good. You made me cum so good; let me give it to you now." And she pulls her fingers out and runs them over her clit & plunges them in again, mashing the palm of her hand against her clit; 4 fingers in. And Esther's pulling Frankie's hair by the roots. "I'm taking you baby, I'm taking you. Do you want it, baby?"

"Yes I want it, sweet baby. Give it to me, honey. Don't stop. Fuck me, baby, fuck me." Esther's arching her back and trembling & hips thrusting up & Frankie's fingers sliding out wet, sticky, rubs her cunt on the outside, stroking & then strokes her fingers back into her vagina, wet and full & ripe.

"Do it to me, do it to me, baby."

Frankie goes down and her tongue licks the clit & their bodies sweating, and then she felt it, waves of Esther's vagina, contracting, tightening on her fingers as she cums. Esther's pulling Frankie's hair, crying with release, sweat runs down her face, and her stomach & chest heaving and raising up so her butt comes off the bed, her back arched as she's orgasming.

Esther has cum. Cum so good. Cum hard. Cum sweet.

And the women held each other mightily, for an eternity.

Daylight's fire addresses the window.

Sun streaks boxes piled in a kitchen with dishes not done. A suitcase half-packed on a closet floor. Esther was leaving town; it was just a one-night stand. Would be a memory soon.

They'd both been despised, and they'd both been to the ends of the earth.

Frankie's first woman-memory here.

A pleasure recall of hot cum in an anonymous night —one filled with action and danger & risk, and good sweet cunt leading her on and on thru a star-filled night; something to remember in an old album of photo-memories.

Yes, she sucked sweet nectar from a passion fruit.

Like I say, it was those days when Frankie was still single. Those days between old loves & new loves yet to be.

DO THE SLANG, SLANG, YES!
Chapter One

"What do you get when you cross a Chinaman with a nigger?"
"A Nigganese."
—Old ghetto humor

Little is known about Chinese to non-Orientals. They are pictured working in Chinese laundries from sunup to sundown; even the children shelling peas in family restaurants; and mopping floors in the ever-present Chinese grocery.

Melody was a special individual.

Wilson was her last name.

The slant-eyed beauty walked thru San Francisco's Chinatown. Past a sign in crooked letters in a laundromat which said: WASHEY MACHINE 25¢. Behind the counter a Chinese daughter counted out boxes of dimes and nickels.

Farther down the block, Melody walked into her favorite restaurant, paid a dollar for some pork buns and green tea in a metal pot & china cup; selected a table and sat down with a satchel of books beside her. She stared out the window at the moving pageant of Asian people who thronged the narrow sidewalks of Grant Street. The restaurant had tile floors, a few tables, & a counter. Populated by Orientals. She alone was different. Slanted eyes, high cheekbones in a brown face.

'Here in Chinatown are no memories from my youth; but of my mother's people. I have heard tales of the sweatshop labor, the sewing factories in which Asian women work 16 hours a day for $2 per hour—far less than the American minimum wage. There are glimpses of this culture impressed on my mind thru my mother's telling, not of my own eyes, or experience.'

She sat watching the street thru the steam foggy window munching the sweet hot dough until the liquid syrup inside with chunks of pork met her lips.

Tiny room, turquoise-blue walls. Milk crates on the floor substitute as shelves. Teacups & a matching ceramic teapot with Mandarin characters on its round sides. A shelf full of textbooks. A radio. Stereo music machine and popular song albums.

Melody Wilson masturbated that morning. It gave her a relaxed feeling. A sense of relief. It also unclogged the drain of her soul. After the cum, she'd cried. Was it lonesomeness? Was it joy at being free? Her mind was on a fast track, spinning like a record at the wrong speed. —She didn't know. She dressed—hurriedly. Her class at the university was at 9. There was no time to think; that was lucky. This morning exercise paid off later; for she would feel more self-centered; the feeling of owning herself, and not bits and fragments stretched from here and there between her paranoias, & worries of what others thought of her. Her self-consciousness in a crowd. Giving herself bodily pleasure was an investment in power. No longer at the mercy of waiting for another human being to come along to have sex with, she could jerk off when and how she pleased.

The 24-year-old woman moved rapidly thru her tiny room. Stockings, a sleeveless blouse, sandals, skirt & sweater combination.

Her face was the color of brown chocolate; eyes like almonds, 5 shades darker than the yellow people of her mother's lineage.

Her life had many compartments, like a pomegranate.

Melody Wilson had tried to explain herself to others upon numerous occasions. "If one parent is a particular race, and a child is raised with them, assimilating their unique culture & language—in this case, Chinese—they don't just suddenly, at age 15, go off saying they're black; —no, you carry that first elementary shit around with you." And, upon other occasions commented, "It is hell enduring the constant rejection for something you are but don't look like; over and over. I look black to some black people, but it is the Chinese that I am in my spirit. I speak Cantonese; I know the customs, learned from my mother, but I'm not one of them."

At this time, it was apparent that Melody was having a fast life. Running & running. No one knew if it was to be a quick life—burnt out fast & hard like a Chinese firecracker, or was she to endure for passing generations to make her acquaintance and pass the test of time. One fact was certain: she lived fast.

'I have felt rejection too much during my childhood. Now I am a lesbian. Among women I feel accepted. Wanted. But am afraid of it.'

School, job, a very few friends, very many sex partners; thus she turned the time clock of her days.

'I've been told I have a speeded-up personality. I have no resting place. No home among Chinese, & I feel alien among blacks. They are the opposite of Chinese in behavior.'

Melody slowly settled among the nomadic woman-oriented society of lesbians in the gay bars, groups, and parties of the 1970s. Females like herself of the same age, with no roots, traveling among the hazards of life with a succession of partners down life's stream, stopping to clutch each other like an island in a torrent of time & events. She spent her sexual energy.

'I have carried around this burden in my soul from day 1. My psyche, my biological body are stitched together from two pieces of fabric: yellow silk and black ebony. —It has kept me running since.'

There is a Dance of Life. Some of us don't get to participate. Others dance at a frantic pace. Such was she.

Door to the blue room slammed shut.

Melody Wilson's days passed in a flurry. Fast pace. Too fast to think or be herself.

DO THE SLANG, SLANG, YES!
Chapter Two

It was hard to piece a story together from the few women who knew her. Bits & pieces of a puzzle. Like a butterfly, she passed thru their lives.

Melody was half-Chinese & half-black & looked neither. Appeared to be a native of some South Seas island. Or a Filipina. Her mother's father had practiced kung fu in the basement of his house in the outer Richmond district; he was 70 years old. As a girl, she'd seen her grandfather only once. The Chinese side of the family had disowned them. Her father was Mr. Wilson, & they had his last name.

Neither the black man nor his yellow wife had known what they were getting into when they brought this baby into the world.

African hair, enough kink to it so it stood up on her head; jet-black in color and very luxuriant. It grew down her back very, very fast, not like slower-growing Afro hair.

Evening.

An off-night at the club. Wednesday.

Two black sisters talking, sit in a booth, laugh: "I'm hot! The next nigga who come in here, I'm gonna grab her & fuck her!"

The other, eyeing a figure who has just breezed in the door replies, "Suppose it's a Chinese?"

"Then I'll do the slang slang!"

Melody made one of her occasional visits to lesbianland. That night she made the acquaintance of the black woman, very much a lady. Feminine style. She left early, and Melody lingered in the club. Had been on the run all day; still wearing the same stockings, panties, bra, sweater & skirt. The tavern was nearly empty by 1 A.M. But she didn't leave. Sat sipping one of many drinks. Jukebox gold & blue played its tunes. An older woman had stood at the pinball machine playing for nearly 5 hours straight. She wore a black leather coat, trousers. Her hair was short. Most evenings she could be found here—her name was Sonny. She'd shot the first silver ball up the tunnel around 8 P.M., and at 2 A.M. when they turned up the houselights, she'd shoot the last.

When Sonny came over and introduced herself, she could see at once that Melody was a flirt. The older dyke slid into the booth; the skin of her white face was wrinkled, her eyes held a softness to them; bleary, blue, gazed across the table at the pretty young femme. There was a glint down deep in Melody's brown eyes that beckoned to women and made them want to follow her.

They talked.

The dyke was flattered by the attention Melody showed her. She was polite. She was caring—or seemed to be.

Sonny bent over the table. "You afraid I'm gonna screw you or something? I mean, you wanna screw or something like that? I just want to be your friend. If you wanna screw, that's fine. Anything goes!" the older dyke said. "I had 2 beers and this." She pointed to her glass; it was vodka. Melody smiled, her slanted eyes closed a second. She herself had had nearly 8 drinks. It didn't show. She carried her liquor well.

The two exchanged phone numbers, Melody hastily jammed Sonny's into her purse and it was immediately lost there amid tissue paper, lipsticks, eyeliner sticks, & mascara compacts; and a string of pearls, which she had decided was too much in addition to the other adornments she wore, and had removed & thrown into her purse. Then she fluttered out into the night; red lights of her car fled into the distance.

Sonny went back to the pinball machine. Fifteen minutes till closing. The starkly beautiful woman was etched strongly into her memory; her chest felt funny. Her nostrils quivered, her fingers pinched the knob and a silver ball shot up the tube and slowly fell down, down, winding its way amid the colorful lights and mazes.

A woman nearer Sonny's age came up, stood beside her, and watched the game as she spoke. "I hear she's a hooker, that gal. A hooker for women." Sonny stopped, hand in midair, and turned her head to gaze at her friend; a smile spread over her face, then she turned and went back to the game. "Ha, ha. It might look good, kid, but watch out. She'll go to bed with you, but she wants something for it." The woman made her cutting remark.

"I got her phone number; she didn't write no price tag next to it," Sonny said defensively.

"She's bad news—that's what I hear."

Sonny replied, "I did a lot of shit when I was young, too, but it didn't go nowhere. If you're poor, you gotta do something."

Sonny dealt dope for a living, when she wasn't parking cars in a lot on Broadway. Another silver ball went up the tube, then bounced down from light to light, blinking scores. Soon the two dykes were laughing at something else.

Melody was a femme who also preferred femme women.

The next afternoon, she went by the house of the black sister that she'd met last night in the bar. She wore high heels, quite the lady in a blouse and pleated skirt. Her hair done—relaxed and straightened with a hot comb; books under her arms. She was between classes on a busy schedule; had had only 4 hours' sleep.

Parked her car in the street of a sunny Oakland neighborhood. Consulting a piece of paper with the address, she went up the steps & stood at the door ringing the buzzer.

Janice let her into her apartment; a front bedroom one story above. In it was a brass bed, a colorful rug, cabinets. Cozy.

Janice was pretty. She stripped out of her clothes quickly—they had only 45 minutes before Melody had to be back in school. Short pubic hairs covered her genitals. Full breasts, round; taut, hard nipples. Melody undressed. The skin under her undergarments was yellowish brown, lighter than her face and hands, for she often was in the sun. She placed her clothes on the dresser. Curvaceous; walked to the bed. The two women held each other and lay back on the sheets. Expectant, Melody lay beside her. The two explored each other's pussies with their hands. The dazzling rings on Janice's fingers soon glistened wet with juice. She parted Melody's kinky jet-black pubic hair and folds of the lips of her labia to find that secret sensual spot. Melody reached down and began to stroke her partner's cunt with her fingers. Janice's dark brown thighs spread wider; she encircled Melody's body gently and drew her to her. "OHHHHHH!" she exclaimed, her full lips opened; teeth gritted, her tongue flicked out for a second, eyes closed in ecstasy. It had been a long time. The bed began to rock. They loved each other with fingers and tongues. Then, they took turns, one rolling atop the other. Thighs interlocking, they humped each other. They rolled & rocked. Finally Janice's feminine hand began working between her thighs until Melody's hips thrust forward involuntarily, it was so good; brought to a fire-hot climax.

Forty-five minutes later, Melody exited, breathless. Her brown face flushed under newly applied makeup. Slant eyes arched with fresh eyebrow pencil. Off again on her busy schedule, she walked down the street to her car; a slight smile twitching at the corners of her mouth.

Once a relative on the black side of her family confronted Melody and said, "My uncle told me you and that Janice Watkins girl who lives over there on Sacramento Street are lovers."

"How does *he* know? Was he in my bedroom?" Melody replied calmly.

And the butch in the black leather jacket fed many dimes into the pay telephone of the club. One dime many times over that is. —The phone on its stand in the turquoise room rang & rang. The room was neat. Its occupant was seldom home.

DO THE SLANG, SLANG, YES!
Chapter Three

All this was at the time when Melody was working her way thru college.

She went thru the bars, the streets, the university, to & from her jobs in an office, and at a grocery store; with books under her arm.

She slept maybe 4 hours per night.

Had much sex, but never got close to anybody.

Melody realized she could control people thru her body, but was too busy even for this.

Where was she going in such a hurry?

What goal was she chasing? —This elusive butterfly who was a goal in herself to the many lesbians who desired her? Had no goal. —She was running…running.

Chinatown.

A tea & pastry shop filled with Asians. Mostly youth, lounging on plastic chairs; clean-cut, yellow skin—fair; black hair in traditional cut; long for girls, down the back; bowl cuts for the boys. Melody sat amid them, identical slanted eyes; her black hair in tight curls of Africa down to her shoulders. Her physique the same as an Asian, shape of her arms & legs rounded; torso longer than African or Caucasian, but her skin, brown. She spoke Chinese as well as they did, from years of conversing with Mrs. Lu Wilson, her mother. The well-dressed woman in lady slacks and sweater to match sat at tea, a cookie in one hand; a patient expression on her face, inherited from a lineage of people enduring eternally.

As the restaurant bustled with the comings and goings of the students, Melody thought about the few others she'd known like herself. They'd met down life's corridors.

'There was Yolanda. She turned out very fair, almond eyes, the same as mine, but tall. Too tall to be Chinese, 5'9". Her black parent was very fair-skinned. Then Bobby. He was white, but with slanted eyes. His mother was white, his father Chinese. He was like any other white boy except for his Oriental eyes—and his eyebrows arched up in little slants. People couldn't figure him out. Was he a white person who accidentally resembled a Chinese? When they joked about it, if he explained himself, suddenly his white buddies at work would realize they weren't talking to a white person like themselves at all, but somebody half-Chinese. Half an alien race, and they didn't understand it. And it made them uncomfortable. Melody chuckled to herself.

Teacups clattered against the plastic tables. Low, the drone of Chinese dialects hummed in the air. She understood. It was her language; but those around her did not know she understood. They did not know she was one of them. It's funny, sitting in a crowd, hearing people talk about you, making remarks about the clothes you're wearing, your hair, or the books you're carrying—in a foreign language, thinking they are hidden by the language barrier;—and knowing just what they are saying.

There is much mixing of the black & white races; their products are considered black. (Brown in complexion.) But much less mixing of Asian & white, or Asian & black. Products of these liaisons during the war, born in Asian lands, left behind by soldier fathers, are disowned by their people. Few are born here. They are beautiful. Some are confused. They are rare. There are such people as Afro-Asians. Aryan-Asians; but far between, thus we have little unity. No mutual support.

The Asian side is part of their heritage they are not able to express, for the Chinese/Japanese/Pacific Rim community is notorious for excluding those not purely of their race. Among blacks, these half-black sisters & brothers are taken in more readily; but if a person has been raised by her Oriental parent and identifies more closely with that bond, outside her home & memories is a vast community of Asians to whom she cannot relate because they won't accept her. Tho she speaks the language, knows the customs, had inherited thru the genes some of the temperament of an Asian; either thru the blood, or thru environment by constant contact with that parent & aunts & uncles & nieces & nephews—if she's lucky—during her formative years of childhood thru adolescence; still, her visible features & skin color &, probably, her lack of "family," being partially disowned, divides her from "her people." Mother & daughter are close, loving, and accepting of one another; but the huge society of Asians disowns its own. Is embarrassed by these children, tho she speaks fluent Mandarin and lifts the rice cup.

This unique breed of people—product of the mixture of races is the wave of the future.

Melody Wilson had inscrutable eyes beaming thru their slanted folds. Held herself quite properly. The brown woman had driven upon occasion thru the suburbs in which was a heavy Asian concentration. She saw the Chinese with their clean-cut lives. Out in their front yards, tending to lawns, cutting the grass & hedges. Their neat houses with wind-chimes and potted plants. The Chinese youth on their way home from high school, and band practice, and scout-troop meetings. She knew their strict attention to community approval; how important it was what others thought of them, and respect for their family. Above all, not to bring disgrace to the family. Nor to be startlingly different. In such a community, no wonder anyone like herself stood out. There was no place for her in Chinese culture with her full lips, brown skin, her tightly curled hair. She was ostracized. She was nothing.

Melody had been raised back in the 1950s when mixed-marriages were even more taboo in AmeriKKKa due to its racist policies. The black side of her family had frowned upon her father for getting a slang-slang wife. Disliked by that side of the family. But it was into black culture, and white, that she would blend. The Asian world of her mother remained inaccessible. And thus was planted the seed of sadness. It was that in her heart which she longed to be most—the blood of the mother who had raised her.

Next evening, the neat blue room held two occupants. —And Melody took her phone off its hook.

Tonight it was Faye, a friend from the university.

At home in her own bed sex was complete.

Toys—3 dildos. And accessories. One ancient type made of hard plastic, 5" and slender in diameter having a strap to tie around the waist; another of soft rubber complete with a harness which wrapped around the body with straps around each thigh to hold it snugly in place. The last toy was a vibrator. Lubricant—including strawberry jelly in a jar, which might be licked off her partner's body in a delicious sensual play, once intercourse was finished. Plus magazines full of naked women which Melody had purchased from a dirty bookstore; plus a not-too-complete lesbian sex manual.

They lay down on the bed. Setting was perfect. Large mattress. As a backdrop, soft music. Heat was turned on so they could play naked on top of the covers without getting cold.

Faye lifted her sweater off over her head, as Melody's brown fingers helped undo her bra. Her tits were large. Stripped off her panties, one slender smooth leg, then the next, stepping out of the silk sheath; as a warm female aroma filled the air. Melody lay back on the blue quilt & spread her legs; cunt hot and inviting. Faye lay down upon her, between her sleek thighs. Equally handsome as pretty, she had removed the rings from her fingers, setting them on the nightstand. Her probe was strong, examining the pussyfolds. She touched Melody's sex firmly, hands stroked the hair around Melody's outer lips, wrinkled skin blackened at the edge and pink inside like the folds of a flower, until she found her clit. Her two hands stretched the skin aside, then she put her face down on Melody's pussy and began to stroke the clit with her tongue, licking, while alternately sucking, drawing it out with little sucks, embracing it with her lips. Took her time. Used care. Soon the brown woman moved on the bed, moaning.

The two women locked in an embrace, Faye having slid back up to shower Melody with kisses tasting of her own cunt. Tongues probed each other's mouth. Soon her fingers were going in and out of Melody's vagina. Melody's hips thrust forward slowly, then back steadily as Faye penetrated her with her index & 3rd fingers with growing momentum, like a train chugging. A hot stream of lust coursing toward a climax.

They held each other fierce until their rapid breathing subsided.

Melody desired to take Faye now. She reached to the nightstand, opened the jar of strawberry lubricant, scooped some out on her fingers, slid it down the dildo; warming it. With shy smiles, Faye helped her into harness.

The black leather harness had silver studs—quite

butch. Very erotic. The woman helped fasten the straps around her thighs. Soon the toy stuck out of her crotch—7"; its base pressed firmly against Melody's clit. As Faye lay back on the bed, spreading her legs to be taken, Melody knelt above her; a masculine feeling empowered Melody. Her sleek brown skin beaded with perspiration, she mounted. On top, her ripe breasts pressed down against her her lover's breasts. As her cock entered the hairy hole of Faye's vagina, a thrill of passion licked hot thru her clit. Faye's thighs surrendered to her thrust; Melody pressed the cock in. Slowly plunging into her lover; soon the motion grew rapid, her naked butt thrust up & down in air. And the woman beneath her moaned, her painted fingernails clawed Melody's back, cumming.

Eating the strawberry jelly off in a romantic interlude together—from their thighs, cunts, faces, & hands with feathery licks, was a satisfying conclusion to the evening.

She lived at a fast clip.

"NO! NO!" her mother had cried in Chinese when she had caught her daughter with her chubby child hand inside her panties playing with herself. The parent was unable to speak English, so Melody had grown up bilingual.

Now, as an adult, she had a high sex drive, perhaps to relieve the extra burden of tension she felt.

Born of 2 races. Speaking 2 languages & having few others like herself to share them with. Leading the dual life of a lesbian somewhat in the closet.

Sex, often repeated with many partners.

Not joyous, but almost as if required. Mandatory.

Melody indulged herself in lesbian fuck books. Knew no better release than a good solid fuck.

Something in her uneasy life patterns fueled her sexual energy. While her normal sexual impulses built up several times per week, and experienced a cyclonic rise—hormonally, at certain times of the month in which she might have a lot of sex for a week, then none for days later; still an added, overall push of sexual need was added on to these basics. Her uneasy situation in life left her on the cutting edge of a constant ever-changing sexual well from which she drew many exploits.

Often she was afraid of what abyss her sexual energies might plunge her into next.

Whatever it was she carried around in her brain, it was in her panties as well.

Melody had started making self-love (putting on a masturbatory show for herself using her mother's lace lingerie in front of the mirror) when she was very young. Putting objects between her legs. Her first sexual experience with another person was as a child with other girls her age, examining each other's hairless sex parts with their dirty little fingers. Her first intercourse was as a teen with a teenage lesbian.

In her teenage years she had used a carrot for a dildo, or a hot dog, shoving it in and out of her.

Melody enjoyed sex and came quickly.

She went to see pornographic movies sometimes, and read sex books to see if there was some position she hadn't tried yet.

Tonight the blue room had only one occupant.

The young woman lay, back flat on the bed, knees

spread, her hands working the vibrator whose low hum emanated, & which drained the electric current in the old house & made her lights flicker whenever switched off or on.

Now, mature, she had prepared herself for her needs. Far from the haphazard spur-of-the moment implements used for lust in her teen years, she now had a collection of feathers, tit clips, oils, lubes, photos, restraint ropes, lace nighties, & dicks.

Selected one of the rubber sex aids; she penetrated herself with it, guided the dildo into her vagina while fantasizing being seduced by a woman lover who would rip off her blouse, so the buttons popped off, to expose her breasts and then greedily stimulate them, sucking, licking, & squeezing. Melody lay on the blue bedspread; put the rubber object in until its shaft was all the way inside her. Pushed it in and out a while. Then set it down on the sheet. Next she reached out, took the vibrator again, which she had put aside, and played with her nipples with one hand while moving the vibrating long object between her legs over her clit. Built herself up to the high plateau. A rush of energy pulsating, rolling out, as if from a volcano within her body. At last, ready, picked up the mucus-wet rubber cock & slid it firmly into her cunt and began to fuck herself with it, while with the other hand used the vibrator humming & buzzing against her clit; working the two toys together for an intense orgasm—followed by a second orgasm. So hot, still bursting with cum, she continued to hump on the bed, pressed her discharge- & lube-soaked thighs together, uttering a low moan, mouth open wide, spine arched,—she tried to reach a climax still another time; to enjoy rapture as long as possible, to savor it, until she couldn't empty herself any longer; and, the reward, her wet flower burst forth in cum; ecstasy. Nostrils open, heart beating fast in her chest; lips gulping for air.

In the blue room, she masturbated alone. Sometimes tears accompanied this, in her isolation. A mixture of freedom of emotional release & sadness that there was no partner to share her physical joy.

DO THE SLANG, SLANG, YES!
Chapter Four

The tubes to the heater of her car were busted. The windshield was cracked; it was cold driving. Melody came into the club, her brown skin cold to the touch.

Tonight this startlingly pretty woman wore a tweed suit; skirt & jacket; a scarf fluttered at her neck. Chinese face framed with African curls.

Women walked to and fro. Red room. Bar 40 feet long against one wall. A fireplace with artificial logs; chairs facing it. Some booths.

Soon she got up and began to dance alone. It looked good. Melody had style.

The patrons of the bar saw a beautiful female, so instead of taking a quick shortcut to the ladies' bathroom, many went the long way 'round, so they could get a better view of Melody.

When would she find a woman to give her the love she needed & not imprison her?

Red-lit. Photos in glass frames on the wall. Women in T-shirts, cues in their hands, shot pool.

A woman yelling in a loud voice which wasn't hers, letting off aggression from the world. Finally she'd found a free space to vent it.

Jukebox played one song after another. Three-minute-long tunes.

When the sister had first gone to gay clubs, on occasion straight men there had harassed her. She had been surprised that no dykes around her had stood up and fought for her. Not enough loyalty among gay women. Melody didn't like the bars that much; she thought it brought out the worst in people instead of the best—like that drunk woman yelling now. She preferred to meet women at the university or in a social group centered around a specific activity, such as dance lessons.

Melody was not very aggressive.

Her father, an ebony-colored black man; burly and worldly-wise once stated, "Men come up and mess with Melody on the street; she won't tell them to go to hell, she won't do nothing but smile and be polite. She gets that from her mother; that's how the Chinese do. But you can't be that way over here. She gets a lot of stuff from her mother's side. My family won't have nothing to do with me or my ex-wife. It split the family apart. Melody's the spittin' image of her mother. But darker and come out with worse hair. She's pretty now, but her face will fall early. Chinese women's faces crack; they lose their looks in middle age."

A tall woman approached.

Marcia wore a striped shirt, blue jeans; a knife was strapped to her right hip. Was tall, blonde. Hair curly & short. The knife at her side was no joke, she'd whip it out and use it in a minute. The sight of that knife being waved in their direction quieted the most loudmouthed enemies.

"Can I buy you a drink? What's your name?"

The feminine creature perched on the bar stool answered politely. Inevitably, one of the first questions in their conversation was, "What nationality are you?"

"I'm Afro-Asian." Melody replied in a melodic tone.

Melody appraised Marcia quietly, with a masked expression as if her face were a veil. She had been raised by her mother to be polite, to be accommodating. —In China this was only etiquette, no more. But these actions were misinterpreted by Western culture, and many women were amazed after receiving such good treatment from Melody to find the coldness underneath.

They should know better than to chase an elusive butterfly.

You have to sit and let a butterfly come to you and sit upon you and rejoice for its short season of beauty!

Melody sat now in the booth.

She put Marcia's phone number in her purse—promptly lost it.

When people passed by the booth, they responded to her beauty; smiled at her, spoke even if they didn't know her. Inside, Melody was not beautiful, & eventually, when her patience wore out, when she was tired of smiling and nodding her head & being polite, she would become unpleasant. Melody had learned early how to use her good looks for opportunity; yet it was not money or success which truly were her goals—she wasn't sure what she wanted nor who she was.

As she grew older, the world would begin to pass her by and no longer speak. She would have more freedom just to be. To be left alone. To be herself and not put up on a pedestal and worshiped for only her surface looks. Free. And not twisted this way and that by the expectations of others. The world no longer wishes to possess a woman with a cracked face. Her beauty would fall. And then Melody would have the option to reach out to the world, by speaking wisdom, by actions; or, to sit quietly, unmolested, and observe.

Red lights streaked the booth. The evening of their second date, Marcia bought her drinks.

Melody anesthetized herself with alcohol.

Pillbox hat, skirt, & sweater in pink. This woman sat, drank 10 vodkas & orange juice and didn't even get drunk.

Marcia told a buddy later; "You realize how much that woman's costing me? I might as well bring 2 fifths over and set them in front of her. Instead of going out to a bar and drinking, we could stay at home and save all that money!"

A week later, Marcia told her buddy, "Melody's got problems."

"She's a beautiful woman; she's probably spoiled."

"I don't know what's wrong." Marcia sounded sad.

Melody's unhappiness was catching. And thus her private blues became the blues of the world.

Later, Marcia had taken the knife out of the sheath on

her side, pressed the steel tip to her own throat, contemplating suicide; alternately, begging Melody for her touch. For the sex again, hot, like it was in the beginning, hot stuff that made her feel real butch, or like a real man, like she had power in the world;—and the love, too. The couple cuddliness. —She had thought emotion was behind it, but was wrong. Melody had offered her nothing of her emotions, only her body, and her intellect in pleasing conversations. Under it she was cool, appraising her situation. The tall woman was physically strong. She had a knife. She held a job. She was smart. But she was weak with beautiful women and crawled on her knees.

"Please don't beg," Melody told her.

The woman couldn't help herself. She'd give all for the rape of her touch. Melody sat, independent, feet propped up on a chair, uncommunicative, stern,—like a soldier in the Red Army. Marcia talked and begged and tugged on her sleeve: "Come on, baby, let's go to bed. *Please!*" But Melody sat like a little emperor; would give nothing, would say nothing.

She was a butterfly flying off in zigzags. To those involved with her, it was painful when she'd break off the relationship abruptly to go flitting off.

Actually, Melody was running down blind alleys & bumping into locked doors. Was losing more than she gained by not trying to hold friends or make a solid relationship.

She had a variety of jobs. In an office; as a night clerk in a grocery store; was a go-go dancer; a cocktail waitress in a slinky gown.

One love affair after another had a bitter end. Thru the flurry of years of romances, it was becoming apparent that the feminine Melody wanted a woman as feminine as herself. She spoke of that lady, Marcia, who had passed into the background of her fast days: "She's a super butch in bed. It's awful. She wants to play this stud role. Gets on top, throws my legs back, jams her clit in my pussy & fucks. Doesn't do anything for me. She thinks the rougher she is, the stronger it makes her."

Another troubling incident occurred within this blue-grey passage of time. She met a woman employed at the same office as herself who had savings & owned her own house. She gave Melody, who wasn't working full-time at the moment, $500 to help her thru a semester in school. The woman appeared to be well off, sporting a mink coat & drove a foreign-made luxury car, but in actuality had just worked for many years in the relatively average pay position & saved her money; spending it judiciously on a few showy items. In an extravagant gesture, the befurred, bejeweled lady stud claimed she didn't want it back, that it was a gift. But 2 weeks later they were no longer sleeping together, and the woman wanted Melody to pay her back.

"You told me it was a gift," Melody stated. She hated arguments. Also she didn't have any money, she was just barely paying her bills for rent, phone, books, tuition, supplies, & gasoline for the car by working two part-time jobs, the other being a cocktail waitress, which kept her up until 2 A.M.

A month later, she received a summons from the

District Attorney's office. Frightened, Melody went down to the courthouse wearing the best of her modest dresses, with matching shoes and purse. The other woman was there speaking outrageous lies about Melody's character, which didn't pertain to the case. The brown woman stood before the bench; a glimmer of fire thru her slanted eyes. The judge listened. When the woman was finally subdued, having talked herself out & presented her case, the judge turned to Melody to hear her side. She said, "The $500 was for services rendered. We were lovers—we went to bed together. I gave her body massages, cooked her meals, and accompanied her on a business trip. She was not satisfied when the arrangement terminated; now she wants her money back." Then simply shut her mouth.

The judge ruled in favor of the defendant.

One day Melody took a dog that she had acquired to the vets. It was a pocket-sized dog, tiny, which fitted in perfectly with her minuscule living quarters. Chi Chi walked proudly, plume tail in the air, into the waiting room to get her rabies shot.

The doctor was a woman.

The doctor smiled at Melody; blond hair fell to her shoulders, grey eyes twinkled; her white coat over a pleasing physique. The Doctor asked her, "would you like to go to lunch with me? Are you busy?"

"No, I have a class this afternoon. I bring my lunch."

The doctor smiled, her eyes twinkled. Both women were the same size. They stared at each other for a moment, together holding Chi Chi firmly on the silver countertop where she'd received her injections.

"Well, maybe you could bring your lunch in sometime and we can eat together."

The veterinarian aroused her. She was strong. She had an efficient manner, she didn't cling. She had strength both inside and out. She paid attention to Melody in a cool way, not overpowering. Allowing her space. Freedom. The attractive woman was flattered. She looked at the vaccination tag around Chi Chi's neck afterwards—it turned her on.

Her heart was elated.

After meeting the doctor for lunch several times, Melody became a ship sailing in drunken circles.

The woman was three years older, 33. Sandy blond hair. Like many of the privileged upper classes, this white woman had light colored hair and eyes. They went to dine in expensive restaurants. The doctor drove a Mercedes-Benz. Melody was impressed. The doctor treated her well. She was turned on by the sense of power the woman had, both financially and in skill. The doctor took her to bed. White & brown flesh meshed. Arms & legs entwined. Both women lusted for each other and gained satisfaction. The relationship lasted awhile.

Also, the woman was kind. She cared for the little animals who came to her for help on their leashes and in their portable cages.

The veterinarian wasn't ready for marriage either. So the two women were free spirits. A happy pair, seeing each other & sleeping together when they could, nights, in the luxuriant apartment the doctor leased. Both women twisted their thighs, fitting together; probing tongues thick & juicy, rolling their sex against each other's sex in wet lust; their hips thrusting to orgasm.

The next thing everybody heard, Melody was living in Marin County, across the water, the richest suburb in America. And commuted to town in a Mercedes-Benz.

DO THE SLANG, SLANG, YES!
Chapter Five

The chapters of her life opened up and folded closed.

Four years later, at 34, Melody ran into Sonny again. The butch wore the same style clothes & haircut. Lines etched deeper in her pale skin. She played pinball. She had changed little. The lithe Afro-Asian had recently broken up with her latest love, a doctor. Her mouth was solemn. Eyes reflected a nervous drain.

She had graduated from the university with a Bachelor of Arts, not certain what field she wanted to pursue. Her new apartment back over the bridge in the City was terribly small & much cheaper—emotionally—than the one she'd shared with her lover the doctor across the water. Her future was uncertain.

Melody looked across the smoky tavern at Sonny playing pinball; bleary blue eyes focusing a shot. 'I'm going to be old like that one day. Will there be someone to want me?'

When Sonny finally noticed the beautiful younger woman perched on a red vinyl bar stool, she came over. They conversed about times past & present.

Then Melody put her hand on Sonny's jacket and said, "Come on."

The old butch looked down at her a moment, somber; lower lip trembled, hands shook. "You mean... with you?"

And Melody had gotten off the bar stool, turned, and was walking out. A smile played briefly in the corners of her full lips as she looked back over her shoulder. Sonny banged down her glass on a table, sloshing the drink; threw a farewell to her pals, and followed her out of the bar.

Their first night, the 53-year-old woman came to Melody's room wearing black leathers. Hair longish, masculine. She smiled, revealing a chipped tooth; eyes glistened. Her lips were soft. They sat together on the side of the bed. The living room & bedroom were the same—one space, with a tiny bath off to one side, and a kitchen on the other. For this she paid an exorbitant $710 per month. Worth the price, for the serenity of living alone. It was summer. Melody was darker brown, tanned by the sun. Her African hair fell in curly black ringlets down her neck. She wore a blouse, toreador pants. Shapely feet now bare. The old butch; lines around her mouth spoke of the weathering of the world. Wore a man's blue shirt, sleeves rolled up showing hard & muscular forearms; grey-white skin. Trousers of black leather.

Soon the butch was laughing; talking about herself; yet pleasantly aware of the brown hand gently massaging her thigh. It felt good. Stimulation, yes, but even just plain touching, which she seldom got enough of.

'I'm going to do her a favor. A big favor. She's so old, she couldn't even beg or buy it from the girls back in the bar—I'm going to lie down and let her use me, in whatever way satisfies her. Why not?—I've been told I have a beautiful body, over and over and over again. And I do what I want with it. Because she's so old and lonely, I'm going to do it. Because I'm going to make a special evening for her in her life. I'm going to let her put her cunt in my mouth and cum. Because she's lonely and not getting it.' It was a compassionate thought.

Melody struck the woman gently, a tap between her legs. "Come on, Daddy!" She whispered with amusement. Melody knew how to get a butch hot. —It was different than with a femme.

They were behind closed doors. The studio room bathed in red lights. Blue bedspread so inviting. Soft music. A female waiting to be taken.

The old dyke was embarrassed to take off her clothes in front of women. She felt inadequate, ashamed of her body. Her T-shirt hadn't been washed. Her feet stank.

"I'm not the world's best lover," Sonny said sheepishly.

Melody playfully struck her hand against the butch's fly, hitting the black leather front right over her clit. "Come on! Don't be so shy!"

Melody's slant eyes appraised her friend a moment; then she said simply, "I want you to enjoy yourself,

Sonny. Nobody's comparing you as a lover to any other butch." And the dyke felt her stomach clench with desire, and her sex grow hot with lust. Suddenly her once-handsome face filled with longing.

"Oh, my God!" Sonny breathed. Her arms reached to encircle the slender woman's body, pulled her down; her hard fingers undid the blouse. Sonny's lips reached Melody's in a kiss as she undid the bra. Melody's cleavage spilled from the lacy cups. Squeezing her nipples with her wrinkled hands, breathing hard, Sonny bent her head and proceeded to flick her tongue in feathery touches down Melody's stomach.

For one last moment, she looked bashfully into Melody's eyes. Melody seemed to read her mind. "I want you, Sonny. I want you just the way you are, baby." Melody's soft hands took the lapels of Sonny's blue shirt and pulled her close, then ran her fingers down the butch's crotch. "Anything you want to do to me is fine. Put it where you want it."

Red lights streamed down on them in the small room. With this new feeling of power, Sonny grew red hot. Her pink skin turned prickly. Her sex knotted up. She unzipped her pants and came out of the black leathers.

"OK, Sonny, come get it." Melody whispers across the inches of space between them, eyes closed. Lay back on the pillow, arms open, inviting. "Come on, honey." She licked her fingertips and touched her breasts so the spit glistened wet on her nipples. Melody lay back, tits glistening ripe and full. A sob in her throat, Sonny came to her; it had been such a long time since she'd had a woman as beautiful as this one. So starved for hot, erotic sex!

Her boxer shorts, shirt, & pants lay in a heap on the rug. Naked white dyke flesh. Sonny reached out and cupped Melody's upper arms with her hands. Breathing hard, Melody's lips parted for Sonny's insistent tongue. Sonny pushed her farther into the bed. They embraced in a long enduring kiss.

Naked flesh of her butt, got between her legs, pressing her cunt to Melody's thigh, and Melody's cunt pressing to her leg. They rolled around, kissing.

Sonny took control, cupping Melody's luscious tits, put her lips to them and sucked the pert dark brown nipples. Melody felt the butch woman's fingers going to her pussyhole; stroking, probing thru the nest of wet curly hairs, met brief resistance, then pushed in. A bolt of sexual ecstasy raced up her. Cradling her body with one strong arm around Melody's waist, Sonny shoved her fingers in into the knuckles; bending them in her vagina, stroking her G-spot. Melody felt her heart in her throat.

Fingers came out dripping with pussyjuice & spit, removed them to stimulate the outside of her cunt, & her clit. Head buried on Melody's breasts, sucking, going from one to another, hungrily as if she was sucking milk out of them; and then again, one, two, fingers, then three, penetrated Melody, who moaned and writhed on the bed.

The woman was taking her so fine. Sonny loved her long and hard. On top, thighs locked together they rolled and humped. She changed from a pathetic old dyke into an experienced lesbian stud. Her pale old hands, slippery tongue, & hot-driving clit making pleasure.

Now the butch wanted to put it in the woman's mouth first before topping her. And she said so.

They climbed off the bed. Sonny stood on the floor, holding onto the headboard of the bed so Melody could french her. And Sonny could thrust her hips fast, hard-driving her sex into that waiting mouth without losing her balance. Melody got down on the floor before Sonny, knelt between her legs, and pressed her mouth up to the woman's crotch, fingers mixed back the pubic hairs so she could suck Sonny's cock better; and soon located her clit & began licking. It was hard. Sonny held onto the bedboard and humped. Sex wet with lust moving against Melody's face. The stink of sex filled Melody's nostrils. The forceful motions of Sonny's cunt in her mouth. The two framed in moonlight, pumping faster, faster, until she busted a nut.

Red lights. Incense burned on the bureau.

They climbed back on the bed. The old dyke wanted to get it again. "I can still cum, honey. Don't worry! I'll satisfy you. Let me get on top of you and I'll make us cum together—you know how!" Melody only smiled.

First Sonny slid down her lover's body to put her head between Melody's thighs and sucked her. One hand reached up to fondle a breast. Other fingers worked in & out of her pussy. Then pulled her fingers out, wet, and kissed the warm thighs, slender and brown. Melody moaned.

Sonny climbed back up over a stretch of sheets. Her

lover's brown arms snaked around her butch, pulling her down on top of her. With index & middle fingers, Sonny reached down between her legs, parted her pubic hair, her clit exposed. Melody hiked her legs back, spread wide so Sonny could press her clit full down on her own juicy cunt. Melody allowed one big long kiss, tongues mixing together in joy, in abandon, then turned her face away.

The old dyke fumbled about till she felt her sex touching Melody's pussy. "Is it in the right place, honey?" she whispered hoarsely. "Can you feel it, too?"

"A little lower...Ohhhuhhhh!"

And the dyke was grinding steadily. "Oh, I can feel it!" Melody arched back, her eyes closed happily.

In a while, Sonny rose up, one hand on either side of Melody; just stopped to look at what she had. Smile on her face as her eyes swept the length of her slender legs, hips, breasts, up into her smooth young face, so pretty.

"UH OH, baby, ohhhhh...." Sonny could only moan, her semi-short straggly grey hair pushed back against her head; freckled old pale back glistening with sweat. Rose up on her arms; as Melody reclined, spreading her thighs to accommodate. Sonny began to fuck her masterfully.

Dyke's wet sex in Melody's pussy pumping up/down, hips going around and around screwing her; bracing herself up on her hands, toes dug into the mattress. The bed was rocking. "Can you feel it good, baby? Are you gonna cum?"

"YES, HONEY! DON'T STOP!"

Dyke started up fast, then slowed, like an engine

chug-chug-chug, then fast bam-bam-bam in red-hot energy; prolonging the delirious moment of orgasm. Under the red lights, Sonny worked, sweat pouring off her, trying to judge their climax so it would be simultaneous; then, gazed down into her lover's face, wrapped in each other's love they headed to the peak; topping her, breathing wild in triumph, the bed shaking up & down; naked their cunts lunged fierce to orgasm; a groan emitting from the butch's throat, while Melody hollered.

After a fifteen-minute rest, Sonny reached to the nightstand drawer upon Melody's response to a question she'd asked in her mature, calm tone. The butch dyke took out a playtoy. "Is this one OK?"

"Use the flesh-colored one." Melody's slant eyes flickered closed, a smile spread over her lips.

Sonny poured lubricant from a small bottle, applied it to the toy which she strapped to her hips, and worked the gel down into Melody's cunt, and put it in her.

The old woman was so nasty, and she loved it. Talked nasty to Melody: "I'm sliding 8 inches into your pussy; it's rubbing my clit & driving me wild." As she did it to her slow & easy.

"Roll around on your stomach, baby." Sonny pants after a good series of driving fucks.

Melody lay facedown on the sheets; her ripe round ass upturned, her smooth sweat-glistening female back.

Sonny knelt, one hand snaked under Melody, over her warm brown belly, fingers searched thru woolly pubic hair to her pussylips, now so wet & big. Melody's ass began to rise up in back like a dog as Sonny rubbed;

clit contact bringing Melody to greater heights. Pushed fingers of her other hand past the round moons of her ass, into her pussyhole, & beat in & out.

Finally, when the woman was red hot, burning with desire & begging; Sonny stops, pours lube directly from the bottle onto the rigid pink cock bobbing out of her crotch; holding the tool in her fist aims it down at Melody's ripe luscious ass, and puts in into her butthole, while working her fingers in her discharge/lube-soaked cunt, to a frenzy of scorching desire.

They played with toys amid the sheets; and the slant-eyed woman demanded only that Sonny be satisfied. Oh, it was good! So good! Until 3 A.M.

When they were thru with that session, Melody's whole body was sore from being used by Sonny all night long. The dyke was the kind of lover you know you've been with afterward—all day. Melody could still feel her body rock like the sea, felt that the dyke had done something real to her.

DO THE SLANG, SLANG, YES!
Chapter Six

Melody had worked part-time jobs while finishing school. Now she had only a full-time job as a secretary. Her college degree wasn't being used. Salary was low. Just covered rent, payments on a newer car, food & clothes. Since she & the doctor had split up, her standard of living had dropped. (The doctor had picked up most of the bills & all the extras, such as trips to the Bahamas & Hawaii.) Now she had to pay for everything herself.

Sonny earned $1,000 per week some weeks. —How else could she make that kind of money but by dealing drugs? She could afford to spend $100 on a woman each and every night of the week.

Her ex-lover, who secretly still carried a torch for Sonny and wanted her back, took her aside and informed her, "Watch out for that gal you've been seeing. *Melody?* Is that her name? I know the type! She's no good.... Sonny, I know you've got some good in you; don't let nobody hurt that good in you. Just be careful of her—that's all. I've known you a long time...I've see her action before.... I'm just telling you.... When she starts stomping on your heart with those high-heeled shoes, tell me, & I'll go over to her house and kick her ass."

The days passed. Sonny dialed the phone asking could they spend an evening together? She was a generous woman; free-spending & kind. She paid Melody's telephone bill the first of that month,—It was high, with calls across the water to the doctor. Or she'd pay her car note. Melody never asked for help, but Sonny wanted to. She wished she could give more. But the Afro-Asian sister needed her independence. She wanted no strings attached. She dreaded feeling obligated. Because Sonny was kind, Melody was her lover far longer than she ordinarily would have been. Butches and how they liked it in bed just didn't turn her on anymore.

Melody said, "Yes." To anyone else, she might have said, "I won't be home this evening, sorry." And just calmly sit reading a book while the phone rang and rang panic-struck off its hook.

Sonny waited for those precious evenings of excitement. The night was dark. The house was still. She walked up the front path; sound of crickets in the grass. Went up the front steps to the row of bells of the apartments.

When Sonny got to the door, the apartment was

dark, a dim blue light shone. Melody ran back across the rug; the naked rear end and back of her shapely body dove under the covers.

Sonny guaranteed her partner's satisfaction. Faithfully would work her over. Massage her. Lick her. Fuck her. Lie down for her. —So the brown femme could mount her butch-style in an aggressive romp. Beat off her pussy with lightning strokes of their favorite purple dildo. —Whatever turned her woman on. That was a promise.

The butch dyke's heart leapt in her throat. In the privacy of the small room, she undressed while her lover waited. Sonny was in control; there was no hurry. This woman was not going to change her mind or fade away. Sonny was promised time. Time to enjoy herself. That her physical needs be fulfilled. She wouldn't be put out the back door at midnight like a stray cat. —She didn't have to leave until the next morning. She could cum as much as she was able; and could do anything she wanted with Melody.

Melody's love was for free, despite the lies of gossiping tongues. The little room was cozy. This was not a hit-or-miss liaison, but one Sonny could be sure of. And this increased her feeling of potency.

Black leather jacket over the back of a chair that sat across the room. Melody lay naked in bed under blue sheets. To the old woman, this smooth still-young body was a miracle. Coming out of her own clothes she said only, "*Yes*. Yes, baby, Yes!" Melody lay back spreading open thighs, under the blue light, and gave Sonny a treat. Drew a filmy veil over her shoulders, then opened it slowly, to expose her ripe breasts. Sonny was a hard butch. And she wanted to fuck her hard. Red hot thrills of passion bolted thru her old cunt & hairs on the back of her neck prickled and sweat rolled down her armpits. Sonny leaned over Melody and lifted the veil, groping her full tits with her lips & fingers, squeezing their ripe fruit, sucking the hard brown nipples. Pushed Melody's thighs open wider and masterfully penetrated her cunt with 3 strong fingers into that wet canal up to the last row of the knuckles of her hand, in/out, in/out, in/out in such a manner that the palm of her hand banged against Melody's clit, bang, bang, bang; while simultaneously sucking her nipples. Melody thrust her pelvis up against her lover's hand, the red-hot bolts of finger fucks pistoned inside her pussy, deeper, harder; breath forced out of her nostrils in short pants. Her body, sleek, brown, sweat-drenched rose and fell like a bucking bronco. Sonny banged her clit & penetrated her. Melody's slant eyes were closed in ecstasy.

Blue lights shone down upon the two, their hair mussed in a soulful kiss. Bed creaked as they romped about.

It was the best loving Sonny had known for years.

"This is for you, babe, the way you like it." Sonny breathed in her ear. A shiver of excitement filled Melody. Stillness hit the room. Melody's full lips shut closed tight, to restrain her joy, eyes began to bubble wickedly. —Then Sonny lay down on her back so the young woman could be dominant and top her. Melody's soft breasts hung down, nipples touched against the butch's white ones. Hot from head to toe, with arms wrapped around each other, Melody began moving her wet pussy against her partner's thigh; Sonny under her, working as a bottom. thrusting her ass upward to move her clit against Melody's brown thigh, which was locked between her legs.

Mouths open, French kissing, tongues circling as the motion of their bodies continued faster, faster, to orgasm.

Mutual sharing.

Finally, Sonny loved Melody one last time. "Get on top of me!" the young woman cried. Sonny climbed between Melody's legs, which were now stretched up in the air, spread wide; red polish glistened on her toes to match her fingertips which now ran feather touches over Sonny's back. Began to rub cunt-to-cunt. "OH FUCK! FUCK!" At the height of passion, a few more lunges until the cum was worked out of them. The evening was complete. They lay breathing hard in each other's arms. White & brown bodies wrapped together.

They lusted.

Underneath this was a kind of love—they cared what became of each other. Whenever Sonny could help Melody—when the pretty woman would allow her to —she did. And Sonny knew no night would have to be spent alone. Melody would see her, if her body was in need. Or her soul.

Sonny knew better than to press her for more than she had to offer. Didn't demand any more of a relationship, but was thankful for what she had.

This was the secret: not to demand.

So, for a period of time, Sonny had a friend whose services she could depend on.

Over the next few years, they had a relationship; seeing each other twice a week on average. Melody didn't want any more than this.

She liked Sonny, but it wasn't exactly what she was looking for.

Wanted her independence yet craved security…. Needed to be alone…yet sometimes at night, reached out across an empty bed and felt the bottom drop out of her stomach.

Finally, after several years, the old dope dealer struck up a relationship with a woman who wanted to enjoy her company 7 nights a week. This woman dragged her off to the altar. The old wedding bell day, the old ball & chain. They got married, and her involvement with Melody ended.

Thirty-seven years of age.

Melody's sex life began to slow down. Now the encounters were few, but full.

Butches & femmes floated thru space as if in a dream.

One would be in her life a few weeks before she'd move on. A day of heartbreak for the other & then it would be over. That's how it was. Melody never stayed in one place long.

Perfumed, Melody floated like a graceful butterfly thru their lives.

Her face was beautiful, & many used her for her looks to cum quickly. To enhance their status among others in the gay social world by escorting her on their arm, & realized only later, painfully, that they hadn't touched her at all. By then she was gone.

The racial conflict produced a great deal of physical energy within. To Melody it was nothing to have 2 or 3 sexual encounters per day. She danced at gay parties nonstop all night. Worked 2 jobs sometimes, 15 hours per day, and went without sleep for weeks and weeks until she'd finally collapse in a bout of the flu.

She didn't need anybody, but she used everybody. —Not with diabolic intent; just as a convenience, without thinking. Trying not to think about it…

Melody wasn't a hustler. She lived so fast, so far out on the edge, that she didn't have time to use people.

As she grew older, she began to analyze how she felt upon being treated as a sex object; of being desired for her beauty, her breasts & hips. And having to perform. Melody began to watch her actions; listen to herself respond in her programmed ways—the coquettish wink, the tinsel laugh; tried to decide was it false; a protection; or was it part of her femininity which she wanted to keep?

The world was cold and wearing on her nerves. The weather vane had shifted from south to north. It might be easier to be a man. To drop the flirting. To leave the skirt and substitute trousers. To cut off her hair.

The butterfly dragged her wings….

Long ago she had abandoned heterosexuality. Men's sexuality was a threat to her; it meant power over her because males were still superior in the world. "I wouldn't be with another man, not for a million dollars!" She said and meant it.

Lesbians had sought her eagerly. —"What a Lady!"

Women who don't know themselves. Women with no power but their sex & beauty flit thru this world.

How would she find an anchor, yet not be tied down?

Make a home that was not a prison?

Lesbians crowded her and made demands of her. Men and women wanted to put her in the prison of their power; to smother her. To *cling* to her. Women seemed worse—they'd been trained from the cradle to cling, to be a homemaker, to be a nurturer—an emotional soil in which a family was supposed to grow—and thus they drained her dry. Women did not have great freedom of moving about, working in the world, or getting things from the world to satisfy themselves. It had been stripped from them, so, having no other spheres to operate in, they clung to other women and smothered and sucked them lifeless.

DO THE SLANG, SLANG, YES!
Chapter Seven

Morning. Thirty-minute ritual of tea, seated by her window watching the dawn, was precious to her. —Also, the rites of evening. Lay back on top of the covers, her hands touching her breasts & genitals. She might caress herself for 40 minutes, squeezing her ripe breasts; work the vibrator fast, faster, in and out of her hole, rubbing her clit as it hummed, surrendering, then holding back, teasing herself; prolonging the delicious moment before giving up into an orgasm; hips thrusting out of control into the air. Then, when the last sex-power was drained out like electricity thru fingers and toes, she'd crawl under the covers in the pleasantly heated room and go to sleep.

Experiencing herself as her own lover.

So many avenues of power were denied her. She

longed for expression in so many areas of her life, but could make none—her job, her future, the amount of money she earned, her safety in the street, her dealings with other women. This one, masturbation, was one area she could master!

The ways of the world are sad.

Everybody wants a happy ending. Sometimes—rarely there are happy endings. And these, only to an extent, —for there are always stray ends to be tied up. Missing persons to be found. —Perhaps not until we stumble across them in heaven when the veils of this earth's blindness are lifted off our eyes. One of those unsolvable problems in her lifetime would be her racial heritage; —that she had no outlet to express the hidden Chinese self which was the core of her. And that she would always look like an advertisement for a travel tour around the world. But in time Melody learned to love herself and what she was and where she'd come from, and to find a power emanating from the core of her, more radical than even sex or race. Many people will not understand this story. They will pass it off as a "nasty book,'" with a shrug of their shoulders. It is not the fuck scenes, but the tale told between the lines which is of utmost importance. It should make you cry. It should make you dance!

For many years, Melody was callous & didn't love from her heart. Finally she had a breakthru. Met a woman, a Chinese lady like a flower. Who wore low-cut dresses which showed her bosom, and high-heeled boots that accentuated her legs. Makeup, and hair styled at a fashion salon. This aging butterfly and her younger flower fell in love. Sex really means a lot, yet it means nothing to the depth of the relationship between people & loyalty & commitment; and how much they need one another. Sex is adjustable. Can redefine itself around these all-important axes.

Both of them were still beautiful. They both had taken women for granted & used them. Now, in their late 30s and 40s respectively, they could still entice; and had wound into each other's desire.

As a young adult, and even into her 30s, Melody's relationships were barren, because she put nothing into them. Her soul had drifted on over the years on the fringes, crying in secret; "Let me in!" She had lived as the kept flower of a dope dealer who had iron gates over her windows and doors; with a doctor in a house on a lofty hill. With coeds from the university. She had met & loved women she'd worked with in proper jobs like offices; & in the hazardous outer fringe of strip-show bars.

Time had passed, thru which God uncovered the heart of her.

Nothing can separate us from the love of God.

Melody would have the desires of her heart because she'd held onto life for a long long time.

Age 50.

Lesbians saw her again in the bars. The years had not yet ruined her face. Battle scars in her soul had mended. The war of oppositions that had raged within her had come to a truce. She had a few more years of fineness left. When she had been young, she had been old—a bag lady who packed up a few possessions in shopping bags in a panic and moved out at midnight down the backstairs. Now that she was aging, Melody had become young at heart. And rich in spirit. Her laugh was sincere. When she sexed a partner, it was not as a machine, but with caring from her heart, to which rhythm she moved her hips & hands.

Ms. Melody Wilson was well-dressed. Trim. Figure superb. Her face which she turned towards her lover was happy... Alive. She had seen rough times. Violence of dykes in barroom brawls. The brutality of men. Over the years, strength grew within her. Had replaced fear & hate. Strength. A smile stretched over her lips. She was cool people. Melody tapped her delicately painted fingernails on the bar, deep in thought. She had even learned to defend herself physically over the years. With Defense Training. Did not look for a fight, nor did she run from fear. Violence is all an ego game. Melody just went about the business of living.

She sat stoically. Feet in high-heeled boots with lacy tops propped up on the rungs of the chair. A sex symbol in her youth, now her brown face was lined; she had a tougher femininity. Timko, her mate, was a Chinese femme; a rarity in this gay bar. The two sat side by side. Timko had not yet lost her looks, tho her face was falling in age. Melody told a friend, 'When I first met Timko, I wanted to fuck her, even tho she was a lady like myself. She brought out the butch in me. I wanted to do everything to her that's been done to me. That's how I want her. Maybe I'm turning into a butch, but I still like my pretty clothes, my femininity. I just don't want to get hard like a man. I've had them all...women, butches, femmes;

all races; it's all the same." She said, "I want a feminine woman. It brings out the butch in me." Melody smiled. "I see Timko, and I want to be strong for her, and reach out to her, and love her. Because I know how much I wanted someone to be strong for me. To reach out to me. To cum with me." She put her arm around her Chinese woman. Brown & yellow, they sat in the dim light of the tavern. Ladies. Faces painted. In skirts. "I'll always want my femininity," Melody said.

They were exact replicas of each other. Stylish. Well-mannered. Fancy skirts, tight sweaters. Leather coats. Hair piled on their heads. The two women would come in often and sit in a booth together sipping drinks; minding their own business. They worked, went out to social events with separate sets of friends. They lived together. Who knows what they did in bed?

They fitted their mouths to the expression of love. They touched fingers thru to the spirit. They caressed the wounded heart back; to live again.

Fifty-year span of time. The long hurt was over for Melody Wilson. Her place was in the sun.

Had fluttered thru the years as a butterfly; a glamorous star. Now she had settled down to earth sucking nectar from the flower chosen to be her mate.

The world talked about them bad. Blacks said; "A sistah can have a Natural, but not a natural bone in her body." Grumbling about Melody, in her African hairdo.

Sling slang. Yin yang.

Some said she had no class; others said she had no shame.

Some said she did the yin yang.

Folks called her a hooker for women. Others said; "Oh, that one from the Islands somewhere? Is she Jamaican?" But they only revealed their own ignorance about her situation.

The same music played then as plays now. Urging everybody to *"PARTY DOWN!"*

As a child she had adapted to adults' fierce looks, and their selfishness. Terrified, she had frozen up; feeling withdrew from her, and she had moved like an armored tank thru her school years. She'd sat like a puppet, manipulating her body so that she'd feel no pain while gaining every advantage.

As a teenager, she had anesthetized herself with alcohol.

Adult; surrounded herself by a community of women; in this safety she had begun to let herself feel once again.

Feeling had come back into her body; she felt powerful.

In the years, steeplechasing, laddering upward out of the earth, she had touched thru to the finite soil of her heart.

She had learned who she was.

Discovered love inside.

Had love to share.

REFLECTIONS OF A LESBIAN TRICK
(AN ARTICLE)

"There ain't nothin' like the real thing, baby,
ain't nothin' like the real thing."
—A popular song from the 1970s

When I first started paying prostitutes to have sex with me in earnest, I would go once a night 7 nights a week, or twice some nights.

Did it cunt-to-cunt, used fingers & tongue. Got sucked off. Didn't put much cock in whores, saved that for my girlfriends. And had them talk dirty while cumming.

First time actually used a prostitute was in my late teens.

Had been using their services off and on, but had been poor. So it was nothing like the intensity of that time frame between 1973 and 1975, when I finally had lots of money and practically no bills.

So, I had in this particular period of heavy action over 300 paid encounters—sex for cash, with just about 30 different ladies—because I frequented the same ones.

This was joy to a pussy rider and cunt jockey like myself.

The way I dress is rough. Construction boots, trousers, shirt, & jacket. Very male. I was 32.

A butch lesbian, very close to the man-side in sex response.

I had always been attracted to glamorous showgirl types. Many of my lovers-for-free had been strippers, go-go dancers, or prostitutes. Both lesbian and bi.

Had been surviving in a kitchenette room in a bad neighborhood in the heart of the ho stroll—a hustling area where whores pick up their "dates."

Then I got one of the few good-pay jobs of my life. Telephone sales—12 hours a day, 6 days per week screening credit applications by phone for major department stores and banks; which brought me $125 to $150 per shift. $800 a week sometimes, which was damn good for an unskilled dyke in the early 1970s.

I was always horny and psychopathically lonely. Had more money than I'd ever seen before!

I remember it was an intense period of loneliness—in which I wasn't meeting women in lesbian bars; and having a high sex drive was killing me.

Saw these glamorous hookers stand on my corner, bare legs in high heels, tits soft under tight satin zip-front dresses that barely reached down to cover their cunts.

Many were very young. Pretty faces. Makeup & wigs. And not of legal age.

Wanted to fuck bad.

Reflections of a Lesbian Trick | 331

See these glamorous women and had the price in my wallet.

My love life had failed. —Gave my presents to a lesbian; my affections & time spent, yet she goes off with another dyke. Maybe my approach to women is crude. My underarms stink? I'm clumsy in bed? I don't know the reason.

But she's gone. And feeling the wild wind of isolation blow thru me, soon I found myself fucking my heart out; saliva, cum, and cuntjuice and sweat all over the bed. "CUM ALL OVER ME BABY! RUB IT! RUB IT! FUCK IT! FUCK IT!" Then my head burrowed in the space between a hooker's wig, her salty-tasting neck, & shoulders after orgasm, to rest a moment—before she threw me off her.

And sometimes I'd take her ass in my strong & gentle hands and push my face in her cunt hair, and probe her wet pussy and lick & suck her off as well—and me having to pay an additional price.

Sally—I found out later her real name was Linda—stood against the white wall of the fast food joint, lit by streetlamps. The youngest & prettiest of that group of hookers.

I went up to her, embarrassed because I didn't have a dick, and wasn't a man. In society's eyes, I wasn't supposed to have a woman.

Asked her, "Will you go with me? I have the money!"

And she replies; "You're blowing my mind! I have to think about this! Nobody's ever asked me to do that before—to be with a woman!"

Turns out she was young & not experienced.

We got down two hours later, in my kitchenette room, 15 by 10 feet, small, that holds a bed, armchair, & sofa. In the presence of another, older, whore; a black brassy woman of 23 with big tits and a round ass who I used later; who sat in the armchair like a queen on a throne, nose sedately stuck up in the air, superior; & watched us fuck to make sure I wasn't going to kill my "date."

The girl takes half her clothes off—rolls her dress up so I don't get tits, just access to cunt, belly, thighs, legs, & ass. She lies down on my bed. I suck her pussy for a few minutes of the 20-minute time; then I show her how to spread her thighs & get my cunt up on hers and slide around in her cunt, screwing to a climax.

CUM HARD! REAL HARD! PUSSY REAL GOOD! PUSSY SO SWEET!

After a few dates, the girl gives in to my demands; kneels down before me to service me orally until I cum all over her face & in her mouth. —I've broke the ice in her. —And she's broke luck with me. That means I'm her first trick of the evening.

Buying prostitutes is simple—the philosophy of the whore, "Money Spends." So no matter if you are old, young, a dyke, or a man, nor what your problem is, if you have money, you are as good as anyone else.

Now, I'm a freak trick,—being lesbian. So some women disdain me. But there are plenty who'll service a woman.

Why would a he-dyke go outside the arc of fire from the lesbian campsite into the shady straight world of prostitutes?

To me it meant control. —Doing something about my sex needs. It meant seeing something I want—a piece of cunt standing up on the corner selling herself, and me buying it. Go home with it for 30 minutes, experience her erotic looks, her nasty talk; work out a sweat on her, bust a nut between her legs and, then, that sexual part of my life, at least, will be at peace.

Now, I could have spent a whole night sitting up in a women's rap group or a gay bar, & it's just a turn of fate if I'll bed some broad. —Yes, by this time, bitterness of 20 years of lesbian life had taken its toll. I wanted to pay. I wanted to cut all strings of emotion & not be hurt anymore.

First thing I notice about whore-fucking is the freedom.

No emotional ties. I'm not hurting in my heart over her.

Later, this turns into a kind of hollowness, cumming and cumming with a multitude of females & never get hold of nothing real. But it took 2 years to see that. And the Freedom! The Power! Tricking released my ties of need to lesbians, as each whore released my cum.

I started to know about power after passing a folded $20 bill to a girl—a piece of green paper that meant nothing, —I had hundreds more stashed away in the bank; knowing as she silently takes off her clothes, that I'm having power over this woman—for a half-hour, renting her. Power over her cunt, which is arousing enough in itself. I finger-fuck her hard, and let her lick me; jam my cunt up in her face; and she is hot & sexually provocative and lust streams thru me, & while I'm thrusting my hips in and out, driving my cunt in her mouth, cumming; I have the power to give her another $20—which means little to me, and let me top her, and ride, for a second climax.

These women are so-called "straight," & this is a heterosexual environment. Some have never done females before. Others have a bulldyke trick in their past, but it is rare. A few are lesbians themselves, & their love wasn't any better than the straight girls.

All women down on the ho stroll must keep up a straight front because females get no respect, and a female with no man is an outlaw, & in physical jeopardy. So she might invent & claim a fictitious man as her pimp. Also, a female who represents a man like myself is a threat, but also a source of money.

So, when they stand together in a ho cluster under neon streetlights smacking gum & blowing cigarette smoke & talking ho talk, they all agree the idea of sucking cunt is distasteful.

But when you get them home, in privacy, out of the prying eyes of their stable sisters, their pimps, and their pimps' nephews and brother spies who ride by periodically to check up on them; what they do in bed might be a different story.

I tasted, picked, and chose. And found some who opened their love-of-sorts to me; who would cum with me themselves, but wouldn't dare tell nobody about it.

So, yes, there was the element of scorn, especially in the group, against lesbians. Each is too proud to admit it publicly—that they gave themselves to a dyke.

This wore on my weak self-esteem. I felt self-conscious about not having a dick I could put in them. Having only my nasty cunt to fuck them with.

And after a while—after months of tricking continually—some hated sucking it so much, I began to look at my cunt as their punishment. So I couldn't wait to get her back to the privacy of my yellow-lit room. —Enough light to see the expression on her made-up face—and degrade her.

I was a trick they had to turn if they wanted to break luck at 9 P.M. And I was the customer they had to accept at 5 A.M., to fill their quota at the end of the evening.

I liked the idea that I was degrading them. —To them that may or may not be true.

Some, I liked the idea I was loving them. (In a moment of weakness.)

I'd like to say I used my strap-on cock in them, my handcuffs; romanced them, put my fingers in their vagina and worked the cuntjuice out of them and timed it so we got off at the same time; but that's for lesbian lovers. It wasn't mutual, it was one-sided. Me cum.

I have shared countless orgasms with lesbians picked up in gay bars. Very seldom shared orgasms with hookers. I used their bodies. They spent my cash.

Only a few were real lesbians. —I met three. Two of them with the same bona-fide lesbian pimp. And their love was no better nor worse than straight hookers.

So here's these hookers having sex with another woman instead of a man (whom they dislike also).

We always talk business first:

"I'll take you, baby, I go with women! Sure, I'll go with you, honey! What do you want to do? Just tell me!"

"I want to get off twice, once in your mouth and once using your cunt. Can you spread your legs wide so I can get my cunt up on yours?"

"I can get in any position you want! I'm a dancer! Come on, baby!"

"Pay Me" is the rule of the whore.

After cum, to try & cuddle is useless on the ho stroll.

So, being a trick, you start to get cold emotionally.

Tricks get jaded & twisted. A regular girl I date loses her cool. No longer aloof, comes begging me to fuck her, to strap it on & take her, to let her kneel down and suck me off—do anything I want to do because she needs $20. She's desperate. —Her old man has got a drug jones, he's lying up on the sofa back at their apartment having cold sweats & hallucinating, needs money for a fix to neutralize his demons.

And I see her need as she's seen mine. And I'm cold, as she has been cold. I tell her I'm choosing another girl —for now, but come back at the end of the evening, I'll go again. —Maybe.

See her desperation & feel even more powerful—in a fake way. And she glares at me out of false eyelashes and heavy mascara, knowing I'm a motherfucker and hard. Hard. And I know I mean nothing to her but the twenty-dollar bill. —What can be harder?

Walking up the corridor to the room where we turn the date, I stick my fingers down in my trousers & under the elastic band of my boxer shorts & keep jacking my clit up and down to be ready for her when we lie down on the mattress together, because for $20 there is no foreplay, no caresses.

I have pumped my heart and soul into so many lesbian bitches, but nowadays, at work on my job, all I can think about is the cream. The slit of her vagina. Hot meat. Rubbing cunts. My own cum.

I'm not thinking about girlfriend & dates, and asking ladies for their phone number. My boxer shorts are soaking. I could smell my own cunt as I drove back to the ghetto, screech tires into the parking lot, ran down the block & went cunt shopping; arranged to meet one back at my kitchenette. And now I fuck hard and fast in the semidarkness on my mattress; she fakes moaning and humping her hips up to meet mine & a light touch of her fingernails on my back.

BANG BANG! SO GOOD!

Put my underwear back on and fall asleep.

That's 10 P.M.

If I feel insecure & blue at 4 A.M. —I'll go again. That's when the last straggler leaves the strip, before the dusk light of dawn breaking at 4 or 5, and then the street is deserted.

Delving down past the surface of the lesbian community you can find a lot of dykes who live with semi-hookers, hookers, strippers, & other lesbians who work the sex industry.

Many of us have had the love of these women, getting it free, maybe being paid by, or kept by them. Especially in the late fifties and sixties when open gays had such a hard time finding work, whereas a femme dyke could work the sex trade & make lots of easy money.

In those days, being a lesbian meant you were an

outlaw. And only outlaw women were bold enough to frequent the bars & take on a dyke & her way of love. Before Stonewall, there were no lesbian rap groups nor politics. There were B-girls, and hustlers who were easy to find for a butch dyke. And nice secret closeted lesbians who didn't know each other, living out lives of isolation and sexual frustration with no access to other women.

Were you scared when you went down and did it?

Of what? My life, my cunt, my wallet, or my ego? —That they wouldn't do it?—Of being refused? Yes, I was scared at first but it fell into a routine. Prowling the streets in my truck looking for women is always exhilarating, fearful, and gut-wrenching.

Were you scared of violence? Yes. *Police?* Yes! *Disease?* I was too stupid to think of that. —This was the seventies, remember? Before AIDS, when herpes was barely heard of. I washed myself up immediately after. The girls smelled clean. —I just chose girls who looked clean on the surface. I caught some infections & had health problems, but I'm still alive.

Did you have any moral consideration?

What is that?

Did you feel guilty about doing it?

Hell, no!

Did any woman ever approach you and ask you to be her man?

Yes, two. One was very young and had a child, and she didn't turn me on, which was weird, because she was very loving in bed. I didn't want the responsibility. In loneliness later I regretted this. Another was too old—

near my age, and didn't look good enough. There was another. —I just didn't want involvement. Only if one had been fast, hot, and full of game would I have wanted it. And those I couldn't get.

Did any whores want to freak out with you?

Yes. Every now and then, I'd pay one and wind up spending hours with her for just $20. Freaking out together in some motel room. It was a nice surprise, always. Sucking & licking the hell out of her clit, her brown legs wrapped around my shoulders and her torso hung over the bed. When we freaked out, I'd use my cock, get them up on all fours and fuck them from behind & reach around and rub her clit with my hand. It was the hand job on their clit they liked more; and I got them off.

Did you frequent trick pads?

After I moved off the stroll and kept coming down at night, I had to use the trick hotel—so there was more fear, more threat of violence, & of the police. I had to go upstairs to the second floor & here's this man at the desk who proved to be OK. Nonjudgmental. He smiles, hands me a scrap of towel to mop cumjuice off my face and cunt, or hers. Too many other people are around, going & coming. Too illegal. Some girls had their own motel room, which was a good reason to frequent them more. Some girls I'd never had before wanted me to do it in the truck, but we never did. A couple of trick pads would not rent to two women for an hour. One man screamed at me and was going to throw us out bodily. —The same hatred of lesbians that's too familiar.

How did you feel when you were finished?

That is the essence of tricking. —She's up off her back, rolls up her pantyhose & zips up her dress and is gone. I wash up, piss, put on my underwear, crawl under the covers & fall asleep in the absence of woman. —Just her perfume remains in the air. Feel satisfied, but empty. A lesbian pickup would still be lying there touching me. —It's the emptiness after that made me finally get out of total tricking and try to make a relationship again. It's fine to have sex, free and anonymous if I have some emotional backup from some woman somewhere. It took a year for this feeling to really make me realize I had to go looking for my heart again, too.

Do whores kiss?

Never. Only the few that wanted me to be their man.

Do whores take checks?

No!

What did the police do?

I'd be ready for a woman all day at the office; in fantasy rubbing her sweet cunt up against my clit. Slide my dyke-cock into her, pumping, her holding my ass tight, pulling me into her & talking dirty: "Cum, baby! Cum for me! I want to take your cum, baby! Bust a nut for me, baby! Fuck me!" Hot & cold chills run down my spine—just to get down to the ho stroll and see a flood of police vehicles. Spotlights, red lights revolving atop squad cars smash the brick walls with crimson red color & painted girls in high heels with bare legs are being escorted into the back of paddy wagons. The street is too hot, so I have to go home & seal myself behind walls with the door shut in isolation, instead of the night wind in my hair surrounded by glamorous and cold and untouchable pay ladies.

Police harassment happened on a regular basis. Hookers and tricks need a neutral territory where they can work & we can play & not be afraid of going to jail.

Did you know of other lesbian tricks?

One of my prostitute girlfriends I was living with when I was poor had an older dyke who was one of our sources of income. She used a vibrator on my girl to penetrate her and never took off her own clothes. I think she must have jerked herself off after my woman had left. Another lesbian who hooked for a living off and on, who I lived with for a time, had a regular jane, old, wrinkled, who annoyed her because part of it—it was a $75 date—was that my woman had to go out with her to dinner and a lesbian club, and then they'd go back to her condominium in a senior-citizens' development and go to bed and she'd take too long to reach orgasm, so we figured we were losing money by the hour. But we would both rather have the jane than a man, so we were stuck with it.

Were you ever a prostitute yourself?

For a year. I did it. I wasn't a hardcore prostitute, not every day. I lay down for men, fucked, or jacked them off by hand. Never let them shoot in my mouth. I accepted money & food & things I needed to survive.

If a woman wanted to pay you to lie with her, would you do it?

Now? It's not a part of my life. I'm too old! I'm not in demand! I'm not poor!

Did any hookers ever cheat you out of your money?

Yes. Twice for $20. One got up and left before the time was up & left me hot, horny, panting, & not having cum. One ran off on me before we even got started, and my clothes are still on. And once for $100. I knew her well, and later got the hundred back. She reduced her regular price of $20 down to $10 for ten more dates until it was made up, and she was pissed about that.

Did you do Golden Showers?

With a lesbian, yes. With a hooker, yes. It was emotionally scintillating & a libido charge, & sex wasn't as important. It was a mind-fuck. I'd rather get my clit swollen hard and cum with the mind-fuck.

Did you carry weapons?

Yes. Various knives, or guns,—.38-caliber revolvers, at various times. Had ten years of karate & judo training which made me more mentally aggressive. I had an idea what to do if attacked.

Were you ever attacked or raped by men or pimps while pursuing hookers?

No, not in pursuit of hookers. The ho strolls and Tenderloins and Gold Coasts & Times Squares are populated areas, well-lit, and a lot of people around and police riding. It's up in a strange trick pad or using a girl's hotel room if I didn't know her where I worried most. I'd carry the gun sometimes & always had the knife.

Did a whore you'd paid ever come live with you?

Yes. Twice I rescued hookers from the street; the youngest was 18. I drove her crazy with my need, paid her for sex each time we did it, but wanted to hug her and kiss her and shit, and she soon left.

So the whore stroll is dangerous for a lesbian trick?

Anywhere is dangerous for a lesbian, trick or not. Lesbian or not. Shit happens:

Reflections of a Lesbian Trick | 343

"MOTHERFUCKING BULLDAGGER! GODDAMN BULLDAGGER! YOU NO MAN! YOU A PUSSY-HATING BITCH! GODDAMN BITCH WITH A PUSSY AIN'T GOT NO COCK! DRESSED UP LIKE A MAN! I'LL TAKE YOU OUTSIDE AND HAVE A PIECE OF YOU AND EVERY MAN IN HERE HAVE A PIECE OF YOU, BITCH! PUSSY SUCKIN' BITCH! YOU BETTER COME SUCK MY COCK, BITCH!"

An item passes from one man to the other—silver glint of a razor. My knife is open and I'm running back into the shadows.

"YOU AIN'T NO MAN! YOU CAN'T DO NOTHIN' ABOUT IT, ANYWAY! YOU GONNA SUCK MY COCK TONIGHT, LESBIAN CUNT! YOU AIN'T A MAN, YOU AIN'T A LADY! YOU GOT MAN CLOTHES ON. YOU REPRESENTING A MAN TO CATCH LADIES. YOU MIGHT FOOL THEM, BUT YOU CAN'T DO NOTHIN' UP AGAINST ME, LESBIAN BITCH!"

It's all a game. Dominance & submission. Humiliation. Fear. Courage. And Victory. It's all a game, emotions racing thru the heart; rehearsed lines to bait the trick. Life experience is where a square learns game, ceases being a square, and becomes a Player. A Player of the Game. No wonder the whores told me, "Go get some game in you, so you can pull a fast lady." It's all about hurt, rage, anger, and acting out that anger. Acting & reacting.

So when I get a woman—a regular—I pay her $40 up front and she's happy at first. And we get to a hotel and I take the bitch hard. Use my strap-on and fuck her cunt with my rod. Don't say nothing, just feel her body sweat, & turn hot, & she's holding back her emotions & not feeling what I'm doing to her. Then take her cunt from behind, get her up on all fours & ram it into her. Then push it in a different hole—her ass, ass-fucking; and I cum that way first. Then take the cock off and fuck her cunt-to-cunt. Then she kneels, a submissive, goes down on me, my cunt all over her face, for the second time, cum hard. And feel the angry emotions and the pain of life wash away from me.

After, we don't look at each other.

It's borderline times like this I realize I should be building myself up as a lesbian, not tearing myself down as a trick.

Carrying the .38; set it down under my jacket so the woman don't see it and be afraid. We undress, make small talk, and lie on the bed. Believe me, I have had these thoughts about feeling impotent, wanting to penetrate her, wanting to find a lesbian who will spread her legs wide enough for me to get my cunt up against hers; who will suck pussy right and get their whole mouth into it & swallow everything I've got, juice, sweat, blood; menstrual blood; cum shot of my small female ejaculation; and not turn her face away.

The root lies in my own inadequacy & frustration. It's been a year out here as a trick; 1973 is coming to a close, and 1974 is around the bend. I go to the gay bars, but still don't have a real girlfriend to call my own.

Maybe if I had a hard dick attached to me and was a man, it would be better between me & women.

Now I'm taking her, mad. She wants to get finished.

Reflections of a Lesbian Trick | 345

All my money is going to some pimp. I know these girls run game down on me for my money, and it comes on—as it has to, between a trick and a whore—the anger. The anger upsetting the power balance & dominance & control that levels between us. I'm between her legs screwing her cunt with my clit. She looks away—anywhere but at me, because this ain't the real thing. I'm not her lover, not even her friend. Am I angry enough to be the one to stick a knife in her heart and see her blood all over my sheets?—The ultimate control?

For 20 minutes, she is a possession. We've drawn down a tattered window shade, fucking on a mattress, taking cunt. To fuck. To fill her cunt with my fingers, or the strap-on dick. To impregnate—which I can't do. The ultimate possession is to kill. To destroy—or to give life. So how far do I want to go with it?

All these feelings stir up.... The ultimate control is to kill someone.... Life on the fast track leads you in strange ways...to hold life or death over her. To simply reach over the side of the bed, get my gun, hold it to her head, insult her verbally, slap her face till she bleeds, fuck her orally until I can't cum anymore, and since I can't pump semen into her, pump .38-caliber bullets into her head instead. As a lesbian butch, don't think this hasn't crossed my mind. I won't, tho. She feels me cum & pushes me off. And I know my days as a trick need a much more human balancing point. Murderous evening. Emotions opened up raw by the fire of sex.

So, it all comes back to why did I take my cunt to the streets in the first place? Why would a lesbian butch become a trick to straight women?

A scene from the Great Lesbian Wars:

Sweet young girl stands at the bar with friends. Bad butch comes up to her, looks her in the eye, smiles, touches the girl's arm; "Hi! Would you like to dance with me?"

BAM!

The butch holds her face, blood rushes thru her fingers.

The girl's screaming: "THAT MAN PUT HIS HANDS ON ME! WHY DO THEY LET MEN IN HERE? THIS IS SUPPOSED TO BE A BAR FOR LESBIANS ONLY!"

"I'm not a goddamn man!"

Then she sees for herself. Takes a closer look. "Oh, gosh! She's a dyke. I thought it was a man."

A friend tells the butch, "Women aren't going for the hard look anymore; you should get into the woman-tailored look."

Scene two from the Great Lesbian Wars:

Driving down the freeway with a box of pizza and a single red rose tossed carelessly onto the floor of the truck. Her date was not at home when she rang the doorbell. This is just one time too many. Feels the wild wind of isolation blow over her soul. Drives down the freeway, one hand loose on the wheel, reckless; and it occurs to her: 'If I just let go of this wheel, the truck will crash into a cement freeway abutment and my problems will be over.' Survival is a strong instinct; her strong hands swerve the wheel in time. Down below the freeway some 50 feet, under the viaduct, is a ho cluster—which waits to have a girl chosen from it to do sex services for cash, and this is better than suicide—when the rainbow ain't enough.

So, that's all there is to say about it—money is the center of it, on the surface; followed by the feelings, and the troubles.

Some kinds of tricks are just lesbian butches tired of being ghettoized in isolation. Who go out of their small & stifling territory into a larger one.

I was down there, 2 years passed. Autumn winds blew, girls lost their youth, and I lost more of my naïveté.

I'm hanging out with some winos I knew from Greenwich Village, down on 6th Street, south of Market, which is the skid row of San Francisco, when here comes the lady who watched me and my first date have sex back in my kitchenette room on the ho stroll—to make sure I wasn't a freak trick who liked to kill people.

She's on crutches, looks horrible, & lives in a single occupancy in a skid row hotel, after a decade of big-time hustling earning up to $250 a night. Her tubes are sick & her ovaries are shot. And her face looks bad. I duck into a doorway as she wearily swings her foot in its cast along the gutter. I don't want her to see me see her in this bad condition. I don't want her to be embarrassed. Also, I don't want to hear no more whore lies, nor to get hit up for no more money.

One last note: under the erotic facade of makeup, lip gloss, and glitter, the fast life is about economics. Making $40 per hour instead of $4. And it's about sex—the strongest force in a human being next to death, and fear, and hunger.

White pussy, brown pussy, black pussy; a few times yellow cunt. And most were good.

Fantasy:

A whorehouse for lesbians. It's like the Mustang Ranch, where I went 3 times. The bell rings as you come in, and the girls line up in a circle with smiles on their faces, in sweet short dresses and some in costume-type things. Only this time, too, there's a Madam who's a professional class:—suit, tailored, butch/femme persona, who welcomes you. And she asks what you need, how long you need, how much money you have to spend—and she's really concerned that as a lesbian your needs are met, and that her establishment & her women's requirements are met. And the women line up as before, in a smiling circle, but they're lesbians. They know what you want and how to satisfy you. And when they go home at night, they do the same thing with another woman, so it's more intimate, and more about being understood. And you choose a woman whose appearance makes you hot, and go off in a private room with her, and have a few hours together, not minutes. And the woman under you doesn't have to pretend you're a man, nor treat you like a man. And you don't have to be embarrassed about your body, because she has female bodies exclusively in her lovemaking. And it's all handled in an adult, honest, legal, and compassionate way. Woman to woman.

It all comes down to us. Services for ourselves. It's all about lesbians helping each other. Few of us do.

About women finding places & ways to be able to touch,—slip & slide their wet cunts together—and their hearts.

It's all about women taking power over their sexuality, and their needs. And not having to be so god-awful lonely, or sexually frustrated.

I'm not an expert trick. —Only a now-poor, lonely, horny, antisocial, sexual psychopath who is tired, gentle/mean, egotistical & selfish, & small in stature; and am exploited by the world myself. Bulldyke memories from personal experience.

I'm sure other dykes have had whores; fucked them better, were braver, and not so stupid.

I remember the lesbians of the bars, and the world, amid the party lights, red, blue, & green; and me eating my heart out with the Soul of an Artist,—shy, timid; going up and saying the wrong thing. They'd turn away....

...Yes, I recall what drove me out into the arms of prostitutes in the first place!

You've heard of the writers
but didn't know where to find them

Samuel R. Delany • Pat Califia • Carol Queen • Lars Eighner • Felice Picano • Lucy Taylor • Aaron Travis • Michael Lassell • Red Jordan Arobateau • Michael Bronski • Tom Roche • Maxim Jakubowski • Michael Perkins • Camille Paglia • John Preston • Laura Antoniou • Alice Joanou • Cecilia Tan • Michael Perkins • Tuppy Owens • Trish Thomas • Lily Burana

You've seen the sexy images
but didn't know where to find them

Robert Chouraqui • Charles Gatewood • Richard Kern • Eric Kroll • Vivienne Maricevic • Housk Randall • Barbara Nitke • Trevor Watson • Mark Avers • Laura Graff • Michele Serchuk • Laurie Leber

You can find them all in
Masquerade

a publication designed expressly for the connoisseur of the erotic arts.

ORDER TODAY
SAVE 50%
1 year (6 issues) for $15; 2 years (12 issues) for only $25!

Essential. —*Skin Two*

The best newsletter I have ever seen! —*Secret International*

Very informative and enticing. —*Redemption*

A professional, insider's look at the world of erotica. —*Screw*

I recommend a subscription to **MASQUERADE**... It's good stuff. —*Black Sheets*

MASQUERADE presents some of the best articles on erotica, fetishes, sex clubs, the politics of porn and every conceivable issue of sex and sexuality. —*Factsheet Five*

Fabulous. —*Tuppy Owens*

MASQUERADE is absolutely lovely ... marvelous images. —*Le Boudoir Noir*

Highly recommended. —*Eidos*

DIRECT

Masquerade/Direct • DEPT X74L • 801 Second Avenue • New York, NY 10017 • FAX: 212.986.7355
MC/VISA orders can be placed by calling our toll-free number: 800.375.2356

☐ PLEASE SEND ME A 1 YEAR SUBSCRIPTION FOR $30 *NOW* $15!
☐ PLEASE SEND ME A 2 YEAR SUBSCRIPTION FOR $60 *NOW* $25!

NAME _____

ADDRESS _____

CITY _____ STATE _____ ZIP _____

TEL ( ) _____

PAYMENT: ☐ CHECK ☐ MONEY ORDER ☐ VISA ☐ MC

CARD # _____ EXP. DATE _____

No C.O.D. orders. Please make all checks payable to Masquerade/Direct. Payable in U.S. currency only.

MASQUERADE BOOKS

MASQUERADE

VISCOUNT LADYWOOD
GYNECOCRACY
$7.95/511-5
Julian, whose parents feel he shows just a bit too much spunk, is sent to a very special private school, in hopes that he will learn to discipline his wayward soul. Once there, Julian discovers that his program of study has been devised by the deliciously stern Mademoiselle de Chambonnard. In no time, Julian is learning the many ways of pleasure—under the firm hand of this demanding headmistress.

EDITED BY CHARLOTTE ROSE
50 PLAYGIRL FANTASIES
$6.50/460-7
A steamy selection of women's fantasies straight from the pages of *Playgirl*—the leading magazine of sexy entertainment for women. These tales of seduction—specially selected by no less an authority than Charlotte Rose, author of such bestselling women's erotica as *Women at Work* and *The Doctor is In*—are sure to set your pulse racing.

N. T. MORLEY
THE PARLOR
$6.50/496-8
Lovely Kathryn gives in to the ultimate temptation. The mysterious John and Sarah ask her to be their slave—an idea that turns Kathryn on so much that she can't refuse! But who are these two mysterious strangers? Little by little, Kathryn not only learns to serve, but comes to know the inner secrets of her stunning keepers.

JULIAN ANTHONY GUERRA, EDITOR
COME QUICKLY:
FOR COUPLES ON THE GO
$6.50/461-5
The increasing pace of daily life is no reason to forgo a little carnal pleasure whenever the mood strikes. Here are over sixty of the hottest fantasies around—all designed to get you going in less time than it takes to dial 976. A super-hot volume especially for couples on a modern schedule.

ERICA BRONTE
LUST, INC.
$6.50/467-4
Lust, Inc. explores the extremes of passion that lurk beneath even the coldest, most business-like exteriors. Join in the sexy escapades of a group of high-powered professionals whose idea of office decorum is like nothing you've ever encountered! Business attire not required....

VANESSA DURIES
THE TIES THAT BIND
$6.50/510-7
The incredible confessions of a thrillingly unconventional woman. From the first page, this chronicle of dominance and submission will keep you gasping with its vivid depictions of sensual abandon. At the hand of Masters Georges, Patrick, Pierre and others, this submissive seductress experiences pleasures she never knew existed....

M. S. VALENTINE
THE CAPTIVITY OF CELIA
$6.50/453-4
Colin is mistakenly considered the prime suspect in a murder, forcing him to seek refuge with his cousin, Sir Jason Hardwicke. In exchange for Colin's safety, Jason demands Celia's unquestioning submission—knowing she will do anything to protect her lover. Sexual extortion!

AMANDA WARE
BOUND TO THE PAST
$6.50/452-6
Anne accepts a research assignment in a Tudor mansion. Upon arriving, she finds herself aroused by James, a descendant of the mansion's owners. Together they uncover the perverse desires of the mansion's long-dead master—desires that bind Anne inexorably to the past—not to mention the bedpast!

SACHI MIZUNO
SHINJUKU NIGHTS
$6.50/493-3
Another tour through the lives and libidos of the seductive East, from the author of Passion in Tokyo. No one is better that Sachi Mizuno at weaving an intricate web of sensual desire, wherein many characters are ensnared and enraptured by the demands of their long-denied carnal natures. One by one, each surrenders social convention for the unashamed pleasures of the flesh.

PASSION IN TOKYO
$6.50/454-2
Tokyo—one of Asia's most historic and seductive cities. Come behind the closed doors of its citizens, and witness the many pleasures that await. Lusty men and women from every stratum of Japanese society free themselves of all inhibitions....

MARTINE GLOWINSKI
POINT OF VIEW
$6.50/433-X
With the assistance of her new, unexpectedly kinky lover, she discovers and explores her exhibitionist tendencies—until there is virtually nothing she won't do before the horny audiences her man arranges! Unabashed acting out for the sophisticated voyeur.

BUY ANY 4 BOOKS & CHOOSE 1 ADDITIONAL BOOK, OF EQUAL OR LESSER VALUE, AS YOUR FREE GIFT

MASQUERADE BOOKS

RICHARD McGOWAN
A HARLOT OF VENUS
$6.50/425-9
A highly fanciful, epic tale of lust on Mars! Cavortia—the most famous and sought-after courtesan in the cosmopolitan city of Venus—finds love and much more during her adventures with some of the most remarkable characters in recent erotic fiction.

M. ORLANDO
THE ARCHITECTURE OF DESIRE
Introduction by Richard Manton.
$6.50/490-9
Two novels in one special volume! In *The Hotel Justine*, an elite clientele is afforded the opportunity to have any and all desires satisfied. *The Villa Sin* is inherited by a beautiful woman who soon realizes that the legacy of the ancestral estate includes bizarre erotic ceremonies. Two pieces of prime real estate.

CHET ROTHWELL
KISS ME, KATHERINE
$5.95/410-0
Beautiful Katherine can hardly believe her luck. Not only is she married to the charming and oh-so-agreeable Nelson, she's free to live out all her erotic fantasies with other men. Katherine has discovered Nelson to be far more devoted than the average spouse—and the duo soon begin exploring a relationship more demanding than marriage!

MARCO VASSI
THE STONED APOCALYPSE
$5.95/401-1/mass market
"Marco Vassi is our champion sexual energist." —VLS
During his lifetime, Marco Vassi praised by writers as diverse as Gore Vidal and Norman Mailer, and his reputation was worldwide. *The Stoned Apocalypse* is Vassi's autobiography; chronicling a cross-country trip on America's erotic byways, it offers a rare glimpse of a generation's sexual imagination.

ROBIN WILDE
TABITHA'S TEASE
$5.95/387-2
When poor Robin arrives at The Valentine Academy, he finds himself subject to the torturous teasing of Tabitha—the Academy's most notoriously domineering co-ed. But Tabitha is pledge-mistress of a secret sorority dedicated to enslaving young men. Robin finds himself the utterly helpless (and wildly excited) captive of Tabitha & Company's weird desires! A marathon of ticklish torture!

ERICA BRONTE
PIRATE'S SLAVE
$5.95/376-7
Lovely young Erica is stranded in a country where lust knows no bounds. Desperate to escape, she finds herself trading her firm, luscious body to any and all men willing and able to help her. Her adventure has its ups and downs, ins and outs—all to the undeniable pleasure of lusty Erica!

CHARLES G. WOOD
HELLFIRE
$5.95/358-9
A vicious murderer is running amok in New York's sexual underground—and Nick O'Shay, a virile detective with the NYPD, plunges deep into the case. He soon becomes embroiled in an elusive world of fleshly extremes, hunting a madman seeking to purge America with fire and blood sacrifices. Set in New York's infamous sexual underground.

OLIVIA M. RAVENSWORTH
THE MISTRESS OF CASTLE ROHMENSTADT
$5.95/372-4
Lovely Katherine inherits a secluded European castle from a mysterious relative. Upon arrival she discovers, much to her delight, that the castle is a haven of sensual pleasure. Katherine learns to shed her inhibitions and enjoy her new home's many delights. Soon, Castle Rohmenstadt is the home of every perversion known to man.

CLAIRE BAEDER, EDITOR
LA DOMME: A DOMINATRIX ANTHOLOGY
$5.95/366-X
A steamy smorgasbord of female domination! Erotic literature has long been filled with heartstopping portraits of domineering women, and now the most memorable have been brought together in one beautifully brutal volume. A must for all fans of true Woman Power.

TINY ALICE
THE GEEK
$5.95/341-4
"An accomplishment of which anybody may be proud." —Philip José Farmer
The Geek is told from the point of view of a chicken, who reports on the various perversities he witnesses as part of a traveling carnival. When a gang of renegade lesbians kidnaps Chicken and his geek, all hell breaks loose.

CHARISSE VAN DER LYN
SEX ON THE NET
$5.95/399-6
Electrifying erotica from one of the Internet's hottest and most widely read authors. Encounters of all kinds—straight, lesbian, dominant/submissive and all sorts of extreme passions—are explored in thrilling detail.

STANLEY CARTEN
NAUGHTY MESSAGE
$5.95/333-3
Wesley Arthur discovers a lascivious message on his answering machine. Aroused beyond his wildest dreams by the acts described, Wesley becomes obsessed with tracking down the woman behind the seductive voice. His search takes him through strip clubs, sex parlors and no-tell motels—and finally to his randy reward....

MASQUERADE BOOKS

AKBAR DEL PIOMBO
SKIRTS
$4.95/115-2
Randy Mr. Edward Champdick enters high society—and a whole lot more—in his quest for ultimate satisfaction. For it seems that once Mr. Champdick rises to the occasion, nothing can bring him down.

DUKE COSIMO
$4.95/3052-0
A kinky romp played out against the boudoirs, bathrooms and ballrooms of the European nobility, who seem to do nothing all day except each other. The lifestyles of the rich and licentious are revealed in all their glory.

A CRUMBLING FAÇADE
$4.95/3043-1
The return of that incorrigible rogue, Henry Pike, who continues his pursuit of sex, fair or otherwise, in the most elegant homes of the most debauched aristocrats.

CAROLE REMY
BEAUTY OF THE BEAST
$5.95/332-5
A shocking tell-all, written from the point-of-view of a prize-winning reporter. And what reporting she does! All the secrets of an uninhibited life are revealed, and each lusty tableau is painted in glowing colors.

DAVID AARON CLARK
THE MARQUIS DE SADE'S JULIETTE
$4.95/240-X
The Marquis de Sade's infamous Juliette returns—and emerges as the most perverse and destructive nightstalker modern Newt will ever know.

Praise for David Aaron Clark:

"David Aaron Clark has delved into one of the most sensationalistically taboo aspects of eros, sado-masochism, and produced a novel of unmistakable literary imagination and artistic value."
—Carlo McCormick, Paper

ANONYMOUS
NADIA
$5.95/267-1
Follow the delicious but neglected Nadia as she works to wring every drop of pleasure out of life—despite an unhappy marriage. A classic title providing a peek into the secret sexual lives of another time and place.

NIGEL McPARR
THE STORY OF A VICTORIAN MAID
$5.95/241-8
What were the Victorians really like? Chances are, no one believes they were as stuffy as their Queen, but who would have imagined such unbridled libertines! Follow her from exploit to smutty exploit!

MOLLY WEATHERFIELD
CARRIE'S STORY
$5.95/444-5
"I had been Jonathan's slave for about a year when he told me he wanted to sell me at an auction. I wasn't in any condition to respond when he told me this..." Desire and depravity run rampant in this story of uncompromising mastery and irrevocable submission.

BREN FLEMMING
CHARLY'S GAME
$4.95/221-3
A rich woman's gullible daughter has run off with one of the toughest leather dykes in town—and sexy P.I. Charly is hired to lure the girl back. One by one, wise and wicked women ensnare one another in their lusty nets!

ISADORA ALMAN
ASK ISADORA
$4.95/61-0
Six years' worth of Isadora Alman's syndicated columns on sex and relationships. Today's world is more perplexing than ever—and Alman can help untangle the most personal of knots.

TITIAN BERESFORD
THE WICKED HAND
$5.95/343-0
With an Introduction by Leg Show's Dian Hanson. A collection of fetishistic tales featuring the absolute subjugation of men by lovely, domineering women.

CINDERELLA
$6.50/500-X
Beresford triumphs again with this intoxicating tale, filled with castle dungeons and tightly corseted ladies-in-waiting, naughty viscounts and impossibly cruel masturbatrixes—nearly every conceivable method of erotic torture is explored and detailed in lush, vivid detail.

JUDITH BOSTON
$4.95/273-6
Young Edward would have been lucky to get the stodgy old companion he thought his parents had hired for him. Instead, an exquisite woman arrives at his door, and Edward finds his lewd behavior never goes unpunished by the unflinchingly severe Judith Boston! Together they take the downward path to perversion!

NINA FOXTON
$5.95/443-7
An aristocrat finds herself bored by run-of-the-mill amusements for "ladies of good breeding." Instead of taking tea with proper gentlemen, naughty Nina "milks" them of their most private essences. No man ever says "No" to the lovely Nina!

BUY ANY 4 BOOKS & CHOOSE 1 ADDITIONAL BOOK, OF EQUAL OR LESSER VALUE, AS YOUR FREE GIFT

MASQUERADE BOOKS

A TITIAN BERESFORD READER
$4.95/114-4
Wild dominatrixes, perverse masochists, and mesmerizing detail are the hallmarks of the Beresford tale—and encountered here in abundance. The very best scenarios from all of Beresford's bestsellers.

P. N. DEDEAUX
THE NOTHING THINGS
$5.95/404-6
Beta Beta Rho—highly exclusive and widely honored—has taken on a new group of pledges. The five women will be put through the most grueling of ordeals, and punished severely for any shortcomings—much to everyone's delight!
TENDER BUNS
$5.95/396-1
In a fashionable Canadian suburb, Marc Merlin indulges his yen for punishment with an assortment of the town's most desirable and willing women. Things come to a rousing climax at a party planned to cater to just those whims Marc is most able to satisfy....

MICHAEL DRAX
OBSESSIONS
$4.95/3012-1
Victoria is determined to become a model by sexually ensnaring the powerful people who control the fashion industry: Paige, who finds herself compelled to watch Victoria's conquests; and Pietro and Alex, who take turns and then join in for a sizzling threesome. The story of one woman's unslakeable ambition—and lust!

LYN DAVENPORT
DOVER ISLAND
$5.95/384-8
Dr. David Kelly has planted the seeds of his dream— a Corporal Punishment Resort. Soon, many people from varied walks of life descend upon this isolated retreat, intent on fulfilling their every desire. Including Marcy Harris, the perfect partner for the lustful Doctor....
TESSA'S HOLIDAYS
$5.95/377-5
Tessa's lusty lover, Grant, makes sure that each of her holidays is filled with the type of sensual adventure most young women only dream about. What will he dream up next? Only he knows—and he keeps his secrets until the lovely Tessa is ready to explode with desire!
THE GUARDIAN
$5.95/371-6
Felicia grew up under the tutelage of the lash—and she learned her lessons well. Sir Rodney Wentworth has long searched for a woman capable of fulfilling his cruel desires, and after learning of Felicia's talents, sends for her. Felicia discovers that the "position" offered her is delightfully different than anything she could have expected!

LIZBETH DUSSEAU
TRINKETS
$4.95/246-9
"Her bottom danced on the air, pert and fully round. It would take punishment well, he thought." A luscious woman submits to an artist's every whim—becoming the sexual trinket he had always desired.

ANTHONY BOBARZYNSKI
STASI SLUT
$4.95/3050-4
Adina lives in East Germany, where she meets a group of ruthless and corrupt STASI agents who use her for their own perverse gratification—until she uses her talents and attractions in a final bid for total freedom!

JOCELYN JOYCE
PRIVATE LIVES
$4.95/309-0
The lecherous habits of the illustrious make for a sizzling tale of French erotic life. A widow has a craving for a young busboy; he's sleeping with a rich businessman's wife; her husband is minding his sex business elsewhere! Scandalous sexual entanglements run through this tale of upper crust lust!
KIM'S PASSION
$4.95/162-4
The life of an insatiable seductress. Kim leaves India for London, where she quickly takes on the task of bedding every woman in sight!
CAROUSEL
$4.95/3051-2
A young American woman leaves her husband when she discovers he is having an affair with their maid. She then becomes the sexual plaything of Parisian voluptuaries.

SARAH JACKSON
SANCTUARY
$5.95/318-X
Sanctuary explores both the unspeakable debauchery of court life and the unimaginable privations of monastic solitude, leading the voracious and the virtuous on a collision course that brings history to throbbing life.
THE WILD HEART
$4.95/3007-5
A luxury hotel is the setting for this artful web of sex, desire, and love. A newlywed sees sex as a duty, while her hungry husband tries to awaken her to its tender joys. A Parisian entertains wealthy guests for the love of money. Each episode provides a new variation in this lusty Grand Hotel!

LOUISE BELHAVEL
FRAGRANT ABUSES
$4.95/88-2
The saga of Clara and Iris continues as the now-experienced girls enjoy themselves with a new circle of worldly friends whose imaginations match their own. Perversity follows the lusty ladies around the globe!

SARA H. FRENCH
MASTER OF TIMBERLAND
$5.95/327-9
A tale of sexual slavery at the ultimate paradise resort. One of our bestselling titles, this trek to Timberland has ignited passions the world over—and stands poised to become one of modern erotica's legendary tales.

MASQUERADE BOOKS

RETURN TO TIMBERLAND
$5.95/257-4
Prepare for a vacation filled with delicious decadence, as each and every visitor is serviced by unimaginably talented submissives. The raunchiest camp-out ever!

CHINA BLUE
KUNG FU NUNS
$4.95/3031-8
"She lifted me out of the chair and sat me down on top of the table. She then lifted her skirt. The sight of her perfect legs clad in white stockings and a petite garter belt further mesmerized me...." China Blue returns!

ROBERT DESMOND
THE SWEETEST FRUIT
$4.95/95-5
Connie is determined to seduce and destroy the devoted Father Chadcroft. She corrupts the unsuspecting priest into forsaking all that he holds sacred, and drags him into a hell of unbridled lust.

LUSCIDIA WALLACE
KATY'S AWAKENING
$4.95/308-2
Katy thinks she's been rescued after a terrible car wreck. Little does she suspect that she's been ensnared by a ring of swingers, whose tastes run to domination and unimaginably depraved sex parties. With no means of escape, Katy becomes the newest initiate in this sick private club—and soon finds herself becoming more depraved than even her degenerate captors.

MARY LOVE
MASTERING MARY SUE
$5.95/351-1
Mary Sue is a rich nymphomaniac whose husband is determined to declare her mentally incompetent and gain control of her fortune. He brings her to a castle where, to Mary Sue's delight, she is unleashed for a veritable sex-fest!

THE BEST OF MARY LOVE
$4.95/3099-7
Mary Love leaves no coupling untried and no extreme unexplored in these scandalous selections from *Mastering Mary Sue*, *Ecstasy on Fire*, *Vice Park Place*, *Wanda*, and *Naughtier at Night*.

AMARANTHA KNIGHT
THE DARKER PASSIONS: THE PICTURE OF DORIAN GRAY
$6.50/342-2
In this latest installment in the Darker Passions series, Amarantha Knight takes on Oscar Wilde, resulting in a fabulously decadent tale of highly personal changes. One young man finds his most secret desires laid bare by a portrait far more revealing than he could have imagined....

THE DARKER PASSIONS READER
$6.50/432-1
The best moments from Knight's phenomenally popular Darker Passions series. Here are the most eerily erotic passages from her acclaimed sexual reworkings of *Dracula*, *Frankenstein*, *Dr. Jekyll & Mr. Hyde* and *The Fall of the House of Usher*. Be prepared for more than a few thrills and chills from this arousing sampler.

THE DARKER PASSIONS: FRANKENSTEIN
$5.95/248-5
What if you could create a living human? What shocking acts could it be taught to perform, to desire? Find out what pleasures await those who play God....

**THE DARKER PASSIONS:
THE FALL OF THE HOUSE OF USHER**
$5.95/313-9
The Master and Mistress of the house of Usher indulge in every form of decadence, and initiate their guests into the many pleasures to be found in utter submission.

**THE DARKER PASSIONS:
DR. JEKYLL AND MR. HYDE**
$4.95/227-2
It is a story of incredible, frightening transformations achieved through mysterious experiments. Now, Amarantha Knight explores the steamy possibilities of a tale where no one is quite who—or what—they seem. Victorian bedrooms explode with hidden demons!

THE DARKER PASSIONS: DRACULA
$5.95/326-0
The infamous erotic retelling of the Vampire legend.
"Well-written and imaginative, Amarantha Knight gives fresh impetus to this myth, taking us through the sexual and sadistic scenes with details that keep us reading.... A classic in itself has been added to the shelves." —*Divinity*

PAUL LITTLE
THE BEST OF PAUL LITTLE
$6.50/469-0
One of Masquerade's all-time best-selling authors. Known throughout the world for his fantastic portrayals of punishment and pleasure, Little never fails to push readers over the edge of sensual excitement.

ALL THE WAY
$6.95/509-3
Two excruciating novels from Paul Little in one hot volume! *Going All the Way* features an unhappy man who tries to purge himself of the memory of his lover with a series of quirky and uninhibited lovers. *Pushover* tells the story of a serial spanker and his celebrated exploits.

THE DISCIPLINE OF ODETTE
$5.95/334-1
Odette's was sure marriage would rescue her from her family's "corrections." To her horror, she discovers that her beloved has also been raised on discipline. A shocking erotic coupling!

BUY ANY 4 BOOKS & CHOOSE 1 ADDITIONAL BOOK, OF EQUAL OR LESSER VALUE, AS YOUR FREE GIFT

MASQUERADE BOOKS

THE PRISONER
$5.95/330-9
Judge Black has built a secret room below a penitentiary, where he sentences the prisoners to hours of exhibition and torment while his friends watch. Judge Black's House of Corrections is equipped with one purpose in mind: to administer his own brand of rough justice!

TEARS OF THE INQUISITION
$4.95/146-2
The incomparable Paul Little delivers a staggering account of pleasure and punishment. "There was a tickling inside her as her nervous system reminded her she was ready for sex. But before her was...the Inquisitor!"

DOUBLE NOVEL
$4.95/86-6
The Metamorphosis of Lisette Joyaux tells the story of a young woman initiated into a new world of lesbian lusts. *The Story of Monique* reveals the sexual rituals that beckon the ripe and willing Monique.

CHINESE JUSTICE AND OTHER STORIES
$4.95/153-5
The story of the excruciating pleasures and delicious punishments inflicted on foreigners under the leaders of the Boxer Rebellion. Each foreign woman is brought before the authorities and grilled. Scandalous deeds!

CAPTIVE MAIDENS
$5.95/440-2
Three beautiful young women find themselves powerless against the debauched landowners of 1824 England. They are banished to a sexual slave colony, and corrupted by every imaginable perversion. Soon, they come to crave the treatment of their unrelenting captors, and find themselves insatiable.

SLAVE ISLAND
$5.95/441-0
A leisure cruise is waylaid, finding itself in the domain of Lord Henry Philbrock, a sadistic genius. The ship's passengers are kidnapped and spirited to his island prison, where the women are trained to accommodate the most bizarre sexual cravings of the rich, the famous, the pampered and the perverted. An incredible bestseller, which cemented Little's reputation as a master of contemporary erotic literature.

ALIZARIN LAKE
SEX ON DOCTOR'S ORDERS
$5.95/402-X
A chronicle of selfless devotion to mankind! Beth, a nubile young nurse, uses her considerable skills to further medical science by offering incomparable and insatiable assistance in the gathering of important specimens. No man leaves naughty Nurse Beth's station without surrendering exactly what she needs!

THE EROTIC ADVENTURES OF HARRY TEMPLE
$4.95/127-6
Harry Temple's memoirs chronicle his amorous adventures from his initiation at the hands of insatiable sirens, through his stay at a house of hot repute, to his encounters with a chastity-belted nympho!

JOHN NORMAN
TARNSMAN OF GOR
$6.95/486-0
This legendary—and controversial—series returns! *Tarnsman* finds Tarl Cabot transported to Counter-Earth, better known as Gor. He must quickly accustom himself to the ways of this world, including the caste system which exalts some as Priest-Kings or Warriors, and debases others as slaves. A spectacular world unfolds in this first volume of John Norman's million-selling Gorean series.

OUTLAW OF GOR
$6.95/487-9
In this second volume, Tarl Cabot returns to Gor, where he might reclaim both his woman and his role of Warrior. But upon arriving, he discovers that his name, his city and the names of those he loves have become unspeakable. In his absence, Cabot has become an outlaw, and must discover his new purpose on this strange planet, where danger stalks the outcast, and even simple answers have their price....

PRIEST-KINGS OF GOR
$6.95/488-7
The third volume of John Norman's million-selling, controversial Gor series. Tarl Cabot, brave Tarnsman of Gor, searches for the truth about his lovely wife Talena. Does she live, or was she destroyed by the mysterious, all-powerful Priest-Kings? Cabot is determined to find out— while knowing that no one who has approached the mountain stronghold of the Priest-Kings has ever returned alive....

RACHEL PEREZ
ODD WOMEN
$4.95/123-3
These women are sexy, smart, tough—some even say odd. But who cares, when their combined ass-ets are so sweet! An assortment of Sapphic sirens proves once and for all that comely ladies come best in pairs.

ALIZARIN LAKE
SEX ON DOCTOR'S ORDERS
$5.95/402-X
Beth, a nubile young nurse, uses her considerable skills to further medical science by offering incomparable and insatiable assistance in the gathering of important specimens. No man leaves naughty Nurse Beth's station without surrendering exactly what she needs!

THE EROTIC ADVENTURES OF HARRY TEMPLE
$4.95/127-6
Harry Temple's memoirs chronicle his amorous adventures from his initiation at the hands of insatiable sirens, through his stay at a house of hot repute, to his encounters with a chastity-belted nympho!

AFFINITIES
$4.95/113-6
"Kelsy had a liking for cool upper-class blondes, the long-legged girls from Lake Forest and Winnetka who came into the city to cruise the lesbian bars on Halsted, looking for breathless ecstasies...." A scorching tale of lesbian libidos unleashed, from a writer more than capable of exploring every nuance of female passion in vivid detail.

MASQUERADE BOOKS

SYDNEY ST. JAMES

RIVE GAUCHE
$5.95/317-1
The Latin Quarter, Paris, circa 1920. Expatriate bohemians couple with abandon—before eventually abandoning their ambitions amidst the intoxicating temptations waiting to be indulged in every bedroom.

THE HIGHWAYWOMAN
$4.95/174-8
A young filmmaker making a documentary about the life of the notorious English highwaywoman, Bess Ambrose, becomes obsessed with her mysterious subject. It seems that Bess touched more than hearts—and plundered the treasures of every man and maiden she met on the way. Incredible extremes of passion are reached by not only the voluptuous filmmaker, but her insatiable subject!

GARDEN OF DELIGHT
$4.95/3058-X
A vivid account of sexual awakening that follows an innocent but insatiably curious young woman's journey from the furtive, forbidden joys of dormitory life to the unabashed carnality of the wild world. A coming of age story unlike any other!

MARCUS VAN HELLER

TERROR
$5.95/247-7
Another shocking exploration of lust by the author of the ever-popular *Adam & Eve*. Set in Paris during the Algerian War, Terror explores the place of sexual passion in a world drunk on violence.

KIDNAP
$4.95/90-4
P. I. Harding is called in to investigate a mysterious kidnapping case involving the rich and powerful. Along the way he has the pleasure of "interrogating" an exotic dancer named Jeanne and a beautiful English reporter, as he finds himself enmeshed in the crime underworld.

ALEXANDER TROCCHI

THONGS
$4.95/217-5
"...In Spain, life is cheap, from that glittering tragedy in the bullring to the quick thrust of the stiletto in a narrow street in a Barcelona slum. No, this death would not have called for further comment had it not been for one striking fact. The naked woman had met her end in a way he had never seen before—a way that had enormous sexual significance. My God, she had been..." Trocchi's acclaimed classic returns.

HELEN AND DESIRE
$4.95/3093-8
Helen Seferis' flight from the oppressive village of her birth became a sexual tour of a harsh world. From brothels in Sydney to harems in Algiers, Helen chronicles her adventures fully in her diary. Each encounter is examined in the scorching and uncensored diary of the sensual Helen!

THE CARNAL DAYS OF HELEN SEFERIS
$4.95/3086-5
P.I. Anthony Harvest is assigned to save Helen Seferis, a beautiful Australian who has been abducted. Following clues in her explicit diary of adventures, he pursues the lovely, doomed Helen—the ultimate sexual prize.

DON WINSLOW

THE INSATIABLE MISTRESS OF ROSEDALE
$6.50/494-1
The story of the perfect couple: Edward and Lady Penelope, who reside in beautiful and mysterious Rosedale manor. While Edward is a true connoisseur of sexual perversion, it is Lady Penelope whose mastery of complete sensual pleasure makes their home infamous. Indulging one another's bizarre whims is a way of life for this wicked couple, and none who encounter the extravagances of Rosedale will forget what they've learned....

SECRETS OF CHEATEM MANOR
$6.50/434-8
Edward returns to his late father's estate, to find it being run by the majestic Lady Amanda. Edward can hardly believe his luck—Lady Amanda is assisted by her two beautiful, lonely daughters, Catherine and Prudence. What the randy young man soon comes to realize is the love of discipline that all three beauties share.

KATERINA IN CHARGE
$5.95/409-7
When invited to a country retreat by a mysterious couple, the two randy young ladies can hardly resist! But do they have any idea what they're in for? Whatever the case, the imperious Katerina will make her desires known very soon—and demand that they be fulfilled...

THE MANY PLEASURES OF IRONWOOD
$5.95/310-4
Seven lovely young women are employed by The Ironwood Sportsmen's Club A small and exclusive club with seven carefully selected sexual connoisseurs, Ironwood is dedicated to the relentless pursuit of sensual pleasure.

CLAIRE'S GIRLS
$5.95/442-9
You knew when she walked by that she was something special. She was one of Claire's girls, a woman carefully dressed and groomed to fill a role, to capture a look, to fit an image crafted by the sophisticated proprietress of an exclusive escort agency. High-class whores blow the roof off!

N. WHALLEN

TAU'TEVU
$6.50/426-7
In a mysterious land, the statuesque and beautiful Vivian learns to subject herself to the hand of a mysterious man. He systematically helps her prove her own strength, and brings to life in her an unimagined sensual fire. But who is this man, who goes only by the name of Orpheo?

BUY ANY 4 BOOKS & CHOOSE 1 ADDITIONAL BOOK, OF EQUAL OR LESSER VALUE, AS YOUR FREE GIFT

MASQUERADE BOOKS

COMPLIANCE
$5.95/356-2
Fourteen stories exploring the pleasures of release. Characters from all walks of life learn to trust in the skills of others, only to experience the thrilling liberation of submission. Here are the joys to be found in some of the most forbidden sexual practices around....

THE MASQUERADE READERS
THE VELVET TONGUE
$4.95/3029-6
An orgy of oral gratification! *The Velvet Tongue* celebrates the most mouth-watering, lip-smacking, tongue-twisting action. A feast of fellatio and *soixante-neuf* awaits readers of excellent taste at this steamy suck-fest.

A MASQUERADE READER
$4.95/84-X
A sizzling sampler. Strict lessons are learned at the hand of *The English Governess*. Scandalous confessions are found in *The Diary of an Angel*, and the story of a woman whose desires drove her to the ultimate sacrifice in *Thongs* completes the collection.

THE CLASSIC COLLECTION
PROTESTS, PLEASURES, RAPTURES
$5.95/400-3
Invited for an allegedly quiet weekend at a country vicarage, a young woman is stunned to find herself surrounded by shocking acts of sexual sadism. Soon, her curiosity is piqued, and she begins to explore her own capacities for cruelty.

THE YELLOW ROOM
$5.95/378-3
The "yellow room" holds the secrets of lust, lechery, and the lash. There, bare-bottomed, spread-eagled, and open to the world, demure Alice Darvell soon learns to love her lickings. In the second tale, hot heiress Rosa Coote and her adventures in punishment and pleasure.

SCHOOL DAYS IN PARIS
$5.95/325-2
The rapturous chronicles of a well-spent youth! Few Universities provide the profound and pleasurable lessons one learns in after-hours study—particularly if one is young and available, and lucky enough to have Paris as a playground. A stimulating look at the pursuits of young adulthood.

MAN WITH A MAID
$4.95/307-4
The adventures of Jack and Alice have delighted readers for eight decades! A classic of its genre, *Man with a Maid* tells an outrageous tale of desire, revenge, and submission. This tale qualifies as one of the world's most popular adult novels—with over 200,000 copies in print!

MAN WITH A MAID II
$4.95/3071-7
Jack's back! With the assistance of the perverse Alice, he embarks again on a trip through every erotic extreme. Jack leaves no one unsatisfied—least of all, himself—and Alice is always certain to outdo herself in her capacity to corrupt and control. An incendiary sequel!

MAN WITH A MAID: THE CONCLUSION
$4.95/3013-X
The conclusion to the epic saga of lust that has thrilled readers for decades. The adulterous woman who is corrected with enthusiasm and the maid who receives grueling guidance are just two who benefit from these lessons!

CONFESSIONS OF A CONCUBINE III: PLEASURE'S PRISONER
$5.95/357-0
Filled with pulse-pounding excitement—including a daring escape from the harem and an encounter with an unspeakable sadist—*Pleasure's Prisoner* adds an unforgettable chapter to this thrilling confessional.

CONFESSIONS OF A CONCUBINE II: HAREM SLAVE
$4.95/226-4
The concubinage continues, as the true pleasures and privileges of the harem are revealed. For the first time, readers are invited behind the veils that hide uninhibited, unimaginable pleasures from the world....

LADY F.
$4.95/102-0
An uncensored tale of Victorian passions. Master Kidrodstock suffers deliciously at the hands of the stunningly cruel and sensuous Lady Flayskin—the only woman capable of taming his wayward impulses. A fevered chronicle of punishing passions.

CLASSIC EROTIC BIOGRAPHIES
JENNIFER III
$5.95/292-2
The further adventures of erotica's most daring heroine. Jennifer, the quintessential beautiful blonde, has a photographer's eye for details—particularly of the masculine variety!

JENNIFER AGAIN
$4.95/220-5
One of modern erotica's most famous heroines. Once again, the insatiable Jennifer seizes the day—and extracts from it every last drop of sensual pleasure! No man is immune to this vixen's charms.

JENNIFER
$4.95/107-1
From the bedroom of a notoriously insatiable dancer to an uninhibited ashram, *Jennifer* traces the exploits of one thoroughly modern woman as she lustfully explores the limits of her own sexuality.

THE ROMANCES OF BLANCHE LA MARE
$4.95/101-2
When Blanche loses her husband, it becomes clear she'll need a job. She sets her sights on the stage—and soon encounters a cast of lecherous characters intent on making her path to sucksess as hot and hard as possible!

PETER JASON
WAYWARD
$4.95/3004-0
A mysterious countess hires a tour bus for an unusual vacation. Traveling through Europe's most notorious cities, she picks up friends, lovers, and acquaintances from every walk of life in pursuit of pleasure.

MASQUERADE BOOKS

RHINOCEROS

ROMY ROSEN
SPUNK
$6.95/492-5
A scintillating tale of unearthly beauty, outrageous decadence, and brutal exploitation. Casey, a lovely model poised upon the verge of super-celebrity, falls hard for a insatiable young rock singer—not suspecting that his sexual appetite has led him to experiment with a dangerous new aphrodisiac. Casey becomes an addict, and her craving plunges her into a strange underworld, where bizarre sexual compulsions are indulged behind the most exclusive doors and the only chance for redemption lies with a shadowy young man with a secret of his own.

CYBERSEX CONSORTIUM
THE PERV'S GUIDE TO THE INTERNET
$6.95/471-2
You've heard the objections: cyberspace is soaked with sex, piled high with prurience, mired in immorality. Okay—so where is it!? Tracking down the good stuff—the real good stuff—can waste an awful lot of expensive time, and frequently leave you high and dry. But now, the Cybersex Consortium presents an easy-to-use guide for those intrepid adults who know what they want. No horny hacker can afford to pass up this map to the kinkiest rest stops on the Info Superhighway.

AMELIA G, EDITOR
BACKSTAGE PASSES
$6.96/438-0
A collection of some of the most raucous writing around. Amelia G, editor of the goth-sex journal *Blue Blood*, has brought together some of today's most irreverant writers, each of whom has outdone themselves with an edgy, antic tale of modern lust. Punks, metalheads, and grunge-trash roam the pages of *Backstage Passes*, and no one knows their ways better...

GERI NETTICK WITH BETH ELLIOT
MIRRORS: PORTRAIT OF A LESBIAN TRANSSEXUAL
$6.95/435-6
The alternately heartbreaking and empowering story of one woman's long road to full selfhood. Born a male, Geri Nettick knew something just didn't fit. And even after coming to terms with her own gender dysphoria—and taking steps to correct it—she still fought to be accepted by the lesbian feminist community to which she felt she belonged. A fascinating, true tale of struggle and discovery.

TRISTAN TAORMINO & DAVID AARON CLARK, EDITORS
RITUAL SEX
$6.95/391-0
While many people believe the body and soul to occupy almost completely independent realms, the many contributors to *Ritual Sex* know—and demonstrate—that the two share more common ground than society feels comfortable acknowledging. From personal memoirs of ecstatic revelation, to fictional quests to reconcile sex and spirit, *Ritual Sex* delves into forbidden areas with gusto, providing an unprecedented look at private life.

DAVID MELTZER
UNDER
$6.95/290-6
The story of a sex professional living at the bottom of the social heap. After surgeries designed to increase his physical allure, corrupt government forces drive the cyber-gigolo underground—where even more bizarre cultures await him.

ORF
$6.95/110-1
He is the ultimate musician-hero—the idol of thousands, the fevered dream of many more. And like many musicians before him, he is misunderstood, misused—and totally out of control. Every last drop of feeling is squeezed from a modern-day troubadour and his lady love.

TAMMY JO ECKHART
PUNISHMENT FOR THE CRIME
$6.95/427-5
Peopled by characters of rare depth, these stories explore the true meaning of dominance and submission, and offer some surprising revelations. From an encounter between two of society's most despised individuals, to the explorations of longtime friends, these tales take you where few others have ever dared....

THOMAS S. ROCHE, EDITOR
NOIROTICA: AN ANTH. OF EROTIC CRIME STORIES
$6.95/390-2
A collection of darkly sexy tales, taking place at the crossroads of the crime and erotic genres. Thomas S. Roche has gathered together some of today's finest writers of sexual fiction, all of whom explore the murky terrain where desire runs irrevocably afoul of the law.

AMARANTHA KNIGHT, EDITOR
SEDUCTIVE SPECTRES
$6.95/464-X
Breathtaking tours through the erotic supernatural via the macabre imaginations of today's best writers. Never before have ghostly encounters been so alluring, thanks to a cast of otherworldly characters well-acquainted with the pleasures of the flesh.

BUY ANY 4 BOOKS & CHOOSE 1 ADDITIONAL BOOK, OF EQUAL OR LESSER VALUE, AS YOUR FREE GIFT

MASQUERADE BOOKS

SEX MACABRE
$6.95/392-9
Horror tales designed for dark and sexy nights. Amarantha Knight—the woman behind the Darker Passions series, as well as the spine-tingling anthologies *Flesh Fantastic* and *Love Bites*—has gathered together erotic stories sure to make your skin crawl, and heart beat faster.

FLESH FANTASTIC
$6.95/352-X
Humans have long toyed with the idea of "playing God": creating life from nothingness, bringing life to the inanimate. Now Amarantha Knight, author of the "Darker Passions" series, collects stories exploring not only the act of Creation, but the lust that follows....

GARY BOWEN
DIARY OF A VAMPIRE
$6.95/331-7
"Gifted with a darkly sensual vision and a fresh voice, [Bowen] is a writer to watch out for."
—Cecilia Tan

The chilling, arousing, and ultimately moving memoirs of an undead—but all too human—soul. Bowen's Rafael, a red-blooded male with an insatiable hunger for the same, is the perfect antidote to the effete malcontents haunting bookstores today. *Diary of a Vampire* marks the emergence of a bold and brilliant vision, firmly rooted in past and present.

LAURA ANTONIOU, EDITOR
NO OTHER TRIBUTE
$6.95/294-9
A collection sure to challenge Political Correctness in a way few have before, with tales of women kept in bondage to their lovers by their deepest passions. Love pushes these women beyond acceptable limits, rendering them helpless to deny anything to the men and women they adore. A volume dedicated to all Slaves of Desire.

SOME WOMEN
$6.95/300-7
Over forty essays written by women actively involved in consensual dominance and submission. Professional mistresses, lifestyle leatherdykes, whipmakers, titleholders—women from every conceivable walk of life lay bare their true feelings about explosive issues.

BY HER SUBDUED
$6.95/281-7
These tales all involve women in control—of their lives, their loves, their men. So much in control that they can remorselessly break rules to become powerful goddesses of the men who sacrifice all to worship at their feet.

RENÉ MAIZEROY
FLESHLY ATTRACTIONS
$6.95/299-X
Lucien was the son of the wantonly beautiful actress, Marie-Rose Hardanges. When she decides to let a "friend" introduce her son to the pleasures of love, Marie-Rose could not have foretold the excesses that would lead to her own ruin and that of her cherished son.

JEAN STINE
THRILL CITY
$6.95/411-9
Thrill City is the seat of the world's increasing depravity, and Jean Stine's classic novel transports you there with a vivid style you'd be hard pressed to ignore. No writer is better suited to describe the unspeakable extremes of this modern Babylon.

SEASON OF THE WITCH
$6.95/268-X
"A future in which it is technically possible to transfer the total mind...of a rapist killer into the brain dead but physically living body of his female victim. Remarkable for intense psychological technique. There is eroticism but it is necessary to mark the differences between the sexes and the subtle altering of a man into a woman."
—The Science Fiction Critic

JOHN WARREN
THE TORQUEMADA KILLER
$6.95/367-8
Detective Eva Hernandez gets her first "big case": a string of vicious murders taking place within New York's SM community. Eva assembles the evidence, revealing a picture of a world misunderstood and under attack—and gradually comes to understand her own place within it.

THE LOVING DOMINANT
$6.95/218-3
Everything you need to know about an infamous sexual variation—and an unspoken type of love. Mentor—a longtime player in scene—guides readers through this world and reveals the too-often hidden basis of the D/S relationship: care, trust and love.

GRANT ANTREWS
MY DARLING DOMINATRIX
$6.95/447-X
When a man and a woman fall in love, it's supposed to be simple, uncomplicated, easy—unless that woman happens to be a dominatrix. Curiosity gives way to unblushing desire in this story of one man's awakening to the joys of willing slavery.

LAURA ANTONIOU WRITING AS "SARA ADAMSON"
THE TRAINER
$6.95/249-3
The Marketplace—the ultimate underground sexual realm includes not only willing slaves, but the exquisite trainers who take submissives firmly in hand. And now these mentors divulge the desires that led them to become the ultimate figures of authority.

THE SLAVE
$6.95/173-X
This second volume in the "Marketplace" trilogy further elaborates the world of slaves and masters. One talented submissive longs to join the ranks of those who have proven themselves worthy of entry into the Marketplace. But the delicious price is staggeringly high....

MASQUERADE BOOKS

THE MARKETPLACE
$6.95/3096-9
"Merchandise does not come easily to the Marketplace.... They haunt the clubs and the organizations.... Some are so ripe that they intimidate the poseurs, the weekend sadists and the furtive dilettantes who are so endemic to that world. And they never stop asking where we may be found...."

DAVID AARON CLARK

SISTER RADIANCE
$6.95/215-9
Rife with Clark's trademark vivisections of contemporary desires, sacred and profane. The vicissitudes of lust and romance are examined against a backdrop of urban decay in this testament to the allure of the forbidden.

THE WET FOREVER
$6.95/117-0
The story of Janus and Madchen—a small-time hood and a beautiful sex worker on the run from one of the most dangerous men they have ever known—*The Wet Forever* examines themes of loyalty, sacrifice, obsession and redemption amidst Manhattan's sex parlors and underground S/M clubs. Its combination of sex and suspense led Terence Sellers to proclaim it "evocative and poetic."

MICHAEL PERKINS

EVIL COMPANIONS
$6.95/3067-9
Set in New York City during the tumultuous waning years of the Sixties, *Evil Companions* has been hailed as "a frightening classic." A young couple explores the nether reaches of the erotic unconscious in a shocking confrontation with the extremes of passion.

THE SECRET RECORD: MODERN EROTIC LITERATURE
$6.95/3039-3
Michael Perkins surveys the field with authority and unique insight. Updated and revised to include the latest trends, tastes, and developments in this misunderstood and maligned genre.

AN ANTHOLOGY OF CLASSIC ANONYMOUS EROTIC WRITING
$6.95/140-3
Michael Perkins has collected the very best passages from the world's erotic writing. "Anonymous" is one of the most infamous bylines in publishing history—and these steamy excerpts show why! Includes excerpts from some of the most famous titles in the history of erotic literature.

LIESEL KULIG

LOVE IN WARTIME
$6.95/3044-X
Madeleine knew that the handsome SS officer was a dangerous man, but she was just a cabaret singer in Nazi-occupied Paris, trying to survive in a perilous time. When Josef fell in love with her, he discovered that a beautiful and amoral woman can sometimes be wildly dangerous.

HELEN HENLEY

ENTER WITH TRUMPETS
$6.95/197-7
Helen Henley was told that women just don't write about sex—much less the taboos she was so interested in exploring. So Henley did it alone, flying in the face of "tradition," by writing this touching tale of arousal and devotion in one couple's kinky relationship.

ALICE JOANOU

BLACK TONGUE
$6.95/258-2
"Joanou has created a series of sumptuous, brooding, dark visions of sexual obsession, and is undoubtedly a name to look out for in the future."
—Redeemer
Exploring lust at its most florid and unsparing, *Black Tongue* is a trove of baroque fantasies—each redolent of forbidden passions. Joanou creates some of erotica's most mesmerizing and unforgettable characters.

TOURNIQUET
$6.95/3060-1
A heady collection of stories and effusions from the pen of one our most dazzling young writers. Strange tales abound, from the story of the mysterious and cruel Cybele, to an encounter with the sadistic entertainment of a bizarre after-hours cafe. A complex and riveting series of meditations on desire.

CANNIBAL FLOWER
$4.95/72-6
The provocative debut volume from this acclaimed writer.
"She is waiting in her darkened bedroom, as she has waited throughout history, to seduce the men who are foolish enough to be blinded by her irresistible charms.... She is the goddess of sexuality, and *Cannibal Flower* is her haunting siren song."
—Michael Perkins

TUPPY OWENS

SENSATIONS
$6.95/3081-4
Tuppy Owens tells the unexpurgated story of the making of *Sensations*—the first big-budget sex flick. Originally commissioned to appear in book form after the release of the film in 1975, *Sensations* is finally released under Masquerade's stylish Rhino*ceros* imprint.

SOPHIE GALLEYMORE BIRD

MANEATER
$6.95/103-9
Through a bizarre act of creation, a man attains the "perfect" lover—by all appearances a beautiful, sensuous woman, but in reality something far darker. Once brought to life she will accept no mate, seeking instead the prey that will sate her hunger for vengeance. A biting take on the war of the sexes, this debut goes for the jugular of the "perfect woman" myth.

BUY ANY 4 BOOKS & CHOOSE 1 ADDITIONAL BOOK, OF EQUAL OR LESSER VALUE, AS YOUR FREE GIFT

MASQUERADE BOOKS

PHILIP JOSÉ FARMER
FLESH
$6.95/303-1
Space Commander Stagg explored the galaxies for 800 years. Upon his return, Stagg is made the centerpiece of an incredible public ritual—one that will repeatedly take him to the heights of ecstasy, and inexorably drag him toward the depths of hell.

A FEAST UNKNOWN
$6.95/276-0
"Sprawling, brawling, shocking, suspenseful, hilarious..." —Theodore Sturgeon
Farmer's supreme anti-hero returns. "I was conceived and born in 1888." Slowly, Lord Grandrith—armed with the belief that he is the son of Jack the Ripper—tells the story of his remarkable and unbridled life. His story begins with his discovery of the secret of immortality—and progresses to encompass the furthest extremes of human behavior. A classic of speculative erotica.

THE IMAGE OF THE BEAST
$6.95/166-7
Herald Childe has seen Hell, glimpsed its horror in an act of sexual mutilation. Childe must now find and destroy an inhuman predator through the streets of a polluted and decadent Los Angeles of the future. One clue after another leads Childe to an inescapable realization about the nature of sex and evil....

DANIEL VIAN
ILLUSIONS
$6.95/3074-1
Two tales of danger and desire in Berlin on the eve of WWII. From private homes to lurid cafés, passion is exposed in stark contrast to the brutal violence of the time. Two sexy tales examining a remarkably decadent age.

PERSUASIONS
$6.95/183-7
A double novel, including the classics *Adagio* and *Gabriela and the General*, this volume traces desire around the globe. Two classics of international lust!

SAMUEL R. DELANY
THE MAD MAN
$8.99/408-9
"Reads like a pornographic reflection of Peter Ackroyd's *Chatterton* or A. S. Byatt's *Possession*.... Delany develops an insightful dichotomy between [his protagonist]'s two worlds: the one of cerebral philosophy and dry academia, the other of headless, 'impersonal' obsessive sexual extremism. When these worlds finally collide...the novel achieves a surprisingly satisfying resolution...." —Publishers Weekly
For his thesis, graduate student John Marr researches the life of Timothy Hasler: a philosopher whose career was cut tragically short over a decade earlier. On another front, Marr finds himself increasingly drawn toward shocking, depraved sexual entanglements with the homeless men of his neighborhood, until it begins to seem that Hasler's death might hold some key to his own life as a gay man in the age of AIDS.

EQUINOX
$6.95/157-8
The Scorpion has sailed the seas in a quest for every possible pleasure. Her crew is a collection of the young, the twisted, the insatiable. A drifter comes into their midst and is taken on a fantastic journey to the darkest, most dangerous sexual extremes—until he is finally a victim to their boundless appetites.

ANDREI CODRESCU
THE REPENTANCE OF LORRAINE
$6.95/329-5
"One of our most prodigiously talented and magical writers." —NYT Book Review
By the acclaimed author of *The Hole in the Flag* and *The Blood Countess*. An aspiring writer, a professor's wife, a secretary, gold anklets, Maoists, Roman harlots—and more—swirl through this spicy tale of a harried quest for a mythic artifact. Written when the author was a young man, this lusty yarn was inspired by the heady days of the Sixties.

LEOPOLD VON SACHER-MASOCH
VENUS IN FURS
$6.95/3089-X
This classic 19th century novel is the first uncompromising exploration of the dominant/submissive relationship in literature. The alliance of Severin and Wanda epitomizes Sacher-Masoch's dark obsession with a cruel, controlling goddess and the urges that drive the man held in her thrall. This special edition includes the letters exchanged between Sacher-Masoch and Emilie Mataja, an aspiring writer he sought to cast as the avatar of the forbidden desires expressed in his most famous work.

BADBOY

JULIAN ANTHONY GUERRA, EDITOR
COME QUICKLY: FOR BOYS ON THE GO
$6.50/413-5
The increasing pace of daily life is no reason a guy has to forgo a little carnal pleasure whenever the mood strikes him. Here are over sixty of the hottest fantasies around—all designed to get you going in less time than it takes to dial 976. Julian Anthony Guerra, the editor behind the phenomenally popular *Men at Work* and *Badboy Fantasies*, has put together this volume especially for you—a man on a modern schedule, who still appreciates a little old-fashioned action.

MATT TOWNSEND
SOLIDLY BUILT
$6.50/416-X
The tale of the tumultuous relationship between Jeff, a young photographer, and Mark, the butch electrician hired to wire Jeff's new home. For Jeff, it's love at first sight; Mark, however, has more than a few hang-ups. Soon, both are forced to reevaluate their outlooks, and are assisted by a variety of hot men....

MASQUERADE BOOKS

JOHN PRESTON

MR. BENSON
$4.95/3041-5
A classic erotic novel from a time when there was no limit to what a man could dream of doing.... Jamie is an aimless young man lucky enough to encounter Mr. Benson. He is soon led down the path of erotic enlightenment, learning to accept this man as his master. Jamie's incredible adventures never fail to excite—especially when the going gets rough!

TALES FROM THE DARK LORD
$5.95/323-6
A new collection of twelve stunning works from the man *Lambda Book Report* called "the Dark Lord of gay erotica." The relentless ritual of lust and surrender is explored in all its manifestations in this heart-stopping triumph of authority and vision from the Dark Lord!

TALES FROM THE DARK LORD II
$4.95/176-4
The second volume of acclaimed eroticist John Preston's masterful short stories. Also includes an interview with the author, and an explicit screenplay written for pornstar Scott O'Hara.

THE ARENA
$4.95/3083-0
There is a place on the edge of fantasy where every desire is indulged with abandon. Men go there to unleash beasts, to let demons roam free, to abolish all limits. At the center of each tale are the men who serve there, who offer themselves for the consummation of any passion, whose own bottomless urges compel their endless subservience.

THE HEIR•THE KING
$4.95/3048-2
The ground-breaking novel *The Heir*, written in the lyric voice of the ancient myths, tells the story of a world where slaves and masters create a new sexual society. This edition also includes a completely original work, *The King*, the story of a soldier who discovers his monarch's most secret desires. Available only from Badboy.

THE MISSION OF ALEX KANE

SWEET DREAMS
$4.95/3062-8
It's the triumphant return of gay action hero Alex Kane! In *Sweet Dreams*, Alex travels to Boston where he takes on a street gang that stalks gay teenagers. Mighty Alex Kane wreaks a fierce and terrible vengeance on those who prey on gay people everywhere!

GOLDEN YEARS
$4.95/3069-5
When evil threatens the plans of a group of older gay men, Kane's got the muscle to take it head on. Along the way, he wins the support—and very specialized attentions—of a cowboy plucked right out of the Old West. But Kane and the Cowboy have a surprise waiting for them....

DEADLY LIES
$4.95/3076-8
Politics is a dirty business and the dirt becomes deadly when a political smear campaign targets gay men. Who better to clean things up than Alex Kane! Alex comes to protect the dreams, and lives, of gay men imperiled by lies.

STOLEN MOMENTS
$4.95/3098-9
Houston's evolving gay community is victimized by a malicious newspaper editor who is more than willing to sacrifice gays on the altar of circulation. He never counted on Alex Kane, fearless defender of gay dreams and desires.

SECRET DANGER
$4.95/111-X
Homophobia: a pernicious social ill not confined by America's borders. Alex Kane and the faithful Danny are called to a small European country, where a group of gay tourists is being held hostage by ruthless terrorists. Luckily, the Mission of Alex Kane stands as firm foreign policy.

LETHAL SILENCE
$4.95/125-X
The Mission of Alex Kane thunders to a conclusion. Chicago becomes the scene of the right-wing's most noxious plan—facilitated by unholy political alliances. Alex and Danny head to the Windy City to take up battle with the mercenaries who would squash gay men underfoot.

JAY SHAFFER

WET DREAMS
$6.50/495-X
Sweaty, sloppy sex runs throughout this collection of super-hot, hypermasculine sex-tales from one of our most accomplished Badboys. Each of these stories takes a hot, hard look at the obsessions that keep men up all night. Provocative and affecting, this is a night full of dreams you won't forget in the morning.

SHOOTERS
$5.95/284-1
No mere catalog of random acts, *Shooters* tells the stories of a variety of stunning men and the ways they connect in sexual and non-sexual ways. A virtuoso storyteller, Shaffer always gets his man.

ANIMAL HANDLERS
$4.95/264-7
In Shaffer's world, each and every man finally succumbs to the animal urges deep inside. And if there's any creature that promises a wild time, it's a beast who's been caged for far too long.

FULL SERVICE
$4.95/150-0
Wild men build up steam until they finally let loose. No-nonsense guys bear down hard on each other as they work their way toward release in this finely detailed assortment of masculine fantasies. One of gay erotica's most insightful chroniclers of male passion.

BUY ANY 4 BOOKS & CHOOSE 1 ADDITIONAL BOOK, OF EQUAL OR LESSER VALUE, AS YOUR FREE GIFT

MASQUERADE BOOKS

D. V. SADERO
REVOLT OF THE NAKED
$4.95/261-2
In a distant galaxy, there are two classes of humans: Freemen and Nakeds. Freemen are full citizens; Nakeds live only to serve their Masters, and obey every sexual order with haste and devotion.

IN THE ALLEY
$4.95/144-6
Hardworking men—from cops to carpenters—bring their own special skills and impressive tools to the most satisfying job of all: capturing and breaking the male sexual beast. Hot, incisive and way over the top!

SCOTT O'HARA
DO-IT-YOURSELF PISTON POLISHING
$6.50/489-5
Longtime sex-pro Scott O'Hara draws upon his acute powers of seduction to lure you into a world of hard, horny men long overdue for a tune-up. Pretty soon, you'll pop your own hood for the servicing you know you need....

SUTTER POWELL
EXECUTIVE PRIVILEGES
$6.50/383-X
No matter how serious or sexy a predicament his characters find themselves in, Powell conveys the sheer exuberance of their encounters with a warm humor rarely seen in contemporary gay erotica.

GARY BOWEN
MAN HUNGRY
$5.95/374-0
By the author of *Diary of a Vampire*. A riveting collection of stories from one of gay erotica's new stars. Dipping into a variety of genres, Bowen crafts tales of lust unlike anything being published today.

KYLE STONE
FIRE & ICE
$5.95/297-3
A collection of stories from the author of the infamous adventures of PB 500. Randy, powerful, and just plain bad, Stone's characters always promise one thing: enough hot action to burn away your desire for anyone else....

HOT BAUDS
$5.95/285-X
The author of *Fantasy Board* and *The Initiation of PB 500* combed cyberspace for the hottest fantasies of the world's horniest hackers. Stone has assembled the first collection of the raunchy erotica so many gay men cruise the Information Superhighway for.

FANTASY BOARD
$4.95/212-4
The author of the scalding sci-fi adventures of PB 500 explores the more foreseeable future—through the intertwined lives (and private parts) of a collection of randy computer hackers. On the Lambda Gate BBS, every hot and horny male is in search of a little virtual satisfaction.

THE CITADEL
$4.95/198-5
The sequel to *The Initiation of PB 500*. Having proven himself worthy of his stunning master, Micah—now known only as '500'—will face new challenges and hardships after his entry into the forbidding Citadel. Only his master knows what awaits—and whether Micah will again distinguish himself as the perfect instrument of pleasure....

THE INITIATION OF PB 500
$4.95/141-1
An interstellar accident strands a young stud on an alien planet. He is a stranger on their planet, unschooled in their language, and ignorant of their customs. But this man, Micah—now known only by his number—will soon be trained in every last detail of erotic personal service. And, once nurtured and transformed into the perfect physical specimen, he must begin proving himself worthy of the master who has chosen him....

RITUALS
$4.95/168-3
Via a computer bulletin board, a young man finds himself drawn into a series of sexual rites that transform him into the willing slave of a mysterious stranger. Gradually, all vestiges of his former life are thrown off, and he learns to live for his Master's touch....

JOHN ROWBERRY
LEWD CONDUCT
$4.95/3091-1
Flesh-and-blood men vie for power, pleasure and surrender in each of these feverish stories, and no one walks away from his steamy encounter unsated. Rowberry's men are unafraid to push the limits of civilized behavior in search of the elusive and empowering conquest. One of gay erotica's first success stories.

ROBERT BAHR
SEX SHOW
$4.95/225-6
Luscious dancing boys. Brazen, explicit acts. Unending stimulation. Take a seat, and get very comfortable, because the curtain's going up on a show no discriminating appetite can afford to miss.

JASON FURY
THE ROPE ABOVE, THE BED BELOW
$4.95/269-8
The irresistible Jason Fury returns—this time, telling the tale of a vicious murderer preying upon New York's go-go boy population. No one is who or what they seem, and in order to solve this mystery and save lives, each studly suspect must lay bare his soul—and more! Never has a private dick worked so hard!

ERIC'S BODY
$4.95/151-9
Meet Jason Fury: blond, blue-eyed and up for anything. Fury's sexiest tales are collected in book form for the first time. Follow the irresistible Jason through sexual adventures unlike any you have ever read....

MASQUERADE BOOKS

"BIG" BILL JACKSON
EIGHTH WONDER
$4.95/200-0
From the bright lights and back rooms of New York to the open fields and sweaty bods of a small Southern town, "Big" Bill always manages to cause a scene, and the more actors he can involve, the better! Like the man's name says, he's got more than enough for everyone, and turns nobody down....

1 800 906-HUNK

THE connection for hot handfuls of eager guys! No credit card needed—so call now for access to the hottest party line available. Spill it all to bad boys from across the country! (Must be over 18.) Pick one up now.... $3.98 per min.

LARS EIGHNER
WHISPERED IN THE DARK
$5.95/286-8
A volume demonstrating Eighner's unique combination of strengths: poetic descriptive power, an unfailing ear for dialogue, and a finely tuned feeling for the nuances of male passion.

AMERICAN PRELUDE
$4.95/170-5
Eighner is widely recognized as one of our best, most exciting gay writers. He is also one of gay erotica's true masters—and *American Prelude* shows why. Wonderfully written, blisteringly hot tales of all-American lust.

B.M.O.C.
$4.95/3077-6
In a college town known as "the Athens of the Southwest," studs of every stripe are up all night—studying, naturally. In *B.M.O.C.*, Lars Eighner includes the very best of his short stories, sure to appeal to the collegian in every man. Relive university life the way it was supposed to be, with a cast of handsome honor students majoring in Human Homosexuality.

EDITED BY DAVID LAURENTS
SOUTHERN COMFORT
$6.50/466-6
Editor David Laurents now unleashes another collection of today's most provocative gay writing. The tales here focus on the American South—and reflect not only Southern literary tradition, but the many contributions the region has made to the iconography of the American Male.

WANDERLUST:
HOMOEROTIC TALES OF TRAVEL
$5.95/395-3
A volume dedicated to the special pleasures of faraway places. Gay men have always had a special interest in travel—and not only for the scenic vistas. Wanderlust celebrates the freedom of the open road, and the allure of men who stray from the beaten path....

THE BADBOY BOOK OF EROTIC POETRY
$5.95/382-1
Over fifty of today's best poets. Erotic poetry has long been the problem child of the literary world—highly creative and provocative, but somehow too frank to be "literature." Both learned and stimulating, *The Badboy Book of Erotic Poetry* restores eros to its rightful place of honor in contemporary gay writing.

AARON TRAVIS
BIG SHOTS
$5.95/448-8
Two fierce tales in one electrifying volume. In *Beirut*, Travis tells the story of ultimate military power and erotic subjugation; *Kip*, Travis' hypersexed and sinister take on film noir, appears in unexpurgated form for the first time—including the final, overwhelming chapter.

EXPOSED
$4.95/126-8
A volume of shorter Travis tales, each providing a unique glimpse of the horny gay male in his natural environment! Cops, college jocks, ancient Romans—even Sherlock Holmes and his loyal Watson—cruise these pages, fresh from the throbbing pen of one of our hottest authors.

BEAST OF BURDEN
$4.95/105-5
Five ferocious tales. Innocents surrender to the brutal sexual mastery of their superiors, as taboos are shattered and replaced with the unwritten rules of masculine conquest. Intense, extreme—and totally Travis.

IN THE BLOOD
$5.95/283-3
Written when Travis had just begun to explore the true power of the erotic imagination, these stories laid the groundwork for later masterpieces. Among the many rewarding rarities included in this volume: "In the Blood" —a heart-pounding descent into sexual vampirism, written with the furious erotic power that has distinguished Travis' work from the beginning.

THE FLESH FABLES
$4.95/243-4
One of Travis's best collections. *The Flesh Fables* includes "Blue Light," his most famous story, as well as other masterpieces that established him as the erotic writer to watch. And watch carefully, because Travis always buries a surprise somewhere beneath his scorching detail....

SLAVES OF THE EMPIRE
$4.95/3054-7
"*Slaves of the Empire* is a wonderful mythic tale. Set against the backdrop of the exotic and powerful Roman Empire, this wonderfully written novel explores the timeless questions of light and dark in male sexuality. Travis has shown himself expert in manipulating the most primal themes and images. The locale may be the ancient world, but these are the slaves and masters of our time...." —John Preston

BUY ANY 4 BOOKS & CHOOSE 1 ADDITIONAL BOOK, OF EQUAL OR LESSER VALUE, AS YOUR FREE GIFT

MASQUERADE BOOKS

BOB VICKERY
SKIN DEEP
$4.95/265-5
So many varied beauties no one will go away unsatisfied. No tantalizing morsel of manflesh is overlooked—or left unexplored! Beauty may be only skin deep, but a handful of beautiful skin is a tempting proposition.

JR
FRENCH QUARTER NIGHTS
$5.95/337-6
A randy roundup of this author's most popular tales. *French Quarter Nights* is filled with sensual snapshots of the many places where men get down and dirty—from the steamy French Quarter to the steam room at the old Everard baths. In the best tradition of gay erotica, these are nights you'll wish would go on forever....

TOM BACCHUS
RAHM
$5.95/315-5
The imagination of Tom Bacchus brings to life an extraordinary assortment of characters, from the Father of Us All to the cowpoke next door, the early gay literati to rude, queercore mosh rats. No one is better than Bacchus at staking out sexual territory with a swagger and a sly grin.
BONE
$4.95/177-2
Queer musings from the pen of one of today's hottest young talents. A fresh outlook on fleshly indulgence yields more than a few pleasant surprises. Horny Tom Bacchus maps out the tricking ground of a new generation.

KEY LINCOLN
SUBMISSION HOLDS
$4.95/266-3
A bright young talent unleashes his first collection of gay erotica. From tough to tender, the men between these covers stop at nothing to get what they want. These sweat-soaked tales show just how bad boys can really get—especially when given a little help by an equally lustful stud.

HODDY ALLEN
AL
$5.95/302-3
Al is a remarkable young man. With his long brown hair, bright green eyes and eagerness to please, many would consider him the perfect submissive. Many would like to mark him as their own—but it is at that point that Al stops. One day Al relates the entire astounding tale of his life....

CALDWELL/EIGHNER
QSFX2
$5.95/278-7
The wickedest, wildest, other-worldliest yarns from two master storytellers—Clay Caldwell and Lars Eighner. Both eroticists take a trip to the furthest reaches of the sexual imagination, sending back ten stories proving that as much as things change, one thing will remain the same....

CLAY CALDWELL
ASK OL' BUDDY
$5.95/346-5
Set in the underground SM world, Caldwell takes you on a journey of discovery—where men initiate one another into the secrets of the rawest sexual realm of all. And when each stud's initiation is complete, he takes his places among the masters—eager to take part in the training of another hungry soul...
STUD SHORTS
$5.95/320-1
"If anything, Caldwell's charm is more powerful, his nostalgia more poignant, the horniness he captures more sweetly, achingly acute than ever."
—Aaron Travis

A new collection of this legend's latest sex-fiction. With his customary candor, Caldwell tells all about cops, cadets, truckers, farmboys (and many more) in these dirty jewels.
TAILPIPE TRUCKER
$5.95/296-5
Trucker porn! In prose as free and unvarnished as a cross-country highway, Caldwell tells the truth about Trag and Curly—two men hot for the feeling of sweaty manflesh. Together, they pick up—and turn out—a couple of thrill-seeking punks.
SERVICE, STUD
$5.95/336-8
Another look at the gay future. The setting is the Los Angeles of a distant future. Here the all-male populace is divided between the served and the servants—guaranteeing the erotic satisfaction of all involved.
QUEERS LIKE US
$4.95/262-0
"This is Caldwell at his most charming."
—Aaron Travis

For years the name Clay Caldwell has been synonymous with the hottest, most finely crafted gay tales available. *Queers Like Us* is one of his best: the story of a randy mailman's trek through a landscape of willing, available studs.
ALL-STUD
$4.95/104-7
This classic, sex-soaked tale takes place under the watchful eye of Number Ten: an omniscient figure who has decreed unabashed promiscuity as the law of his all-male land. One stud, however, takes it upon himself to challenge the social order, daring to fall in love. Finally, he is forced to fight for not only himself, but the man to whom he has committed himself.

CLAY CALDWELL AND AARON TRAVIS
TAG TEAM STUDS
$6.50/465-8
Thrilling tales from these two legendary eroticists. The wrestling world will never seem the same, once you've made your way through this assortment of sweaty, virile studs. But you'd better be wary—should one catch you off guard, you just might spend the rest of the night pinned to the mat.... A double dose of roughstuff, available only from Badboy.

ORDERING IS EASY

MC/VISA orders can be placed by calling our toll-free number
PHONE 800-375-2356/FAX 212-986-7355/E-MAIL masqbks@aol.com
or mail this coupon to:
MASQUERADE DIRECT
DEPT. BMRBA6 801 2ND AVE., NY, NY 10017

BUY ANY FOUR BOOKS AND CHOOSE ONE ADDITIONAL BOOK, OF EQUAL OR LESSER VALUE, AS YOUR FREE GIFT.

QTY.	TITLE	NO.	PRICE
			FREE
			FREE

We Never Sell, Give or Trade Any Customer's Name.

SUBTOTAL	
POSTAGE and HANDLING	
TOTAL	

In the U.S., please add $1.50 for the first book and 75¢ for each additional book; in Canada, add $2.00 for the first book and $1.25 for each additional book. Foreign countries: add $4.00 for the first book and $2.00 for each additional book. No C.O.D. orders. Please make all checks payable to Masquerade Books. Payable in U.S. currency only. New York state residents add 8.25% sales tax. Please allow 4-6 weeks for delivery.

NAME _____

ADDRESS _____

CITY _____ STATE _____ ZIP _____

TEL( ) _____

E-MAIL _____

PAYMENT: ☐ CHECK   ☐ MONEY ORDER   ☐ VISA   ☐ MC

CARD NO _____ EXP. DATE _____